THIS BOOK WAS DONATED BY

FRIENDS
OF THE
HOPEWELL

PUBLIC
LIBRARY

LETTER FROM POINT CLEAR

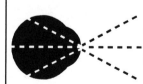

This Large Print Book carries the
Seal of Approval of N.A.V.H.

LETTER FROM POINT CLEAR

DENNIS MCFARLAND

THORNDIKE PRESS

An imprint of Thomson Gale, a part of The Thomson Corporation

THOMSON

GALE™

Detroit • New York • San Francisco • New Haven, Conn. • Waterville, Maine • London

THOMSON

GALE

™

LIBRARY OF CONGRESS CATALOGING-IN-PUBLICATION DATA

McFarland, Dennis.
  Letter from Point Clear / by Dennis McFarland. — Large print ed.
    p. cm. — (Thorndike Press large print reviewers' choice)
  ISBN-13: 978-1-4104-0314-8 (hardcover : alk. paper)
  ISBN-10: 1-4104-0314-9 (hardcover : alk. paper)
  1. Brothers and sisters — Fiction. 2. Alabama — Fiction. 3. Domestic
fiction. 4. Large type books. I. Title.
PS3563.C3629L48 2007
813'.54—dc22   2007034709

Published in 2008 by arrangement with Henry Holt and Company, LLC.

Printed in the United States of America on permanent paper
10 9 8 7 6 5 4 3 2 1

For Michelle and Katharine and Sam

CHAPTER 1

First, Ellen's letter to Willie:

My sweet guy,
I hope everything's continuing to go well for you and that you had a great Fourth. You can tell me all about it when we talk Tuesday night. I'll be by the phone at 9:45, so if your plans change, get your counselor to call me and let me know the new time.

July 4 was the day when your grandfather always celebrated his birthday, you know, so I've been thinking about him this week. I talked on the phone to Bonnie, who's still in Alabama, and we admitted to each other that we were missing him and feeling a little sad. It's odd, because Daddy wasn't the best company in the world. Of course, he mellowed quite a bit before he died. Anyway, I was very aware of his being gone this past week.

I went to the pond yesterday, and the crazy lady who lives in the house on the other side was playing some New Age music — what your Uncle Morris calls "ear candy." Soon she glided down through the trees in a long white robe, promptly let it fall to the ground, and entered the water naked, like a big white bird in a dream. I believe she was having some kind of special New Age moment. Just when I was thinking I would have to leave, she went inside and stopped the music. Then it was really beautiful. You could hear the ocean over the dunes, and I swam all the way around the perimeter.

It's lovely being down here, but I think you would be bored. I work in the mornings. Then I go swimming, read, eat dinner, listen to the ball game if there's one, and go to bed. Dull. But I'm getting a lot done. I think by the time you come home, I'll nearly have enough poems for a new book.

I love you and miss you and can't wait to hear your voice Tuesday night. If you need help with anything, be sure to ask for it. That's as much a sign of maturity as not needing help — if not a greater sign. Most adults still don't know how to ask for help, and they get themselves into a lot of trouble because of it. I know this, because I'm one of them from time to time.

Have a blast, my sweet guy. Drink some milk, eat an apple (or other fruit), brush your teeth, *blah blah blah.*

I love you very much,

M

And Morris's most recent e-mail message to Ellen:

Dear E —

Is it a conversation if only one person is talking?

You've probably noticed that Ted Williams's remains are back in the news again. An artist has created a shrine of some kind to Williams's severed head (on display in a NYC gallery), rekindling the endlessly fascinating cryogenics debate. Is this what people mean when they say, Dead but not forgotten?

What do you hear from Willie? I still don't understand how you and Dan could send him away like that. I HATED camp as a boy. As far as I can tell, camp takes everything that's already hard

9

about life and makes it harder. If Willie's miserable, just pull him and send him to Richard and me. I know I said no before and now I'm saying yes, which is probably annoying, but some things have unexpectedly changed and Richard's not going to Chicago after all. We're here in Ipswich through the middle of August. Willie could come up and go canoeing with Richard, which would take some of the pressure off me. Come to think of it, what's husband Dan doing for the next few weeks? I'm sure by now he's manicured most of the hillside, straight to the edge of the marsh. There are only just so many weeds that can be whacked in the world, and besides, don't they have environmental laws about such things on the Cape? Send Dan to us. I'll stick a canoe paddle in his hands and make Richard very happy.

I had an idea: When we come down for our long weekend on the 19th, why don't we swing by Willie's camp and bring him with us? Do you think they would release him for three days, or do they have ideas about how contact with the outside world might affect his incarceration? It would be so nice to have a thirteen-year-old around for the weekend, an ally when Dan's onslaught of shellfish dinners begins. Somebody to eat cheeseburgers with while the rest of you all are cracking open crustaceans and sucking out the innards.

Are you getting any work done? (Sorry. Idle curiosity.) Did you think of Daddy this past week? It would be gratifying, someday, to learn whether or not he was really born on the Fourth of July. I don't know why it matters. Somehow it does, though. Would also be nice if Bonnie would someday make known her intentions (I refer here mostly, but not solely, to Daddy's ashes). Will you please send me something to read, or at least recommend something? I find everything I lay my hands on disappointing this summer (I refer here mostly, but not solely, to books).

xxoo,

Morris

p.s. Cafe Martelle finally reopened on Saturday, and there's a big sign in the window that reads UNDER "NEW MAN-AGEMENT," further evidence that most people think quotation marks are for decoration and don't have any particular meaning.

Ellen Owen, middle-aged poet of *Marsh Light* and *Mirror in the Woods,* sat at a battered drop-leaf table by a triptych of double-hung windows and stared at her brother's message on the screen of her laptop until Morris's words began to go blurry and jumbled. She closed the lid of the computer, shut her eyes, and saw in the darkness a clear image of herself at the table in the small room: wearing a baggy white T-shirt, pink jogging shorts, and sky-blue trainers, a possibly too-thin woman with a bad haircut. A reckless pre-vacation visit to the beauty salon and an untried stylist had resulted in straight chin-length hair, unflattering, matronly, the color of dark mahogany, much too red, and entirely artificial-looking. The last few days, she'd noticed herself avoiding mirrors — both here in the little cabin, where she came in the mornings to work, and in the main house a hundred yards up the hill — and she hadn't quite managed not to interpret this symbolically, a cowardly evasion of truth. Now she opened her eyes, turned toward the window by her right elbow, and asked herself why oh why had she begun her letter to Willie — already mailed yesterday — with *My sweet guy?* She should have avoided a salutation that would embarrass him, should any of his buddies be looking over his shoulder. At least, she thought, she'd had the presence of mind to sign the letter M rather than Mommy.

She gazed down a tunnel in the locust trees to the lime-green grasses of the marsh. This view, meticulously tended by "husband Dan" in summers past, boasted a ragged periphery, a change Ellen thought she liked, even with its gentle threat of occlusion. She'd withheld from her brother the fact that Dan was not with her at the Cape house — that she and Dan had decided to spend the six weeks apart — for she wanted to spare herself Morris's voluminous opinions. Willie did know his father had remained in town, but not why. With Willie you could say, Daddy's staying behind to take care of some things, and that was enough of an explanation. With Morris the result would be twenty rapid-fire questions and an hour of debate.

Across the cabin's small central room, three other windows looked onto an expansive slope of lawn that led up to the main house, an antique Greek Revival so essentially Cape Cod with its white clapboard walls and roof of cedar shakes, its rambling side porch, wide parson's door, many dormers, and clothesline stretched between whitewashed posts, it had been featured over the years in no fewer than four coffee-table books of photography. Some two hundred years before, a half-dozen acres had been cleared of trees in this spot, providing most of the lumber for construction of the house, but only a small portion of the acreage — a circle hugging the house and the long slope to the cabin — was still dedicated to lawn. A perennial garden had been planted near the porch, which faced south, and beach grass about two feet tall had taken over the rest of the original clearing, so that the overall impression was one of fields, which changed in color with the seasons and gradually rolled to the edge of the abutting salt marsh. A single towering horse chestnut stood in the side yard twenty feet from the parson's door and — happily, to Ellen's thinking — humbled the house on its hilltop. A small grove of locust trees provided shade around the three-room cabin, which had been used by previous owners as a place for guests but which was now Ellen's private retreat. She loved everything about the cabin, its weathered shingles and unpainted wooden interior walls and black potbelly stove, but she valued most its artistic usefulness: Something about its removed position, in this larger dramatic scene, she found encouraging to poetry. This was especially true when the main house was filled with people, and music and voices drifted down the hill, or near the end of a day, when an upstairs window ignited with the sudden yellow fire of a light switched on inside.

Beneath the chestnut tree was a turn-around of crushed clamshells, where now, to Ellen's surprise, sat a black pickup truck beside her own car. She moved to the cabin windows and could see, indecipherable from this distance, gold lettering on the driver's door. Few unsolicited visitors found their way to the house, at the end of a long driveway through the woods, marked by homemade PRIVATE signs; the drive itself was at the end of a narrow dirt road, whose sharp ruts and heaves discouraged explorers. Ellen felt in her stomach what she gauged to be a normal flutter of butterflies — a woman alone in a remote place, encountering a surprise visitor — but in the next moment she recalled having scheduled a noontime appointment with the local chimney sweep. A kindly man in his sixties by the name of Gaston, he would have knocked at the front door, let himself in, and gone about his business of inspecting the flues. It made sense that she'd forgotten about him, for the weather had been unusually and consistently hot; the thought of an evening fire hadn't crossed her mind.

Up the hill and five minutes later, she found Gaston kneeling at the cold living room hearth, resting on his heels and holding a clipboard, already making out the bill. "I'm going to have to order a part for that damper upstairs," he said by way of a greeting, when she came in. "But both flues are clean enough, good for another year. No need to waste your money on that. Just give me forty-five dollars for the house call."

He tore the invoice from the clipboard and passed it to her, smiling, a dot of soot at the tip of a very red nose. "Thank you," she said. "I'll write you a check. Gaston, are you sunburned?"

"Can you imagine that?" he said. "Spent my whole life out here and still can't tolerate more than a minute of sun. Had to be up on a roof yesterday and forgot to bring my hat."

He began to push himself up from the hearth.

"You should wear block," she said, moving across the hall and into the kitchen, where she kept her checkbook in a drawer and where, now, she noted in herself an impulse she often disparaged in others, the impulse to adopt a maternal air with older

16

persons.

She'd taken a chair at the kitchen table and was writing Gaston's check when he appeared in the doorway. "Easy for you to say," he said. "Can't tolerate sunblock either. Makes me break out in a rash. You've done something to your hair."

"Yes," she said, not looking up.

"And where's Dan?" he asked, as if he were ticking off items on a list of changes — new hairdo, absent husband.

"Dan didn't come down this time," she answered, still not looking up. "Too many things to do in town."

"You mean you're out here all by yourself?" he said.

She stood and handed him the check, which he fastened to his clipboard. "Yes," she said. "All by myself."

He turned and took one step into the hall, then returned to the kitchen door and said, "You don't get lonely?"

She looked at him as he stood in the doorway holding his clipboard with both hands against his chest, expectantly, like a schoolboy, his shirttails hanging out of baggy blue carpenter's jeans. Sunlight fell onto the broad planks of the hall floor behind him and cast a glow that lit up the short wisps of white hair at the back of his neck. The bank of windows to his immediate left offered its usual spectacular view of the marsh, a shimmering blue-and-green tangle of water and odd-shaped islands. Now Ellen recalled that Gaston's wife had died a year ago last spring. "Well," she said at last, "if I did get lonely, I could just go home. It's only a two-hour drive."

She meant to show sympathy by alluding to their very different circumstances, their different sorts of solitude, and something in the way he paused and then nodded pensively made her think he understood. "I guess that's true," he said. "I like that husband of yours. I hope you'll give him my best when you talk to him. I'll be back when the part for that damper comes in, but it's likely to take a few weeks. And now I'm headed to the harbor, to get myself a bite to eat. Hot as it is, I think I'll call it a day."

"Gaston," she said, as he turned again to leave, "you've got soot on your nose." His remedy, swatting at his nose as if he were shooing a fly, accomplished nothing, so she shook her head and said, "You want me to get it for you?"

Gaston signaled his consent by craning his neck forward. Beneath the kitchen tap, she wet a corner of a paper towel, then wrapped it around two fingers. Approaching him, she thought she detected apprehension in his eyes. "I'll be very careful," she said softly, but he stood in the hall and kept his head so perfectly still, it was as if he really did think that any slip he might cause her to make would result in injury.

In the ten seconds it took to wipe away the soot, she saw his eyes fill with tears. She pretended not to notice and simply said, "There you go," allowing him to turn away quickly and leave through the screen door.

She followed him as far as the front stoop. "Is that a new truck?" she asked. "I don't think I recognize it."

"Bought it around Christmastime," he called matter-of-factly, without turning back. With the distance of the side yard between them, he waved, then climbed into the truck and drove away.

As she returned down the slope to the cabin, she thought, *Of course it isn't true.* She couldn't "just go home," as she'd so glibly put it to Gaston. She'd isolated herself by design — in truth, Dan had acquiesced to the arrangement with some bitterness; you couldn't honestly call it a mutual decision to separate — and she'd been lonely and generally out of sorts almost every day since she got there. Contrary to what she'd written Willie, she hadn't got a lot of work done, and her time alone on the Cape hadn't been especially lovely. Though the shady cabin stayed cool enough during the day, and she'd been able to sleep all right in the house with the help of an electric fan, the weather had been so hot that the water in the bay was unpleasantly warm; if you wanted to swim you *had* to go to the pond, which was nearly always overrun with people and a pestilence of biting greenheads. Yesterday, after the New Age woman had finally stopped the horrid music, Ellen had swum around the perimeter in an effort to escape the screaming and crying of unhappy children. She missed Willie, missed Dan, and loneliness had been the reason she'd impulsively asked her brother Morris down for a visit on the nineteenth, which now she regretted, not least because it would mean explaining to him the nature of Dan's absence.

It also wasn't true, as she'd likewise written to Willie, that her father, dead now ten months, had mellowed; he'd suffered a series of mild strokes, had been very ill for a year before he died, and had been heavily medicated. Now Ellen was worried about Bonnie, who, more than a year ago had abandoned an acting career in New York to go to Alabama and help take care of their father near the end, and who had still not returned, apparently kept in Alabama by a new romance, a subject on which she'd been uncharacteristically mum. In their telephone calls, Bonnie's chatter had had a disquieting dreamy air. Ellen had told herself that her younger sister was in love, cause enough for alarm, given her track record with men, but that dreaminess: Was it born of Bonnie's being lost or found? Ellen couldn't tell. When they'd talked on the Fourth, Bonnie had said she thought the well water at the Point Clear house was making her sick; Ellen told her to buy bottled water and Bonnie had said, "Oh . . . oh, yeah . . . I didn't think of that." And yes, it was extremely annoying that Morris first said no and now, too late, was saying yes to Willie's spending some time with him and Richard in Ipswich. Willie hadn't been thrilled about going to camp but had chosen it over spending six weeks at the Cape house with little to do; Ellen would have liked to have had the option of his spending part of the time with Morris, who had a swimming pool, whose house was walking distance from a town full of amusements, and who evidently had nothing better to do with his summer than to pester her with e-mails. As she entered the cabin, the room's cool dark

21

shade seemed an immediate comfort, but she couldn't help but think — as she took up her station at the table and gazed again down the tunnel through the locust trees — that her great need for a change, and her selfish pursuit of it, had spoiled the summer for the people she loved most in the world.

"I have an idea," said Morris Owen, somewhere in the middle of the tidal portion of the Ipswich River. He was speaking to Richard's back, since Richard was perched at the front of the canoe. "I'll say a few words and phrases descriptive of a visit to Wellfleet, and you just free-associate."

"That's funny," said Richard, meaning it wasn't.

Both men — each forty and fit for his age, darkly tanned, not tall, not short, not heavy, not thin — wore only swim trunks, Richard's green, Morris's yellow. In the modest hold between them, a liter of Evian, two orange life vests, and a squeeze bottle of sunscreen. It was late afternoon, a solid blue sky overhead, and very hot.

"Okay," Morris said, his paddle balanced sideways across his knees. "What comes to mind when I say *The restorative fellowship of family?*" After a silence in which a gull glided low over the water alongside the red canoe, Morris said, "Nothing at all? Okay, what about *Three days of free lobster, bluefish, oysters, clams, and champagne?*"

"Paddle, Morris," said Richard, in a monotone. "Please paddle."

"Hmm," said Morris, "that's an odd association, but all right. What about *A pleasant change of routine, a refreshing variety of canoeing partners?*"

"Morris, I'm not playing."

"I'm only trying to help you understand your feelings."

"I don't need any help understanding my feelings," said Richard. "I feel that I don't want to go to Wellfleet on the nineteenth. I feel that I'm happy where I am. I feel that you shouldn't have accepted the invitation on my behalf without checking with me first, and I feel that now you can just go by yourself."

"Rich," Morris said, his tone shifting suddenly, "do you realize that we're the only fools on the river? Did you check the tide table?" Morris leaned over the side of the canoe, peering into the gray-green water to see if he could see bottom. "I agreed to go canoeing," he added, "not portaging."

"Yes, I checked the tide table," said Richard. "It's just the heat. Most people can't take the heat."

"All right," Morris said, straightening up. "Let's see. What about *Shy in groups even when unconditionally fond of individuals?*"

"Okay, okay," said Richard, "I'll go with you to Wellfleet already. Now will you please paddle? I'm breaking my back here."

Morris smiled, kept smiling, as he returned his paddle to the water. As they moved forward, he concentrated for a while on a narrow strip of untanned skin above the waistband of Richard's trunks. Presently he was distracted by a second seagull, the briny smell of the water, a fiery breeze, and a single white cloud like a small mistake near the horizon. He stayed silent for such a long time that Richard was obliged to turn and look at him. Morris smiled again, still, after fourteen years, in love.

Back at the house in Ipswich three hours later, Richard fired up the grill on the deck for steaks. Morris took him a cold Bass Ale, Richard's favorite despite what Morris considered its very unfortunate name. A gin and tonic in hand for himself, he descended the short flight of wooden steps to the swimming pool and took a chair at a glass-top table; from this lower plane, he gazed upward and observed Richard's ribbed undershirt and his seersucker Bermuda shorts, mid-thigh length, very unfashionable. People sometimes said that he and Richard looked alike, a remark he couldn't fathom, given Morris's own full head of thick brown hair and Richard's salt-and-pepper fuzz with sunburned landing strip on top. Morris sipped his drink and soon turned his attention, bit by bit, to the physical hour — it was his favorite time of evening, when the pool, as if it had stored light in its depths throughout the day, now began to emanate a pale aquamarine toward the dusk under the maples and birches; when the venerable shiplike house he and Richard had bought together a decade ago seemed to stand taller, cool white in a landscape bullied all afternoon by the sun, and the wrinkled leaves of the rugosa roses along the western fence turned nearly black, a perfume like cloves wafting clear out to the road. At last he contemplated the tomato plants beyond the pool at the end of the lot, which, despite the recent heat, were evolving too slowly to suit him, and for a moment this delay on the part of the tomatoes seemed to him his most serious complaint. Sometimes, as now, he inquired of himself whether or not he felt any guilt in the face of his extraordinary good fortune in life and love, and the answer always came easily back the same: No.

This particular *no* invariably led to an angling for substantial grievances, and after about a minute, he called to Richard, "Ellen's been on the Cape now for ten days and she doesn't answer my e-mails."

"But I thought she wrote and invited us down on the nineteenth," said Richard.

"I mean besides that," said Morris. "That was one measly logistical e-mail."

"How many e-mails have you sent her?" asked Richard.

"I don't know, it's not like I *count* them," said Morris. "Fifteen, I guess."

Richard stepped to the deck railing and peered down at Morris. After what felt to Morris like a thorough viewing, Richard said, "Maybe you should cut back a bit."

"Why would I do that?" said Morris. "Are you suggesting that if I wrote less she would respond more? That doesn't make any sense."

Richard took a wire brush to the grill, producing a terrible screech. "It makes sense to me," he called, over the noise.

Morris waited for the rasping to cease, then said, pensively, "No, something's up. I can tell. I can feel it."

"They're on vacation," said Richard. "Willie's away at camp and the two of them are alone. They're probably having fun. Not

26

focusing on things like e-mail."

"No," said Morris again. "Something's definitely up. If I don't hear from her soon I'll put in a call. I mean, I know it wouldn't come as a shock to learn that Ellen was unhappy, but if she's so unhappy she's not answering my e-mails, it means that something's definitely up. Something big. I should have phoned her on the Fourth."

"The telephone works both ways, you know," said Richard.

"Does it?" said Morris. "Is that what it means when it makes that little ringing noise?"

"She's only been gone ten days," Richard said. "Bonnie's been in Alabama for a year, and how often do you hear from her?"

"That's different," said Morris. "It's a given that something's up with Bonnie. Something's always up with Bonnie. Any day now we're going to find out what kind of a jam she's got herself into, what's really detained her in Point Clear. And besides, they don't have e-mail in Alabama. The state legislature passed a bill banning the Internet."

"That's not true."

"Well, it very well could be true. Places doesn't stay as benighted as Alabama by accident, you know. You have to enact laws."

Richard made no reply, a pointed silence with which Morris was familiar and which said, *Don't be such a snob.* It was true that he took satisfaction in having escaped the state of his birth, even though the escape hadn't been his own doing — his father had sent him and Ellen to boarding school in Connecticut when they were adolescents. But Morris figured he could take credit, at the very least, for having had the good sense to stay away. He believed that if a person had spent the better part of his boyhood in Alabama, he would not be enchanted, as so many Yankees apparently were, with the hideous sanctimony known as *southern hospitality:* a kit of pleasant manners that included a knife for backstabbing. He found equally revolting what seemed to be a growing body of lightweight literature that portrayed the South as chock-full of characters who couldn't be more colorful if they tried, who never uttered a phrase that wasn't picturesque, and who, despite the unmentionable crimes of their bigotries, were good-hearted folks through and through. Thank God Ellen had escaped Alabama as well, for Morris wouldn't have been able to bear it if she'd taken up writing poems about the charms of crawdaddies and mimosa trees and swamp-side shanties,

Spanish moss and the like. At least, if she had to be so enthralled by the natural landscape, she was enthralled by one worthy of Thoreau rather than Faulkner. He reminded himself to go gently with Ellen, even in mental exercise, as she had never quite forgiven him for remarking that the title to her first book, *Marsh Light,* sounded like a lo-cal dessert topping. The sad truth about Ellen, Morris had decided, was that if she worked hard for the rest of her life, she might attain the status of a tiny bubble in the overly inclusive waters of American verse. Her poetry was pretty, usually formal, often rhymed, which Morris had never held against her. He actually admired that about her, that she clung to such lifesaving devices in a lagoon of flotsam and jetsam, but the poems were often — well, one might as well face it — a bit decorative. In an effort to render justice to nature, she went after this dangerous and beautiful thing with the sharp weapons of her word painting, captured it, by God, and then invited the reader to view it in its new confines. Morris wouldn't have begun to know how to fix the poems. He wouldn't have made Ellen's choices. To have continued to *reject* the writing of poetry, as he himself had done since the age of sixteen, was in his opinion

29

the afterglow of an ineffable wisdom.

He sometimes thought Ellen should never have married a man as wealthy as Dan Kepperstan, despite Dan's good looks and kindheartedness, when she already had money enough of her own; it had had the effect of removing a thread that bound one to the rest of humanity. At his most cynical, Morris thought her turning to poetry after Willie was born smacked too much of a rich lady's taking up an improving hobby. Morris — who, like Ellen, had come at the age of twenty-one into an equal share of a trust established by their paternal grandfather — had taken pains, for the betterment of his character, to keep one foot in academia. Teaching put him regularly among people; he liked to think that, by instructing college students to read and write sensibly, he helped produce grown-ups better equipped for life; and happily he was spared, as Ellen was not, a product that lingered within sight. Of course Morris tried to keep such criticism and self-congratulating to himself, out of the reach of the dreaded snob watch of Richard, who sometimes chided Morris, unfairly, for being too disparaging of friends and family.

As Morris finished his drink, he returned his thoughts to Ellen's recent mysterious silence. Whatever was wrong, he imagined it somehow connected to the unnaturally protracted period of mourning she had been putting everyone through since their father died last autumn. Morris could only guess what life had been like these past ten months for Dan and Willie; he doubted that either of them could have been sufficiently sensitive, not in the face of so important a grief as Ellen's. Granted, it was sad for one's father to die, even if the father happened to be Roy Owen, drunken, narcissistic, and not especially interested in his children. But for some reason, Ellen had to be the saddest, had to grieve deepest and longest; there had been something, Morris thought, decidedly proud and exclusive about it.

"Hey, Morris," called Richard, from the deck. "How about coming up here and hooking up the radio. I want to get a score in the Sox game."

When Morris gained the deck, Richard smiled at him and said, "Why the long face? What have you been thinking about down there by the pool?"

"I've been thinking about something you don't understand," said Morris.

"That's not surprising," Richard said.

"What you don't understand," said Morris, "is that my view of people I love is actually more balanced than it appears."

"Okay," said Richard, "but why do I have the feeling I'm coming in on the middle of a conversation?"

"I think I have a fairly firm grasp of what's good about people," Morris said. "I can't help it if their faults are more interesting than their virtues."

Richard reached for his beer, upturned the bottle to his mouth, and drained it. "Well," he said, "thank you for clearing that up."

CHAPTER 2

Morris gave his sister another day to respond to his proposal about bringing Willie to the Cape. When no response came, he telephoned both the house and the cabin but was required to leave a voice message at each. In other words, Ellen was declining to take his calls. He saw her in his mind's eye, listening coldly by an answering machine. In a lame effort to console, Richard proposed that Ellen hadn't answered the house phone because she was down at the cabin and she hadn't answered the cabin phone because she was working. It occurred to Morris to ask Richard why he was always taking Ellen's side, but he knew Richard would laugh at him, and that would make him angry.

"So why doesn't Dan answer the phone?" said Morris.

"He's out mowing the lawn," said Richard, and Morris then asked him why in the world Richard was wasting his prodigious gifts in little ol' Ipswich, Massachusetts, when he could be making a fortune on the Psychic Friends Network.

The following day, Ellen telephoned in the evening, all business, and though she concentrated almost entirely on plans for the impending visit to the Cape, she managed somehow to sound unwelcoming. She thought it a good idea for Morris to bring Willie when they came down on the nineteenth, and she'd already spoken about it to Willie, who'd said he would love to. She'd contacted the camp office and persuaded the director to make an exception to a rule that did indeed prohibit visits home. She gave Morris detailed directions to the camp and to the camp office, as well as the name of the person Morris needed to see; there would be a simple form to fill out, and Morris should let someone at the office know what time on Friday they planned to come for Willie. "I told them Willie's uncle was visiting from out of town," she said, "and it was Willie's only chance to see him. So when you get there, don't say anything about having just driven over from Ipswich."

"Well, what *should* I say?" asked Morris.

"Say about what?"

"I mean, what if somebody asks where I'm from?"

"What does it matter?" she said. "As long as it's someplace far away. Besides, nobody will ask."

"You don't know that," said Morris.

"Morris," she said, "this was your idea, bringing Willie. Do you now think it's going to be too difficult for you?"

"Don't be testy," said Morris. "You know this kind of thing makes me nervous."

"What kind of thing?" she said. "What kind of thing is it?"

"Oh, you know," he said. "Little lies. Little plots."

After a pause, she said, "I'm sorry, Morris, but they have a rule, and it was the best idea I had for persuading them to break it."

"Don't worry," he said, "I'll be fine. I would walk through fire for Willie, you know that. Why don't you answer my e-mails?"

"I couldn't possibly answer all of them," she said. "I'm trying to get some work done down here."

That night, in bed, in the dark, Morris said to Richard, "It was her tone. You would have thought we'd invited *ourselves* to Wellfleet. You would've thought our offer to drive a hundred miles out of our way to bring Willie was somehow an inconvenience to *her.*"

"It's not really a hundred miles, is it?" said Richard.

Morris closed his eyes and allowed nearly a full minute to pass in silence.

At last, keeping his eyes shut, he said, "You know, Richard, that trick of pretending to miss the point is awfully tired by now. You've overused it. It doesn't even annoy me anymore."

A few days later, one day before they were to travel to Wellfleet, Ellen telephoned again. "There's something you should know," she said to Morris, who had taken the call on a cordless phone by the pool. It was midafternoon; Richard had left Ipswich at four in the morning to go fly-fishing with their septuagenarian next-door neighbor, and Morris had decided to use the day for reading a book he'd been putting off, a novel written by a colleague at his university. When the telephone rang, he'd just set the book aside after about a hundred pages and had begun to feel inexplicably blue, an emotion that didn't correspond in any obvious way to the rather lighthearted events portrayed in the book. "I'm sure there are many things I should know," he said to Ellen. "But what's on your mind?"

"Dan and I decided to separate for these

six weeks while I'm down here," she said. "It's complicated and I really don't feel like going into it, but I thought you should know. Willie will probably mention it tomorrow when you pick him up — I mean, he might mention the fact that Dan didn't come with me."

"Okay," said Morris. "But just tell me — is it Oprah issues or Jerry Springer issues?"

"I have no idea what you mean," said Ellen.

"I mean is it like *He's emotionally unavailable,* or like *He's having an affair with our transsexual mailman?*"

This question made her laugh, which surprised Morris.

"As far as I know," she said, "he's not having any affairs. I guess I'd have to say that I've never known anybody quite as loyal as Dan."

"I agree," said Morris, "but something about the way you say it makes it sound like a weakness. Loyal like a dog."

"Well, I don't mean to," she said. "Here's the thing — since you're going to be bringing Willie down with you, I decided I should invite Dan too."

"Are you telling me this because it's going to be awkward?" asked Morris.

"No," she said, "I'm just giving you the

lay of the land. I don't expect it to be awkward. But I think not to invite him would feel like a punishment."

"To him, you mean."

"Well, yes, to him, but also to everyone, especially Willie. What are you and Richard up to today?"

"Richard's gone fishing, and I'm reading Stanley Meacham's novel. What does Willie think about this separation thing?"

"Willie thinks Dan couldn't come to the Cape because of work."

"You might've come up with something more imaginative than that," Morris said.

"What would you have told him?" said Ellen.

"I don't know, but that's not even trying. When did work ever keep Dan from doing anything? What are y'all hoping to achieve with this?"

"We didn't set a specific goal, Morris," said Ellen. "We just thought a little break from each other might spark a needed change."

"You mean like *Absence makes the heart grow fonder?*"

"I suppose you think that's trite," she said, "but yes, something like that."

"I don't think it's trite," said Morris. "I have doubts about its working, but I don't

38

think it's trite. I don't imagine this was Dan's idea, was it?"

"I'll answer that," she said, "but before I do, I would like for you to recall something I said at the beginning of this conversation."

"It's complicated and you don't feel like going into it," said Morris.

"Right," she said. "No, it wasn't Dan's idea. It was mine. Have you talked to Bonnie?"

"Not lately," he said. "I'm conducting a test to see how much time will pass if I don't phone her and wait for her to phone me instead."

"And how long has it been?"

"A month and five days," said Morris.

"I think you should call her," Ellen said. "I'm vaguely worried."

"Yes, well, that would be the natural response where Bonnie's concerned," said Morris. "But I don't think I'll phone her. I prefer worrying vaguely to worrying specifically."

"Do you really?" said Ellen. "I'm just the opposite."

"I've been vaguely worried about you, for example," Morris said. "Now I'm worried in a specific way, about you and Dan, and I don't think I prefer it."

Morris heard her sigh, after which she

said, "That's very sweet."

"I don't mean it to be sweet," he said. "I mean to express my irritation with you."

"I know," she said. "But it's still sweet. Is Stanley Meacham's novel bad?"

"Of course," said Morris, "but there are many ways of being bad. This is bad in a way that makes you *feel* bad."

Afterward Morris took a swim, then lay flat on his back on the sun-warmed paving stones alongside the pool. He turned his head and gazed at the telephone resting on the glass-top table a few feet away; he found himself actively suppressing an urge to phone Dan. "That would be inappropriate," he said aloud, then looked at the sky, which was a uniform sky-blue. To Ellen, six weeks alone at the Cape house would mean time to think, time to read and write, what she would call time to be with herself. To Dan, six weeks in town without Ellen or Willie would mean nothing but loneliness. Certainly he could go into the office and pretend to work — what he occasionally called "showing some leadership" — meaning he would put on a suit and tie, go downtown, and say hello to the younger partners in his private equity firm to whom he long ago turned over all practical responsibilities. Dan had never been a great reader of books, and any thinking he might do in Ellen and Willie's absence would mostly concern how much he missed them. In all inward capacities, Dan would simply be waiting: a period for him of purposelessness and extreme dejection. At last Morris thought, Maybe Dan *is* something like a dog.

"I'm sure it was all very quiet and civilized," he said to Richard that evening at dinner. "Ellen and Dan have never yelled."

Morris and Richard were eating inside, at the dining room table. Earlier, Richard had brought home two rainbow trout, from a trout-stocked river whose purity was carefully regulated for the benefit of both the fish and the humans who ate them; he'd cleaned and gutted the trout on the deck, which, Morris thought, would probably reek for the next year or so. Morris was having a cheeseburger.

"Why couldn't Willie stay home with Dan?" Richard asked. "Then she would have time to herself but Dan wouldn't have to be so lonely."

"I don't know," said Morris. "My guess is that Ellen wouldn't think it a proper separation if Dan got to keep Willie. Dan might enjoy himself too much, when the whole point is for him to contemplate his considerable shortcomings."

"That's harsh," said Richard.

"Well, Ellen can be harsh," said Morris.

"I meant your saying it was harsh."

"Oh."

Morris left the table and took his plate into the small Pullman-style kitchen. Earlier, Richard had come home from fly-fishing in the usual beatific state, reeling from the punch of a natural high, and this last remark took Morris by surprise. Morris returned to the dining room door, leaned against the frame, and stared at Richard, who had stopped just short of coming to the dinner table in waders — he hadn't changed out of his river clothes, or bathed, and he still wore his khaki fisherman's cap.

"I'm sorry you think me harsh," said Morris, "but I can't help seeing the thing from Dan's point of view. If he and Ellen weren't feeling close enough, Dan's solution would be to find a way of spending *more* time together, not less. From Dan's vantage, this separation is probably just the next logical step for Ellen to take. She's grown more and more withdrawn since Daddy died, and now she's actually geographically withdrawn. I don't imagine Dan would see one kind of distance as a cure for another kind."

"I agree," Richard said, continuing to eat meticulously, tediously, the way one had to eat rainbow trout.

"You do?"

"Yes. And the next time Wesley and I go fly-fishing I want you to come."

"Is that why you agreed with me? Because you want me to come fishing?"

"No," said Richard. "I agreed because you're right. Even if it's not what Dan thinks and feels — even if it's just what you feel — it's right. And I want you to come fly-fishing because you need to get some kind of spiritual life."

"Oh, God," said Morris. "Haven't we been over this before? Everything that has a meditative element isn't spiritual, Richard. Some people meditate on the toilet."

Richard put down his special fish knife and fork. He wiped his mouth with a linen napkin, folded it, and laid it to one side of his plate. "Just think about it," he said. "Consider it."

"All right," Morris said, "but remember this: Most spiritual disciplines don't provide the immediate reward, as this one does, of putting food on the table. And I don't think they usually include the big rush you talk about getting when you feel a strike on the line."

"Just consider it," Richard repeated. "Now tell me — how did Ellen seem?"

"It's interesting you should ask," said Morris, returning to the table and taking his chair opposite Richard. "She seemed strangely unperturbed. Imperturbable. Almost cheerful. Not at all what I expected. And entirely different from how she seemed the last time we talked."

Richard turned toward an open window, nodding, as if he understood something. For a moment Morris wondered what it was, but then Richard said, "Can you feel that little shift in the air? I think we're about to get a change in the weather."

Some hours later, deep in the middle of the night, Morris startled awake at a familiar and frightening sound. Suddenly the upstairs room jumped with a flash of white light, and he realized that a clap of thunder had awakened him. Richard slept, snoring in his boxer shorts, on his stomach, on top of the covers. Morris heard a second rumble of thunder in the distance, then the wheezing of the window screens as wind rocked the sugar maple by the road. He climbed out of bed to put the windows at half-mast. Lightning blitzed the room a second time, and for an instant Richard looked like a hairy corpse somebody had dumped onto the bed. Morris went to him and gave a nudge, to interrupt the snoring. In a deep corpselike voice, Richard said, "What?" but didn't otherwise stir or open his eyes. Morris returned to the other side of the bed and propped pillows behind his own back, thinking he might need to read to fall asleep. Just as Morris was about to switch on the lamp, Richard turned toward him, eyes still shut; he swallowed, licked his lips, swallowed again, and muttered, "I learned a new loop knot today. . . ."

They went in Richard's car, the Land Rover, because it handled better on wet roads, and Morris took the steering wheel because Richard hated driving in rain. Along the way Richard was quieter than usual, and Morris worried that he was having second thoughts — or, more precisely, second resentments — about the long weekend in Wellfleet. Morris comforted himself by reflecting that Richard was not inclined to nurse any sort of grudge; once Richard accepted a situation, he accepted it fully, much the way he loved people, fully, as if he'd admitted them to a special club with an irrevocable membership. In any case, Morris didn't mind the silence, for it allowed him to devote his thoughts more thoroughly to Willie, whom he adored and whom he hadn't seen for several weeks. He recalled Willie's last visit to Ipswich, a sleep-over near the end of the school year, and specifically he recalled a moment, at bed-time, when he'd gone to the downstairs guest room to say good night and found Willie lying not in the bed but in the middle of the carpet by the bed, on his back, staring wide-eyed at the ceiling. The door to the room was open, so Morris discovered Willie without the barrier of having to knock. The boy was lost in a reverie, which Morris would have found endearing enough, but what he found enviable was Willie's utter lack of chagrin at having been caught at it. When he entered the room and took a seat on the edge of the bed, Willie acknowledged him with the briefest shift of his eyes. Small for thirteen, he sported a new summertime buzz cut and wore nothing but black knee-length basketball shorts, slung low and revealing an especially promi-nent pair of hip bones. Morris adopted Willie's contemplative demeanor and asked him if he intended to sleep there on the floor rather than pampering himself with the indulgence of an actual bed.

For an answer, Willie had said, "A hypo-chondriac is somebody who pretends to be sick when they really aren't, right?"

"Not exactly," said Morris. "They don't

pretend to be sick, they *imagine* themselves to be sick. Why do you ask?"

Willie said he'd overheard his father call Willie's Aunt Bonnie a hypochondriac. Morris had known at once that this could refer only to Bonnie's adventures earlier in the year in Point Clear, when, having taken up the position of nursemaid to their dying father, she'd begun to acquire some of the old man's symptoms, even though he'd had nothing contagious. Morris and Ellen had worried for a while that somebody would have to go to Alabama to administer to the old man *and* to Bonnie. "Well, I'm afraid your father was right," said Morris to Willie, "but *hypochondriac* doesn't paint the whole picture. Sick is only one of the things Bonnie occasionally imagines herself to be."

"It made my mom mad," said Willie.

"That's surprising," said Morris. "She probably just didn't like Dan saying it. Sometimes we don't like other people saying things, even when we know them to be true."

Willie had looked at Morris and nodded, as if he understood exactly what Morris meant and possibly had some recent experience of that kind. He told him that his mother had said that Bonnie's ability to empathize was part of what made her a

47

good actress. Given the look of skepticism on Willie's face, Morris saw no need to refute this idea. In the last ten years, Bonnie had landed only one role in a production that could be considered legitimately off-Broadway, and Morris recalled that Willie hadn't been allowed to go see his aunt in the play, for the role had required her to appear naked onstage. "Well, I do think Bonnie has a natural gift for drama," Morris said at last, without any obvious irony, though he believed he saw the hint of a smile cross Willie's face as the boy continued to gaze at the guest room ceiling.

On the drive to Southborough, that was how he remembered Willie most vividly: a rail-thin half-naked boy, afloat on a Turkish carpet of greens and golds and eight-pointed stars, peering upward, vacantly but for a trace of amusement at the corners of his mouth.

Midmorning, when they reached the outskirts of the town, the rain stopped, the sky brightened, and Morris noticed that the streets and bordering lawns took on a restrained matte quality. Willie's summer program had occupied the campus of a boys' prep school, and when its Tudor-style buildings came into view, Morris felt his heart inside his chest, quickened by both the prospect of seeing Willie and the small administrative task it entailed.

But Morris found the camp office easily, following Ellen's excellent directions, everything there went smoothly — nobody questioned him about his place of residence — and soon Willie appeared at the office door. Morris resisted the urge to say how the boy had grown, though that did seem immediately to be the case, and not only in the physical sense. On their way back to the parking lot, where Richard had waited with the car, Morris and Willie were accosted under a colonnade by an astonishingly large black kid who greeted Willie as "Piss ant" and then kindly relieved him of his duffel bag. Willie introduced the kid as Khalid Jackson, of Durham, North Carolina, known to all his friends as Kool-Aid. Morris allowed the two boys, a comical-looking duo, to walk ahead, as he pondered how feasible his own summer camp (and boyhood in general) might have been if he'd had Willie's knack for identifying the biggest, toughest kid around and making of him a best friend.

At the car, when the second of Willie's uncles was introduced, Khalid said, "Y'all sure must be brothers."

Morris naturally thought this a conclusion drawn from their both being uncles, and that it would require a tiresome explanation, but Khalid quickly added, "Man, y'all *look* alike."

"Don't say that," said Willie. "He doesn't like it."

"I can't help it if they look alike," said Khalid, scowling at Willie. The kid turned back to Morris and said, "I have a cousin, lives in Virginia, he looks so much like me, people don't know what to think."

Morris, not quite sure how to use this information, nodded reflectively.

Willie said, "I don't have any cousins."

"That's too bad, cousins can come in handy," said Khalid, prompting Morris to even deeper, murkier reflection.

Willie was settled into the rear seat, and, because the rain had stopped, Richard took over the driving. As Richard began to pull the car out of the parking lot, Morris turned to Willie and saw Khalid through the back window. The kid had removed his baby-blue sock cap, freeing a bramble of light brown hair, and now stood at the curb, using the cap as a flag and waving good-bye to the rear end of the Land Rover. Morris found this strangely moving and said to Willie, "I like your friend. Is he your roommate?"

"I wish," said Willie. "He swears a lot."

"Really?" said Morris, not sure if there

was a connection between the wish and the swearing.

"It already got him into trouble," said Willie, "but he said he can't help it. He said he couldn't stop even if he wanted to."

"What kind of trouble?" asked Morris, genuinely curious about the punishments this sort of high-tone boys' camp meted out. "What's the penalty for swearing?"

This triggered an outpouring of camp news from Willie, during which Morris had only to interject the occasional follow-up question. Nobody got into trouble for a casual *damn* or *hell,* but there was a rule banning vulgar language, and since Kool-Aid had been caught not once but twice calling a fellow camper a name heard in just about every hip-hop song on the radio — and even though Kool-Aid had only been *kidding* — he was scratched from a weekend trip he'd signed up for, a trek into Boston to see the Red Sox play, a high price to pay since it would have been Kool-Aid's first major-league game. Willie's actual roommate, Carl, from Ohio, was okay, though he was suffering serious homesickness, which made him a little too desperate to make friends; Carl's idea of reaching out was to offer to let you use his soap-on-a-rope in the shower. In general, camp was also okay,

51

though the thirteen-year-olds were the youngest group, which was never a lot of fun. The RA for Willie's living group was a nice guy but deeply in love with one of the female counselors and couldn't spare much extra time for the boys. Willie had signed up for a role in a pared-down version of *Much Ado About Nothing,* having been promised by the director a sword fight, and now, more than a week into rehearsals, it was looking as if there wouldn't be any sword fighting after all, and the costumes were nothing but white bedsheets they wrapped around themselves so they looked confusingly like ancient Greeks.

Abruptly, Willie concluded his report with, "Why didn't Dad come get me?"

This question, entirely reasonable but lacking in tact, took Morris aback. "That's a good question," he said after a pause. "I hadn't even thought of it. I believe, when we made the plan, we didn't know your father would be coming down. Are you disappointed?"

"No, no," said Willie — apparently he'd grasped the potential rudeness of his own question. "I just thought it would've been closer for him than for you guys."

"He's right about that," said Richard to Morris, which Morris thought a disagreeable contribution.

"Well, I suppose we're all doing more or less what we've been told to do by your mother," Morris said to Willie, then turned and faced forward. He was aware of Richard's reproachful glance coming his way, but he leaned toward the windshield, feigning an interest in the changing weather.

As they drove southeast, the sky brightened more and more and Morris used this as a tool against any tendency in himself toward peevishness. He was grateful they'd got a jump on the worst of the Friday traffic. He was grateful when Richard engaged Willie for a while on the topic of the sports he'd been playing at camp. Soon Willie put in his earbuds and retreated into the world of his music. He made no other reference to his father, and none to his parents' separation, though Morris remained certain that the boy hadn't bought that flimsy business about Dan's staying home to work. When they reached the bridge over the canal at Bourne, the bottleneck was negligible, and they made good time all the way to the rotary at Orleans, the official start of the Outer Cape, where Salt Pond came into view beneath a silver-white glare of sky.

They stopped in Eastham for sandwiches and reached Wellfleet around one in the afternoon. On the narrow muddy road through the woods to the house, Morris envisioned their arrival, himself the author of this small splintered family's reunion: Ellen and Dan would rush out of the house into the clamshell driveway to greet them, loud and frenetic, full of gratitude, hugs, and laughter.

But once Richard had navigated the long rutted driveway and pulled the car into the apparently deserted turnaround beneath the horse chestnut, there was the silence of the tomb. No Ellen, no Dan. The house was not only empty but also locked. Morris, who'd brought his own key, opened the door and stood back as Willie passed through into the front hall. Morris turned to Richard and said, "Where do you suppose they are?"

"Probably Dan didn't get here yet," said Richard. "And Ellen's out running errands."

Exasperated, Morris said, "What if I hadn't thought to bring my key?"

"But you did bring it," said Richard, one hand on the screen door.

"But what if I hadn't?" said Morris.

Twenty minutes later, Willie came bounding down from his upstairs room, shouting, "I hear a car!" and was out the front door.

Richard quickly followed, Morris more slowly. Dan's beige Mercedes, a 1970-something classic that Morris found a touch precious, was parked in the turnaround. As Willie and Richard greeted Dan, hugs all round, Morris, feeling unthinkably petty, lingered at the base of the porch steps and watched; he believed that Dan, curly-headed, handsome, and unnecessarily tall, held on to each of the two others a bit too long. And when Dan swaggered over to Morris — smiling, even teary-eyed — and pulled Morris into a bear hug, Morris whispered into his ear, "I love you too, Dan, but I can't breathe."

"Sorry," said Dan, releasing him and turning back to Willie.

He engaged Willie in a few seconds of that shadowboxing thing straight men like to do, which came to an abrupt end as Richard appeared from around the car, carrying Dan's leather suitcase, which was surprisingly large and obviously heavy. Dan relieved him of it, blushing. Then, his free arm around Willie's shoulders, he started up the porch steps. "Where's your mom?" he said, and kissed Willie's temple.

"She's not here yet," Willie answered.

"Not here yet?" Dan said. "Where is she?"

"No one knows," said Morris pointedly,

from behind them.

"She's not down at the cabin either?" asked Dan.

"No," said Morris. "As you can see, her car is gone."

Forty minutes after Dan's arrival, Morris sat at one end of a long gold sofa in the living room, a pair of expensive field glasses pressed to his eyes, and gazed through a panel of tall windows down at the salt marsh, which was filling with water, about two-thirds of the way to high tide. "I've never understood what all the fuss was about," he said generally, to the room. "I mean, first of all, he was a baseball player. It's not like he was Jonas Salk or something. And second of all, he wouldn't have been so all-fired great if he'd had to bat against today's pitchers. I wonder where Ellen can be?"

"I don't think she's out there in the marsh," said Richard, from the other end of the sofa, then winked at Willie, who was playing solitaire on a rug near the cold hearth.

It was now two o'clock. Twice in the last half-hour, a shaft of sunlight had pierced through the low sky, lit up a circle in the dismal duck-strewn marsh, then faded away. Morris had dialed Ellen's cell phone three times to no avail — service was unreliable almost everywhere on the Cape except the main highway. Richard, apparently unfazed by the disappointing state of things, had taken a root beer from the fridge and settled with a fishing magazine on the sofa. Willie had found a deck of playing cards, each with a different picture of Elvis Presley, and lit on the nearby rug. Dan, who'd arrived with about a dozen bags of groceries in the trunk of the Mercedes, was already up to his elbows in the concoction of several marinades for tonight's seafood dinner; he'd moved all his fixings to the dining table a few feet away so that he might carry on a dreary conversation with Richard on the topic of Ted Williams, who, though dead, would not quite go away. The topic of his cryogenically frozen remains, which had caught Morris's attention in an idle moment earlier in the month, now struck him as soporific. For the last few minutes, to distract and calm himself, he'd been searching the far side of the marsh for herons, which sometimes nested in the pine trees there. He was thinking of Ellen's eleventh-hour confession yesterday over the telephone (why had she withheld from him this important information until the last minute?); of how she and Dan had taken what might have been a reasonable idea (a week or two apart) and turned it into something absurd (*six* weeks); and of the curious weight and size of Dan's suitcase (surely it held more than a three-day weekend's necessities). Then, through the field glasses, he saw the blurry vertical stripes of Dan's shorts. He lowered the binoculars and found Dan staring down at him; his hands were covered with something shiny and brown, and he held up his arms, bent at the elbows, like a surgeon entering an operating room.

"You're not serious, are you?" he said to Morris, in apparent disbelief.

"Serious about what?"

"About Williams not batting as well against today's pitchers."

"Of course I'm serious," said Morris. "Today's pitchers are stronger, they pump iron, take any number of performance-enhancing supplements, they throw harder, and the minute they start to feel the least little bit tired, the manager replaces them with a fresh one."

"But Morris," said Dan, visibly distressed. "Williams would be even *better* if he were playing today."

"I think so too," said Richard, treacherously chiming in. "But you say why first, Dan."

"Because," said Dan, "he was always sixty points or more ahead of his peers — no, I shouldn't say peers. He had no peers. Sixty points ahead of his colleagues. Simple logic dictates that that disparity would be a constant. Home-run records and batting averages are generally higher today, so if Williams was sixty points better than his colleagues today, he would obviously be batting better today than he did in his own time."

Morris shifted a few inches to his left and returned the field glasses to his eyes. He said, "I have no idea what you just said."

"I get it," said Richard. "It's simple. He's saying that if Williams was better than his fellow players in his own day, he would be better than his fellow players today. And since everybody is generally better today, he would be that much better too."

Morris scanned the stand of pines beyond the marsh and began wondering about sleeping arrangements. Would Dan stay with Ellen in the master bedroom? Would he be asked to bunk in with Willie? Would he be banished to the cabin down the hill? If Dan didn't sleep in the room with Ellen, how would they explain it to Willie?

"Why is everybody generally better to-day?" asked Willie from the floor.

"A lot of reasons," said Dan, returning to the dining table. "They've definitely juiced the baseball in some way. And there are a lot more hitter-friendly parks to play in."

"Well, right," said Richard, "and think about this: The way they set up the pitching rotation these days, batters face a fifth-in-the-rotation starter in twenty percent of the games. A guy who usually isn't all that good."

Morris spied a great blue on a bough of a pine. It lifted one wing, then turned its head, lowering its bill balletically, as if to inspect something beneath the wing. Morris said, "Willie, come look, quick. It's so beautiful."

Willie moved next to Morris on the sofa and took up the binoculars.

"Straight across there," said Morris excitedly. "You see that tallest pine?"

"Yeah," said Willie.

"Okay, now move an inch to the right. There's a slightly smaller tree with a dead patch near the top. Do you see it?"

"Yeah," said Willie again.

"Okay, now just three branches down from the dead patch, look for a —"

"Oh, yeah, I see it," said Willie, as if it

were the umpteenth sighting of the day. "That's beautiful," he added, handing the binoculars back to Morris.

Willie returned to the rug by the hearth. Morris watched for a moment as the boy resumed his card game. After a few seconds passed, Willie looked up at Morris and said, "Do you think Ted Williams would take steroids if he was playing today?"

Morris stood and went to the windows, where he might get a better bead on the great blue. "I don't know," he said coldly, fine-focusing the glasses. "You'll have to put that on your list of questions to ask him when they thaw him out."

Soon Morris went to the kitchen telephone and tried Ellen's cell phone again, still to no avail. He opened the freezer and began emptying ice trays into a stainless steel mixing bowl, which he would put into the freezer after refilling the trays. He suffered a persistent fear of running out of ice, an idiosyncrasy he traced to his southern boyhood. After a minute Richard came into the kitchen, carrying a blue plastic tumbler and looking around at the cabinets quizzically. He opened one and another of them and finally took down a bottle of scotch.

From the sink, Morris said, "What are you doing?"

"Dan wants another scotch," said Richard.

"*Another* scotch?" said Morris. "I didn't know he'd had one already. He's drinking scotch at two-something in the afternoon?"

Richard gave Morris a *back-off* glare, which prompted Morris to add, "That's not like Dan."

Richard leaned close and whispered, "This is bound to be a little tough for him, don't you imagine?"

Morris thought of the overlong hugs in the driveway. He turned off the tap and put the last of the ice trays into the freezer. "Richard," he said, as Richard was about to leave with the tumbler of scotch. "Seriously. Where do you think Ellen can be?"

"I don't know," he said. "It's a wide wide world out there."

"What's that supposed to mean?"

"It's just that we never said exactly what time she should expect us," said Richard, his tone revealing the great depth and breadth of his patience. "We never specified a time, Morris. It's not even two-thirty yet, and you're acting as if we need to put in a call to the state police."

"You're right, you're right," said Morris. "I just wish she'd get here. I'll be more relaxed once she's here, and something's obviously wrong with Dan."

"Morris," said Richard, "something's always wrong with somebody. It's the nature of things. Dan's going to have his drink and then we're going to take Willie out in the canoe. It's high tide. The sky's clearing. Any second now, the sun's going to come out."

Half an hour later, Richard, Dan, and Willie trooped down the hillside to the cabin, where they found Dan's caution-yellow canoe, carried it over their heads to the edge of the marsh, and launched it through a patchwork of reeds. The sun did come out, a warm breeze stirred the horse chestnut, and a half-dozen pale blue butterflies appeared in the perennial garden, visiting Ellen's crop of peach-colored daylilies. Morris took the field glasses outside and followed the canoe's progress west into the center of the marsh and south toward the bay. The water trembled white like something molten under the sun, and for a moment Morris forgot his several local fears and the alarms of the world at large, absorbed by the beauty of the boat with its three beloved human silhouettes.

When at last Ellen arrived and moved to his side, putting her arm around his waist, he neglected at first to be annoyed with her. She wore sandals and a gauzy pink sundress with kangaroo pockets, her hair was wind-blown, and she'd clearly been weeping.

"Oh, is that Willie out there in the middle?" she cried.

"We've been here for almost two hours," Morris said. "What's wrong? Where have you been?"

Ellen pulled sunglasses from a pocket of her dress and put them on. "I've been to the post office," she said. "And then I took a long walk on the beach at Brush Hollow. Do you want to sit in the garden?"

"The benches will be wet," said Morris.

They carried chairs from the dining table into the garden and found a spot near a young birch, where there was mottled sunlight. Once they were seated, Ellen handed Morris an envelope. "I found this in my post office box about an hour ago," she said.

It was a letter from Bonnie.

Point Clear
    Monday afternoon

Dear Ellen,
You'll be mad at me for doing things this way, but I think you'll eventually under-stand this choice along with some others I've made. After you've read this and

64

had some time to think, we'll talk. Last Saturday, I married the man I've been seeing down here for a while. I know it seems sudden and you'll have your feelings hurt about me not telling you and not inviting you or Morris to the wedding. And now I'm afraid my explanation will hurt your feelings even more but I don't know any other way except to tell the truth and expect that we're all grown-ups and capable of handling difficult things. You and Morris have always looked at me and my life as a kind of train wreck. You're both happily married and successful in your chosen work. I know my failure at a career and my failures at love must look pathetic to you by comparison. While I was down here taking care of Daddy, I realized that I'd been trying my whole life to make myself into somebody he and you and Morris would approve of. Coming down here to take care of Daddy was mostly just another bid for his approval. Which didn't work. Half the time he didn't know who I was and when he did recognize me he'd ask me what in the world did I want. But while I didn't get the love from him I'd hoped for, I got something else by being here. I can't explain it fully because I don't understand it fully myself. When Daddy died, I felt this weight lifted from my heart. I felt alive. I've already mentioned to you that I've fixed up the house and thrown a lot of old stuff out. And after a few weeks of living here on my own, I began to feel, for the first time in my life, that I was really home. Then I began to feel that new doors were about to open for me and that my life was about to take some kind of a wonderful turn. One day in January, shortly after New Year's, I was sitting on our beach wrapped up in a blanket by the pier — which needs some repairs by the way. It was pretty cold and hardly any people. Some fishing boats out on the bay had been sort of hypnotizing me. Then from out of nowhere a man walked up and said hello. He said he was a preacher at a church not too far away and that he often took walks when he was trying to figure out his sermons. I know it sounds mystical, Ellen, but I felt that when he looked at me he *saw* me. And afterward I thought the reason he saw me wasn't just because he had the eyes for it but also, for the first time ever, I was somebody definite to be seen. I've never felt with anybody the way I feel when I'm with him. He's already given me more than I can say. We were married Saturday in his church, which is called the Church of the Blessed Hunger, and isn't that a beautiful name? It's a reference to the Sermon on the Mount, when Jesus said, "Blessed are they who hunger and thirst after righteousness." Oh, Ellen, I want so much for you to be happy for me! I think that once you've gotten to know Pastor (Pastor Vandorpe, that's his name), you'll put aside all your first thoughts. But I know it will take time. I also know that if you and Morris had come down here for the wedding, which was very small by the way, just his parents from Florida and a couple of other witnesses, I would have been worrying the whole time about what you and he were feeling and thinking. It's not your fault, I'm the one that puts you there in my mind. But I hope you can understand and forgive me for whatever pain this causes you. I'm hoping you'll talk to Morris for me too. He hears you in a way he doesn't hear me. Please don't pick up the phone right away. Write me first if you like. Pastor and I are right here, not going anywhere. A honeymoon was out of the question, since the church is just in the middle of a big fund-raising campaign for the new Christ Center. I realize there's a lot to fill in, but I didn't want to spring everything on you over the phone. It's been so horrible keeping this big secret from you, the engagement I mean, the last couple of times we talked. Ellen, I'm happy, that's what I want you to know. And I hope knowing that will affect all your feelings.

Love,
Bonnie

During Morris's silent reading, he uttered, "Oh . . . my . . . God," three different times, and when he finished, he said, "Well, for starters, somebody has got to teach her about paragraphing."

"Please don't make a joke right now, Morris," said Ellen, reaching for the letter, which she placed in its envelope and returned to the pocket of her dress.

"Well, I don't know what to say," Morris said. "I don't know what to say because I don't know what to think. I don't know what's more astounding, that she considers herself a grown-up or that she calls her new husband Pastor."

"And don't be acerbic," said Ellen. "We've got to think about what to do."

"Do?" he said. "What's there to do? Legally, she *is* a grown-up. She's married. Maybe Pastor Vandorpe is just the thing for her. How do I know? She didn't even say what denomination he was. And what in the world is a Christ Center?"

"There's an awful lot she didn't say," said Ellen. "Don't you have the impression that they're living together in the house?"

"Of course they're living in the house. Do you think he just happens to take walks on the beach in Point Clear? As far as I know, it's the only place to walk on Mobile Bay where there are multimillion-dollar homes."

"Oh, Morris, now please let's not immediately assume the worst."

"Okay," he said. "Let's assume the best. Let's assume that Bonnie found a really good psychopharmacologist in Alabama who put her on a really good antidepressant. Let's say that at his insistence she ditched the Ativan and completely stopped smoking dope. Let's say that the Church of the Blessed Hunger is not a fundamentalist sect of the Christian Right but is just a nice little Episcopal parish with a quirky name. Let's say that Bonnie, despite her long history of getting involved with men who took advantage of her, whom she supported financially without exception, has finally met someone who loves her true and true. *Sees* her, as she puts it. Sees the kind, lovely woman she is, beneath all the neediness and self-delusion. Let's say —"

"I'm going for a walk," said Ellen suddenly, standing up. "I'm going to walk along the marsh and try to flag down the canoe."

As Morris watched her hurrying away down the slope, he wondered if perhaps he should have offered to go with her, but he imagined that just now he wasn't the right kind of company. Though she was only two years his senior, she still tended to take with him a big-sister tone, retained from their childhood. It was almost a game they played: He would misbehave; she would correct. There was, in it, a subtle implication that he somehow needed her more than she needed him. But he knew she relied on him in a certain way too, and he regretted not having told her how pretty she looked in the garden, with her newly brown shoulders and pink sundress.

Chapter 3

She told Morris that she'd found the letter in the post office box and then taken a walk on the beach at Brush Hollow; aside from being true, there was enough cause and effect in it to waylay further questions, even from Morris, who habitually probed things deeper than they required. Morris would think it typical of her to withdraw into solitude for the purpose of digesting a surprise; she generally wanted to think about things before she talked about them, while he was more inclined to learn what he thought from what he heard himself say. What wouldn't occur to Morris was that she took the long stroll by the ocean specifically to postpone her encounter with *him*. Morris had a way — actually, he had several — of making everything his own, and she wanted the hour or so at Brush Hollow, not solely to digest Bonnie's news but also to hold it in her own hands before it inevitably became mostly Morris's.

She knew too, even as she stood reading the letter in the post office, that she would cry, and she wanted to get the bulk of that done in private, this in consideration of Dan. Morris, to give him his due, had always been good about tears, while Dan reacted to tears the way most people react to blood. In the aftermath of her father's death last year, Ellen eventually had taken to crying in secret, to avoid Dan's panic response. Whenever he got fed up with her dark moods or irritability and confronted her, she made an effort not to cry, for at the first sight of tears, he would drop whatever charges he held against her. Then he would resent the tears, and she would resent their effect on him. She had known, throughout these past difficult months, that she was too sad, and recently she'd come to see that it was unreasonable for her to expect Dan to understand something she herself didn't. The decision to separate might not have been entirely mutual, but the impulse behind it, in her mind at least, was made of mutual stuff: It was as much her effect on him as his on her that prompted the idea. And now she believed that some benefit, even after only three weeks, had already come of it.

At first, Morris's proposal to bring Willie down for the weekend had thrown her. How could she say no to seeing Willie when she missed him so? How could she have Willie down and bar Dan, when she knew Dan missed him just as much? Even when Morris and Richard were planning to come without Willie, she'd worried it would look too much like a family gathering that pointedly excluded Dan. She'd been irked at Morris for putting her into this particular stew — it seemed to her, without pausing to assemble any evidence, that putting her into a stew was another of his idle pastimes. Even after she'd cleared the way for Willie to come, which cheered her, the problem of what to do about Dan kept her in a funk. That condition, she'd been obliged to observe, evaporated the minute after phoning Dan to invite him for the weekend — or, more accurately, the minute after he accepted. Her spirits had continued to brighten ever since, the basis to her belief that the separation, brief as it was, had already turned a profit. And despite all her complaints against Morris, she was also obliged to observe that it was he who'd originated this happy change. The last few days, an essential part of her better self had been restored, the capacity to notice and love the extraordinary natural beauty that surrounded her, and she'd intended to thank Morris for his role.

Then came Bonnie's letter, or, as she immediately began to think of it, Bonnie's letter *bomb*. Ellen had anticipated something like this, but the overtones of salvation that had usually accompanied Bonnie's romantic entanglements had never been quite biblical. And Bonnie, though she'd always tossed herself suicidally into love, had never submitted to a religious ritual. (She'd married once before, at the age of twenty, but the ceremony took place in a courthouse somewhere in Westchester County, New York, to which she returned in the light of the next day to seek an annulment.) Ellen hadn't found the zeal of her sister's letter as troublesome as a sense she had that Bonnie, in the telling, was actually muffling her emotions: What came through — what Bonnie had allowed to come through — was much more the smoke than the fire. Despite the fatalistic note she'd attached to meeting Pastor Vandorpe, despite the connections she'd drawn between his arrival and the death of their father, she'd meant to be persuasive and consequently she'd soft-pedaled the intensity of her feelings. Ellen would rather have had a giddy letter from her sister, silly and head over heels. Instead, Bonnie had clearly labored over the writing and held too much back. Ellen sensed a fear behind that, and she thought it something other than Bonnie's fear of her and Morris's reactions to the news.

That smaller, more obvious fear — of their reactions — saddened Ellen. Bonnie's leaving her out of the wedding didn't so much provoke hurt feelings as it did a deep disappointment in herself. Bonnie, sweetly, had tried to let her off the hook with *I'm the one who puts you there in my mind,* but there was still the fact of the hook: Bonnie had plenty of reason for leaving her and Morris out. Ellen often had seen herself as reserving judgments of Bonnie, of cautiously sorting what could be let go from what needed constructive criticism. But here she'd been lumped together with Morris, and if she wasn't only disappointed but a little hurt, it was because of this. She supposed Morris's proximity did have the effect of making her underestimate her own tendency to find fault, and yet she would have hoped Bonnie could see a difference between them.

Now, halfway to the cabin, she lost sight of the bright yellow boat as the locust trees rose up and blocked the view, and this coincided with a particular notion: Of course it would be necessary for Bonnie to lump Morris and her together, regardless of any difference she might see between them, for she couldn't very well send an invitation to one and not to the other. By the time Ellen rounded the cabin and started through the tunnel in the woods, at which point the canoe reappeared, she'd added this, her being left out of her own sister's wedding, to a list of unhappy outcomes for which Morris could be held accountable. In the next moment, however, that train of thought seemed clattering and empty. If Bonnie's desire for her had been deeper, it could have absorbed Morris and his flaws.

The canoe, about a hundred yards from shore, moved at a good clip south, toward the mouth of the marsh and the intrusion of the bay. If Ellen meant to make herself seen and heard, she would have to walk some distance south along the periphery. The path she would normally have used for this was, at high tide, under water, so she had to negotiate, in dress and sandals, the dry ground just inside the edge of the woods, a shelf of land cluttered with brush and poison ivy. After a minute of the fancy footwork this demanded, she found herself laughing aloud — something about the ridiculous sense of urgency that seemed to have her in its grip. When at last she came up even with the canoe, she quickly removed her sandals, stepped off the ledge, and waded into the ankle-deep water, a springy mat of cordgrass and peat beneath her feet, a scurrying of mud crabs. She began to wave the sandals, one in each hand, in extravagant arcs; an easterly wind thrummed the acres of water and tall green grasses, gulls plunged and soared, the yellow canoe the sole visible craft, now advancing along a passage between two islands. She called out all three names, *Dan, Willie, Richard,* twice each, in rapid order, and — the wind in her favor — all three heads turned in her direction, but not simultaneously; Willie, nearest the bow, appeared to prompt the two others.

They executed a turn in the narrow passage and began paddling out of it, toward her, and Dan briefly jabbed the paddle skyward in a kind of salute. Of course she felt herself welling up, but she had already determined that tears, precisely tears, would not be what greeted them.

Afterward, no one would quite recall how the topic of the Dalai Lama got introduced or who introduced it, but near the midpoint of the evening, Morris was heard to say, "Oh, Christ, the Dalai Lama, why doesn't somebody just throw a net over him?"

They'd been treated to a marvelous sunset. The afternoon sun had overly warmed the house, but by the end of dinner, and once darkness had fully settled in, a breeze began to churn the sheers over the open doors to the sleeping porch. This same breeze bore the scent of the marsh at low tide, prompting Morris to remark that it reminded him of home, an uncongenial reference to Mobile Bay. Earlier, after Ellen had flagged down the canoe, Richard and Willie had once again taken up the voyage, but Dan accompanied Ellen on a long walk through the woods, during which she shared with him the news of Bonnie's letter. His response, a single "Oh-h-h," had carried for Ellen a satisfying ring: She'd taken the silence that followed it as a kindness — he'd indicated his breadth of understanding, his grasp of the implications, but he would wait awhile before tossing his own thoughts into the hat. This reading of the moment, colored by her gladness at seeing him, hadn't been completely undermined when, a minute later, he'd confessed that he'd had two scotches in the afternoon and that the boat had made him feel woozy. Back at the house, Dan had devoted himself to the dinner preparation, refusing all offers of help;

Morris had dragged a chaise longue into the garden and finished Stanley Meacham's novel; Ellen had taken a luxurious bath, shaved her legs, and washed her hair. When Willie and Richard returned from the marsh, they'd each taken a turn in the outdoor shower, then put on dry shorts, lain down on separate beds on the sleeping porch, and fallen asleep.

A while later, when the group gathered at the long pine dining table in the main room of the house, Richard and Willie had added clean white T-shirts to what they were already wearing; Dan still wore the striped shorts and polo shirt he'd arrived in; but Ellen and Morris had descended the front stairs attired for a more formal occasion — she'd put on the best dress she'd brought with her, pale blue silk with spaghetti straps, and he'd put on what he called his "better khakis" and an Oxford-cloth sport shirt the same shade of blue as Ellen's dress. Dan of course had gone all out with the cooking; he'd served oysters on the half shell, grilled local bluefish, fresh corn on the cob and sliced tomatoes, risotto with bay scallops, and two very expensive wines; he'd prepared cheeseburgers for Willie and Morris. What to do about Bonnie had dominated the dinner conversation even when not being spoken of directly, so that departures from it, such as the Dalai Lama, had a distinct air of diversion.

"Oh, don't tell me," Dan said to Morris, from the head of the table. "You don't like the Dalai Lama."

Dan's tone was both exasperated and amused, and something about it made Ellen uneasy; she stood and started to clear the table, removing the almost empty wine bottles first. A light with a soft beaded shade hovered low over the center of the table, and Ellen knocked her head against it as she reached for the bottles. For a moment after she'd left the room, the shadows of the tall wine goblets swung eerily back and forth across the tablecloth.

"Of course I don't like the Dalai Lama," said Morris.

"I've never heard of anyone who didn't like the Dalai Lama," said Dan.

"You mean apart from Chairman Mao and several million Chinese."

"What did the Dalai Lama ever do to you?" asked Dan.

"I'll tell you later," Morris said. "There are children in the room."

Willie had already left the table and joined Richard on the sofa, where they'd switched on a lamp at either end and begun to play backgammon. Willie said, "I'm thirteen, Morris, and everybody else in the room is way over twenty-one."

"I stand corrected," said Morris, turning to Willie for a moment. "There is only one underage person in the room, and he is an adolescent."

"Just ignore him," said Richard to Willie, then, to Dan, "Just ignore him."

"Let me say this," said Morris. "Should I bump into His Holiness on the road of life, I would have a bone or two to pick with him."

"That's my Morris," said Richard.

During this exchange, Ellen made three trips between the table and the kitchen, continuing to clear the dishes. At last she returned to her seat and sat down in so apparent a fog that Morris glared at her and said, "What?"

"Oh, nothing," said Ellen. "I was just thinking."

"I can see that," said Morris. "And somehow *a penny for your thoughts* doesn't seem adequate."

Dan looked at Ellen, which called him back to the dominant topic. He turned to Morris and said, "Well, what did you plan to do with the house in Point Clear anyway?"

"I don't know for sure," said Morris. "Vaguely, I suppose we planned to sell it. I suppose we were waiting for Bonnie to come back from Alabama. To come back to her senses, as it turns out. Now I'm not sure what we'll do."

"This isn't about the house," Ellen said, to no one in particular. Then she looked at Morris and said, "Is it?"

"Well, it's about the house and some other things," Morris answered. "Mostly it's about this *parable* Bonnie seems to be living in."

"Yes," said Ellen, thoughtfully.

"Or *psycho*-parable," added Morris.

"It's a familiar pattern, isn't it," said Ellen. "The undiscovered actress. The undiscovered person. At long last discovered."

"Nicodemus waiting in the tree," said Morris. "Jesus comes rambling along the road. Looks up. *Sees* him. Invites him to sup with him, as I recall."

"Yes," repeated Ellen.

After quite a long pause, in which Morris and Ellen appeared to have entered a common daydream, Dan said, "How much do you think the house is worth?"

Morris, startled for a moment, said, "Oh, I think we could get close to two million probably."

"In *Alabama?*" said Dan.

"Shocking, isn't it," said Morris.

"I wish you hadn't brought in Jesus," said Ellen, softly to Morris.

"Sorry," said Morris.

From the sofa, Richard complained that Willie, who had handily beaten him a second time, was too clever by half. As they began resetting the board for a third game, he said, "I guess this sounds like blasphemy under the circumstances, but has it crossed either of your minds that you may be making a mountain out of a molehill?"

"What do you mean?" Morris asked, turning in his chair.

"Just what you think I mean," answered Richard. "Maybe this is Bonnie's chance for happiness. You can't know."

"I was thinking something like that too," said Dan, "but I didn't want to step on any toes. I was also thinking that maybe Bonnie could buy out your interests in the house. I mean, assuming she and her husband want to go on living there."

"Dan," said Ellen, "I already told you. This isn't about the house."

"What does Jesus have to do with it?" asked Willie.

"Much too much, I'm afraid," said Morris. "Much more than we would like."

83

Willie said to Richard, "What does he mean?"

"He means that this man, the man Bonnie's married, is a preacher."

"What's wrong with that?" asked Willie.

"Nothing," Richard said. "But there are suspicions in the air. Many many assumptions and suspicions."

"She quotes the Sermon on the *Mount* in her letter," said Morris.

"Well, it's not a bad sermon," said Richard.

"And in the next breath mentions fund-raising," added Morris.

Willie said, "I still don't understand. Shouldn't we be happy that Aunt Bonnie's finally gotten married?"

"Well, that's exactly the question, isn't it," Richard said, and high-fived Willie. "Shouldn't we be happy?"

Ellen shook her head, then shrugged her shoulders. "Maybe it's true," she said. "Maybe we're letting our imaginations run wild."

"If our imaginations were running wild," Morris said, "we would be thinking that Bonnie had pulled herself together and found a proper husband."

"Oh, what in the world could be more proper than marrying for love?" said Richard. "If anything's clear, it's clear that she's in love with the man."

"Can I just say one last thing about the house?" asked Dan, turning to Ellen. "I get it that the house isn't the main thing. But if you all three own it equally, and she's decided to make it her permanent home . . . well, wouldn't she have talked to you about it first? I mean, I think it's an indication that she's afraid of you and Morris, not just afraid of what you think, but —"

At that moment, from somewhere deep in the woods around the house, a din of yips and howls rose up, lasting about thirty seconds, and during which everyone sat frozen — serious, if wide-eyed — except for Willie, who grinned from ear to ear. When the sound faded away, he whispered, in a horror-movie voice, "Coyotes."

Ellen said, "That's the loudest I've ever heard them," then turned to Dan and said, "What's your point?"

Dan appeared taken aback, as if he had either forgotten his point or thought it already plain. "Well, you say this isn't about the house," he said, "and what I think you mean is that it's not about money. But it *is* about the house in one sense — the house is the physical thing that still ties you three together as a family. At the very least it represents your relationships to one another. And if Bonnie was planning to live there with her new husband and didn't talk to you about it, it means she must be *afraid* to talk to you about it."

"I see what he's saying," said Richard.

"We all see what he's saying," said Morris. "It's just so . . . I don't know . . . obvious."

"Maybe so," said Dan. "But I think it's a question of focus."

"Okay, Dan," said Morris. "Let's focus. Bonnie meets a man, an evangelical preacher, and falls in love. Soon they're living together in the old family homestead. Until today, we —"

"You don't know all of those things for sure," Richard said.

"These are safe assumptions," said Morris sharply. "Until today, we have only some cloudy notion that she's involved with somebody, no more than that. But lo and behold, they've gotten married. She lets Ellen and me know about it after the fact. No, she lets Ellen know and asks Ellen to let me know. Even if she'd told us about this Vandorpe person earlier, even if she'd asked our permission about his moving into the house, what would we have said? No? Sorry, Bonnie, but we forbid it?"

"Well, you might have said —" Dan began.

"She kept us in the dark until after the wedding because she didn't want us at the wedding," said Morris. "It's that simple. No, it's not that simple. She didn't want *me* at the wedding."

Surprising everyone, Morris stood, tossed his napkin onto the table, and left the house through the front door. Richard said "Excuse me" to Willie and followed him.

Willie moved from the sofa to the table, where he took Morris's chair, opposite his mother. The three of them sat silently for a few seconds. Willie folded his hands on the tabletop. The low-hanging light at the table's center lent the scene a grave significant air, a summit meeting or a séance.

At last, Dan said, "What'd I say?"

He looked at Ellen, who had the face of someone who'd chanced onto something she'd been searching for but now didn't find it pleasing. "It wasn't anything you said," she answered, almost dismissively, as if Dan's question was so wide of the mark it didn't merit consideration.

"Well, what did he mean by —" Dan began, but at that moment Morris came back through the front door.

He moved next to Willie and put his arm around the boy's shoulders. "Richard's out in the yard looking at the stars," he said. "He asked me to ask you to join him. There's a constellation or two he thinks you might know."

Willie glanced briefly at his mother, then rose from the table and went outside, carefully closing the screen door without a sound.

Morris sat at the table and met Ellen's eye. "You do realize," he said, "that we have to go down there."

She reached for his hand, held it a moment, then stood and started gathering what was left of the silverware. "Yes," she said. "I realize."

"We must see what's what in Point Clear."

"Yes."

Once Ellen had left the room, Morris turned toward Dan and smiled, thinking how like a passenger Dan looked, how not like a driver.

But Dan peered at him through narrowed eyes, as if he was trying to read Morris's mind. "I get it," he said, nodding slowly. "You think I don't, but I do. You meant she didn't want you and Richard there, you and Richard together, that's what you meant."

A few minutes past midnight, the house was dark except for a lamp in the master bedroom and a light in the master bath. In the sky, the stars had faded because of a three-quarter moon high over the salt marsh. Morris and Richard lay on the four-poster bed in one of the upstairs rooms, talking softly. The room's decidedly feminine decor — the bed's lace-skirted canopy, which matched the curtains over the windows; the wallpaper of pink roses and ribbons — made the two men, in their underwear, atop a floral-patterned chenille spread, look strangely brutish.

"Where did you go?" asked Morris, studying the mahogany ribs on the canopy's underside.

"We took a walk along the marsh," answered Richard. "The moon came up."

"That's nice. What did you talk about?"

"I mostly listened," said Richard. "He talked about himself. About what the last three weeks were like."

"Isn't Dan great?" said Morris. "It's so refreshing when somebody that filthy rich also has an agreeable personality."

"I love Dan," said Richard. "For richer or poorer."

"I do too," said Morris. "In sickness and in health."

"And I love Willie."

"Willie's the most. I wish I could go back

in time and *be* Willie."

"We're lucky, aren't we."

"Lucky in many ways," Morris agreed. "What did Dan say?"

"He's been taking muscle relaxants to get to sleep. He said he's been suffering a bad case of monkey-mind."

"Ah," said Morris, "monkey-mind."

"Swinging between hope and resentment, he said. He said he couldn't even watch the baseball games because it made him miss Ellen and Willie too much."

"It shows," said Morris. "I mean, that he's not been sleeping well."

"He said that last night he packed a bag, and about halfway through he realized he was packing as if he was staying for the rest of the summer. He'd been invited for the weekend, but he'd got it into his head that when Ellen saw him she'd have a change of heart and he'd end up staying. So he unpacked and packed a smaller one for the weekend. Then, this morning, he packed the larger one again and brought it. Just in case."

"Good for him," said Morris.

"He called it a *crazy fantastical hope*."

"That's what he said? Those were his exact words?"

"Yes. He meant it as an example of how

pathetic he was."

"Dan's about the least pathetic person I know," said Morris.

"I agree," said Richard.

"And you, of course," Morris said. "You're not pathetic either."

"What have I got to be pathetic about? Tell me what you mean to accomplish by going to Point Clear."

"I don't think we'll know for sure until we get there."

"You're going to take a look around."

"Yes. To verify my many suspicions and assumptions."

"Or not."

"Okay, or not, but either way that's not my main concern."

After a few seconds of silence, Richard said, "Your main concern is what you *don't* suspect or assume."

"Sometimes you astound me," Morris said. "Yes, exactly." After a pause, he added, "Ellen said she smells fear in Bonnie's letter."

"Fear?"

"Well, Ellen thinks the letter has a looked-over-the-shoulder quality," said Morris. "Which isn't quite the right way to put it, but I understand what she's getting at."

Ellen, at that moment sequestered in the

master bath and wearing only a cotton summer robe, was staring into the medicine chest mirror and applying a rose-scented facial cleanser, a component of a bedtime ritual so entrenched that it required absolutely nothing of her conscious mind — a good thing, since every corner of her conscious mind was occupied by Dan, who waited for her, in bed, on the other side of the door. Mostly, she'd been asking herself, again and again, what she felt about one thing and another: the new overabundance of food in the refrigerator downstairs; Dan's overlarge suitcase, which, without advice or consent, he'd carried upstairs and placed at the foot of her bed; his overdrinking, which, admittedly, was for Dan only more than one glass of wine with dinner. What exactly did it *mean,* his waiting for her in the next room? What did it mean that she'd brought three different sleeping ensembles into the bathroom, and that she would presently mull over what particular message they each conveyed? She took it as a positive sign that twenty-one days, though short on the calendar, felt long when she'd seen Dan that afternoon. To banish him from the bedroom would overstate something she didn't quite believe — that by sleeping separately they would somehow honor their original plan of separation, already clearly broken by her inviting him for the weekend. What would be the point? She could sense his fidgetiness now as he waited for her under the covers, a familiar and pleasurable feeling. But of course she needed to talk first. She didn't want things to unfold between them by default. If they were to be back together, and sooner than planned, she wanted to talk, for talking about it would make it real and deliberate, rather than something that "just happened." She turned on the tap in the sink and held her wrists under the warm water for a minute. She dampened a clean cloth and removed the cleanser from her face and neck and forehead. She started to brush her hair, which was beginning at last to reach a respectable length.

But after only a moment she put down the brush, turned her back to the mirror, and leaned against the vanity. The separation, which had been directed at her marriage only, seemed, she realized now, to have caused a shift in a neighboring property, where the death of her father had pitched its dark tent, and the change had come in the cleanest possible form: For several days, she'd simply forgotten to think about her father. She imagined there was still more to feel — the strings that bound up the loss of a father one never actually had were fairly tangled — but even as she tried to think of him now, he seemed the least interesting thing at hand, and she wondered if the new ordeal facing her, Bonnie, might have shoved him aside. In any case, she believed she was glad about Dan's waiting for her in the next room, glad in her sense of his fidgetiness under the covers. She'd brought with her into the bathroom a plain cotton nightgown with a scalloped neckline, a pair of white panties and a T-shirt, and silk tap pants with a matching top. Recalling Dan's opposition, in bed, to fabric of any sort — in bed he was thoughtful but no-nonsense — she put on the panties and T-shirt. She brushed her teeth and rinsed with mouthwash, switched off the light, and opened the door.

A single lamp burned on the nightstand nearest Dan, who rested on his side, the covers down around his waist, his bare back turned to her. He didn't stir. She thought maybe he'd fallen asleep, which she greeted with both disappointment and relief. Then, as she took two steps toward the bed, he rolled onto his back, smiled, and said, "Hi."

She sat on the edge of the bed and looked at him. He put his hands behind his head. "Last night the thunderstorm woke me up," he said. "I went into your study to close the window in there, and the wind had blown a couple of things off your wall . . . you know, behind your desk, where you have all those pictures tacked up. I'd seen those things before — the ballerinas, the field of wildflowers, the lake in Scotland, all the others. And I'd always thought they were just things you loved. Beautiful things. Good things. But last night, I thought maybe they were things you —" He stopped, shut his eyes tight, then added, "I don't know . . . things you maybe longed for."

An hour later, in another upstairs room but at the opposite end of the house, Willie was dreaming that he was alone and paddling the yellow canoe in the marsh; he heard a swooshing of wings, and a great blue heron swooped down so close to his head that he tried to swat it away with the paddle, at which point, looking up at the sky, he saw the ceiling of his bedroom at the Cape house and was consumed by an urge to pee.

The floor beneath his bare feet inevitably creaked here and there, but he knew a few especially noisy spots to avoid in the hallway. Moonlight streamed through the small bathroom window so that he didn't need to switch on a light. When he was done, and as he stepped back into the hallway, he recalled that in the dream his hair had been very long, and he wondered what that meant. A boy in his dorm at camp had a book called *A Dream Dictionary,* which you could use for interpreting dreams. There'd been a lot of talk about what different body parts signified — genitals, no surprise, were always about sex; sucking on nipples meant you were spending too much money — but Willie hadn't heard anything about long hair. Now he noticed a faint glow of light falling onto the floor at the end of the hall where the hall made an L toward his parents' room. He heard, also faintly, his father's voice, and something new and odd about it drew Willie, on tiptoe, to that corner. The door to the room stood open two inches, and he saw now that the light spilling onto the floor was candlelight. The narrow opening looked like a vertical strip that had been razored out of a larger picture of his parents' room. In it, he could see his father and mother sitting at the foot of the bed, his father in boxer shorts, his mother in a white T-shirt. Willie thought of a certain kind of religious painting, for he could see that his mother was holding his father in her arms, his father's head resting on her shoulder, her own head bowed over his. The only truly fascinating thing about all this was his father's voice. Willie still couldn't understand any of the words — his father spoke too soft and low — but, this close, Willie was able to confirm the spectacular instinct he'd had a moment before: His father was crying.

CHAPTER 4

A Thursday morning of brilliant sun, and the shadow of a passenger jet glided over the bay, then rippled across the white strip of beach in front of the house, the great oak in the yard, and the several angles of the dark green roof. Bonnie Owen Vandorpe, situated in a rattan chair on the porch and reading a wizened paperback of *The Power and the Glory,* looked up from the book and squinted at the glare of the bay, dimly aware of some flickering in the natural light and a faraway whisper of displaced air. Her young husband, Pastor, who lay on a matching couch nearby, smiled at her from over the top of a thick spiral notebook, into which, for the last half hour, he'd been entering thoughts for next Sunday's sermon. From inside the house there came a heavy crash — Macy, the housekeeper, had dropped a cast-iron skillet onto the kitchen floor and let out a whoop, leaping backward to protect her toes. Cricket, the old family bird dog, bolted from under the kitchen table and into the living room, where he startled the orange cat, who'd been sleeping in an easy chair and who now rocketed through the open window onto the porch, sailing over the back of the rattan couch and upsetting Bonnie's almost empty aluminum tumbler of tea; a few drops splattered onto Pastor's notebook and along one leg of his khaki shorts. Bonnie, quickly out of her chair, cried, "China!" (the cat's name) and began making a fuss with a paper napkin, but Pastor sat upright on the edge of the couch and waved her away. She knelt near his feet and wiped a puddle from the painted wood floor, sensing, as she did this, his gaze, and when she looked up at him, he leaned forward enough to kiss her brow; he smiled again and said, "The peaceable kingdom." He kissed her a second time and added, "I think I'll head over to the church and work on this in my office."

He stood, slipped out sideways between her and the couch, then stepped to the screen door and shooed the cat into the yard. He moved through the interior doorway, into the darkness of the house, and Bonnie said softly to herself, "Well, *bye* then."

Macy — who had cooked and cleaned for the Owens since before Bonnie was born — immediately appeared at that same threshold, plump, white-haired, and flushed. She wore a pink candy-striped apron, which she now untied and removed. She was running late for the vet's, she told Bonnie; Cricket was supposed to get his distemper shot at noon, she would have to race over there pronto, and was there anything Bonnie needed her to pick up in Fairhope?

Bonnie pondered this question for a moment, then sighed and shook her head, as if she *wished* she needed something from Fairhope. At last she said, with more than a little hopelessness, "Nothing I can think of, Macy."

"What's wrong?" asked Macy.

"I don't know," said Bonnie.

Macy stepped forward and laid first her palm on Bonnie's forehead, then the back of her hand. "Hmm," she said. "Feels to me like there's something on your mind but you ain't quite ready to say what it is."

"I want your opinion about something," said Bonnie, mostly ignoring Macy's diagnosis. "Do you think Pastor's happy living here with us?"

"Oh, Lord, Bonnie," said Macy, "let me get back to you on that. I can tell you he's plenty happy to have home-cooked meals set on the table for him every day. Now, I'm gonna be late."

After Macy left, Bonnie remained in the same spot on the porch floor, sinking back onto her heels and feeling abruptly alone. She stared at the threadbare cushions of the couch, at their pattern of olive-green palm fronds and red monkeys, and made a mental note to have some new slipcovers sewn for the porch furniture. The last several months, she'd undertaken a cosmetic restoration of the house, which had not only occupied a good bit of her time and energy but had also taught her some important lessons. One late afternoon around Thanksgiving last year, she'd found herself, as she often used to find herself, a little overmedicated — she'd had a day in which she'd felt unusually and relentlessly afraid, and she'd swallowed an extra Ativan and then smoked a joint — and as she wandered the rooms of the old house at sunset, she'd encountered them so bluntly, so acutely, she'd finally seen into the heart of their ugly ambiguous character. She'd understood their problem, and in some critical breakthrough way she identified with them. The spirit of her mother, who'd died giving birth to Bonnie thirty years earlier, lingered profoundly in the rooms, successfully lingered, because her mother's taste hadn't been contemporary but had run to a bygone era, which, it now turned out, was timeless and true. The trouble came from her having left the scene so long ago, and since then, odd people — Bonnie's father the oddest among them — had added tacky incongruences to the rooms, insulting everything good established by her mother. Heavy glass ashtrays and cardboard coasters with advertising logos rested on delicate tea tables of inlaid cherry. A large gloopy oil painting, a deep-sea fishing scene given to Bonnie's father by a business associate, occupied a wall of the living room alongside five handsome black-and-white prints depicting the cathedrals of Europe. All that was needed to set things right, Bonnie had seen at last, was to rid the house of what indicated the father and keep what indicated the mother. Over the next few weeks she'd tossed out yards of revolting shag carpeting and then had the beautiful oak floors refinished; pulled down dozens of plastic miniblinds and replaced them with white sheer drapes; filled two vans from Goodwill Industries with cheap knickknacks and sorry-looking furniture, including her father's large metal rubber-topped desk from the library; she'd had the wallpaper cleaned in the dining room and other rooms newly painted. In this way she'd purged the house of the dead father, and to her surprise the result was something brighter and broader than improved rooms. She'd been given a sense of her place in the world, a sense that attached somehow to her having "restored" her mother, the mother she'd never known. What was more, she felt she'd hit on a principle she could apply to other areas of her life, and she began to experiment with going for longer and longer periods without drugs, a phase of her development that happened to coincide with the appearance of a young preacher who approached her one cold day on the beach and introduced himself.

Now from her spot on the porch floor (where she felt inexplicably stuck), Bonnie could still see him lying before her on the rattan couch, a little schoolboyish with his white polo shirt tucked into his shorts, his beaded Navaho belt, his bare legs crossed at the ankles. Clean-shaven, tan, smelling of a pine-scented aftershave, his longish black hair tucked behind his ears, his bright blue eyes both guileless and intrusive beneath thick eyebrows, he radiated physical beauty, a thing Bonnie sometimes felt must be endured as much as enjoyed. *He can't work here,* she thought, and then, *He's too young for me,* but these fears, failing to find anywhere to lodge, seemed to die almost as quickly as they were felt. The last several weeks her mind had been dispensing with most fears in this fashion, an effect, she believed, generated by her happiness. Her happiness — new, admittedly, but also strong, the way some new things could be — didn't blot out her fears. It simply *rendered* them (like, as Pastor had said, boiling water did to fat in a pot on the stove), so they might be seen for what they truly were. Then they could be felt thoroughly and do what most fears were supposed to do: pass. Pastor said to her, early on, months before they were married, that if she meant to "get better," the catchall term he used for every kind of spiritual progress, she would need to give up her long love affair with fear. He'd said, rightly, that she'd neglected herself spiritually, and this neglect had made her vulnerable to whatever powerful force might want to step in to administrate her inner life. Bonnie had recognized *powerful force* as a reference to the Devil, but Pastor had wisely refrained from using the actual word on her. Fear, he'd said instead, had become her Lord and Master, because she'd neglected to nurture any other thing, and of course because she'd neglected to make any definite decisions along these lines. We belonged to God, he told her, and our be-longingness to God was the core of our true nature. If we didn't know that, then every-thing else we thought we knew about our-selves was but a house without a founda-tion, a scary place to live. Every time the wind blew it rattled our walls. Terrified night and day, he said, we stand vigilant at the windows, certain that some bad weather's going to come along and blow us away. And what chance does a person have, under those circumstances, for any degree of hap-piness?

Such talk revealed him to Bonnie but also showed the depth of his immediate under-standing of her lifelong trouble. It had for her several startling qualities — she'd found it more comforting than threatening, for example — but most startling was that it often came, not simultaneously, but in conjunction with, lovemaking. Equally startling, the lovemaking itself had com-prised for four full months nothing more than kissing and fondling, never sleeping in the same bed if Pastor stayed overnight at the house, and the ease with which he moved from physical affection to this other kind, a caring for her soul, made even the novelty of it feel to her like part of the romance. The first of June, they got engaged, and through a ritual of holding hands and joining together in prayer, he'd declared them married in God's eyes; the ceremony to follow in a few weeks would be the joyous public expression of such. This meant they could have what Bonnie privately thought of as real sex, but when at last it happened — the reservoir of desire so deep, the terrain of friendship already explored so great — it didn't feel like real sex at all but something she'd never experienced with any of a half dozen lovers from the past: it felt like *real* sex.

Pastor's question — What chance does a person have, under those circumstances, for any degree of happiness? — first put to her months ago, returned to Bonnie now in his lovely, calming voice, and she leaned forward and laid her head on the cushion of the couch. She thought, *He's going to leave me, he's going to leave me for sure,* but she recalled without delay that she belonged to God, who would never leave her, and that God was the well of her happiness, not Pastor Vandorpe. Fear, so long allowed to burn unchecked inside her, continued to sputter out these desperate flaming arrows, but the difference today was that they

106

seldom ignited anything. In a way, even their hot little sting served to remind her of how she had changed.

She *had* changed, though she worried occasionally that she had too directly substituted God for the various medications she used to use to stay afloat; she worried about becoming too dependent on God, which was actually a more palatable way of worrying about becoming too dependent on Pastor, God's resident proxy. Not long ago she'd expressed to Pastor her concern about overdependence on God, and he'd told her that God was not a drug and a person couldn't overdose on Him. But secretly she enjoyed thinking of God as a drug — after all, if you couldn't overdose, what was the harm? — and what she liked most about the God-as-a-drug idea was that you couldn't run out of it.

A breeze, warm and damp, came through the screens of the porch, and she stood, moved to the screen door, and gazed out at the yard and the bay. Here was the ancient live oak of her girlhood, the hundred-armed monster erupting from the ground by the brick wall that abutted the promenade, its myriad of long gray beards (Spanish moss) swinging in unison toward the house. Here was the modest lawn, bare and scorched in spots, a patchwork of green, gold, and gray, that stretched between the porch and the wall with its black wrought-iron gate; the stone promenade; the blinding strip of beach beyond; and the ailing pier that jutted into the water, at its end an empty boat shed with a tin roof so noisy in rainfall you could hear the racket from the house. For a moment Bonnie wondered where the cat could have got to, and then she was jolted by the sound of a voice behind her. When she turned, she saw Pastor standing in the doorway. "You scared me to death!" she cried. "I thought you'd left for the church."

"You didn't think I'd leave without saying good-bye, did you?" he said, clipping his cell phone onto his belt. "I had to change my shorts. Do you by any chance want to come with me today?"

"Oh," she said, "do you want me to? I mean, today especially?"

"Just if you want to," he said. "How are you feeling anyway?"

This referred to her breakfast-table complaint of queasiness, which she'd felt recurrently the last three weeks or so. Now, however, she felt strangely caught by him at something.

"I guess I'm about the same," she said.

He looked at her, tilting his head side to

side, as if to get a couple of different angles on her, then said, "You probably ought to stay home then, I guess."

She wanted to explain that this little lie wasn't the old kind she used to tell regarding her physical condition; one of the several ways she'd "got better" over the past few months, since knowing Pastor, was that she wasn't nearly so prone to maladies brought on by her mind. That old kind of lying — which had to do with her health and which wasn't, technically, lying at all, since she experienced it as truth — was the product of her being the victim of what he called a false reality. She didn't so much bear false witness, he'd said, as she bore witness to something false. She really *had* been feeling queasy lately but it generally passed by this time of the day and the reason she'd pretended still to feel about the same was because she didn't right now want to leave the house. She'd been actively ignoring the obvious explanation for the queasiness, while speculating that the tap water was to blame — a speculation, she'd noticed, that always elicited a tolerant look from Macy. But all this was way too complicated to explain to Pastor, and she wished he wouldn't leave either, so she went to him and put her arms around him. As he pulled her closer, she whispered, "Don't go, Pastor. It's quiet here now."

He put her at arm's length, a hand on each of her shoulders. "You think that's why I'm going over to the church . . . because the cat splattered my shorts with tea?" he said. "Why, on a different day, that cat flying through the window might've been my inspiration, sweetheart. I'm just looking for a change of scenery because I'm not getting anywhere with my sermon."

To Bonnie's ears this only confirmed her fear that he couldn't work at the house, and she figured her disappointment showed on her face, for he drew her to him again and kissed her on the lips, a consolation kiss if there ever was one. "Why don't you take your book down to the beach and soak up some of that sunshine?" he said. "It might do you some good."

"Maybe I will," she said, smiling and feeling, ridiculously, that she was smiling bravely. Just as he was about to turn, she almost blurted, "What's it about, Pastor — the sermon, I mean?"

" 'Every branch in me that beareth not fruit he taketh away,' " Pastor answered, in the special overly enunciated voice he used for quoting scripture. " 'And every branch that beareth fruit, he purgeth it, that it may bring forth more fruit.' "

"Which means?" she asked.

"Well, that's the very question I'm wrestling with, Bonnie girl," he said. "What do you think it means?"

Before she could stop herself, she shrugged her shoulders. "I don't even know who's speaking," she said. "It sounds like a psalm."

"No," said Pastor, "not a psalm, but I'll give you a hint. The verse before it goes, 'I am the true vine, and my father is the husbandman.' "

"Husbandman?" said Bonnie. "That's a funny word."

"Well, just plug *gardener* in there," said Pastor. "I am the true vine, and my father is the gardener."

"Okay, let's see," said Bonnie. "If he's speaking in metaphors . . . and he's talking about one of his favorite subjects, himself . . . I'm going to have to take a wild guess and say it's Jesus."

Pastor laughed — genuinely, she thought — and said, "Bingo. Now talk to me about the next verse. Every branch that beareth not fruit —"

His cell phone went off — strains of the Hallelujah Chorus that indicated Edith Busby, senior minister secretary at the church — and he pressed a button to silence it. "She's probably just calling to remind me about Prayer Team at noon," he said.

Bonnie, happy to evade the Bible verse question, kissed him and said, "Go. You should go."

"I'll be home for supper," he said. "What's Macy cooking tonight?"

"I don't know," Bonnie answered.

"Well, it's bound to be good whatever it is," he said, "you can count on that." He gave her one of his big bear hugs and turned to leave. From inside he called, "Be good, now."

This time Bonnie followed him through the sprawling dark house, past the living room and dining room, down the long hallway past the bedrooms, past the library where her dead father's ashes rested in an urn on the mantel, and into the kitchen; she stood at the Dutch door of the mudroom, at the corner of the house where they parked the cars and where Macy had her small apartment. She called out, "Bye-bye, husbandman. Wifewoman will miss you while you're gone."

He waved from behind the steering wheel of his shiny new fire-engine-red open-top Jeep (her wedding present to him), and it made her think of his leaving on safari. She watched as he maneuvered the car into the driveway with one hand and rigged a headset to his ears with the other. The oystershell driveway, which ran nearly a quarter mile from the house to the road, bisected a flat open field, open and green except for a three-car garage, a gardener's cottage with an attached lean-to shed, and two large islands of azaleas, each at the middle of the field's two equal rectangles. Bonnie remained at the door until the Jeep disappeared in the distance through the brick columns at the entrance to the property. She then turned away, moved back through Macy's pristine kitchen and into the dark hallway inside. She paused before a huge mirror in a mahogany frame, thinking, *Something's wrong.* In the dim mottled glass she saw not herself but her older sister, Ellen — and, astonishingly, this older, paler, and entirely unglamorous woman burst into tears.

She did not take her book down to the beach to soak up some sunshine. The sun was oppressive this time of year and she was tired of *The Power and the Glory,* which she used mostly as a prop, something to hold in her hands those mornings when Pastor stayed home to work and she wanted to be near him. She thought the reason Pastor had suggested the beach was because of how she looked, tired and cadaverous. She decided, instead, to take a long bubble bath and wash her hair, the kind of action her theater friends would call *changing your energy*. The bathroom attached to the master bedroom was her favorite in the house. With its tall French windows opening onto a shady terrace, it stayed cool even on the hottest days, and she'd made the most of the huge old white porcelain fixtures — the clawfoot tub, the pedestal sink — by painting everything white except for the floor, which she'd had redone in tiny turquoise glass tiles.

As Bonnie soaked in the tub, she reflected on her morning so far and saw that what Pastor had caught her at, as he'd spoken her name and startled her on the porch, was that terrible skulking peril of thirty-year-old, independently wealthy, and spiritually neglectful women who'd failed to find a clear calling: idleness. That moment, and their ensuing bland exchange, she thought, was mostly about sweet beautiful Pastor in his new home, trying to work out the mystery of his having chosen her. Always kind, always patient — How are you feeling? Do you want to come with me to the church? Why don't you take your book down to the beach? — but conveying unintentionally, with kindness and patience, the need for a situation's improvement. How much longer are you going to continue to feel poorly? When, if ever, will you begin to assume some of the duties of a preacher's wife? Is there anything you can do about that pasty complexion?

The vision of her older sister in the hallway mirror, and the sudden tears, had undone Bonnie, but only temporarily. The thing itself had nothing other than physical content, based on the realities of chronology and a strong family resemblance; after all, she loved Ellen and wouldn't have minded "ending up" like her in any of several ways. But right afterward, she'd been seized by a panicky conviction that her new happiness was already abandoning her. Gratefully she recalled Pastor's once telling her that happiness didn't exclude tears — for that matter, happiness didn't exclude unhappiness — and the lasting result of the horrible moment at the mirror was not only that she'd found her way to the bubble bath but that she'd now spent some of her time there "with" her sister, the way they might actually have done as little girls if Ellen hadn't been sent away to boarding school when Bonnie was only three.

Since mailing Ellen the pored-over letter revealing her marriage, Ellen had been very much on Bonnie's mind. She'd imagined Ellen's reading the letter, imagined her talking with Morris about it, imagined her rushing to the telephone despite Bonnie's admonishment not to. More than two weeks had passed since then, longer than Bonnie had anticipated, but Pastor had encouraged her not to interpret the silence. (Again, kindness and patience, but conveying a tacit reminder that she'd opted to ignore his former advice to invite her brother and sister to the wedding and here was an inevitable consequence.) Pastor had said that any meaning she might give to Ellen's silence was just as likely to be the opposite of true, but of course Pastor didn't know Ellen or Morris and couldn't have begun to understand how confusing her choice of a husband was bound to be to them. It had been unfathomable to Pastor, who had no siblings, that Bonnie would get married and not invite her own brother and sister to the wedding. He'd worried that she would regret the decision not to have any family at the ceremony — Pastor's mother and father, in their sixties, had driven over from Fort Walton Beach to be there — and he'd told

116

Bonnie that her brother and sister were to be *his* kin now, too, and he was eager to know them. Bonnie had said she loved them very much, but her connection to them was complicated, and she would be distracted on her wedding day by what she imagined to be their opinions of everything. Pastor said, "Their opinion of me, you mean," but she assured him that Ellen, and especially Morris, were opinionated on most subjects. Afterward, she'd read her letter aloud to him to see if he had any recommendations before she mailed it. He suggested she explain that the fund-raising campaign for the new Christ Center was what prevented their taking a honeymoon. He didn't want Bonnie's sister and brother thinking he was cheap.

She'd described her siblings to Pastor each as happily married, but she'd still not told him the gender of Morris's spouse. She convinced herself that she'd been truthful both to Pastor and in her letter to Ellen. Sadly, she really would have been constantly fretting about Morris's and Ellen's opinions. But she had to admit, too, that her decision also had allowed her to postpone the business of Morris's sexual orientation; at least she hadn't had to deal with it on her wedding day. She hated herself for thinking of

Morris as a problem, as something to avoid or put off, and she reminded herself that Pastor's primary message, always, was love love love, and that whatever he believed about homosexuality would be filtered by that. She was enough at peace with all this, she decided, and perhaps the happiest note in all of it was that none of her worries about Ellen and Morris had developed into anything resembling an obsession. She'd felt a reasonable amount of shame since mailing the letter, but she was living with it, the way one lived with a mildly sprained ankle — it hurt, but not enough to keep you from walking, and the pain lessened with each passing day. She believed she'd made the right decision for herself, and if she couldn't put herself first on her own wedding day, then when could she? She'd thought, off and on these last two weeks, of phoning Ellen, but she'd stopped herself. She meant to give her sister all the time she needed. It would be selfish to rush Ellen for the benefit of her own relief.

Soon it became apparent to Bonnie that she'd sufficiently changed her energy and, as if to confirm this fact, as she stepped out of the bathtub she had a brand-new idea: She would paint her toenails, put on something nice, and walk down the promenade to the Grand Hotel for lunch. After all, she thought, there's idle and there's idle — idle doing nothing and idle doing nothing of substance. She dried off, turbaned her shoulder-length hair in the bath towel, and pulled on a light summer robe. At her dressing table in the bedroom she towel-dried her hair and combed it back over the top of her head and behind her ears. She changed into shorts and a tank top, found the nail polish she wanted and a bag of cotton balls, and went barefoot to the screen porch and took a seat on the rattan couch. After she'd placed a cotton ball between each toe of her right foot and painted three nails, the doorbell rang. She thought, *paper boy, Girl Scout, political canvasser,* and hobbled through the house, walking on the heel of her right foot. About halfway to the door, she thought, irrationally, *Ellen,* which made her heart race.

But of course it was not Ellen. When Bonnie opened the door in the foyer, she saw, to her slight horror, a middle-aged woman whom she immediately identified as someone from the Church of the Blessed Hunger. Large and strong-looking, with short dark-brown tightly permed hair, the woman wore a black-and-white tent dress and shiny pink flip-flops and held with both hands a shoe box filled with peaches. "Hello, Mrs. Vandorpe," she said, with an apologetic smile, "I hope I'm not catching you at a bad time. I'm just coming back from Hogarth's over at Daphne, and I said to myself, I'm gonna take some of these beautiful peaches they had to Pastor and his new wife. I think they call these Majestics, down from Chilton County, and they're supposed to be real good."

Bonnie relieved the woman of the box of peaches and thanked her, and then an awkward moment ensued in which the woman took in Bonnie's wet hair, her shorts and tank top, and the cotton balls between the toes of her right foot; and in which Bonnie saw that the woman meant, despite any deterrent these details might present, to be invited in. At last Bonnie said, "I'm sorry, I know I know you, but I don't remember your name."

"That's all right," said the woman. "It's Ruth, Ruth Delk, Mrs. Robert Delk. You can't very well be expected to know everybody that knows you."

Bonnie rather enjoyed the way this remark made her feel like a celebrity, and she sensed that the woman might be accustomed to taking people, including preachers' wives, as she found them. "Well, Mrs.

Delk," she said, "as you can see, I'm in the middle of painting my toenails. But if you don't mind, you can come sit with me on the porch while I finish up."

"Oh, I don't mind," said the woman. "But are you sure it's not an imposition? I can't stay but a minute anyway."

As they moved through the house toward the porch, the woman oohed and aahed over every little thing: the Chinese umbrella stand by the coat closet, the Persian runner and brass sconces in the hallway, even the awful wagon-wheel light fixture Roy Owen had hung in the library. At the door to the dining room, she paused, stunned by the mahogany extension table, and said, "Would you look at that table! And all those legs jumbled up underneath it. Don't tell me you can make it even longer than it already is."

"I think there are about seven more leaves in the attic," said Bonnie.

"Well, how much fun!" said the woman. "You don't run across something like that every day." She turned her attention to the living room, opposite, and cried, "Oh, my heavens, a grandfather clock!" She went straight across the room and stood next to the clock, running her fingers along one edge of its trunk door and gazing up in awe at its bronze face. "I have *always* wanted to own one of these," she said, as if Bonnie had just given her the clock. "Where in the world did you ever find such a thing?"

Bonnie, who remained standing in the hallway, told her that the clock had been in her mother's family for generations, that it had been made by an English clockmaker named Joseph Park, and that it was very old, from the 1700s. Mrs. Delk shook her head side to side and asked how tall the clock was (a bit over seven feet) and what kind of wood it was made of (walnut). Mrs. Delk said, "Isn't that odd, the way they've written the Roman numeral four. They've got it I-I-I-I instead of I-V."

"Good for you for noticing," said Bonnie. "Nobody ever comments on that. Apparently, it's an idiosyncrasy of early grandfather clocks, I'm not sure why."

"Well," said Mrs. Delk, moving back toward Bonnie and the hallway, "I won't even ask what something like that must be worth."

"Honestly, I don't know for sure," Bonnie said. "I saw a very similar clock not long ago that was eleven thousand and something."

"Eleven thousand dollars!" cried Mrs. Delk. "I know people who live in houses worth less than that."

Bonnie smiled and said, "I could never part with it at any price. Of all the beautiful things that belonged to my mother, it's my favorite."

When at last they stepped onto the porch, Ruth Delk cupped her hands over her mouth and cried, "How do you stand it, it's so beautiful? If I had something like that to look at all day long I wouldn't ever leave the house. I wouldn't get a single thing done."

Once the woman was seated on the porch, Bonnie, still hobbling on one foot and one heel, took the peaches to the kitchen and poured two tumblers of tea from a pitcher in the refrigerator. When she returned, she told Mrs. Delk that coincidentally Pastor's sermon this coming Sunday was going to be about fruit, not realizing until she'd said it how idiotic it sounded.

"About fruit?" said the woman, bewildered.

"Well, sort of," said Bonnie.

After a pause, Mrs. Delk, as if determined to make some sense of Bonnie's words, said, "Well, there's an awful lot of fruit in the Bible."

Bonnie thanked her again for the peaches

and said it was thoughtful of her to bring them.

"Well, you are just quite welcome," said the woman. "Did you know that up in Chilton County they have a Peach Festival every year? Everything is peaches and more peaches in Chilton County. They have a Peach Parade, a Peach Queen, a Peach Contest. I guess they had a bumper crop this year, since the spring weather cooperated. The weather's got to be just right for peaches, you know. If you get warm weather in the early spring and then cold temperatures again after it, it's murder on peaches. The farmers up there'll put hot pots under the trees and use wind machines — just about anything to keep the peaches warm. I'm very grateful for it, too, since it's my favorite fruit. Do you like them, Mrs. Vandorpe? You can be honest."

Bonnie said she loved peaches too.

"Most people don't know it about peaches," said Mrs. Delk, "but they won't ripen and get any sweeter off the tree, not like apples and pears will. The minute you pick a peach it just stops dead. I understand they're very rich in vitamin A, too, which I'm told is good for your eyes and also for your digestive tract. I don't know why I'm yammering on about peaches this way, except that I'm nervous, formally meeting you for the first time in your own home. Tell me about you, Mrs. Vandorpe, that's what I really want. Is that your very own pier out there I'm looking at?"

Bonnie, who had resumed painting her toenails, suddenly recalled precisely who Ruth Delk was — a soprano who stood in the front row of the church choir and about whom Pastor had said, *She's as good as can be but she could talk the ears off a stalk of corn.* Bonnie said, "Yes, that's our pier. I'm afraid it's in need of some attention."

"I can't begin to imagine how much work it must be to keep a place like this up," said Mrs. Delk. "I'm told your father died last year and I was so sorry to hear it. I didn't know him, but I wish I had. I lost my husband Bob two years ago and I'm happy to say my son Bobby and his wife Brenda have taken me in. Of course our house wasn't anything like this, but I couldn't have kept it up by myself. I don't reckon Pastor's got a lot of time for things like piers, what with the church growing the way it is. Have you met my boy Bobby? He's the director of Newcomer Ministry at the church, just about your age, I'd guess."

Bonnie said she'd not met Mrs. Delk's son

but she thought she'd heard Pastor speak of him.

"Well, Pastor and the Blessed Hunger is just about Bobby's whole world," said Mrs. Delk. "I don't mind telling you that he's struggled with some personal problems in his short life, and finding his way to Pastor and the church . . . well, it genuinely saved him. I'm just so grateful his father lived to see him get hisself straightened out and married to a sweet girl like Brenda. That polish is a lovely shade of red. Do you mind if I ask you what it's called?"

Bonnie had forgotten the name of the nail polish and had to lift the bottle to read the label. "It's Revlon," said Bonnie. "Forever Scarlet."

"Well, it's pretty," said Mrs. Delk. The woman suddenly gazed upward and said, "Oh, look, there's one of those slatted porch ceilings I've heard about. I know all about these houses over here, how these rain porches they build around the outside of the screen porch are designed to catch the sea breeze and then how the slatted ceiling lets the air up into the attic and keeps the inside of the house nice and cool. You know, I have a confession to make, Mrs. Vandorpe. Ever since I was a young girl, I've wanted to set foot inside one of these houses. You know, there's only twenty-eight of them, here on the promenade. I used to think about the people who lived in them and what their lives must be like. And here I am, talking to one, and you're just as normal as can be. People are just people and houses are just houses, I guess. Don't bother comparing your insides to other people's outsides, as Pastor would say. You know, I haven't even said best wishes on your marriage. *Best wishes* is the right thing to say, did you know that? Not *Congratulations.* My mother taught me that. My mother was steeped in etiquette: the Emily Post of Point Clear before she died nine years ago. Anytime anybody needed to know the right way to do something, they would call up my mother and she would tell them. And me, I have to think about what side of the plate to put the knife and fork on every time I set the supper table. Of course, most people don't care about such things anymore, etiquette and the like. We've become a very informal society, don't you find. Which is all right, I guess. But, you know, I wouldn't mind knowing just one woman in my life today that was even a little bit like my mother."

"I would have at least gotten dressed, Mrs. Delk," said Bonnie, "if I'd known you were stopping by."

"Oh, honey, did you think I was talking about you? No, no, not at all. I'm the one who broke the rules by not even calling to tell you I wanted to drop in. Of course, that's changed too, hasn't it. It used to be you could drop in on somebody if you happened to be passing their home and it was considered a compliment. Now people can get offended . . . *Why didn't you call me first?* These days, you have to make an appointment to say hello. But look how you welcomed me in, even though you were right in the middle of something. That's a quality of a true Christian, I think. You know, everybody's seen you at services, but nobody seems to really know who you are. Can it be true that you grew up right here in this very house?"

"I did grow up here," said Bonnie, "but I went away to boarding school in Connecticut when I was twelve."

"Connecticut?" said the woman. "Well, that accounts for how much of your accent you've lost. But somebody told me they thought you'd spent time in New York City, of all places."

"That's right," said Bonnie. "I lived there my whole adult life."

"Well, somebody told me that, but nobody

said doing what."

Bonnie, finished painting her toenails, screwed the cap back on the bottle. "I was trying to be an actress," she said. "Trying and failing."

"An actress on the stage?" said Mrs. Delk. "Well, how much fun! You're certainly pretty enough for it. Practically nobody at church can stop talking about how pretty you are."

At that moment the cat came crying at the screen. Bonnie said, "I wondered where you were, China," and got up to open the door.

"Oh, please don't let it in," said Mrs. Delk quickly. "I'm afraid of cats."

"She won't hurt you," said Bonnie. "She's my father's old cat, a hundred years old. She'll just ignore us and go inside the house to sleep."

"Oh, please," said the woman. "They know I'm afraid of them and they always rub up against my legs and it's just awful the way it makes me feel."

Bonnie stepped to the screen and shooed the cat, but it didn't budge and continued to cry — oddly enough, staring directly at Mrs. Delk.

Mrs. Delk said, "You see what I mean . . . see how it's looking at me? It knows I'm afraid of it."

Bonnie opened the screen door a couple of inches and slammed it shut, scaring the cat away, but only about fifteen feet, where she lay down in the sun on the concrete sidewalk outside the rain porch and rolled onto her back. When Bonnie returned to the couch, Mrs. Delk put her hand over her own heart and thanked her. "Bobby says I must've been a cat in a previous lifetime, which accounts for me being afraid, but I don't know why he says it. It doesn't really make sense, and besides, I don't believe in previous lifetimes. But you were telling me about being an actress, Mrs. Vandorpe, and I'm very interested. I have nothing but admiration for any kind of a struggling artist."

"There's not much to tell," said Bonnie. "For every person who makes it, there are dozens — I don't know, maybe even hundreds — who don't . . . and I'm one of those. But it wouldn't be honest for me to pass myself off as a struggling artist. I always had plenty of money from my family. I never needed to work to put food on the table. To tell the truth, I've sometimes wondered if that wasn't part of my problem. I wonder if I mightn't have done better — or at least quit sooner — if I'd had the pressure of needing to make money."

"I think I know what you mean," said Mrs. Delk. "But what made you pursue a career in the theater? I mean, what gave you the idea?"

Bonnie saw in the woman's face something more than casual curiosity — she seemed to be wondering how a person *gets* from Point Clear to a theatrical stage in New York City. "I'm not sure," Bonnie said. "I imagine it seemed magical to me, the theater. You know, a kind of childish make-believe. Since I've come back home here, I've started to think I wasted an awful lot of time. And I was doing it for the wrong reasons."

"The wrong reasons?" said the woman. "Do you mean vanity?"

Oddly, this idea had never crossed Bonnie's mind — her reflections on the subject had been tedious and complex — but this one-word explanation was suddenly appealing. "Yes, I suppose," she said. "That and other things."

"I don't know the first thing about acting," said Mrs. Delk, "but I have noticed, just singing in the church choir, that I have to . . . well, when I get up there in front of all those people, I have to ask myself, *Okay, am I here to praise God or show off my sing-*

ing voice? Do you sing, Mrs. Vandorpe? I thought, being an actress, you might sing."

"I can carry a tune," said Bonnie, "but I'm not ready for the choir, if that's what you're thinking."

"You're probably being modest," said Mrs. Delk, "but that's okay. The choir's not for everybody, which is a good thing too. What would we do if everybody wanted to sing in the choir? Where did you go to church in New York?"

"I didn't," Bonnie said. "I'm afraid Pastor's married himself a heathen. I wasn't really brought up in the church. My mother died when I was born — I mean she died in childbirth — and my father wasn't a churchgoer. Before I went away to boarding school up north I attended the Catholic school here."

"The Catholic school?" said Mrs. Delk.

"In Daphne," said Bonnie. "Kindergarten through sixth grade."

"Was your father Catholic?"

"No," said Bonnie. "Somebody convinced him that it was a better place for me than the public school. He let me go but he never allowed me to join the Catholic church."

"You mean you wanted to?"

"Well, yes," said Bonnie. "I had to study Catholicism and join in prayer every day at school and even attend mass. But when it came time for the sacraments, I was excluded, so I always felt like an outsider. Officially I was a Protestant, you see. I'd been baptized a Presbyterian, which was what my mother was."

"That's what *my* mother was," Mrs. Delk cried, with delight. "I went to the Presbyterian church when I was a little girl. My father was like yours, went to services about three or four times a year, but he was *such* a good man. I don't think you have to go to church to be good, do you? Well, some of us do, I guess. I think *I* have to. And probably my son Bobby does. But I'm just so glad life has settled you down with us at the Blessed Hunger. You couldn't have picked a better place to light."

"Thank you," said Bonnie.

"Pastor makes everything so plain, don't you think?" said Mrs. Delk. "And him without any kind of formal training too. I bet you must feel lucky indeed."

"I do," said Bonnie. "I do feel lucky, Mrs. Delk. With Pastor and . . . well, you see, the thing is, I'm still finding my way around."

The woman looked at her, bewildered again, and smiled sympathetically. "Finding your way around?" she said. "You don't mean Point Clear."

"Not literally Point Clear," said Bonnie. "I mean this is a whole new life to me: my father's dying, me returning to my childhood home, marriage, the Church of the Blessed Hunger. It feels like overnight I'm a preacher's wife . . . and I haven't even been able to muster the courage to stay for coffee hour yet. I'm sure people have been wondering what's wrong with me."

Bonnie had been more candid than she'd intended, and Mrs. Delk appeared to be at a loss for words. Rather than this seeming to Bonnie like any kind of victory, she felt she'd somehow injured the woman. Mrs. Delk, who had not previously touched her tea, now reached for it and took a long drink. At last she said, "Would you mind very much if I called you by your Christian name?"

"I wish you would," said Bonnie.

"Well," said the woman, "I'm sure it's all very new, Bonnie, and an awful lot to adjust to. And here I am, barging in on you, invading your privacy, poking around like a common busybody. I feel a little ashamed of myself, if you want to know the truth, and if I'm not mistaken you were getting ready to go somewhere before I arrived on your doorstep, so now I'm gonna let you go and get yourself dressed."

Bonnie said she was glad Mrs. Delk stopped by, it wasn't an imposition, and that all she was getting ready for was a walk up to the hotel for a bite to eat. It occurred to her to invite the woman to join her, but she could see that it would only further disconcert her.

As Mrs. Delk rose from her chair, she said, "I only hope I haven't made you late."

"Not at all," said Bonnie. "I'm going by myself, so it doesn't matter what time I get there."

"By yourself?" said the woman, turning to leave. "Now, there's something I wish I could do, go eat at a hotel by myself. I lack the self-confidence for it and I don't mind saying so."

As Bonnie followed Mrs. Delk back through the house, she was suddenly sure that walking to the Grand Hotel to eat by oneself was something preachers' wives didn't generally do in Point Clear. She thought, too, that Pastor wouldn't approve, though she couldn't quite think why. She further reflected that Pastor, since moving into the house, had often enough enjoyed eating at the hotel himself. Mrs. Delk peered intently into each open doorway along the hall, as if she meant to memorize everything. When she reached the door at the end, the woman turned to Bonnie and said, "Now, except for Bobby and Brenda, I'm not gonna tell a living soul at the church that I visited with you. I don't want to make anybody jealous."

Bonnie laughed, and Mrs. Delk reached out, touched her cheek, and looked into her eyes. "You dear thing," she said. "Growing up without the love of a mother. I didn't know that."

Surprised, Bonnie felt tears welling in her eyes and only smiled, not knowing how to respond. Mrs. Delk opened the door herself. Sunshine flooded the hall. She stepped onto the stoop outside and into the yard, but when she was only a few feet away, she turned and came back to the door. "Do you mind if I give you one little piece of advice, even though it's not my place to do so?"

"Of course not," said Bonnie.

"I'm sure I don't have to tell you Pastor's special," she said. "He's called by God, and anybody can see that clear as day. People are naturally drawn to that in a man, I guess." She paused, cast her eyes upward, and shook her head. "Oh, my," she said, "I'm getting in deep. I don't know how to say what I want to say."

"No, please," said Bonnie. "Try."

"Well," said the woman, then paused and

took a deep breath. "Sometimes, with a man like Pastor, people just want to be near him. And wanting to be near him, they can get confused and think maybe he belongs to them somehow. They can start to think they have some claim on him. He doesn't affect me that way because I knew him when he was a boy. He had a reputation for being wild, you know, a little reckless when he was a teenager. He grew up and answered the call of the Lord, but when all's said and done he's still just a man. Do you understand what I'm trying to say?"

"I'm not sure," said Bonnie. "But you said you had some advice for me."

The woman nodded and squinted, pulling a determined face. "You and him are married now," she said. "You're his and he's yours. If anybody thinks different — if anybody has opinions about how y'all should and shouldn't be doing things — well, you just don't pay them any mind. Here's what I want to say: You take your own sweet time, Bonnie, and you just find your own sweet way."

An expression of such thorough self-doubt came over Mrs. Delk's face that it forbade any questioning from Bonnie, and she watched the woman walk quickly to her car. She expected her to turn one last time to wave good-bye, but she didn't. Bonnie remained in the doorway and thought, *People* have *been wondering what's wrong with me;* then, after another moment, she peered down at her newly lacquered toenails, so impossibly brilliant-red in the sunshine they made her feet look fake.

She entered the hotel through the door at the end nearest the promenade, which opened into the oldest and original part of the resort. She moved along the narrow pine-paneled hall and smiled at a blond woman who was returning from the pool and who seemed to admire Bonnie's straw handbag. The straw bag, as well as the sandals and white sundress Bonnie wore, was purchased at a swanky boutique in Greenwich Village, and as she crossed the expansive round lobby of the hotel, she reflected that she was dressed more smartly than anyone she would encounter and that her years in New York did give her a reserve of self-confidence to draw on. She stepped inside the double doors of the restaurant, where she was greeted by a young woman in a maroon-colored uniform who looked like an airline stewardess. To make matters clear quickly, Bonnie requested a table for one and added that she did not have a reservation. She was shown to a table near the middle of the large room with its windows overlooking the bay. Naturally her gaze was drawn in the direction of the water, but she was required to look past perhaps thirty other diners, many of whom, both men and women, wore golfing clothes, and all of whom seemed to be staring at her. Before she determined the extent of the role her imagination played in this, a waiter who reminded her of her brother, Morris, arrived with a menu and a glass of ice water, removed (somehow surreptitiously) the extra place setting from the table, and retreated.

On the walk over, Bonnie had envisioned a shrimp cocktail, but now, as she read those actual words on the menu, her stomach turned. Everything on the list of luncheon specials had the same effect, particularly the words *Cajun* and *Creole,* which also seemed to identify the restaurant's dominant and suddenly sickening aroma. She closed the menu and looked away toward the water again. Now there was no question that four women at a table across the room were repeatedly stealing glances at her and that she was the topic of their conversation. *This was a terrible mistake,* thought Bonnie, unduly miserable, then saw that one of the women at the table looked shockingly like Mrs. Delk. She wondered, her nausea now full-blown, if everyone in the restaurant would soon remind her of someone else. She averted her eyes for a moment and when she again gazed in the same direction, the new version of Mrs. Delk — this one heavily made up and bejeweled, her ample figure squeezed into a salmon-colored shirt dress with a gold metallic belt — had left her seat and was coming straight for Bonnie, beaming an uncertain smile. The woman stopped at Bonnie's table, stared down at her with an inexplicably naughty look on her face, and said, in a gravelly voice, "You're Roy Owen's daughter and you better not tell me you aren't."

"Yes," said Bonnie weakly, inwardly wincing at the smell of the woman's gin-soaked breath.

"I knew it!" said the woman. "I saw you at Roy's funeral last September. You didn't remember me then and you don't remember me now."

"I'm sorry," said Bonnie.

"It's Karen Simm," said the woman. "We said hello at the funeral, don't you remember? I almost didn't recognize *you* just now. You look ten years younger than you did last fall, and I said to my friends, I'm gonna march over there and get that girl to tell me her secret."

The woman laughed and glanced back at her own table. Bonnie's feeling of being trapped in a foul-smelling and airless box had now reached such a peak that she could think of nothing to do but stand up — a first step toward getting out — and once she'd stood, she could only repeat, "I'm sorry," meaning she was sorry for more than not recognizing Karen Simm's face or name, meaning she was about to desert Karen Simm in the middle of the restaurant. "I'm afraid I don't feel well," she said.

As if the woman thought Bonnie had offered this as an excuse for not recognizing her, she said, "Karen *Simm,* honey. I taught you piano when you were a little girl."

Bonnie said, "I've got to get some air," turned, and bolted from the room, not stopping until she had reached the terrace outdoors on the bay side of the hotel lobby, and then only because she realized, to her dismay, that she had left her handbag in the restaurant. She moved immediately onto the grass and into the shade of a nearby oak, where she braced herself against the tree's trunk in order to remove her sandals. Even as she did this, fumbling only a little with the small buckles on the straps, she couldn't

think why she was taking off her shoes —
somehow it seemed a sensible reaction to
the impossibility of returning to the restaurant. When next she looked up, she saw her
brother, Morris, wearing a short-sleeved
white shirt and black pants, crossing the
wide terrace toward her and carrying her
straw handbag in his left hand. She felt she
was about to cry, and instead of greeting
him she turned away and started for the
railing at the edge of the seawall.

"Miss!" he called out. "Miss! Your purse!"
Unexpectedly at her side — had she stopped
to let him catch up? — he said, "I'm sorry
you're not feeling well," and Bonnie noted
an inviting, sincere tone in his voice. She
was standing on the hotel's very green lawn,
somewhere between the oak tree and the
seawall, in bright sunlight, and the grass felt
wonderful and cool beneath her feet.

"Thank you," she said, accepting the
handbag. "You look like my brother."

The man smiled, erasing the better part
of his resemblance to Morris, and said, "I
do?"

"Much less so when you smile," said Bonnie.

He stopped smiling.

"There," she said. "Now you look like him
again."

"Your brother doesn't smile?" asked the man.

"I guess he must," said Bonnie. "I hardly know what I'm saying. I don't know what's wrong with me."

"You're not feeling well," said the waiter, kindly. "Do you need some help getting home? Do you want us to call somebody for you?"

"It's only five minutes," she said. "I can walk."

"Well, good," said the waiter. "I have to get back. My tables, you know." He wagged his head, imitating a drunken customer, and said, *"Where's my Tom Collins?"*

"I want to give you some money," said Bonnie.

"That's not necessary, ma'am."

"I want to," she said, already digging in the handbag. She found her wallet, pulled out a bill, and handed it to him.

"This is a twenty," he said.

She took another from her wallet. "Here," she said. "Take another one. What you did is worth ten times that."

He pushed her hand gently back and said, "Thank you, but one's more than enough." He turned, pocketing the twenty, and walked away. Halfway to the lobby doors, he raised one arm and waved, his back still to her.

She observed that the nausea had passed entirely, but then, as she made her way barefoot across the hotel grounds toward the promenade, she looked for a moment at the water, where a man in red swimming trunks was sailing one of the resort's small catamarans close to shore, and she had to shut her eyes; the motion of the boat, the *idea* of the boat, called up seasickness. Once she'd gained the promenade, the afternoon took on an eerie quiet Bonnie had noticed on other days. It was the hottest hour, before any thunderclouds had begun to roll in from the gulf: The houses had a lazy removed quality, set back neatly and with the illusion of safety from the water; there were no people visible, save a single ancient black man in a straw hat, raking the Crowells' beach, two houses up from Bonnie's; the contrast between the deep shade of the promenade and the brilliance of the sand and bay was intense and somehow tiring; not much of a breeze, and even the brown pelicans that perched at close intervals on docks and bare pilings appeared to be sleeping.

Pastor, Bonnie thought, would have been mortified by her behavior on the hotel lawn.

Who was that rich lady in the Jil Sander sundress, suffering a bout of the vapors and pressing twenty-dollar bills on someone who'd done her a simple favor? *It's worth ten times that to me, dahling.* In a pinch, in the throes of the slightest mental imbalance, it was one of several personas she could slip into, and she'd only embarrassed the poor waiter. Pastor, who was always the same wherever he went, would have been mortified. Of course, Pastor had never actually gone much of anywhere, which probably made being the same a little easier. Having a sense of her place in the world, and who she was in it, was still new, she thought; she was bound to backslide now and again. In another moment, she was thinking of her lovely apartment on the Upper West Side of Manhattan, now rented by an agency to a stranger; of its tall front windows, from which you could see the tops of the trees in Central Park; and of her long and errant time in New York. She'd imagined, at the start, that if she chased a career that required her to inhabit roles, it might not matter so much that she was so hopelessly undefined. Over the course of that decade of frustration and disappointment, she'd gradually understood that the truly good actors were those who seemed most thoroughly to know themselves. It was as if they were braver — they had little fear of venturing great distances inside a role, of wholly giving themselves to it — because they were, at some very deep level, anchored.

Bonnie had no anchor. She couldn't venture very far. And now, as she stood in front of the house and unlatched the gate, she thought, *Ironic,* for she felt she had finally ventured far and look where she had ended up: back in her childhood home.

Cricket heard the gate and came barreling around the corner of the house and across the lawn to greet her. She stooped on the sidewalk to scratch his ears, but the old dog's breath made her recoil.

Indoors, she found Macy putting away groceries in the kitchen. When Bonnie sat at the table without a word, Macy stopped what she was doing to take a good long look at her. At last Macy said, "Where did that shoe box of peaches come from?"

"Mrs. Delk brought them by," said Bonnie.

"I don't know any Mrs. Delk," Macy said, "but that's a pretty dress you've got on. Where did you go? Your husband called five minutes ago and I had to tell him I didn't know your whereabouts."

"I walked down to the hotel," answered

Bonnie. "What did he want?"

Macy pulled out a chair catercorner to Bonnie and sat. She wore one of her half dozen floral smock-style tops over a pair of cotton slacks, the only thing Bonnie had ever seen the woman wear apart from an apron. "As far as I could tell," said Macy, "he wanted to know what was for supper. I have the impression that when he's not eating he's thinking about eating. His staying so slim's gonna change when he gets a few years older too, you wait and see. Did you get a piece of tragic news down at the hotel?"

Again Bonnie felt herself welling up. She said, "Oh, what's wrong with me, Macy? What's wrong with me?"

"Why, what do you mean, honey?" said Macy. "There's nothing wrong with you."

"This is the second time today I've burst into tears, and it's hardly two o'clock in the afternoon," Bonnie said. "Pastor left to go to his office. Then this woman from the church stopped over to bring us these peaches, but I think she really came by to get a look at me — so she could report back about the freak Pastor's got himself married to. I went to the hotel and sat down in the restaurant but everything on the menu made me feel sick. Then this woman I've never laid eyes on came over to me and insisted she knew me — I mean, she *did* know me, but I didn't know her."

"What was her name?" asked Macy.

"I don't know," said Bonnie. "Simmons, maybe. Karen something."

"That would be Karen Simm," said Macy. "She gave piano lessons to your sister when Ellen was little. She mistook you for Ellen."

"Oh," said Bonnie. "Well, I practically ran out on her while she was still talking, I got to feeling so sick. But I forgot and left my bag in the restaurant and a really sweet waiter who looked like Morris hunted me down on the lawn and gave it back to me, and I tried to make him take forty dollars."

"Forty dollars?" said Macy. "For bringing you your purse?"

"He would only take twenty," said Bonnie.

"My Lord," said Macy.

With renewed tears, Bonnie said, "I know you and Pastor both think I'm nuts because I'm suspicious of the tap water. And I guess you're right, because you both drink it and it doesn't make *you* sick."

Macy narrowed her eyes, leaned back in her chair, and crossed her arms. "Do you know who you remind me of right now?" she said, after a moment.

"My *mother*," said Bonnie. "You've told me that a hundred times."

"Yeah," said Macy. "But more specific."

"I don't know what you mean," Bonnie said.

"You remind me of her at a very particular time."

"I still don't know what you mean."

"You remind me of her, oh — some thirty years ago or more. Back when she was carrying you."

"Carrying me?" said Bonnie. "Macy, why do you have to be so . . . I don't know what —"

She stopped herself.

Macy continued to glare at her, the hint of a smile on her face.

"Oh, I think you know perfectly well, now, don't you?" said Macy. "Be honest, Bonnie Owen. Mrs. Pastor Vandorpe."

Macy pulled a paper napkin from the napkin holder in the middle of the table, passed it to Bonnie, and told her to blow her nose, which she did. Bonnie said, "But I got my period the night before the wedding."

"Did you?"

"Well, sort of," said Bonnie.

"Sort of."

"I'm *irregular,* Macy," said Bonnie. "I've

always been irregular. I had some spotting the night before the wedding. It didn't amount to much and I just thought it was probably all the excitement and everything."

"Well, spotting ain't a period," said Macy, then left the table to return to putting away the groceries. At the counter, she took hold of two large cans of pork and beans and dropped one of them to the floor, startling Bonnie in her chair. The can rolled across the kitchen and bumped against the grill at the bottom of the refrigerator. "And let me tell you another thing," said Macy.

She waited until Bonnie — who had begun to stare off somewhere in the direction of the kitchen window — looked at her. "What?" said Bonnie.

"I've been wrong on this subject exactly once in my life."

As she passed Bonnie's chair on her way to retrieve the dropped can, she leaned down, kissed the top of Bonnie's head, and said, "I believe my record's something like ninety-eight percent accurate."

CHAPTER 5

Over the weekend Morris had been preparing himself for the foray into Alabama, which, oversimplified, meant girding himself for inevitable brushes with racism, homophobia, unwholesome cuisine, and pandemic bad taste; it was a purely mental exercise that seemed, mysteriously enough, to continue subconsciously even while he slept. When it came time on Monday — the day before they were to fly south — to see to the more physical details of travel, he discovered the zipper stuck on the bag he wanted to use for the trip, and a subsequent overzealous attempt by Richard to unstick it broke the thing irreparably. Penitent, Richard rooted about in the attic of their Brookline townhouse and brought down a half-dozen other bags for Morris to choose from, but none was quite the exact size or style Morris wanted. The ordeal of his rejecting them — that one's too big, that

151

one's too small, that one's too ugly — ended with Richard's making an unseemly reference to Goldilocks and the Three Bears, and Morris left him standing in their bedroom amid a rubble of luggage, went down to the kitchen, and telephoned Ellen. He ascertained, as he'd expected to, that she possessed the "just right" bag, and he drove over to the house in Cambridge around three o'clock in the afternoon to get it. As payment for lending the bag, Ellen asked him to run an errand for her; she was sending a copy of *Mirror in the Woods* as a birthday gift to a friend in Ohio, and would Morris mind stopping at the little post office in nearby Inman Square on his way back to Brookline?

What could he say? It occurred to him, as he searched nearly fifteen minutes for somewhere to park the car in Inman Square, that it was like Ellen to extract immediate favors in return for favors, but he somehow couldn't think of any past examples. At the PO — all plate-glass windows, on a corner — there was no line to speak of, only one other customer besides Morris, but the afternoon had turned unbearably hot, gray, and muggy, and apparently the PO's AC was on the fritz. There were two clerks behind the counter — an older woman, whose head and iron-colored pageboy just cleared the countertop, and a middle-aged woman, tall and (dyed) blond — but of course only one of the clerks was actually helping customers. The short older woman was busy showing a man at the counter several different sheets of stamps, as the other clerk, ten feet back from the counter, sorted through a stack of parcels on a table and tossed them into one or another nearby bin. Morris waited his turn behind a dirty tattered piece of red tape stuck to the floor, where he heard the clerk say to her customer, "Now, these are new: sickle-cell awareness stamps. You want the sickle-cell stamps?"

The customer, a pink-faced man in his fifties, wearing soiled short-sleeved coveralls, turned to see who was behind him; as he glimpsed Morris, Morris noted that the man appeared amused by something that had just occurred to him. The man returned his attention to the counter and with a naughty laugh said, "What, you mean the great white hope?"

He'd spoken in the nasal accent Morris linked with the working classes of East Cambridge and South Boston. The bewildered postal clerk took the man's apparently humorous remark as a rejection of the sickle-cell awareness stamps and pulled a different sheet from her shallow stamp drawer. But the meaning of the remark did not escape Morris.

To the man's back he said, "Hey, mister, that's not funny."

The man turned on him a face gnarled with bitterness, pointed his chin at Morris, and said, "Then don't laugh."

"I'm not laughing," said Morris. "I'm not laughing because it's not funny."

"Oh, yeah?" said the man. "Well, didn't anybody ever tell you to mind your own fuckin' business?"

The man turned back to the counter, where the clerk showed him yet another sheet of stamps. Undaunted, Morris said, "Actually, it *is* my business. You're in a public place and you're making remarks about a disease that happens to kill children, and I find it offensive."

The man wheeled around on Morris now, redder than before, and said, "Oh, is that so? Well, who the fuck made you God, I'd like to know?"

"I'm not God," said Morris. "I'm just another human being, like you."

"Ha!" said the man. "You're nothin' like me, that I can guarantee."

The tall blond clerk, trying, Morris

guessed, to defuse the situation, called out, "No, *I'm* God," and laughed.

As if this somehow supported the man's position, he waved his hand at Morris in dismissal and added, "So go fuck yourself."

Morris, shocked by the apparent depth of the man's rage, said, "Jesus."

"Oh, right, what the fuck do you know about Jesus?" said the man, and turned back to the counter, pushed a bill toward the clerk, then folded and slipped a sheet of stamps into the breast pocket of his coveralls.

Morris, aware of a strong inner impulse to disengage, still couldn't quite keep himself from answering the man's question. He said, "I know enough to know he wasn't white."

The man now strode toward him, and Morris braced himself, catching a sudden whiff of motor oil and body odor. But the man only paused for a second next to him, spoke the inevitable "Faggot," and continued through the open door.

The tall blond clerk had taken up her station at the counter now and called to Morris, "I can help you over here, dear."

In an adrenaline daze, Morris moved toward her, suddenly conscious of Ellen's book in its yellow padded envelope, trembling in his right hand. When he reached the counter, the woman greeted him with a warm smile, which he found curious and baffling. She wore garish gold jewelry that clashed comically with her blue-and-gray postal garb. "I need a minute to calm myself," Morris said, his breath coming fast and short.

"Take your time, dear," said the clerk. "You wanna drink of water?"

"No, thanks," said Morris. "Just give me a minute."

He noticed the woman's mottled complexion, an unnatural rosy-bronze he associated with tanning salons, and felt a tinge of something like sympathy toward her. He said, "Did you hear how that man spoke to me?"

"Oh, he's okay," said the clerk, scrunching up her nose. "He's in here all the time. We know him."

"Well, maybe you know him," said Morris, "but he's a racist, that's for sure."

"You think so?" said the clerk cheerfully, as if Morris had proposed a novel idea.

"He said something about the sickle-cell stamps," said the short older woman, "but I didn't understand what he meant."

"He said that sickle-cell disease was the *great white hope*," said Morris.

"Well, do you think he meant it as racist?" asked the older woman. "I didn't understand it that way. I'd be really surprised if he meant it racist."

"You want that to go first class?" said the blond woman.

Morris placed the small package on the counter and nodded. The clerk studied the mailing label for a moment and said, "Looka there, Ohio, round on the ends and high in the middle."

"What?" said Morris.

"Round on the ends," said the woman, drawing two circles in the air with her index finger. She waved her fingers at Morris and added, "And *hi* in the middle."

"Oh," he said, vaguely grasping her meaning but incapable of appreciating it. As she weighed the package, he half closed his eyes and concentrated on slowing his breath, his blurry gaze focused on the neutral beige of the countertop, which seemed to whisper, *Detach, Morris, detach.* Suddenly there was something Gandhi-like about his baggy khaki shorts, modest leather sandals, and simple white T, washed so many times it had begun to approach the texture of homespun.

"What is it anyway?" he heard the blond clerk ask the older one. "Sickle-cell disease."

"I think it affects black people," answered the other woman, shrugging her shoulders.

"That's two dollars and thirty-one cents, dear."

Morris paid the postage, and the clerk slid his change toward him across the counter. "You know what I heard is supposed to be good for stress?" she said. "Bananas, if you can believe. I saw it on TV."

"Bananas," intoned Morris, nodding slowly, then turned and left the PO.

That evening, as he soaked in the bathtub at home, his head the only body part above water, Morris recounted the afternoon's events to Richard. When he came to the end of the story, he reflected silently that life was sometimes tedious in its relentless parade of lessons. To Richard he said, "I suppose I'm meant to *learn* something from this."

They were in the upstairs bathroom in Brookline, where Morris had filled the ample Roman tub with water as hot as he could stand it and poured in a packet of bath salts from the Dead Sea. Richard, out of the shower some time ago and wearing only a towel, sat on a nearby vanity bench, elbows on knees, chin in hands. He said, "Like what?"

"Well, obviously, the horrible experience

is supposed to show me that Alabama, and the South in general, doesn't have a corner on racism," answered Morris. "Or homophobia. Or ignorant mean-spirited people."

"But you already knew that," said Richard.

"Okay then," said Morris, "I'm *reminded.*"

Morris's tone stemmed from the recent girding-up he'd been doing, a kind of hardening of the heart that sometimes resulted in snappishness, he couldn't quite think why. It felt as if everyone close to him had failed him in some important way and was responsible for his having to go to Alabama.

Richard stood. "You're turning very red," he said, and left the room, closing the door behind him.

Morris had only time to heave a sigh of remorse when the door reopened and Richard's head appeared. "Where do you want to go for dinner?" he asked. "I think tonight you should have your heart's desire."

Nine days earlier, on a Saturday morning, Ellen had phoned Bonnie from Cambridge to say that she and Morris had made reservations on a flight to Mobile. Bonnie needn't meet them at the airport; they would rent a car and drive over to Point Clear a week from Tuesday. She'd kept her voice free of any obvious attitude and simply declared the plans, which implicitly required neither Bonnie's invitation nor her approval; then she asked whether Bonnie perhaps thought it better for her and Morris to take rooms at the hotel.

Before making the call, Ellen had mentally stripped down to the reduced, purposeful self she used for phoning a repairman who'd botched a job or failed to show up. This cold air, already warmed by the sound of Bonnie's voice, evaporated entirely with the frankness of her sister's response. "Of course you shouldn't take rooms at the hotel," she said. "Not unless you mean to punish me."

Ellen said, "Then you don't mind our coming down."

"What could possibly make me happier?" said Bonnie. "I've been afraid you weren't ever going to speak to me again."

"Oh, Bonnie," said Ellen, "I just needed time to sort out my feelings."

"And have you got them sorted out?"

"Not completely," said Ellen. "But enough to know that I'm worried about you and want to see you."

"Well, I do think you'll be less worried

once you see me," said Bonnie.

Ellen detected none of the fear she'd sensed in Bonnie's letter, and even the dreaminess of former conversations was absent, replaced by something like real composure. It was as if Bonnie had been operating earlier beneath the cloud of a question that had now been answered. Bonnie soon suggested they not try to talk about things over the phone but wait until they could do it in person. She laughed as she told Ellen about a postcard she'd received in the mail from Morris, in which he asked whether or not "Rev. and Mrs. Vandorpe" were registered somewhere, as he would like to send a "necessarily belated" wedding gift.

After Ellen hung up the phone, she felt strangely off-kilter. The conversation had assuaged her former worry about Bonnie's being under some kind of psychological duress, but it did not altogether comfort her. Later in the day, as she drove over to Morris's house in Brookline for lunch, she thought that the conversation had returned her to the less desirable state of being vaguely worried about Bonnie and had furthermore blurred her perspective on the situation in general; she'd been readying herself for the trip with a sense of purpose, which now seemed shakier than before.

She found Morris waiting for her outside the townhouse, on the stoop. Though they'd talked several times by phone and made their travel arrangements, it was the first time they'd actually seen each other; she and Dan had only just returned to town from the Cape the day before. Morris greeted her with a hug and a kiss, and as he escorted her in through the front doors, he said, "Well, welcome home. . . . It seems that absence really did make the heart grow fonder, yes?"

He was referring to the fact that Dan had stayed on with her in Wellfleet. "Not only that," she said.

He paused in the foyer. "Meaning what?"

"Meaning," she said, "that I seem to have finally moved on from Daddy."

"Oh," he said, smiling. "High time, I'd say."

"Yes," she said. "I know that's what you would say."

Minutes later, on the terrace of Morris's enclosed garden, she related to him the phone call with Bonnie and Bonnie's surprising equanimity. Across the brick wall at the back of the garden, Morris's pampered yellow and white roses were putting on their second bloom; the brick walkways were freshly hosed clean, the several Chinese ceramic urns gleamed in the sunlight, and Ellen observed in herself an inward objection to everything's being quite so meticulous. Morris served a cold mango soup, which was delicious but minimal, bordering on precious. He said, "She's riding a pink cloud. It's only a matter of time."

"Before what?" asked Ellen.

"Before she realizes she may have acquired a new name but she's still the same old Bonnie."

"Morris," said Ellen, "are you ever worried that your optimism might get the better of you? That you might be in danger of becoming a full-blown Pollyanna?"

Morris laughed and said, "I'm not sure what this means exactly, but that remark sounds an awful lot like something *I* would say."

Ellen assumed he meant her remark was biting and sarcastic, and afterward it gave her something to think about. She imagined she'd spoken only partly out of her desire for more chaos in the garden; in this sense, Morris's garden was classical, a world unto itself, echoing the gardener. Instinct told her the primness of the garden stood for a more reasonably objectionable primness in Morris's personality, but she couldn't quite build a case for the idea.

That night, in bed with Dan, she said, "I've never really minded that side of Morris before, his fastidiousness. He's got plenty of the opposite, too, hasn't he?"

They were upstairs in the Cambridge house. Dan said, "Sure he does, he's got Richard."

That made her laugh but failed to cheer her. She lay awake after Dan had fallen asleep and indulged her mind in a trick she sometimes used for conceiving poems. Before the actual writing, she would conjure a landscape and then turn her mind loose in it to ramble. Here she conjured Morris's fussy little garden in Brookline and moved with little delay to the heart of the matter: Morris refused to let things grow where they would, insisted on conformity to his own vision, and tended to whip everything into shape accordingly; influenced by him in the wake of Bonnie's letter, ignoring more moderate voices (like Richard's and Dan's and even Willie's), Ellen hadn't given sufficient airtime to the possibility of Bonnie's legitimate happiness.

She decided, above all, not to let Morris's outlook prevail in Point Clear — which would require some effort, since they would arrive together, with an apparently shared mission. She would need to stay mindful of her independence. And what *was* their mission, anyway? It had remained undefined, except, as Morris had put it, "to see what's what in Point Clear." More and more, as the time of travel grew nearer, it felt to Ellen that hers was only to see Bonnie, meet the husband, and wish them well. The news of Bonnie's marriage had been a shock, but recovery from shock, Ellen soon saw, was to be less shocked. The trip to Point Clear, plotted in shock as an errand of search and rescue, now felt to Ellen mostly like going to visit her recently married baby sister.

Ellen had also decided to talk to Morris about the question of their mission, but somehow she'd put it off until they were driving in a rental car across Mobile Bay, on their way to Baldwin County. Throughout the trip from Boston, Morris had been at his best: easygoing, helpful, taking charge of details. On the flight he made reference to some deep-in-the-night change of heart and told Ellen he'd managed to cast off his dread of going to Alabama. He said he had deliberately adopted a positive attitude toward everything Alabaman and even toward everything evangelical. Ellen's remark in the garden several days earlier, concerning the anemic state of his optimism, had inspired him, he said; he'd resolved to assume the best until persuaded otherwise by real evidence, and he thought Ellen should do the same. Ellen was able to say honestly that she already had. But it still didn't answer the question of what exactly was their mission, so, in the car, only twenty minutes from Point Clear, she said, "There's something I don't feel sure about."

The words seemed both loaded and understated. Morris, who'd insisted on an expensive Volvo sedan at the airport rental counter, had chosen the causeway for crossing the bay rather than the newer expressway on its tall concrete pilings. The old road from their childhood, built on a low and mostly narrow rise of land, got swamped in every decent storm, and in Ellen's memory it had become a gray strip of asphalt beneath six inches of standing water, through which her father eased his black Coupe de Ville at five miles an hour, afraid he would stall out the engine. Today an overcast sky hung close overhead and turned the bay water a uniform slate, a dull blank canvas silently crisscrossed by gulls and skimmers. Ellen had willfully returned her mind to the question of her and Morris's intentions in Point Clear, for along the causeway, an old gas station or abandoned fishing pier would prompt her into what she thought of as free-floating nostalgia, a cloudy longing but for nothing one actually remembered. The road made her think for example of Whitney's, the tin-roofed shack that had stood on stilts on the south side of the causeway, where their father had taken them every Friday night for supper, where he himself invariably ordered the fisherman's platter and where he invariably forced Morris to eat a fried oyster or shrimp or bite of catfish before allowing him to start his own cheeseburger and fries. As a boy, Morris hated all fish, and the repeated ritual — meant, Ellen supposed, to convert him — had only ensured his lifelong aversion. Still, beneath the hurtful reality, there was for Ellen the pleasant *idea* of Friday-night suppers on the causeway with Father.

Morris, from behind the steering wheel of the Volvo, gazed at her meaningfully and nodded, as if to say, Yes, there's a great deal not to feel sure about.

"What exactly do we mean to do here?" Ellen asked.

Now Morris faced forward, decidedly not looking at her, and smiled. "Getting cold feet?" he said.

"No," said Ellen. "Though I might if I knew exactly what we were here for."

"I'm surprised you came all this way blindly," said Morris. "It's a rather expensive ticket, you know. We could've flown to Paris for half the cost."

"Morris," she said, "you're evading the question."

"I thought we'd agreed that we wanted to come and see for ourselves," he said. "Keeping an open mind, we simply mean to see for ourselves."

"Right," said Ellen, "that's what I thought. It just recently struck me as overly vague."

"It *is* vague," said Morris. "Unavoidably."

"It didn't feel vague when we decided," said Ellen. "It felt necessary."

"I don't think those conditions exclude each other," said Morris. "The trip is necessary. Its purpose is vague."

"Give me a minute to ponder that," said Ellen. "On its face it seems absurd."

"Well, if you think it's absurd I don't know what you're doing here," Morris said.

"And so we've come full circle," Ellen said. "Back to the question of what I'm doing here."

"I don't see why you're asking *me* what *you're* doing here," said Morris. "I thought it obvious what we came for."

They were leaving the causeway and starting up the long hill to Spanish Fort. "But you just said our purpose was vague," said Ellen. "How can it be vague and obvious at the same time?"

Morris said, "This is the most ridiculous conversation I've ever been a part of."

"I'm sure that's not true," said Ellen.

"It is true," said Morris. "I feel as if I'm in an Edward Albee play."

After that, they rode the rest of the way, south on Scenic Highway 98, in silence. A mile from the house, Ellen pulled down the visor on her side of the car, applied fresh lipstick, and brushed her hair.

When Morris took the right turn into the drive and steered the car through the brick columns on either side, he heaved a great sigh. "Oh, Lord," he said softly.

"It's going to be okay," Ellen said, returning the visor to an upright position.

"It seems ages ago we were here for the funeral," he said. "And it hasn't even been a year."

"Yes," said Ellen.

The oyster shells of the drive crunched beneath the wheels of the car. They drew nearer the house, which rested on brick footings over a lattice enclosed crawl space designed to guard against damage from storm surges; white with forest-green shutters and roof, obscured by oleanders and banana trees, elephant ears and palmettos, it seemed to Ellen, despite the raised foundation, closer to the ground somehow, not as tall.

"The field has been mown," she said. "Can you smell the grass?"

Morris nodded and glanced at her, smiling, his eyes marginally wetter than usual. With his occasional knack for saying precisely the right thing at the right time, he said to her, "You look pretty."

Off and on throughout the trip, Morris, regardless of any recent resolutions about optimism, had experienced an uneasiness about everything going too smoothly — which reflected his quite reasonable view about travel that something *always* went wrong; inevitably, given how many humans were required in the making of arrangements, somebody somewhere along the line was bound to screw up. When no snag came from Boston to Point Clear, he deemed it the exception that proved the rule. After he'd parked the willow-green Volvo in a shady spot between the gardener's cottage and the garage, he said to Ellen, "Very suspicious indeed."

"What's suspicious?" said Ellen.

"Here we are, without a hitch."

"Morris, there doesn't always have to be a hitch."

Morris glanced at his wristwatch; it was just after three o'clock. "Well," he said, "the day is yet young."

Earlier, Morris's heart had sunk when he first encountered the horrible damp heat of the airport parking lot, but now, as he stepped out of the car, there was a pleasant sea breeze and the air felt a good ten degrees cooler. In another minute, as he and Ellen lifted their suitcases from the trunk of the Volvo, Macy, the Owens' housekeeper of countless years, came trotting toward them from the mudroom door, singing, "Oh, my goodness, my goodness, would you look who's here!"

She wore an unfortunate smock with putty-colored sci-fi flowers, and she appeared genuinely surprised to see them. Morris, who was surprised though not disappointed to see Macy, had neglected over the intervening months since his father's death to consider the woman's fate. Now, as he watched Ellen and Macy embrace, he supposed it made sense that she had remained at the house — it was the only home she'd known for ages — yet he didn't imagine Bonnie required cooking and housekeeping services, which surely even

Bonnie would see as an extravagance. Morris imposed on the housekeeper a European-style greeting, kissing each of her cheeks, clearly addling her, and she pulled away from him but continued to grasp one of his arms, as if for support. She was short of breath, and Morris thought she displayed an unwarranted degree of excitement.

"Bonnie told me y'all were coming tomorrow!" she cried at last.

Morris only cast a knowing smile in Ellen's direction. There it was, the snag.

Macy released Morris's arm and looked to Ellen. "She told me y'all were coming on Wednesday," she said. "I was planning a special supper and everything."

"Well, here we are today," said Ellen, trying but not quite succeeding at seeming unruffled. "Bonnie made a mistake, I guess."

"I guess she did," said Macy. "Y'all come on into the house. Have you had anything to eat?"

Macy didn't wait for an answer but started for the mudroom door. Half the distance there, she stopped and turned. She glanced quickly back at the house and softly said, "Now I might as well tell y'all before we go inside. Pastor's folks is up from Florida, been here since Saturday. Dropped in without any warning. Bonnie told Pastor he had to have them out by tonight, which he said he would, but now Bonnie's gonna be fit to be tied."

She continued toward the house, Ellen and Morris following behind. "Oh, good," he said, to the back of Ellen's head. "An unexpected treat. We get to meet the curious people who named their newborn infant Pastor."

Inside, Cricket, the old family bird dog, lumbered out from under the kitchen table, his dark-brown ears hanging heavily, and Morris noted that the dog, though he greeted them obligingly enough, quickly showed more interest in their luggage, which they set down on the linoleum. Macy had been baking — a pineapple upside-down cake, three quarters of a pecan pie, and some sort of lattice-crusted fruit pie rested on the tabletop — and the kitchen was hot, despite the ceiling fan whirring overhead. Morris went to push open the swinging door to the hallway, which would draw in some cool air from the bay, but Macy stopped him.

"Oh, honey," she said, "don't do that. Not unless you put Cricket in the yard first. Pastor's mother can't abide dogs."

"I see," said Morris, withdrawing his hand from the door.

Macy poured them tall aluminum tumblers of tea, and they all three sat at the table for five minutes, during which Morris and Ellen learned that Pastor had spent the day in his office at the church and wasn't expected home till suppertime; Bonnie had a three-o'clock doctor's appointment and would probably be back home in another hour or so (no, not sick, just a checkup); and Mr. and Mrs. Vandorpe had walked over to the hotel for their dinner around one o'clock but were now on the screen porch, where Macy had served them dessert and coffee. "Do y'all want to join them out there or what?" asked Macy. "There's a baked ham in the icebox if you want a sandwich."

Ellen asked Morris if he was hungry, and he said he couldn't tell.

"I can't either," said Ellen. "Something about flying."

"Well, let me know when y'all decide," said Macy. "In the meantime I better make a fresh pot of coffee." She stood and moved to the nearby counter. "I've never seen people drink coffee like Pastor's folks do," she added. "Morning, noon, and night."

Morris detected the same slightly impatient tone she'd used when she'd told him Mrs. Vandorpe couldn't abide dogs. Ellen must have noticed it too, for she said, "Macy, come sit back down. I'll make the coffee and when it's ready Morris and I will take it to them on the porch. That will be our entrée, fresh coffee. Are the Vandorpes very old?"

Macy went ahead and quickly got the coffeemaker going with a new pot, then returned to the table and seemed to Morris to be near tears. She said she guessed the Vandorpes were about her own age, in their early sixties, that they'd lived all their lives somewhere right there in Baldwin County, but they'd retired a couple of years ago to Fort Walton Beach. Because Macy recited these particulars as if she were reading out names of the dead from a war memorial, Morris said, "Macy, please tell us what's wrong."

She clasped her hands together on the tabletop and gave Morris a look of great uncertainty. At last she said, "Your daddy and mama were the only kin I ever had. And you kids were like the children I never had of my own. It just about broke my heart when your daddy sent you two away to school up north. I can't tell you how I looked forward to the holidays, when y'all would come home for a while. Having y'all here now . . . well, I guess I'm just feeling the past . . . very strongly feeling the past, I guess."

Morris looked at Ellen, who reached across the table and touched Macy's clasped hands. "Macy," she said, smiling, "what is it really?"

Macy stood and tiptoed to the swinging door; she pushed it open a crack and peered into the hallway, returned again to the table and sat down. In a lowered voice, she said, "Well, if I can't tell y'all, I don't know who I can tell. I overheard Mrs. Vandorpe saying something to Pastor I wasn't supposed to hear. They were out on the porch yesterday morning after breakfast. Bonnie was sleeping late, which she's been doing a lot of, but that's another story. I'd gone into the living room for something and I could hear them through the open windows in there. I'm sure they thought I was still in the kitchen. I know I shouldn't have listened, but I couldn't help myself. I've already been to confession about it."

"The sin of eavesdropping," said Morris. "What kind of penance does that carry?"

"Now you hush," said Macy, "that's between me and God and my priest. I don't want y'all to feel sorry for me; that's not why I'm telling you this. And I don't expect you to do anything about it either. I'm just getting it off my chest so to speak. Because you asked."

"Go on, Macy," said Ellen. "Morris, please don't interrupt."

Macy sat silent for another few seconds and appeared to be either mustering her courage or getting things organized in her mind. At last she said, "Mrs. Vandorpe told Pastor that she and Mr. Vandorpe weren't happy in Fort Walton Beach, that they were thinking about moving back up here. She said they could be quite satisfied in my little apartment off the mudroom. There wasn't any reason in the world why she couldn't do everything I did; she'd been cooking and cleaning her whole life and they wouldn't even have to pay her for it. Mr. Vandorpe could take care of the grounds and they could save that money too, whatever they paid for gardeners. They could move back up here, join Pastor's church, and all be together again."

"And what did Pastor say?" asked Morris.

"He said he'd think about it," Macy answered, shrugging her shoulders hopelessly. "He said he would talk it over with Bonnie."

"And do you think he has talked it over with Bonnie?" asked Ellen.

"No," said Macy. "If he had, I would've

seen it in Bonnie's face right off this morning. She can't hide anything from me, even
when she tries."

"Good," said Ellen. She took a long drink
of her tea and banged down the aluminum
tumbler on the tabletop. "Ready?" she said
to Morris.

"Ready," he said.

As Ellen moved to the coffeemaker for the
new pot, Macy said, "You're not gonna say
anything to them about what I just told you,
are you?"

"Of course not," said Ellen. "We're just
going to visit with them until Bonnie gets
back."

Morris held the hall door open for Ellen
to pass through. He considered inviting
Cricket to come with them to the porch but
decided against it; while he fully intended
to alienate the Vandorpes, he didn't want to
be too aggressive about it. Ellen paused in
the hall, where it was considerably cooler,
and waited for him to close the door. They
heard a metallic crash from inside the
kitchen, and then Macy, calling, "Don't
worry . . . nothing broke!"

"I didn't realize Macy had stayed on with
Bonnie," Ellen whispered.

"I didn't either," said Morris. "But I'm
certainly not having her displaced by any

interloping Vandorpes."

"No," said Ellen. "Of course not."

"You see?" he said. "Not here half an hour and the mission's already starting to take shape. I knew it would."

At the far end of the long dark hallway, he saw the bright rectangle of the porch door, through which two blurry horizontal ribbons trembled, the narrow white one of the beach and the wider gray of the bay. Ellen indicated for him to lead the way, which he did, noting how the many shut doors along the hall created a Victorian atmosphere. When they reached the open double pocket doors to the dining room, he suddenly stopped, stunned. Ellen, at his side, whispered, "Oh!"

Morris turned and peered into the living room opposite. "My God," he said. "It's so beautiful. Did you know about this?"

"She told me she'd thrown some things out and fixed the place up," said Ellen. "But look what she's done! It's brilliant."

"I never thought Sheila would take to this sort of thing," said Rex Vandorpe. "Big fancy house, fine hotel dining. Why, you'd think it was how she grew up. She's been perched out here on this porch since Saturday, waving to every soul that passes by.

She's like a pig in mud, bless her heart."

Morris sat next to Sheila on the rattan couch, whose cushions appeared to have new slipcovers, made from coarse muslin in brick red, and Ellen and Rex sat opposite each other in the matching chairs at either end. A low table before them, fashioned from barn wood, was strewn with coffee things and the Vandorpes' dessert plates. Rex — a wide, handsome, bald-headed man with pale blue eyes beneath thick eyebrows — had addressed his observation about his wife to Morris, accompanied by a wink that seemed to say, Now, ain't I misbehavin'? He was, like the wife, extremely tanned, and he'd apparently spilled coffee on himself, for there was a sizable brown stain near the right pocket of his canary yellow Bermuda shorts.

Morris thought *pig in mud* an especially poor choice of words, since Sheila, by her own admission the victim of an incurable sweet tooth, was on the heavy side, but Sheila didn't seem to mind in the least. She smiled and said, "You know very well I didn't grow up like this, Rex," then turned to Ellen and added, "Rex's solitary idea of something nice is a forty-two-inch TV screen."

"That's not true, sugar," said Rex. "I think

that dress you're wearing is nice."

This remark, Morris couldn't avoid thinking, alluded to the cleavage Sheila's white sundress amply displayed, unusual in a woman her age. She was still very pretty, peroxide perm and all. He imagined that she'd been homecoming queen to Rex's football hero in their day. They were not at all what he'd expected. He supposed he'd anticipated something straitlaced — the parents of an evangelical preacher — and, given what Macy had revealed in the kitchen, also grasping. But they struck Morris as neither.

Sheila rolled her eyes and explained to Ellen that Rex had bought her the sundress yesterday, in the shop at the hotel, and paid twice what he should have for it. "I am *so* glad y'all came a day early," she added. "And I just can't get over the family resemblance. I would know y'all were related to Bonnie if I ran into you anywhere."

Morris noted Ellen's tolerant smile, and he guessed it had to do with Sheila's second repetition in the last ten minutes of the phrase *a day early,* when Ellen had made the situation plain. *She* suddenly struck Morris as straitlaced, serious and severe in her standard travel costume: tasteful black slacks, black T, black flats. Ellen said, "Macy

181

told us you-all lived somewhere around here before moving to Florida."

"We did, we did," said Sheila. "We lived in Fairhope, where Rex was in business for over thirty-five years."

"Oh, come on, Sheila," said Rex, "I sold stoves and refrigerators at Fairhope Appliance for thirty-five years."

"Well, I don't know what that is if it's not being in business," said Sheila.

"You don't have to dress it up," said Rex, "I'm not ashamed of it. I was Salesman of the Year a dozen different times. When I finally quit, old man Gates said his only regret was that he'd never figured out a way to clone me."

"Rex did very well for himself," Sheila said. "And the Lord's been very good to us. We owned our own home . . . nothing like this, of course . . . but nice and adequate and we never wanted for anything within reason. Now, Ellen, Bonnie said you were a poet, of all things. . . . I remember that, but I can't think what she said Morris did."

"Morris teaches English," said Ellen, "to college students. Don't you, Morris."

Morris supposed Ellen meant to prod him out of the pointed silence he'd been maintaining, but before he could speak, Rex said, "Wouldn't you think by the time somebody got all the way to college they'd already know how to speak English?"

He smiled at his wife — apparently he thought he'd been clever and wanted to see if she shared his opinion. Sheila stared out at the bay and shook her head, as if only something that large and forgiving could fathom her plight, but even this, Morris thought, was chiefly for show.

Morris feigned earnestness. "Oh, it's not about speaking English," he said, "it's all about reading and writing it."

"He knows that," said Sheila, "he's just trying to be cute. Anyway, Morris, I guess that must make you a professor."

"Technically, yes," Morris said, "but I've never liked that title with its religious overtones. Don't you think it sounds sort of . . . I don't know . . . borderline hysterical?"

Sheila appeared stumped and blinked her considerable eyelashes three times. She glanced at her husband and reached for her coffee cup. She sipped from it briefly, then turned to Ellen and said, "We were always Southern Baptists ourselves."

Morris let out one delighted bark of laughter, *Ha!,* then pretended to cough, and Ellen cast him a look of reproach. She turned to Sheila and said, "Was Pastor your only child?"

"Oh, yes," said Sheila, "he was the only one, our little miracle. I was already in my forties, you see. We'd completely given up on ever having any children, Rex and me. The doctor told me I couldn't, but we just never stopped praying."

"That baby was the light of our lives," said Rex. "We never knew such love as that. It was like a bolt of lightning. Can I get y'all something to drink? Morris, you want something to drink? This here's a dry house, nothing alcoholic, but I expect there's a Coke or something out in the fridge."

"It certainly didn't used to be a dry house," said Morris.

"This is *their house,* Rex," said Sheila. "You don't have to play the host." She again turned to Ellen. "I'm gonna float off this porch if I don't stop drinking Macy's coffee," she said. "It's just the best I've ever had. I don't know what she does to it."

"Yes," said Morris quickly, "thank God for Macy. How could any of us have managed all these years without her?"

Ellen admirably took up the thread. "Macy was the only mother Bonnie ever knew," she said. "And Daddy certainly could never have gotten by alone."

"I'm surprised he never remarried," said

Sheila, trying, Morris thought, to divert them.

"He wasn't an easy man to live with," Morris said. "Daddy was a little overfond of his whiskey sours. Macy was the only one who could handle him when he got into one of his foul moods. Ellen and I were just saying on the flight down that we hoped Macy would stay on here forever."

"Well, it's her home too, by now," said Ellen.

"As far as we're concerned," said Morris, "the only way Macy will ever leave this house will be by her own choosing. We could no more turn Macy out than we could —"

He'd almost said *Pastor* but caught himself in time. "Well, suffice to say, she's just like family to us."

Morris feared they'd laid it on a bit thick, and he was sure he'd seen Sheila casting significant glances Rex's way. After a moment Sheila sighed impatiently and said, "Well, she sure does make a good cup of coffee. I think Bonnie told me you have a boy of your own, Ellen, is that right? What did she say . . . about twelve?"

"Willie's thirteen," said Ellen.

"Oh, that's a nice age," Sheila said.

"It's a terrible age," said Rex. "All pimples

and hormones, if you ask me."

"Well, there is that," Sheila said. "I forgot. It seemed like Pastor was already a grown-up by the age of nine or ten."

"He was precocious, all right," said Rex, "no doubt about that. Maybe too precocious for his own good."

Morris found this last remark intriguing and was trying to find a tactful way to pursue it when Ellen said, "You must miss him now that you're in Fort Walton Beach."

"Oh, we do," said Sheila. "We surely do."

"It's not that long a drive, though, is it?" asked Morris. "I would imagine you could just drive over and drop in on a whim if you cared to."

"Two hours," said Sheila. "No, it's not long, but I expect as we get older it'll get longer. And I sure am gonna hate being two hours away from my grandchildren."

As if the subject of grandchildren disquieted him, Rex suddenly stood and moved next to Morris, wedging himself on the couch between him and Sheila. He put an arm around Morris's shoulders and said, "Now let's see, if Bonnie's my daughter-in-law, and you're Bonnie's brother, that must make you my. . . . What does it make him, Sheila?"

"I don't think it makes him anything,

Rex," said Sheila. "He could be your friend, though."

"Oh, come on," said Rex. "We won't have time enough to become friends. I want him to *be* something to me. I think him and Ellen have gotta be our in-laws of some kind."

"I don't think so, Rex," said Sheila. To Ellen, she said, "If Rex had his way, he'd be related to every human being in the world. That's just how he is."

Morris shifted a bit on the couch, prompting Rex to remove his arm, and now the big man sat with his hands folded between his legs, as if he meant to control his impulses to grab and squeeze people. After a moment, he stood again. "Come on, Morris," he said, "how's about me and you take a little walk out there on that pier?"

Morris looked at Ellen, though he couldn't think why, for he could see that she was the last person with the ingenuity to rescue him from anything. As if to drive this reality home, she suddenly turned to Sheila and said she would be right back, she needed to visit the bathroom, and excused herself. Morris recalled his pledge of optimism and decided that a walk on the pier might be some kind of an opportunity. He might learn more about Pastor, for example. He stood and moved toward the screen door, which Rex already held open.

"Rex?" said Sheila, drawing out the syllable in a foreboding voice.

"What, Sheila?"

"What are you doing?"

"I'm going for a walk with Morris out there on that pier," he said.

"Well, I'd really rather you didn't," said Sheila. "I'd really rather you stayed here on the porch."

"We won't be long," said Rex, and gently nudged Morris on through the door.

"You better behave yourself, Rex Vandorpe," Sheila called. "Do you hear me?"

"Don't you worry, sugar," said Rex.

Outside, Morris stopped under the rain porch and said, "Should I be afraid for some reason?"

Rex moved alongside him and put a hand on his shoulder. "Hell, no," he said. "She just gets nervous."

They passed through the wrought-iron gate and onto the promenade. "Nervous about what?" Morris said.

"Everything," said Rex. "At home, I switch the coffee around on her. I pour the regular stuff out of the can and put decaf in its place. Come on."

As they crossed the sand toward the pier, Rex said, "Boy, it sure is pretty here, ain't it? Even on a cloudy day like today."

Brown pelicans perched at odd intervals along the southern side of the pier and launched clumsily into flight, one at a time, as Morris and Rex walked toward the small boat shed at the end. Rex said, "No lack of pelicans, that's for sure. Many as they are, it's a good thing they don't make noise. I reckon they're like the giraffe in that regard."

"The odd thing is," said Morris, "I don't recall them from my childhood."

"That's because they weren't here," said Rex. "Or very few. People think it was the DDT we used in the fifties. The stuff got into the water, which got it into the fish, the pelicans ate the fish, and pretty soon they couldn't reproduce. You're too young to remember it, but when I was a boy they'd have trucks come around in the summertime, cranking out big clouds of DDT. Trying to control the mosquitoes."

Inside the boat shed, Rex sat down and dangled his legs over the edge of the pier, into the empty berth. Morris, never much of a leg dangler, sat beside him on the wooden planks, Indian-style. There, under the tin roof, the water below them appeared a murky green and lapped at the hideous encrusted things that grew on the pilings.

Morris looked out over the bay — flat, silver, lazy, nondescript — and was suddenly ambushed by fatigue, a kind of depression made one tenth of travel stress and nine tenths of longing for Richard. He wouldn't have gone so far as to say he already regretted having come, but he suddenly, achingly, wanted to be alone. Most irritating, a boyhood memory was poking and nibbling at his heart, having to do with his father's disappointment over Morris's indifference toward boats and fishing.

Rex didn't waste any time. He said, "It seems Bonnie just recently let Pastor know about your situation, son."

"My situation?" said Morris.

"Your Massachusetts marriage, son, that's what I'm talking about."

Morris, though startled, felt himself plunged deeper into fatigue, which seemed to prevent him from simply standing up and walking away. "I'm happily married to someone I've lived with for fourteen years," he said. "That's hardly a situation and, if I may say so, scarcely any of your business."

"Now, hold on," said Rex. He started to put an arm around Morris's shoulders, but apparently thought the better of it. "I'm on your side, son."

Again startled, Morris said, "You mean

there are sides being taken?"

"Oh, yeah," said Rex and chuckled. "You've been a hot topic between me and my boy Pastor since Sunday night. Me, I agree with what you just said — it's not any of my damned business — but Pastor . . . I'm giving you warning . . . he's very likely to try and change your mind while y'all are down here."

"Change my mind?"

"About your lifestyle," said Rex. "Pastor's gentle as a lamb, always was, even in his wild days. I don't doubt he's got a genuine calling too, as far as that goes. But he's still just a kid. Wants everything his own way like a kid. Now, I love Bonnie to death, but I'm not sure she's the kind of woman who's gonna throw a lot of opposition in his path. He reckons he saved her and now he's gonna save you. Hell, he's gonna save your whole damn family and Macy too, gonna save that poor woman from her Roman Catholicism."

After a moment, Morris said, "Crazy."

"What?"

"Oh, just that in a vague sort of way we came down here to save Bonnie too. There's an awful lot of saving going on."

"Save her from what?"

"Save her from Pastor, I suppose," said

Morris. "She has a history of colossal bad luck with men. And she sprang this wedding on us after the fact."

"And she's got money," said Rex.

"Yes, that's right," said Morris, a little awed by Rex's candor.

Rex, who must have seen it in Morris's face, shrugged his shoulders and said, "I'm a salesman, son. The secret of my success was no bullshit. I might've talked folks into spending a little more than they planned to, but in the long run, I did them a favor. They got a better product with a longer life."

"Well, just for the record," said Morris, "since we're not bullshitting, I don't have a lifestyle, I have a life."

"Gotcha," said Rex, but he didn't appear to think it an important distinction. He looked past Morris and smiled. "Well, lookee there," he said. "I knew she wouldn't be able to stay in that house longer than five minutes with us out here talking."

Morris turned and saw Sheila, with Ellen, already on the pier and coming toward the boat shed. Morris said, "What did you mean before, when you said Pastor might have been too precocious for his own good?"

"Oh, nothing in particular," said Rex. "I just have a notion that if you're smarter than most of the people around you, you can start to *feel* smarter than most of the people around you. Now watch this. Sheila's gonna walk up and ask us what we've been talking about, I'll bet you anything."

The two women were about twenty feet away now, and this time when Morris turned, he saw Sheila wave one arm in the air with some urgency, as if Rex and he were about to set sail and she meant to detain them at the dock. "What are you two yakking about out here?" she called.

Rex Vandorpe threw his head back and swung his legs, laughing. Now he did grab Morris's shoulders, in a one-armed embrace. Morris didn't entirely like it, though he liked even less his reason for not liking it: He was *forty* already, and it made him feel like a little boy.

Ellen could see immediately that something of weight had passed between Morris and Pastor Vandorpe's father. Morris, clamped in Rex's grip, looked up at her from his low spot at the edge of the pier. Perhaps it was partly the material circumstances — he sat cross-legged under the roof of the boat shed where he'd squatted dutifully as a boy, rod and reel in hand, bored to distraction — but Ellen now saw, gazing at her sleepy-eyed brother, a younger softer Morris who seemed to be saying, *I want to talk, and then I want a nap.* She thought she might only have read into Morris's expression those desires because they happened to be her own. Travel of any kind was tiring, but not as much as the improvisation of arrival. The Vandorpes were pleasant enough, but she hadn't planned on them. When Ellen had returned to the porch from the bathroom, Sheila seemed antsy and kept glancing through the screen toward the water. She'd gone on at some length about the shortcomings of her and Rex's little place in Fort Walton Beach, and while she rattled on about tiny bedrooms, too-low ceilings, and a lack of shade trees, Ellen's mind was pulled toward a delayed consideration of the house in which she currently sat, the house of her childhood, now altered by Bonnie's remodeling and the permanent departure of their father. She'd supposed it inevitable that their father's absence would loom large, this first time back in the house since the funeral, yet she could see, based on a glimpse of only two rooms, that Bonnie had diminished his lingering. The sight of the transformed rooms hadn't invoked for Ellen their father's absence. What they'd invoked — and what she'd referred to when she said to Morris, "Look what she's done"

194

— was their mother's presence. She hadn't expected that, any more than she'd expected the Vandorpes. Sheila soon suggested that Ellen and she join "the boys" out on the pier, and as they walked toward the boat shed and Ellen felt the many warped planks rocking beneath her feet, she was struck by what she had expected least of all: that she would be so quickly at peace. The last few days she'd harbored a secret fear that a return to Point Clear would prompt a return of grief. Now it seemed, even in the first hour, that she could lay her fear to rest. It wouldn't happen. Other things would happen, but not that. What was happening for her now was a gray pier, against a gray seascape, under a gray sky. And then Morris's boyish upturned face.

"You just can't stand it, can you, sugar?" said Rex to Sheila. He stood, then gave Morris a hand up. "So afraid you might miss something."

"Well, did I?" said Sheila. "Did I miss something?"

For an answer, Rex put his arm around her waist and kissed her cheek. Then the four of them began moving back toward the house. They walked the length of the pier in silence, and when they reached the stairs to the beach, Morris took Ellen's hand, pulling her gently back. Ellen called to the Vandorpes that she and Morris would be along in a few minutes.

Sheila appeared surprised and disappointed, reluctant to continue without them. She said, "Oh, well . . . okay then." Still, she made no move until Rex turned her by the shoulders and prodded her forward toward the yard.

Ellen sat next to Morris on the wooden steps and watched the Vandorpes' progress. Once they'd reached the shade of the rain porch, the family's old orange cat appeared from beneath a nearby hydrangea.

"Oh, look," said Ellen, "there's China."

They watched as Sheila bent to pet her, and Morris said, "Apparently she can abide cats."

After the Vandorpes entered the house, a neighborhood boy came barreling down the promenade on a bicycle, careened off the stone walkway and executed a skidding U-turn in the sand, then headed back in the direction of the hotel. A breeze stirred the Spanish moss in the great old oak by the wall. Ellen waited for Morris to speak first, and while she waited she was revisited by the earlier memory of those Friday-night suppers on the causeway with their father. This time it came attached to an oddly troubling question: What had their mother been doing on those Friday nights such that she'd never come with them? Ellen was about to put the question to Morris when he began to speak. "Well, it seems —" he said, but stopped, for they heard a clamor of voices coming from the screen porch.

The screen door flew open and Bonnie appeared, barefoot and wearing a waistless ankle-length dress the color of forget-me-nots. Ellen and Morris stood and began walking across the sand, side by side, as Bonnie moved to the gate, pushed it open, and came rushing toward them, beaming and crying, "I guess I must have goofed!"

Not in the least fit to be tied, thought Ellen; then the porch door swung open again and she saw a young man with dark hair step outside onto the sidewalk. "Oh, my, that can't be —" she heard Morris whisper, just before Bonnie reached them and threw her arms around them.

CHAPTER 6

In the morning, Ellen awakened disoriented by a dream she'd been having, in which she (or her life, or her world, or all three) had become a tall elm, whose broad creviced trunk poured forth a galaxy of outward-fanning branches into a black sky. She sat up in bed — not the king-size bed she shared with Dan at home in Cambridge, not the four-poster in Wellfleet, but the iron-barred brass-knobbed single she'd slept in as a girl in Point Clear. The tall casement window to her right was newly adorned with pale aquamarine sheers embroidered with a floral latticework, parted about six inches, and near the midpoint of a bright column of light she could see a silver patch of the bay. Her room was at once much the same and altogether different. The walls had been freshly painted but in a similar cream color, the nasty shag carpet had been removed, and the oak floor beneath it refinished. All the furnishings remained the same, down to the three pictures on the walls: two nineteenth-century Audubon prints, one of trumpeter swans and one of wild turkeys, and a watercolor Ellen had done as a girl, depicting two dozen robins on a field of solid emerald, entitled "Four and Twenty Robins, Feeding on the Lawn."

At bedtime the night before, she'd found in a glass-doored bookcase an old gardening book, published in the 1940s, a slim but comprehensive volume full of ink drawings and charts, explaining everything from the construction of a proper cold frame to the eradication of bagworms and thrips. The book had belonged to her mother, who'd passed it to her as a Christmas present when Ellen was twelve, the year her mother had died giving birth to Bonnie. The chapter on trees began with an epigraph from Walter Scott:

Jock, when ye hae naething else to do, ye may be aye sticking in a tree; it will be growing, Jock, when ye're sleeping.

Her mother had underlined a passage that hailed the immeasurable spiritual value of being with trees and loving them, and which listed among their benefits that they kindled in people cleaner thoughts and higher ideals. Ellen had decided to take the book back to Cambridge as a gift to Willie, though she suspected he wouldn't know what to make of it. She couldn't think what she herself had made of the gift as a girl, but it didn't matter; it had accumulated meaning, yellowing inside a bookcase of her childhood bedroom, unassisted by the will of any human intelligence. That would happen for Willie too, if not in the occasion of the old gardening book then in some other design: Somewhere off in the future, he would walk into a room from his past, his gaze would fall on an object acquired through an act of love, casually received and forgotten, and he would marvel at its previously unnoticed merit. Or so she believed; so she hoped.

She found herself starting down a dreary path having to do with how Willie would fare should she suddenly die, so she climbed out of bed and went to the window, where she drew back the sheers, flooding the room with sunlight. She could smell coffee and bacon even with the bedroom door closed, but she figured she would delay things a bit longer, enjoy her solitude a few minutes more. What she meant to delay was everything concerning Pastor Vandorpe, the Church of the Blessed Hunger, Bonnie's marriage, and especially Morris's many ideas and anxieties. In short, she wished to delay the immediate future, for at the moment she was much more drawn in the opposite direction.

Had she stood at that same window as a girl and admired the smooth fogged mirror of the bay, the craggy black outline of the oak against the sky, the gray pier's unvarying lesson on perspective? Not likely. More probably she'd taken the view and its details for granted, though it might have provided a backdrop for a young girl's thoughts, entirely unrelated to it. Last night, when she'd closed the sheers before bed, she'd seen in her mind's eye a clear image of her mother, moving to a window (in the dining room?) and standing there in silence, looking out at the bay. Her mother had moved to the window right after Ellen's father had left the house to go somewhere, but was it something that happened one particular time or was it something her mother did habitually upon his leaving? Ellen didn't know. What she knew was that Bonnie's restoration of the house not only evoked their mother but, for Ellen, the loss of her. Ellen imagined that over the course of the near-year of mourning she'd just got through, she'd been partly grieving her mother, a grief largely deferred, frozen in

201

time as the grief of a child. Most likely it had been easier for a twelve-year-old girl to "forget" her mother than to go forward without her — and of course the baby, Bonnie, had been less a distraction than an opportune vocation.

Ellen thought of Morris and wondered how it was possible that over the years they'd not had a single talk about the grotesque night some three decades ago when their father had awakened them around two in the morning and asked them to come into the library — where, with what seemed in Ellen's recollection icy indifference, he informed them that they had a new baby sister but that their mother would not be coming home from the hospital. Afterward, Ellen had seen Morris back to his bedroom, adjacent to hers, and then on to bed herself, dreamily resigned to yet another twist in the eccentric and unpredictable world of adults — that for some reason their mother had decided to take up residence at the Fairhope Infirmary.

Now, as if she'd conjured Morris by thinking of him, a very soft knock came at the door. She figured she could ignore it and he would assume she still slept and go away, but the memory of him as a ten-year-old, nodding in flannel pajamas between the capacious arms of their father's library recliner, made her turn from the window and call out, "Come in, Morris."

He entered the room and closed the door carefully and silently, as if he'd been sneaking through the house. He moved to the bed, where he lifted the old gardening book from the bedside table and sat down. He was already dressed for the day, in shorts, sandals, and a red-checked sport shirt; his hair was wet, parted on the side and combed severely across his brow. "How did you know it was me?" he asked, thumbing through the book.

"It didn't occur to me that it would be anyone else," said Ellen. "Smells like breakfast is under way."

He closed the book and laid it aside, apparently seeing in it nothing of immediate interest. "I think Macy's frying bacon and planning to scramble us some eggs in the bacon grease," he said. "I dare say you won't find any organic oatmeal in the cupboard, if that's what you have in mind. Thanks, by the way, for abandoning me last night."

"I didn't mean to abandon you," she said. "I was tired, and I figured that if I went to bed you could follow suit if you wanted."

"What is that you're wearing," said Morris, "a muumuu from the Vermont Country Store?"

"This happens to be a nightgown," said Ellen, "and I'd thank you not to insult it. Willie gave it to me last spring for Mother's Day."

"Well, I don't know how you can sleep in something like that. How *did* you sleep, by the way? I had some trouble myself. Do you think Bonnie's actually singing in the church choir or was it just an excuse to leave us alone with Pastor last night?"

Ellen moved to the bed and sat next to him but said nothing.

Morris gazed out the sunny window. "My God, it's confusing," he said. "I didn't expect him to be so young. Do you think he's really twenty-five? I wouldn't have put him a day over nineteen."

Ellen still didn't respond.

He looked at her and said, "Is it just me, or does he look like the love child of Colin Farrell and Aishwarya Rai?"

"Who's Aishwarya Rai?" said Ellen.

"Only the most beautiful woman in the world," said Morris. "Queen of the Indian film industry. Her most distinguishing characteristic, besides her beauty, is that she worships a Hindu god of happiness who's half man and half elephant. You've really got to get out more, Ellen."

"Morris," she said, "why do you think Mother never came with us when Daddy took us to eat on Friday nights at Whitney's?"

Morris, if surprised, took the question in stride. "That would have been difficult for her," he said.

"Difficult?" said Ellen. "Why?"

"Well, you see, she was dead."

"Oh."

"He didn't start taking us over there until after she'd died."

"Are you sure?"

"Yes," said Morris, "I'm sure. Macy had Friday nights off — that was when she went to mass — so Daddy took us out to eat."

"Then I guess we left Bonnie with —"

"With Susannah or Winifred or . . . what's-her-name."

"Natalie."

"Right, how could I forget Natalie? The chosen one."

"I don't think Natalie was the *only* chosen one, Morris."

"I'm sure you're mistaken," said Morris. "Even Daddy couldn't have — Why are we talking about this? Why are you thinking about it?"

"No special reason," said Ellen. "Back

here in the old room . . . just having some memories."

"Well, they aren't very pleasant."

"No, I guess not."

"You may be interested to know that Pastor has already left for the church," said Morris. "He was wearing cowboy boots and easily the largest belt buckle I've ever seen. Carved leather, the head of an eagle. He said something about needing to get ready for a ten o'clock meeting with the Prayer Team."

"The Prayer Team?"

"Yes," said Morris. "I'm not entirely sure, but I think they meet on a field somewhere outdoors and pray. Afterward they take showers and sit around in towels and watch themselves praying on videotape."

"And where's Bonnie?"

"Sleeping," said Morris. "Macy says that lately she's been sleeping most of the morning away. A sign of depression, if you ask me. What do you think's going on between Pastor and Rex?"

Ellen recalled that yesterday evening, as the Vandorpes were taking their leave around five o'clock, Pastor had hugged and kissed his mother good-bye but hadn't even shaken his father's hand. Still, she said to Morris, "What do you mean?"

"I have the impression that Rex doesn't entirely approve of the wunderkind preacher," said Morris. "Yesterday in the boat shed he told me Pastor was likely to try and save me from my ho-mo-sexuality."

"He actually said that?"

"Surprising, isn't it. Seems Bonnie waited till the last minute to drop the bomb on Pastor about her brother Morris being married to one of the same gender. And apparently Pastor had some discussion with Rex about it. That is to say, they argued."

"Oh, Morris," said Ellen, "I'm sorry."

"Don't be," said Morris. "Rex meant to warn me, for which I'm very grateful."

"But Pastor was so affectionate with you last night," said Ellen.

"Yes, you noticed," said Morris. "All that hugging. Not twenty minutes ago, on his way out, he actually kissed me on the cheek as he passed me in the hall. I think he wants to show me he isn't afraid of queers. Trying to gain my confidence. Setting me up."

"Setting you up for what?" said Ellen.

"Who knows?" said Morris. "The laying-on of hands, I imagine. Now, I really can't talk to you anymore until you've changed into something less comical."

Ellen told Morris he would need to leave the room in that case, which he did, after extracting from her a pledge of not taking longer than half an hour. He returned immediately to say that she should look for him in the library, where he would be contemplating the fate of the marble urn on the mantelpiece, their father's ashes, and he urged her not to indulge herself anymore in stirring up memories; he suggested that poking about in the past was a dubious enterprise and — very pleased with himself — added that there was simply no future in it.

Five minutes later, in the shower, Ellen recalled that their father, after a two-year hiatus from drinking, had again taken up the bottle the night her mother suffered the placental abruption that caused her to bleed to death at the hands of a poorly prepared Baldwin County obstetrician. As far as Ellen knew, her father hadn't lived a sober day for the next twenty-eight years, not until after his third, most severe, and most damaging stroke. She believed she had smelled whiskey on him in the wee hours of the morning when he'd summoned her and Morris to the library as children. She believed, too, that back in her room, as she drifted to sleep in a fog of incomprehension, she'd heard her young brother's weeping through the wall.

■ ■ ■ ■

Morris took a seat in one of a pair of gold wing-backed chairs that faced the fireplace. The library, the exclusive sanctum of their father during his lifetime, had always possessed the makings of a handsome room, obstructed by a haphazard arrangement of ugly furniture and general disorder. Bonnie had evidently seen its potential and, except for the tacky wagon-wheel light fixture that still hung overhead, she'd stripped it to the bare bones, redone the floor in an almost-black finish, and covered its two tall windows with wide-louvered shutters. The degree to which she'd exorcised the room of any trace of its former occupant bordered on aggressive, and Morris most appreciated the way the room's new austerity drew the eye to the cremation urn resting on the mantel, as if to call attention to the former occupant's considerably reduced status. The urn, about eight inches in height and shaped like a ginger jar, was made of dark green marble. It had cost just over $600, he recalled, the highway robbery typical of the funeral industry; divested of its hallowed purpose, the urn should have cost about $50. In his will, their father had requested cremation but had made no stipulation concerning the ashes. After the funeral last year, Morris and his sisters had talked about scattering the ashes over the water somewhere, a tribute to their father's lifelong love of deep-sea fishing, but Bonnie had said she wasn't "ready." Morris had preferred to be done with it — he was thinking mostly of not having to return to Point Clear in the near future — but Ellen had convinced him privately to defer to what she considered Bonnie's even more than usually fragile state. Off and on during the intervening months he'd thought about the ashes, a minor irritant, and at least once he'd dreamed of them, a cloyingly symbol-laden episode in which he dumped them over the bow of a sailboat only to have a gust of wind blow them back into his face. Now, as he sat in the shadowy room and stared at the urn, he saw he didn't care what happened to the ashes. He'd imagined before that he did care, without quite knowing why, but now — possibly owing to the aptness of their current situation, laudably effected by Bonnie — he simply didn't.

Here, and perhaps overall, he'd underestimated Bonnie's capacities. He almost felt as if he didn't know her, she seemed so changed. What he found trickiest was that she'd not changed clearly; she'd gone from something distinct (though ultimately sad) to something not entirely readable. During supper last night — an informal concoction of cold ham, potato salad, and limp green beans, served by Macy at the kitchen table — Bonnie had gushed over the sand-colored Cesarea dishes Morris and Ellen had sent as a wedding gift. Watching her, Morris reflected on the irony of her having said in her letter that she was for the first time someone definite to be seen. He'd thought her definite before, definitely lost, plainly drug-dependent; now she was a little blurry. There was nothing blurry about her physically; she was more beautiful than he'd ever seen her. She'd gained some weight — during her actress years she'd been prone to the emaciated look, often seeming snatched from the jaws of dissipation, desperately pulled together, and worried about the results — and now she appeared much more at home with her natural virtues. She did seem, as Ellen had observed earlier, more composed, but Morris, so far, was having trouble telling what exactly she was composed of. She maintained a familiar youthfulness and even a touch of familiar staginess, but now, no longer attached to blatant self-abuse, these traits were less firmly settled in her personality; it wasn't clear that they still belonged.

At the supper table, she'd reminded him of a teenager embarking on her first solo drive, thrilled to be behind the wheel, projecting for the sake of others an abundant self-confidence but not quite able to keep a speck of fear from her eyes. She'd too frequently changed the subject, as if every topic, no matter what its concerns, might lead somewhere unfortunate, or at least unplanned. Her method of interruption had been to apologize yet again for having muddled the day of their arrival. They discussed the wonderful alterations Bonnie had made to the house, the poor condition of the pier, the good health (despite the advanced age) of China the cat and Cricket the dog, and Bonnie cried, "I just feel *terrible* about getting the date wrong!" Pastor, after saying a grace that included thanks for Morris and Ellen's safe arrival and for the blessing of family love, had retreated into a single-minded spectacle of feeding himself. But eventually they got around to talking about the goings-on at the church, the capital drive for the new building, the necessary addition of a second Sunday morning service, and Bonnie cried, "I wasn't even home when you *got* here!" At first Morris thought her ill at ease on the occasion of their meeting Pastor. Later he had the impression that she kept returning to her mistake because she'd prepared herself for their arrival on Wednesday and couldn't quite bring herself fully to participate in the reality of their arrival on Tuesday. She'd rehearsed and psyched herself up for the next day's matinee, and she wanted to postpone her honest-to-God performance until then.

Morris supposed they would have to sort out the financial complications of the house. Bonnie had clearly sunk a small fortune into the renovations, and though it had been a pleasant surprise, she'd not consulted either himself or Ellen beforehand. Because her money had come from a source separate from his and Ellen's, the three of them hadn't been required formerly to cooperate in financial matters. Their paternal grandfather had established a trust for Morris and Ellen when they were children; after their mother died, their father, mostly for sentimental reasons, conveyed the mother's estate wholly to Bonnie. He'd considered Ellen and Morris already provided for, which was true, but what had come to Bonnie was nearly equal to Ellen and Morris's combined inheritance; fortunately, this mathematical detail had never bred any resentment, since despite the disparities everyone had more than enough. Then came their father's own will, which, aside from a respectable legacy left to Macy, divided everything equally into thirds. The only real property involved was the Point Clear house, and before any sorting out of that could occur, Morris would need first to sort out his feelings about it. He'd never imagined it a place he would want to use; he and Richard already had two houses, and how many houses did a person need? Still, he wasn't yet disposed to see Pastor Vandorpe's name on the deed. At the very least, if there was to be a transfer of Morris's and Ellen's interests to Bonnie, he thought it prudent to wait a few years, to see what the fate of the marriage would be.

He recalled the moment, yesterday afternoon, when Sheila Vandorpe had said to Rex, *It's their house.* Apart from that, there had been no acknowledgment of the odd situation they found themselves in, that Bonnie and Pastor (a person they were meeting for the first time) had taken up what appeared to be permanent residence in a house owned jointly by all three siblings. Last night, after Bonnie announced with overwrought regret her commitment to choir practice and left Morris and Ellen alone with Pastor, the three of them had settled for about an hour on the screen porch. The evening air felt slightly warmer than earlier, and the sky that had threatened rain all day finally delivered. Slouched in one of the rattan armchairs, Pastor made a point of turning off his cell phone, which, clipped to his belt, had rung three times during supper, though he'd declined to take any of the calls; he sighed and seemed to enter a near trance of languid contentment, richly fed, luxuriously sheltered, and confident that he was loved. The light over the bay, doubly softened by dusk and the rain, occasionally flared up white with sheet lightning; now and again a southerly wind segmented the rainfall into vertical panels, which it marched across the water northward toward the delta region at the top of the bay. This play of sea and weather further rewarded Pastor's astonishing good looks — particularly the plundering midnight blue of his eyes — and two or three times Morris caught Ellen openly staring at him. Like his father, Pastor was quick to smile, quick to wink and hug, but, unlike Rex, in an idle or contemplative moment he reverted to an aspect of sadness — altogether winning in Morris's book, since it made the young man's easy pleasure rise apparently from seriousness. He wasn't especially given to religious talk, as Morris had feared he might be, though he sometimes sprinkled his conversation on subjects ranging from Mexican food to local history with scriptural references of the proverbial stripe. Morris thought that even if he hadn't known him to be the minister of an independent church whose seven-hundred-member roster was still growing, he would have taken him for a young man in some sort of successful self-employment. Throughout the evening, Morris was off and on conscious of the "odd situation," Pastor's sudden residence in his childhood home, but he was convinced that it never crossed Pastor's mind.

Around eight-thirty (which felt like nine-thirty, given the shift in time zones), Ellen complained of fatigue, said she wanted to turn in early, and retired so abruptly to her room it struck Morris as a kind of betrayal. Pastor moved into Ellen's spot on the couch, next to Morris. That way Pastor gained a straight-on view of the bay from beneath the eaves of the rain porch, but it also seemed to Morris to reflect a natural inclination to be physically closer with whomever he was keeping company. After a minute or two of silence, Pastor cried, "Are you *saved,* you miserable sinner?" then quickly laughed and slapped Morris on the knee. "Well, isn't that what you expected of me?" he said.

Morris didn't appreciate the joke as much as he would have had it not genuinely startled him. It occurred to him that he might swish limp-wristed across the porch and fire the same question back at Pastor, but he only smiled and said, "Actually, I've made an effort to set aside my expectations."

"That's good, I guess," said Pastor. "You know, Morris, I thought it was wrong of Bonnie to leave y'all out of our wedding. Well, I shouldn't say wrong. I just thought it was a mistake. And one she might regret later on too."

Morris did not say, Bonnie couldn't invite Ellen without inviting me, and if she'd invited me she would have had to invite Richard. He said, "Do you think she does regret it?"

Quite a long silence passed between them before Pastor answered — so long that Morris turned to look at him. It appeared that the question had sent the young man into a study of far wider-ranging concerns. At last, he shook his head and said, "I honestly don't know, Morris. I just hope y'all didn't get your feelings hurt, that's all."

The old bird dog wandered onto the porch and Pastor, leaning forward to scratch the dog's ears, seemed happy to leave the subject there, a relief to Morris, who, after a moment, said, "I like your parents. I understand we might not have met them had things gone according to plan, but I'm glad we did."

"They're decent folks," Pastor said, almost as if he was naming their chief limitation.

"*Folks* is an ambiguous noun," said Morris. "Do you mean they're decent people or decent parents?"

Pastor looked at him and smiled, which Morris took as showing appreciation for the bit of parsing he'd just done. Pastor said, "I meant they're decent people. But since you mention it, they were pretty decent parents too."

"They clearly love you to pieces," said Morris.

"Well, I expect they ought to," said Pastor. "They're my *folks.*"

"It doesn't always work out that way," said Morris.

Before Pastor could respond, Macy appeared at the porch door and announced that she was closing the kitchen unless anybody wanted anything else. Pastor said he wanted a glass of milk but that he would come and get it himself, and Morris seized the opportunity to say good night.

He had spent the next three hours in the bed of his boyhood room, thinking over the events and ramifications of the day and reading E. M. Forster's *Where Angels Fear to Tread,* which happened to be lying on his bedside table. He found the novel clunky here and there but thoroughly captivating. Outside, the rain continued to fall, hard at times, and when at last he fell asleep, he seemed to ride into his dreams on a hump-backed whale whose watery expirations sounded like distant rumbles of thunder.

That morning, on his way to the kitchen for a wake-up cup of coffee, Morris had encountered Pastor in the hallway, who beamed at him, took him by the shoulders, and kissed him on the cheek. "The Apostle Paul tells us to greet all our brothers with a kiss," he said.

Morris, distracted by Pastor's enormous American eagle belt buckle and his elaborately tooled brown and sky-blue cowboy boots, said that if he recalled that verse correctly, the Apostle Paul made an exception for those brothers who had terrible morning breath because they had not yet brushed their teeth. Pastor laughed and said he saw where Bonnie got her sense of humor, and Morris continued to the kitchen, eager for coffee.

Macy had stepped into the yard for something, but the coffee was already made and he helped himself. He took a cup to the screen porch, where after about ten minutes he began to feel lonely, so he had gone to knock on Ellen's door.

Now, as he waited in the library for Ellen to finish bathing and dressing, Bonnie turned up at the door, barefoot, drowsy, unkempt, and wearing what looked like a polka-dotted hospital gown. She staggered toward Morris, and threw herself into his lap, draping her bare legs over one arm of the wing-backed chair and obviously reenacting some bond she believed she'd had with him in their youth. She kissed him near the temple and said, "Your hair's all wet."

"Yes," he said, shifting in the chair to distribute her weight more evenly onto both his thighs.

"Well, what do you think?" she said. "Tell me what you think."

"What I think," he said, "is that none of the women in this family know how to dress properly. Ellen is in the next room looking like Old Mother Hubbard, and you —"

"No," she said, "I mean what do you think

about the library?"

"The library is splendid," he said. "Except for the —"

"Wagon wheel," she said. "I know. Isn't it hideous?" She threw her head back to view the light fixture. "Pastor likes it," she whispered.

"That's no excuse," said Morris, adopting an authoritarian tone. "Some things you just have to take in hand."

She sighed, as if resigned to this troubling universal truth, and said, "I know. Take things in hand. Lay down the law. Draw the line."

"Stick to one's guns," said Morris. "Put one's foot down. Hold one's ground."

"I will, I will," she said, "all in good time. But except for the wagon wheel, you really like it?"

"I really like it," he said. "I like everything, not only the library. You've done a phenomenal job. And squandered a good chunk of your inheritance, no doubt."

She quickly lifted her head and looked directly at him, narrowing her eyes. "We're not going to talk about money," she said.

"Well, we have to talk about it sometime," said Morris.

"I don't see why," said Bonnie.

"Well, because we —"

She clamped her hand over his mouth. "Stop," she said. "If you talk about why we have to talk about it, then we're talking about it."

He removed her hand from his mouth and said, with extreme patience, "We don't have to talk about it this morning. But you're mistaken if you think you can silence me forever. Not on this subject, and not on a number of others."

Her eyes clouded over with tears, but not quite enough to spill over. "You're never going to forgive me, are you, Morris."

"Don't be silly," he said. "I already have."

"You have?"

"Yes," he said. "When I had time to think about it, I saw that your decision made perfect sense. You put your own feelings first. If a girl can't do that on her wedding day, when can she?"

"Oh, my God," she said. "That's exactly what I told myself. But it was unforgivably selfish. If I could do it over, I —"

"But you can't," he said. "I only wish there had been some way for you to have invited Ellen and not me. She's disappointed and hurt, and she blames *me* for it."

"She said that?"

"She doesn't have to say it," said Morris.

"She —"

"She doesn't have to say what?" said Ellen, from the doorway.

As she entered the room, Morris quickly noted a couple of accessorizing touches that Ellen brought out only in the South. With her simple khaki slacks and white silk blouse, she'd put on a string of pearls, something she would never wear during the day in Cambridge, and the prim little open-toed pumps on her feet seemed to belong only to Point Clear — last autumn, she'd worn them to their father's funeral.

"Don't you look beautiful!" cried Bonnie, leaping from Morris's lap and causing him to groan with pain.

She went to Ellen and took her by the arm, delicately, as if she feared she might break, escorted her to the middle of the room, and stood her between Morris and the hearth. "Doesn't she look beautiful?" Bonnie said to Morris.

"She does look beautiful," said Morris, "but have I missed something? Are we going somewhere?"

"I just thought we'd probably walk up to the hotel later for lunch," Ellen said, "and I didn't see the sense in getting dressed twice. Now, tell me what you were talking about. What is it that I don't have to say?"

"What makes you think we were talking about you?" said Morris.

"Gee, I don't know," she said petulantly. "Your tone of voice, maybe?"

"I was just telling Bonnie that of course you were hurt about missing her wedding," Morris said. "That you blame me for it, and that you don't have to say so for me to know it."

Ellen took about five seconds to absorb what Morris had said, during which Bonnie stepped a few feet back from Ellen, eyed her from head to toe, then stepped forward again and adjusted the collar of the blouse and the string of pearls. "Really, Morris," Ellen said at last. "What's it like, being the destination that all roads lead to?"

"Very tiresome," said Morris, smiling. "If you want to know the truth."

"Apparently not tiresome enough," said Ellen, which made Morris laugh.

"Sorry," he said. "Only thirty seconds ago, Bonnie had her hand over my mouth, which is where I guess she should have left it."

"You removed it," said Bonnie.

"Well, I shouldn't have," he said. "What I should've done was to go with Pastor this morning to meet with the Prayer Team. At least it would've been something new."

"He's meeting with the Prayer Team?"

asked Bonnie.

"At ten o'clock," said Morris.

Bonnie, who appeared truly worried, said, "Did Pastor say that something had happened?"

"I don't know what you mean," said Morris.

"They don't normally meet on Wednesdays," said Bonnie. "Something must have happened to someone."

Macy Rosalie Walsh — whose nineteenth-century forebears had been among the idealists who established a Utopian community in the neighboring town of Fairhope — possessed like many of those settlers some definite ideas about how life should be lived. Among these ideas was the certainty that people should eat what's placed before them and do so with gratitude. At Macy's behest, Morris, Ellen, and Bonnie reported to the kitchen and took seats at the table, where Macy set out plates of biscuits already swimming in butter, undercooked bacon, hominy grits, and scrambled eggs spotted brown with grease. The three of them sat silent for a minute, looking troubled, until Macy said, "Well, y'all dig in while it's still hot."

Morris recalled that a nearly identical

scene, made of nearly identical ingredients, had occurred when he and Ellen had come down last year for the funeral. Evidently Macy's strategy here was to choose a path of absolute denial, thereby putting them in a position of repeating what had been, for Macy, a considerable affront, a strategy Morris deemed particularly southern. Ellen had never been much of an eater; she didn't so much eat as repeatedly curb her appetite several times a day, and she'd acquired a skill for creating the illusion of eating — nibbling, rearranging, crumbling, and mashing things with her fork, then covering it all with a napkin. She immediately took this tack at the breakfast table, as Bonnie, who sat opposite her, with Morris in between, only cast Macy a cryptic, desperate look, which Macy seemed easily to translate. The housekeeper sighed and shook her head, and Morris figured he might as well jump in at that moment too. "I'm sure this is all very delicious, Macy," he said, "but since I'm a good fifteen hundred miles from my cardiologist, I think I better pass. If you don't mind, I'll just have a piece of fruit."

"We don't have any *fruit*," said Macy bitterly, then added as an afterthought, "I had some blackberries yesterday but I put them into a pie."

"Oh, that's what I want," said Bonnie. "A slice of blackberry pie."

"Pie," said Macy, slinging a dish towel down onto the counter. "For breakfast."

"Well, it's what sounds good," said Bonnie.

"Honey, if I only ate what sounded good," said Macy, "I'd weigh three hundred pounds."

Morris pointed out that bacon, eggs, and biscuits were not exactly slimming, and Macy said she gave up, she didn't know why she bothered to try and make a special breakfast when she knew the three of them had always had picayune eating habits and she couldn't imagine why she'd expected anything different this morning. She removed her apron and left the kitchen, through the mudroom, and retreated into her apartment.

Ellen asked Bonnie if she thought Macy was really angry, but before Bonnie could answer, the housekeeper returned to the doorway long enough to tell them matter-of-factly that the coffee on the counter was fresh, she'd just brewed it. After Macy was gone again, Bonnie smiled and said, "This is the breakfast she makes for Pastor practically every morning and then tells him he's going to eat himself into an early grave."

They cleared the dishes from the table, scraped the eggs and grits into the garbage, but saved the biscuits and bacon. Ellen and Bonnie each had pie, and Morris helped himself to a piece of Macy's pineapple upside-down cake. Soon Morris was gazing vacantly around the kitchen, noting the cherry-red Formica countertops from his boyhood, the cracked floral-patterned linoleum, the white-painted cabinets, and the old glass pulls and knobs, some of which had been replaced with only near-matching substitutes. At last he turned to Bonnie and asked her whether or not Pastor had said anything to her about letting Macy go.

Ellen did not kick him under the table, but she scowled at him so severely he thought she might have been restraining herself. He said to her, "I don't see the harm in asking."

"What are you talking about?" said Bonnie. "Pastor just gave Macy a raise a couple of weeks ago. He wanted to be sure she'd stay, since she doesn't really need to work anymore. You know . . . after the money Daddy left her."

Morris told Bonnie about Macy's eavesdropping adventure, what she'd overheard Sheila Vandorpe saying to Pastor.

"Oh, that," said Bonnie. "Yes, he mentioned it. But he would never seriously consider allowing his parents to live with us."

"There, you see?" said Morris to Ellen. "Everything out in the open. Doesn't that feel better? And we can set Macy's mind at ease." Then he turned back to Bonnie and said, "Why would he never consider letting them live with you?"

"You don't have to answer that, Bonnie," said Ellen. "It's none of his business."

"Don't be trite," said Morris to Ellen. "What is and what isn't one's business is a highly debatable question."

"I don't mind," said Bonnie. "It's something biblical. Something Jesus said about how the child is supposed to leave the parents. I don't recall exactly, but it's like a moral issue with Pastor. And he doesn't get along all that well with Rex."

"Why not?" said Morris.

"I'm not sure what *he* would say," said Bonnie, "but I think it's because they're so much alike. I've noticed they tend to argue a lot."

"About what, for example?" said Morris.

"Morris, you're grilling her," said Ellen.

"We're just having a conversation," said Morris. "If it makes you nervous for some reason, you can —"

"It doesn't make me nervous, Morris," said Ellen. "I'm just wondering if we mightn't talk for five minutes about Bonnie before you turn our whole visit into something that's about you."

"Is this a new cause you've taken up?" said Morris. "Reining in my narcissism? Well, let me ask you a question, Ellen. Do you think the degree to which our whole visit's about me is something completely within my control?"

"No, I don't, Morris," said Ellen, "I'm sorry. I only wanted to —"

"Okay," said Morris, "why don't we get Bonnie to tell us about her religious conversion."

"For heaven's sake, Morris," said Ellen.

"I haven't had a religious conversion," said Bonnie.

"Well, you're married to a preacher and you're singing in the choir," said Morris. "Surely it's an indication of something."

"I only just started singing in the choir," said Bonnie. "And I'm not sure I want to talk about this. I'm afraid you'll make a joke about it."

"I promise not to make any jokes," said Morris.

"Don't make promises you can't keep," Ellen said.

Bonnie was about to speak, but Macy appeared again at the mudroom door, this time with car keys in hand and a straw hat on her head. "Excuse me," she said, "but Pastor told me just this morning about the two extra places at the supper table. So I'm on my way over to Bruno's."

"What two extra places?" said Bonnie.

"He didn't say," said Macy. "I assumed you already knew."

"Well, I don't," said Bonnie. "Tonight was to be our official welcome-home supper for Ellen and Morris."

"I know it was," said Macy. "It still is, but Pastor said there'd be two extras. Told me right before he left the house. Didn't choose to say who it was, and I didn't figure it was my place to ask. Now, do y'all have any special —" Macy stopped herself.

"Were you going to say needs?" said Morris. "Do we have any special needs?"

"I was gonna say requests," said Macy, "but I ought to have my head examined for even thinking it. Let me take care of tonight's supper first, and then tomorrow y'all can give me your long lists."

As Macy turned to go, Bonnie immediately rose from the table. "I'll be back in a minute," she said. "I've got to find out what's going on."

Morris observed her bare feet as she went, her meticulously polished toenails — something touching and vulnerable about that — and after another moment he heard, from down the hallway, a door slam shut. He looked at Ellen with raised eyebrows.

"She's just calling her husband," said Ellen. "People do it every day. I'm planning to call mine this morning too."

"As it happens I'm planning the same thing," said Morris. "I mean of course Richard, not Dan. But if you'll notice, there's a telephone right over there on the kitchen wall. I definitely think we may be flying into a little domestic turbulence."

"You mean you hope we are," said Ellen. "We haven't been here twenty-four hours and already you're starting to regress."

Morris took a moment to unravel the sense of her remark. At last he said, "Is that an allusion to the Great Eternal Soap Opera of the South?"

"It is," said Ellen.

"My God, you're right," he said. "It's drawing me in, I can feel it —"

"You'll need to be on your guard," said Ellen. "Now, what did Bonnie say earlier, in the library . . . about the wedding?"

"She said she thought I would never forgive her."

"And what did you say?"

"I said I already had."

"That was easy," said Ellen. "She must have been relieved."

"One down and one to go. Now she's worried about you."

"It's not true, by the way," said Ellen, "what you told her about my blaming you."

"Well, you don't want it to be," Morris said, "but I think it's a little true."

"I'm surprised you think something can be a little true," said Ellen. "It's not like you."

"I'm getting less precise in my old age," said Morris. "No one ever tells you what a toll precision takes. It actually ages you. Don't you think it's interesting that Pastor gave Macy a raise? I wonder if he gave it to her with Bonnie's money."

"I don't know what kind of financial arrangement they have," Ellen said.

"And good luck finding out," said Morris. "She's already made a declaration that we're not to talk about money."

"We'll have to talk about it sometime."

"That's what I said when she clamped her hand over my mouth."

"Well, even if he did use Bonnie's money," said Ellen, "it indicates generosity on his part."

"Or enlightened self-interest," said Morris. "Is it possible that you and I came home for Mardi Gras one year after we'd gone away to boarding school?"

"Now look who's having memories," said Ellen. "Yes, we did, but I can't think why. I remember going to some of the parades across the bay."

"You don't mean *parades across the bay.*"

"Excuse me," said Ellen. "I mean parades, comma, across the bay in Mobile."

"But didn't I hate Mardi Gras?" asked Morris.

"Yes. You hated all the carrying-on in the streets. You hated the people on the floats throwing things at you." Ellen paused for a moment, then smiled. "But you loved the marching bands," she said.

"Yes," said Morris, "I did. Don't tell anybody, but I still love a good marching band. It's a weakness."

"What made you think of it?" asked Ellen.

"Macy did," he answered. "When she stood there in the doorway just now, I suddenly recalled a time when she'd been to Ash Wednesday services and came home with a black smudge on her forehead."

"Oh, I remember that," said Ellen. "We were here during Mardi Gras and she came back from mass in the middle of the day.

Bonnie must've been about five, I think, and she saw Macy and started to cry. Said she wanted a black dot on her head too."

"That's right," said Morris. "So Macy pressed her forehead to Bonnie's and left a little smudge. Then you and I asked her to do us too and she touched her forehead to each of ours, right here in the kitchen. God, we were teenagers, Ellen. What could we have been thinking?"

"I'm not sure," said Ellen. "I imagine it was sort of intriguing and beautiful, like a blessing. She shared the blessing of the ashes with us."

"And Daddy had a fit when he saw it."

"He was so ignorant about church," said Ellen. "I guess he thought only Catholics had that ritual and he accused Macy of turning us into little Catholic heathens. Marched us into the bathroom and made us wash our foreheads. Poor Bonnie. You and I probably thought it was funny, but she —"

At that moment, they heard Bonnie's voice from down the hallway. "Ellen!" she cried. "Could you come here for a minute?"

Ellen left the table, the kitchen, and Morris to his thoughts. Vividly he recalled the housekeeper's face as she'd drawn near him that afternoon to press her forehead against his; she'd smiled, but sadly, and a minute afterward he asked her what it all meant, the curious black smudges.

Ellen had got one detail wrong, thought Morris: Their enraged father had marched her and Bonnie to the bathroom, not him. When Macy had answered Morris's question — "Why, it's meant to remind us that we're dust, Morris" — he'd gone straight to the kitchen sink and scrubbed his brow with soap.

CHAPTER 7

Edith Busby, senior minister secretary at the Church of the Blessed Hunger, told Bonnie that Pastor had not yet returned from meeting with the Prayer Team in the fellowship hall. She confirmed that Bonnie was correct, the Prayer Team did not normally meet on Wednesdays, they met on Thursdays, but Pastor had called a special meeting. She did not know why, he had not said why, but no, to her knowledge, nothing bad had happened to anyone. As Bonnie was asking Edith to get Pastor to phone home, the secretary interrupted to say, "Hold on, he's walking in the door right now."

Bonnie heard Edith say, "Mrs. Vandorpe," and then a few moments passed during which Bonnie imagined Pastor situating himself in the privacy of the inner office. She had placed the call at her lamp table in the master bedroom, and when at last he said hello she sat down on the edge of the bed. "What's going on, Pastor?" she asked.

"What are you referring to, Bonnie girl?" he said.

Lately, Bonnie liked being called "Bonnie girl" only half the time she was called it. "Pastor," she said, "please don't treat me like a child."

There was a long silence at the other end of the line, after which Pastor said, "All right, yes, I met with the Prayer Team this morning to pray over your brother. But I kept it completely anonymous. I asked for prayers for somebody who was struggling with homosexuality but I didn't mention any names. Probably half the Prayer Team thought it was myself I was talking about."

"But Morris isn't struggling with homosexuality," said Bonnie. "You're struggling with it. . . . I mean, you're struggling with his. You should be praying for yourself."

"I pray for myself every day, Bonnie. I pray that I may be guided by the Holy Spirit in all that I say and do."

"But how do you know if you're being guided? How do you know you're not just doing whatever you damn well please and because you prayed for guidance you just imagine you're being guided?"

"Say that again."

238

"You understood me."

She had never taken that tone with him before, and as her gaze fell onto the diamond ring on her left hand, she felt a not entirely unpleasant sensation of heat in her face and neck. After another pause — and in an extremely modulated manner meant, she guessed, to instruct by contrast — he said, "I can't tell for sure, Bonnie, not a hundred percent of the time, if I'm being guided. If you're upset with me I'm sorry, but I can't see what harm praying for somebody can do. It's not like God's going to do something or change something just because the Prayer Team asked Him to."

"Then I don't see the point in asking," said Bonnie. "And it *is* harmful, Pastor. It's . . . I don't know . . . invasive. It feels invasive."

"I don't know what that means," he said.

"You don't know what invasive means?"

"I don't know what *you* mean."

"I mean that Morris didn't ask for your prayers," she said. "He didn't ask for them and they're based on a false premise. You're imposing your particular view on him and praying about something that's really none of your business."

"Well, that's the same opinion Daddy put forward the other day," said Pastor, "but I disagree. And the view you say I'm imposing happens to also be the biblical view. And I still don't see the harm."

"It hurts my feelings, Pastor," she said. "That's the harm."

"I don't see why."

"That hurts my feelings too. That you don't see why."

"I'm a Christian minister," he said, after a moment. "You knew I was a Christian minister when you married me. It's one of my duties to pray for those I see living in a condition of sin. I do it out of love. Pure love and nothing else, if that makes any difference to you."

"It doesn't," she said. "Actually, it's worse. It's like people who beat their children and say they're doing it out of love."

"Nobody's beating anybody here," said Pastor.

"No, that's just what you used to do," said Bonnie. "Beat them, stone them, burn them at the stake, whatever. Now you pray for them. Out of love. I guess that's progress."

"I guess it is," he said. "In fact, I'm sure it is. And speaking of hurt feelings, it kind of hurts mine when you say *you* that way, meaning me."

"Well, at least you can see now why I couldn't have my own family to our wed-

ding," Bonnie said, her voice cracking —
infuriatingly, since she'd wanted to get
through without crying.

"Bonnie, you're the one who kept this a
secret until after we were married," he said.

"Are you suggesting that you might not
have married me if you'd known my brother
was gay?"

"Of course not," he said. "I'm just —"

"I couldn't invite my own brother to my
own wedding because I was afraid you'd do
something like this."

"What in the world have I done?" said
Pastor, his voice rising in pitch. "Tell me
what I've done."

"You called a special meeting of the fucking Prayer Team! That's what you've done!"

Another silence ensued, in which Bonnie
thought, *Why did I have to say fucking?* and
then Pastor said, "Well, Bonnie girl, for better or worse, you're the wife of a Christian
minister now. You're the preacher's wife.
I'm sure you don't mean to show such a
lack of respect for one of the sacred institu-
tions of our church and for the fine folks
who practice their faith in this serious way.
I really think we should talk about this when
you're not so upset."

"Good idea!" she said. "Maybe tonight at
supper! Maybe we can take it up with our

mystery guests!"

She slammed the receiver down, which she imagined was an even greater shock to him than to herself. She dialed him back immediately, dreading the hurdle of Edith Busby, but Pastor answered the phone; in spite of everything, the sound of his voice had on Bonnie a watered-down version of its usual calming effect.

"I'm sorry," she said. "I've never done that before. It was a first. It felt strange."

He laughed, which rekindled her anger just as it had started to subside.

"It felt pretty strange from this end too," he said.

"I would like to know who you've invited to supper tonight," she said. "And I would like to know why."

"That seems fair enough," he said.

"I'm glad you think so," she said.

"Bobby and Ruth Delk are going to be joining us," he said.

"You're kidding."

"No, I'm not," he said. "I thought you liked Ruth Delk. I distinctly remember you telling me you liked her."

"Please tell me you're kidding."

"Well, I wouldn't have done it if I'd known you'd react like this," he said. "To be honest, Ruth coming was an accident. I called over to Bobby's to ask him and Brenda and it turned out Brenda's up in Memphis, visiting her folks. And Bobby mentioned Ruth — she lives with them, you know — and it just felt like the right thing to do. To include her."

"But why would you invite people — never mind who — when Morris and Ellen are here?"

"Well, why wouldn't I?" he said. "That's generally when people have company, isn't it? They invite folks over to meet other folks who are visiting from out of town. And I especially wanted Morris to meet Bobby because I think they'll like each other."

"Okay, Pastor," she said. "I'm going to hang up now. Not hang up on you, but just hang up. I need to reflect on all this."

"What are y'all planning to do today?"

"I don't know, but I'm not going to talk about that now," she said. "I'm just going to get off the phone."

"All right," he said. "I was going to come home in a little while to eat, but maybe under the —"

"Do whatever you like," she said. "But I don't imagine we'll be here if you do come."

After she'd put down the phone, she continued to sit on the edge of the bed for another minute or two. The room was dark.

The sun didn't reach that side of the house until midafternoon, and earlier, when she'd got out of bed, she'd been eager to see Morris and Ellen and had neglected to open the shutters. In the gloom, the claret tones of her mother's old Turkish carpet appeared brown, and the walls, which Bonnie had painted a deep blue-green called *Nile,* gave the bedroom a lonely underwater quality. She caught sight of herself in the round mirror of the dressing table opposite. She still wore the nightgown she'd slept in, she hadn't brushed her hair, and she was sitting with her feet resting on the bed's side rail, her arms wrapped around her knees; she was even rocking back and forth a bit — exactly like a drug addict, in rehab, undergoing withdrawal. This image of herself so frightened her she called out Ellen's name and then realized that Ellen probably couldn't hear her, far away in the kitchen, with the bedroom door shut. She moved to the door, opened it, and shouted up the long hallway; she left the door standing open and went into the bathroom to wash her face.

Ellen, who'd left Morris alone at the kitchen table, immediately started down the hall toward the master bedroom. Behind her, in the living room, her mother's antique grandfather clock chimed the half hour, eleven-thirty — which coincided with a succession of thoughts that formed in Ellen's mind as plain and self-evident as the columns on an antebellum mansion: (1) she couldn't tell whether or not Bonnie was happy; (2) she couldn't tell whether or not Pastor Vandorpe actually loved Bonnie; (3) even if Pastor had married Bonnie partly for her money, it didn't rule out his loving her, nor did it rule out Bonnie's happiness; and (4) Bonnie was pregnant. She thus entered the bedroom with a sense of new clarity, even if much of it illuminated what wasn't clear.

She heard water running in the adjacent bath and assumed she would find Bonnie there, but she paused for a moment near the foot of the bed. Here, too, Bonnie had worked her wonders: straightaway Ellen recognized their mother's dressing table with its matching padded bench; Ellen had sometimes been allowed to sit there next to her while she got ready for going out, Ellen thrilled by the mysteries of small sterling silver mirrors and brushes, rhinestone-encrusted combs and barrettes, crystal perfume bottles, lipsticks and tiny pots of rouge, creams and lotions of secret benefits and secret costs. As Ellen continued toward the bath, she noticed a black leather Bible on one of the bedside tables; four ribbon markers of different colors were attached to the top of the spine, but uncountable scraps of paper were stuffed between the pages as well, tagging, Ellen first imagined, passages most relevant and edifying to the household, and then, more hopefully, more charitably, she thought perhaps they were passages most loved. She thought the Bible must surely be Pastor's and not Bonnie's, for she didn't think Bonnie had lived long enough in her new incarnation to have chosen that many verses.

The door to the adjoining bath stood ajar about an inch and she could see a sliver of the pedestal sink but nothing of Bonnie. She knocked lightly and then heard Bonnie's hello from what seemed outside the room. The next moment, she found her sister, through tall open French windows, seated on a concrete bench on a terrace of damp moss-covered bricks. "I'm out here," Bonnie called to her, though of course it was already obvious.

Awestruck, Ellen said, "I'm not sure I even knew this spot existed."

"Well, it was never used," said Bonnie. "The French windows had been painted shut so many times it took two men most of a day to get them working again."

She'd put on a long lilac-colored robe over her nightgown; she scooted to one end of the bench and indicated for Ellen to sit next to her, which she did. The terrace was surrounded on all sides by high trellises, supporting a mixture of pale-pink rambling roses and honeysuckle; a narrow archway opened at the far end into the side yard. "It's so beautiful," said Ellen. And then, "Bonnie, sweetheart, you've been crying."

Bonnie stared into her lap. "Tears of rage," she said softly.

"Pastor?" said Ellen.

"Pastor and myself and the Church of the Blessed Hunger and . . . I don't know . . . the world, I guess."

"That's a lot," said Ellen.

"I know, I've been bottling it up," Bonnie said. "Thoughtful of me to save it until you and Morris got here. I wanted everything to be perfect when you came, and now. . . . Oh, this morning in the library he was so completely sweet and understanding, and now —"

"You mean Morris," said Ellen. "Morris was sweet and understanding."

Bonnie nodded. "He told me he'd already forgiven me about the wedding — which I don't deserve, by the way — and the last thing I wanted was for you and him to come down here and be subjected to unpleasantness."

"It's been perfectly pleasant so far," Ellen said, lying only a little. "Married couples quarrel, Bonnie. Dan and I have just come through a whole year of quarreling. Well, I don't mean incessantly, and it's not always like that, thank God . . . not that extreme . . . but you can't always control —"

"I'm not talking about just any quarrel," said Bonnie. "I'm talking about Morris."

"Oh," said Ellen. "You're quarreling about Morris."

"Apparently," said Bonnie.

"This is going to be a source of conflict? I mean now, while we're here visiting?"

"I didn't think so," said Bonnie. "But maybe it is."

"But Pastor's been so kind to Morris," Ellen said. "Affectionate, even."

"Oh, yes, I know, that's Pastor's way," said Bonnie. "He can annihilate you with kindness and affection. He can assassinate, exterminate, and hang you out to dry with it."

"Do you think maybe you're overstating it a bit?"

"No, I'm not," said Bonnie. "It's like the

Eighth Wonder of the World, how small he can make you feel by heaping praise on you . . . blinding you with the beacon of his love."

"We're talking about you now, right?" said Ellen. "About how Pastor has sometimes made you feel."

"Of course we are," said Bonnie, and looked again into her lap. "Sorry."

After a moment, Ellen said, "Practically speaking, Bonnie, what do you think it means . . . whatever these feelings are that Pastor has about Morris?"

"Practically speaking, it means he called a special meeting of the Prayer Team this morning," said Bonnie.

"To pray about Morris?"

"Yes."

"Oh, dear."

"That's what I thought too," said Bonnie. "Oh, dear."

"I don't see why he had to call a special meeting," said Ellen.

"I know," said Bonnie. "It's like a flipping emergency or something."

"What else?"

"Nothing else so far," she said. "It's my fault, really."

"Why do you say that?"

"I gave Pastor more information than he

needed. I think it's the marriage that totally sends him over the edge."

"That would have come out in any case," said Ellen. "Morris doesn't exactly keep his marriage to Richard a secret."

"But I should have told him sooner," said Bonnie. "I dreaded it. I was afraid of it. I sprang it on him three days ago."

Ellen also felt more time might have helped, but she didn't think Bonnie's self-reproach needed encouragement. "Well, if Pastor continues to be kind and affectionate to Morris," she said, "and then goes to church and prays for him, I don't see how that can hurt him. That's all we really care about, isn't it? That Morris doesn't get hurt?"

"It's not all *I* care about," said Bonnie.

After a pause, Ellen said, "Yes, you're right. In your position, I would care about more than that too."

"After all, you and Morris will be going home in a few days," said Bonnie, making it sound almost like an accusation.

Ellen nodded and waited for a moment, to see if Bonnie had anything to add. A bumblebee flew in through the archway, loud and menacing, dive-bombed two or three honeysuckle blossoms in a perfunctory way, and scribbled over the top of the trellis and out of sight. Ellen said, "Have there been other things like this? I mean, is this the first obstacle of this kind you've run into? I mean, between you and Pastor, is this —"

"I understand the question, Ellen," said Bonnie. "You mean, given who he is and who I am, you'd assume there would be lots of problems like this."

"Well, yes, frankly," said Ellen. "It's one of the things I've wondered about. One of the things I've worried about. Vaguely."

"There really haven't been," said Bonnie. "There have been some things I could've turned into obstacles, but I've chosen not to. Things he believes that don't make sense to me but that I don't really care about."

"Like what?"

"The theological stuff," said Bonnie. "I just figure it's part of his faith and I haven't really worried about it. He's been so helpful to me, Ellen. I mean, look at me: I'm truly a changed person. I had nothing going on in the God department and Pastor gave that to me . . . gave it to me at exactly the right moment. I went to Catholic school for seven years as a kid, Ellen. My only idea of God was the Great Scorekeeper in the Sky. Pastor introduced me to the unconditional-love side of things, and that's been enough for me. It still is. If other stuff comes later, then that's okay. But I'm doing fine with the love part right now, and I leave the rest to other people. Do you know what I mean?"

"I think I do," said Ellen. "I'm just not sure that's how it works."

"What are you saying?"

"I'm not sure you can just sign on for part of it, the part you like, and pretend the rest of it doesn't exist."

Bonnie looked crushed. "You're still mad at me about the wedding," she said. "I don't blame you."

"No, no," said Ellen. "I was hurt, Bonnie, of course I was hurt. We'll never get that day back, your wedding day, and I wasn't there for it. But I immediately saw the position you were in. On one side you had to worry about Pastor's feelings about Morris. And on the other side you had to worry about our feelings about Pastor. That's an awful lot of worry on your wedding day. I would say an unfair amount."

Ellen guessed she'd shown the kind of sympathy that had the power to undo people, for in the next moment Bonnie threw her arms around her and began sobbing into her shoulder. In these last two or three minutes they'd touched on some rather large themes, she reckoned — matters of faith, forgiveness, and (in an oblique way) prejudice and sin — but underlying all of it, stoking the emotions, there was still the undeclared item: During one of Bonnie's valleys rather than one of her peaks, Ellen whispered into her young sister's ear, "How far along are you, sweetie?"

Bonnie pushed back and held her at arm's length. "How did you know?" she said.

Ellen shrugged, prompting a new round of tears. "I've been so happy," Bonnie cried. "Just when I thought I couldn't be any happier, I found out about the baby. It seemed like such a gift, such a bonus. Now everything feels so horrible."

"Do you mean, now that you've had this quarrel about Morris?"

Bonnie sat up straight, reached down for the hem of her robe, and wiped her eyes with it. "I wanted you to see how happy I was," she said. "I'm so disappointed that this is what you get to see instead: a blubbering idiot. I should've talked to you more, Ellen. I've behaved as if I was working on some kind of secret project. I had an idea I was making this enchanting picture of myself, this beautiful picture, my new life. I was going to unveil it and blow you away." She pressed her hands flat on either side of her head and then dug her fingers into her hair as if she might start to tear it out. "I've been so stupid about everything," she said.

Rudely left to his own devices, Morris found his sunglasses and his cell phone and dragged a collapsible chair from under the rain porch out onto the beach. He figured he had about an hour before the sun would become more punishing than pleasant. He unfolded the chair — a vintage model of heavy wood and colorful striped canvas — and set it near the pier, about ten feet from the water. As usual, the beach was virtually abandoned; he'd always felt that the strip of sand between the yards and the piers was mostly for show, something that had to be crossed in order to get to the real deal: motorboating and the serious pier life it begat among the faithful. Two houses down toward the hotel, a white-coated staff of six was preparing a luncheon party beneath a commodious pavilion at the end of a next-generation pier; wider and longer than the others, it was rigged on both edges with an array of antique-style streetlamps and had ceiling fans in the pavilion. Once Morris had got himself settled in the chair, he gazed out at the bay and cloudless sky, blue and paler blue with a mediating white-blue mist at the horizon. He removed his shirt and sandals and wondered briefly what degree of scandal he would foment by also removing his shorts. He dialed the number in Ipswich, allowed the telephone to ring a ridiculous number of times, and then felt unreasonably let down when the answering machine finally picked up. He supposed Richard would be out *fishing,* a sorry excuse for not being at home when he was needed, and Morris left a terse voice message to that effect. Morris knew Richard was staying in Ipswich and not in town, but he phoned the Brookline house anyway, where he was greeted by another answering machine. It was pointless to try Richard at work at the private library and foundation in Boston where he'd served as CFO for fifteen years; the odd self-appointed hours he kept there included almost none during the summer months. No, Richard was most likely standing in some stupid river somewhere, like some dreamed-up male character in a Hemingway story.

Half a minute later, Morris's cell phone rang: Richard, explaining that he'd been out at the back fence harvesting tomatoes and hadn't got to the deck in time. The tomatoes had finally come into their own, he said, perfectly ripe all at once and so delicious you wanted to eat them like apples, sun-warmed, right off the vine; so plentiful he was doling them out to the neighbors, and he didn't know which he preferred, the wonderful red heirlooms Morris had planted for the first time this year or the little yellow ones called Sun-gold. Morris thought impatiently that Richard was riding some kind of tomato high, the way he rambled on about them — after all, Morris wasn't there to enjoy the tomatoes, so wasn't it impolite to belabor the subject?

"Where are you now?" asked Morris, when Richard paused for breath. "On the deck?"

"No, by the pool," said Richard. "In the shade. It's hot here. Where are you?"

"On the beach. Alone."

"Why alone? Where's everybody else?"

"Otherwise occupied," said Morris. "Bonnie went to her room an hour ago to phone her husband at the church. After about five minutes, she summoned Ellen to the bedroom, and neither of them has emerged yet. I suppose they're female-bonding. I'm catching little whiffs of trouble in paradise this morning."

"What kind of trouble?"

"I have no details," said Morris. "There's an odd tension in the air, though. From the beginning, but slowly building."

"And aside from that, how are things?"

"I'm finding it hard to read . . . the situation, I mean. Bonnie's beautiful but blurry. Pastor's even more beautiful but a bit inscrutable. I would almost say about him that what you see is not necessarily what you get . . . there are hidden ambitions lurking beneath the surface. But his being so absurdly good-looking muddies everything. I've found myself missing entire sentences when he speaks."

"You'd best come home right away," said Richard. "Your next phone call will be to tell me you've joined his church. You've decided to sing in the choir."

"Bonnie is," said Morris. "Singing in the choir; no joke."

"I imagine she has a lovely soprano," said Richard. "And what about your many suspicions and assumptions? How's that playing out?"

"Equally difficult to tell," said Morris. "For a wedding present, Bonnie gave him a new car. He gave her a Bible with all his favorite verses marked. That seems to signify a kind of inequality, but the church is apparently huge and hugely successful. I would think he makes a good salary. He didn't move in with Bonnie out of a house trailer, as I'd imagined."

"Do you like him?" asked Richard, ever simplifying.

"No, not quite," said Morris, surprised by how quickly the answer came. "It's complicated."

Morris silently weighed the wisdom of sharing with Richard the business Rex had broached yesterday in the boat shed. In some ways the most intriguing detail at hand, it was the sort of thing that would distress Richard; he would perceive it as Morris's being in a kind of danger, and then he would worry. "We met the parents," Morris said.

"They're there?"

"Were here," said Morris. "Briefly."

"What were they like?" he asked, but Morris could tell that his interest was already waning.

"Surprising, actually," he said. "They live in Fort Walton Beach and I imagine their Floridian friends think of them as loads of fun. They're certainly very tan. Tanner than you or I. Tanner than anyone I've ever met. You should see what Bonnie's done to the house. She's renovated and done a spectacular job."

"Really?" said Richard — and then, again simplifying, "I miss you."

"How is it that you can still break my heart with a little sentence like that?" Morris said. "I say to you what the butler said to the errant upstairs maid: 'Come down here at once.' "

"Are you serious?"

"Hang up the phone, get in the car, drive to Logan, and get on a plane."

"I'll give it some thought," said Richard, but Morris believed that whatever thought he gave it would be casual.

After a pause, Richard added, "Willie and Dan are coming to dinner."

"That's nice," said Morris.

"They're spending the night and we're going to Crane's tomorrow. Water temperature's supposed to be in the high seventies. By the way, do you know where that paddleball set is, the one we bought last year?"

"I think it's in the closet under the stairs."

"No, I looked there already."

"The garden shed?"

"No. Looked there too."

"Well, try the trunk of my car. That's a possibility."

"And did you tell me the red umbrella's broken?"

"No, the red one's fine," said Morris. "The orange one was broken but I threw it into the trash already."

Morris wished the conversation had not degenerated into domestic platitudes before it ended, though he supposed ending it was easier that way. He'd planned to sit in the sun for a while, but once he'd said good-bye to Richard, he saw that he'd also planned to be discovered there on the beach by now by one or both of his sisters. Besides, he hadn't thought to bring a drink with him and he was thirsty. He collected his things and headed back to the house.

Cricket greeted him at the gate. Inside the yard, he knelt on one knee and stroked each of the dog's velvety ears, pulling them between the fingers of his free hand. "At least *you* love me," he said.

Moving from the glare of sunshine into the darkness of the house rendered him practically blind. He shuffled along the hallway slowly, his hands out before him. He peered into the kitchen — no one there — and moved on to the master bedroom, buttoning his shirt as he went. Inside the room, which was cool and shuttered like a chapel, he spied a bottle of spring water on his mother's old dressing table. He took several large gulps directly from the bottle and then noticed, on the bed, a pair of slacks and a blouse, laid out carefully as to prevent wrinkles; he would have sworn they were what he'd seen Ellen wearing earlier.

He heard female laughter from the direction of a closed door he identified as a bathroom door. He moved alongside it and cocked his head: muffled voices, unintelligible words, more laughter. He rapped one knuckle against the painted wood. After a moment came Bonnie's voice, singing, "Who is it, please?"

"Who do you think?" said Morris. "The Abandoned One, back from the leper colony. What's going on in there? And why has Ellen shed her clothes?"

After another pause, he heard Bonnie again: "You may enter."

He opened the door into a lovely steamy white room — white walls, white fixtures — with a floor of turquoise glass tiles. There was a sweet smell, a mix of roses and lavender, and in the cavernous clawfoot bathtub, mounds and mounds of bubbles, overflowing the rim and dripping onto the floor. Bonnie's head poked out of the suds at one end of the tub and Ellen's at the other. He saw right away that they were each very red-faced, and while Ellen appeared to be blushing, Bonnie appeared to have been weeping.

"What's going on in here?" he said. "I thought maybe you two were bonding somewhere, but I never imagined anything like this."

"Have a seat," Ellen said, wiping soap bubbles from her eyes. "Bonnie's acting out a fantasy and I'm assisting her."

"Okay," said Morris, sitting on the closed toilet lid. "I think that's all I really want to know about that."

"A *childhood* fantasy," said Ellen.

He was sure that embarrassment accounted for at least part of Ellen's blush: she'd gone along with Bonnie for the ride and was even having fun, but nevertheless she felt compromised before him, naked under the bubbles.

"Where have you been?" she asked him. "You look sweaty."

"On the beach," he said. "I phoned Richard. He's harvesting bushels and bushels of tomatoes. Dan and Willie are going to Ipswich tonight for dinner and a pajama party."

"That sounds like fun," said Ellen.

"Maybe, if we hurry, we could go to that party instead of the one we're having here tonight," said Bonnie.

"We're having a party?" asked Morris.

Ellen explained that Pastor had invited a couple of people to join them for supper: the director of Newcomer Ministry at the church, who was bringing his mother. "Apparently the mother's quite a magpie," said Ellen. "But benign, according to Bonnie."

"Director of Newcomer Ministry," said Morris. "Do you think there's a plot afoot? He's coming to recruit us? Is that the idea?"

"We don't know what the idea is, actually," said Ellen. "Only that it's Pastor's."

After a moment, Bonnie said, "Morris," and waited for him to answer, her eyes moving back and forth from him to Ellen and back again.

"What, Bonnie, dear?" he said.

"I'm going to have a baby."

"Is this another part of the fantasy?" he asked.

"No," said Ellen. "It's true, she really is. I guessed it. Can you even begin to imagine how beautiful it will be, Morris?"

"Assuming Pastor's the father," he said.

Bonnie threw a wet washcloth at him, which he batted away with both hands. "Yes," he said, "I can just begin to imagine how beautiful."

He smiled at them both and noted that Ellen's face had visibly relaxed, its natural color restored.

Bonnie said, "Do you want to get in, Morris? There's plenty of room."

"Is *that* part of the fantasy?" he asked.

"No," said Bonnie. "Now I'm just impro-
vising."

"I'll take a rain check," he said, but he
continued to visit with his sisters a few
minutes more. He wanted to postpone a
direction his mind was fighting to go,
concerning all a baby signified. Also, he
liked the feeling of the beautiful room with
the beautiful women in the tub and the
atmospheric suggestion that — certain
temporal details rearranged — this was how
things might always have been, the three of
them in the big old house, and no crazy
grown-ups to bother them.

CHAPTER 8

In truth, he was happy not to go back to
the house to eat. He'd thought it the right
thing to do, with her brother and sister visiting, but given all he had to get done by suppertime, a sandwich in the office seemed a
better option. Among the many things Bonnie didn't yet understand or appreciate was
this: how much, on a daily basis, he had to
get done. His extra meeting with the Prayer
Team had made an already full day even
fuller. He needed to put the finishing
touches on the Pastor's Message for the
Blessed Hunger Web site, and then he had
back-to-back appointments in the afternoon. The architects were coming to go over
some revisions in the blueprints for the
Christ Center. Mike Jordan, the Pastoral
Care minister, wanted to consult with him
about a couple of situations. For some
reason, Edith had scheduled a meeting for
him with Butch King, the Buildings and

Grounds man, though he was sure that, whatever Butch's problems were, he needed to take them up with Henry Allen, the church administrator. Likewise for Jo Staples, the membership secretary, who was dropping by to see him at three-thirty. Some of the staff members who'd come on board around the same time Pastor had taken over — hard workers, every one — had gotten accustomed to daily contact with him, and now that the church had grown the way it had, and employed a staff of nineteen, they were reluctant to give up that close relationship. They would generally come in to talk, he would listen, and then send them to see somebody else. They seemed happier with this rigmarole, even though it wasted everybody's time and breath. He strove to keep in mind that the church was in the midst of a major transition and people always needed an ample period of adjustment. Most ticklish along these lines was the adjusting the congregation needed to make. Folks who'd been used to bringing their personal and spiritual problems to Pastor sometimes got their feelings hurt when they called to make an appointment and Edith referred them to Mike Jordan instead. Pastor himself had to practice patience on a regular basis (and of course ask for God's help in this regard), since so few of them seemed to understand that there was a limit to how thin he could spread himself. He had recently joked at a supper with the Men-in-Christ group that there were no bounds to what God could do, but so far God had not seen fit to grant him one thing he sorely needed, the ability to be in two or three places at the same time.

After his bothersome talk with Bonnie, he asked Edith to order him the pork plate combo from Whisker's, a barbecue joint down the road. He told her to let him know when it got there — he was already hungry — but he didn't want to take any phone calls for a while. And he asked her to please check the air-conditioning; it was freezing in his office. Edith, who'd recently declared without an ounce of modesty that she was going through the change, sometimes played fast and free with the thermostat.

The sun shone directly on his office window, and the blind was creating a jarring pattern of stripes across the top of his desk. He closed the blind, and then the small office with its oak paneling was so dark he needed to switch on the desk lamp. He spent the next fifteen minutes at his computer screen, ruminating and struggling with the Pastor's Message. It was a monthly thing, mostly meant to express gratitude for everybody's help, to ask for prayers in a number of different areas, to encourage the hard work and dedication of the various lay ministries, to give updates on the progress of the Christ Center and any other big projects that might be going on, and to squeeze in as many plugs for Christian giving as possible without sounding avaricious. Bonnie's phone call had rattled him such that he was second-guessing his phrasing and choice of words in the simplest matters, and this month he was obliged to write a sentence or two about his recent marriage. *Thank you for your prayers and support at this joyous time and for welcoming Bonnie into the community* — that was all he needed to say, easy enough, and yet, every time he read it over it troubled him. In the first place, he wasn't feeling especially joyous at the moment, and because Bonnie had been so slow to get active in the life of the church, the last part of the sentence rang false. To most of the congregation, she was still that beautiful mystery woman who sometimes, but not always, showed up for one of the Sunday services, who never stayed for coffee hour but could be seen kissing Pastor good-bye. Hardly a coffee hour transpired that several people didn't tease him about her, and since the wedding they'd begun to say things like, "Where's that pretty new wife of yours we're all dying to know?" Usually it was the women of the church who made such remarks, but occasionally one of the men had slapped him on the back and accused him of *keeping her under wraps* or *keeping her all to yourself,* followed by a wink. He sensed that Bonnie's disinclination to take up her role as the preacher's wife had fanned the always smoldering flame of gossip, which was not surprising since Bonnie's situation possessed all the right elements — she'd been living up north and she was rich, glamorous-looking, and noticeably older than him — and it would certainly occur to the common mind that she thought she was too good for the rest of them. Pastor had breathed a sigh of relief when Bonnie told him she was going to try the choir, but last night, when she'd come home and got into bed, after attending her first and only practice, she'd said she didn't think she would go back.

"Why not?" he'd asked her.

"Oh, I don't know," she said. "I just don't think I'm going to enjoy it."

"You didn't like Jeannie?"

Jeannie Hart was the music director.

"Oh, no, I liked her fine," Bonnie said. "It wasn't anything like that. Everybody was really nice."

"Well, don't you think you might give it a little more time?"

She shrugged and said, "Sometimes you can just tell, right off the bat, if something's going to work for you or not. I might try it again after the baby comes."

That was the newest thing, a growing list of procrastinations that fell under the category of "after the baby comes." She would join a Bible study group after the baby came. After the baby came she would start attending coffee hour. He'd suggested that with her theater background she could be a valuable resource for the young people's programs, and she'd agreed to think about it after the baby came. He'd hoped she might give the Media Ministries folks some tips when they purchased a fancy ETC lighting board for lighting the worship services, but Bonnie wanted to wait until after the baby came. All of which was completely cockeyed, since, after the baby came, she would have less time and less energy.

Last night, when she'd returned home from choir practice, he'd been in a happy mood, on the verge of falling asleep. He was very pleased about her brother and sister visiting at last, and relieved that Morris seemed as normal as he did, like a regular guy, especially when he wasn't trying to be clever. Ellen was a little on the quiet side, kind of reserved, but he figured she was tired from the traveling. He'd enjoyed their company. He guessed he was hungry for family — growing up as he did an only child — and he appreciated the family feeling Morris and Ellen's presence gave the house. Bonnie practically idolized them, and Pastor had been concerned that the highly educated poet and the college professor might see him as not up to their level or, even worse, not up to Bonnie's. But on meeting them, Pastor didn't find them the least bit la-di-da. They seemed like down-to-earth folks, even if the earth they were down to wasn't like most people's. On their earth you didn't ever worry about paying the bills or even have to work for a living. The greatest luxury of wealth — which was not having to give any thought to money — could produce some serious spiritual consequences, and in Pastor's judgment that was part of the affliction Bonnie was still recovering from. You were more likely to turn to God if you didn't know how you were going to put shoes on your children's feet, and you were more likely to be grateful to Him for the food on the table if you weren't in a

271

position to take it for granted. But Morris and Ellen had given every indication, in what little time he'd spent with them, that they were ready to accept him as he was, even if he wasn't what they might have imagined as a husband for Bonnie. Last night, he'd got into bed filled with gratitude, his favorite feeling. When Bonnie came home and said, after only one practice, she didn't think she'd be returning to the choir, he'd pretty quickly let the subject drop, because it made him angry. In terms of causing people to talk, it would have been much better for her not to try the choir in the first place than to go once and not return.

Then, today, he'd been out of sorts and distracted throughout the morning, especially during Prayer Team. Three days ago, when Bonnie had finally got around to telling him the little secret about her brother, Pastor had known right away where to take it. He figured a man married to another man was a fairly distant point down a long road, and prayer was the only hope for something like that. He was afraid that organizing prayers for the state of Massachusetts would stir up political feelings in the Prayer Team, so he'd kept it personal and specific. He'd given them a single praying point: entreaties on behalf of one who was struggling with the sin of homosexuality. They'd asked for a name and he'd said he wanted to keep it anonymous. They asked whether it was a man or a woman, and he told them it was a man. For the next half hour Pastor's brother-in-law, Morris, became *he* and *him* and *this person.* The team had undertaken this particular problem only a time or two in the past. Regularly they prayed for the bereaved, the sick, those undergoing surgery or chemotherapy and radiation, those seeking jobs, those suffering the scourge of addiction, soldiers injured or killed in battle, the recently divorced, or those who needed healing in their relationships. The more detail provided in the prayer request, the better. If they were to go to God for a creative miracle, it helped if they could ask for a liver or a heart or a stomach to be made whole again, an infection to be rooted out and cleansed, a compulsive craving for drugs or alcohol to be lifted. Pastor had been impressed with how thoroughly shot through with love the team's prayers were that morning. The word *abomination* was never spoken. Nobody brought up Sodom or Gomorrah. And Moody Ellis, the team leader and the most eloquent among them, had even thought to pray for the friends and family of *this person,* that their tolerance and compassion might pave for him a path to recovery through Christ's love.

Still, Pastor could tell that the team was a little thrown at having been gathered for a special meeting and then given only what he gave them. Such occasions were usually a response to sudden and time-sensitive events — heart attacks or strokes, car wrecks or boating accidents — and chief among Pastor's distractions during the meeting was the nagging doubt that maybe he'd overreacted. He worried that he might have been provoked by how passionately his father had criticized him the night Bonnie made her revelation. Pastor was kicking himself for sharing the information about Morris with his father. He'd gone to him as a son, seeking advice on a family problem, and suddenly they were having a knock-down-drag-out over spiritual affairs. Pastor had hardly uttered two words when his dad began to lecture him on how Pastor needed to look after his own salvation and take the log out of his own eye before he started losing sleep over the speck in somebody else's. He went on to say that people came in many varieties but they were all made by the same God, and Pastor needed to stop running around trying to save everybody who wasn't just like himself. No matter what scripture Pastor cited, his dad fell back on "That's just your interpretation," implying that Pastor's interpretation was wrong, even though the Bible was not ambiguous on this subject. His behavior had all the earmarks of a personal attack, and Pastor thought he'd been unduly cutting. Also, it had seemed like the argument stood for something larger — his dad's disapproval felt to Pastor like a blanket disapproval. Pastor hoped he hadn't called a special meeting of the Prayer Team just because his dad had hurt his feelings, and yet he couldn't deny that there was an aspect to it that felt like he was staking out his own position, against his dad, and was seeking outside support for it.

So Bonnie's phone call, and her extreme reaction, only made everything worse. She'd spoken to him in a way she'd never spoken to him before, almost contemptuously. She'd always had the power to addle him with her strange moods and attitudes, and an encounter like the one on the phone left him so doubtful of everything he almost felt as if the Devil was messing with him. He doubted the wisdom of marrying a woman so different from himself. He doubted the wisdom of marrying a woman so rich. (He knew there were people who thought he might have married her for her money, especially after the gift she'd made to the Christ Center campaign, but he was acquainted with the problem of the camel passing through the eye of the needle and, ironically, he'd married Bonnie *despite* her money.) And he was second-guessing, in general, his response to the big news that she had a brother living in a so-called "gay marriage." He still didn't see the harm in praying for Morris. He already liked him, and it was painful to see him so hamstrung by spiritual error. But now Pastor was questioning the wisdom of inviting Bobby Delk to supper. Maybe that was going overboard.

Worst of all — and this was the part that brought the Devil to mind — he'd thought off and on throughout the morning prayer meeting, about a man from ten years ago, a man who lived alone in a house down a dirt road about a half hour east of Spanish Fort. The house was known among the boys at Pastor's junior high school as a place where you could drop in on a Friday or Saturday night, smoke free dope, and drink free beer. After you were sufficiently ripped, and if you were too weak to resist the dares and egging on from the other boys, you could pick up a flavored rubber from a bowl on the kitchen counter and slip off down the hallway to a room — completely dark inside, completely empty save a single chair — and get blown, no questions asked, no talking of any kind. Pastor had once got as far as the chair, but when it came time to drop his pants, he'd bolted. In physical terms, Pastor could recall only that the man was middle-aged and dark-complected, but the memory of him had come calling during Prayer Team, a madness and a mystification. Drinking and smoking dope and running wild had been the three prevailing winds of Pastor's young life before he was strong-armed by the Lord. A thrill-seeking self-abuse had been the primary quicksand out of which the Lord rescued him. He didn't oppose reflecting on that period. He was fully familiar with most of its ins and outs. But in this morning's recollection, he'd glimpsed in himself a quieter kind of conduct, one he couldn't count as fully departed: a disposition for edging up to temptation and then turning tail at the last minute.

On second thought, this unbidden memory, confounding as it was, didn't hold a candle to Bonnie's insinuation that by praying for her brother, and praying for him out of pure love, Pastor was somehow allying himself with a history of oppression. Pastor believed that even if it was some people's nature to desire their own kind, as naturally as he himself desired women, it was all the more reason to bring Christ's love to bear on it. Christ's love was the only thing strong enough to reverse such a powerful fixation. Whatever feelings you had about homosexuality — and what man didn't have some feelings about it? — it was perfectly clear that nothing good or useful could come from persecution. Pastor didn't have a persecuting bone in his body, which Bonnie knew, and that was why her remarks had been so hurtful and unfair.

Now he reached for the double-hinged picture frame that rested just beyond the border of the desk blotter. In the right side was a photo of Bonnie and him on their wedding day, smooching after Mike Jordan (who'd married them) said, "You may kiss the bride." In the left side was a snapshot he'd taken of her on the beach last spring. She was wearing jogging shorts and sneakers and a baseball cap, standing with one foot in the sand and one foot planted on a washed-up stump of a tree, her hands on her hips, as if the old stump were a creature she'd just slain. In the background a little Windsurfer skimmed close to the shore, with striped sails of blue and yellow and red and purple. Bonnie was beautiful, beaming to beat the band, and as he continued to gaze at the picture, he recalled that over in England — or in Scotland, maybe — that was what *bonnie* meant: beautiful. He returned the frame to its position on the desk and returned his attention to the keyboard. He wrote, *Thank all of you for your thoughts and prayers around my recent marriage to Bonnie Owen, originally of Point Clear. We have entered holy matrimony —*

He stopped, afraid that *holy matrimony* might be a Catholic expression. The chief disadvantage of having spent no time in a seminary was that he sometimes felt he was picking his way through a minefield. When he stuck to the Bible and to his own reflections and experiences, he felt secure enough in preacher's robes, but if he ventured very far from scripture, he was apt to get something wrong. He recalled a bumper sticker he saw from time to time on the cars of 12-steppers and reminded himself to keep it simple.

God has blessed us with a special love, he wrote. *Our hearts are full of hope and gratefulness.* He changed *gratefulness* to *gratitude* and saved the document, done.

He moved to the door to the outer office, opened it, and asked Edith how long did Whisker's say that pork combo was going to take. She said she would give them a ring and check on it. He told her that when she was done with that, would she please call over to the Delks' house and see if she could get Bobby on the phone.

"Well, I don't think prayers ever hurt anybody," Dan said. "Do you?"

Ellen switched the phone from one hand to the other, then reached down with her free hand to slip her shoes off her feet. She was sitting on the bed in her room again, alone, just back from the hotel restaurant. The short walk home had been hot but, fortunately, Macy had closed the windows in the house and turned on the air-conditioning. Ellen dropped one pump to the floor, then the other. "No," she said to Dan, "but it casts a pall over everything. Knowing he feels that way."

"I can't say it's surprising," Dan said. "I mean, how did you expect him to feel about it?"

"I would like to have been surprised," she said, and thought how off-putting it was to share a concern with someone, only to have them imply that you should have anticipated it, as if anticipating it would have made it not so. "And besides," she added, "it's confusing. In person, he's been nothing but kind."

"I imagine from where he stands," said Dan, "praying for Morris is also being kind."

"I get that," Ellen said. "But do you see what I'm saying? You wouldn't like it if people were praying for your . . . well, essentially praying for you to stop being you."

"I thought you told me Morris didn't know about the prayer meeting."

"He doesn't," Ellen said, trying not to sound as frustrated as she felt. "I guess I'm just worried, Dan. And Bonnie's pregnant, by the way."

"By the way?" he said. "That's big."

She heard him call out to Willie that his Aunt Bonnie was going to have a baby. "She's already eleven weeks," Ellen said.

"Wow," said Dan, "that was quick."

"I only hope not too quick," she said.

"I know what you mean," Dan said. "It kind of seals the deal, doesn't it. And a little soon, probably."

"Exactly," she said, disarmed at last by an overdue taste of empathy. "But you should see the house. She's redone the whole thing and it —"

"Hold on," he said. "Willie's reaching for the phone. I'll say good-bye when he's finished."

After a pause on the line, Willie said, "Hi, Mom. What's going on?"

"Not much," she said. "I miss you."

"Miss you too."

"What have you and Dad been up to?"

"Baseball, mostly," he said.

"You mean you've been to the park?"

"No, Mom," he said, "they're on the road, remember?"

"Oh, that's right," she said. "When you get down here where nobody cares, the details kind of leave your mind. How are they doing?"

"Terrible," he said. "They dropped two out of three to the Rays."

"Two out of three to Tampa Bay?"

"Yeah," he said, "but the Rays are better than people think. They've brought up some really good rookies."

"Well, I understand you guys are driving up to Ipswich tonight."

"We are?"

"I think so," she said.

She heard Willie call out to Dan: "Dad, are we going to Ipswich?" Then, back on the line: "Yeah, apparently. That's cool. Listen, Mom. Have you seen *The Grapes of*

Wrath?"

"You mean the movie with Henry Fonda?"

"No, Mom, not the movie, the book. I'm supposed to read it before school starts, remember? Have you seen it anywhere?"

For an instant, she thought Willie was asking if she'd seen it there, in Point Clear — evidence of the displaced state of her mind. "I assume you've looked on the shelves in the library," she said. "In the S's."

"No, I already took it from there," Willie said. "A week ago. It's somewhere in the house but I can't find it."

"Have you asked your father?"

"Yeah," said Willie. "He doesn't know. Mom, my cell phone's ringing and I think I better take it. It might be important."

"Okay, sweetie, I love you and miss you and can't wait to see you."

"Me too," he said. "Here's Dad."

"I told him yesterday we were going to Ipswich," said Dan. "You never know what penetrates and what doesn't. So you were saying that Bonnie's fixed up the house?"

But Ellen was still stuck on Steinbeck. "You can't find Willie's book?" she asked.

"Don't worry," he said. "I also told him yesterday that if he didn't find it we'd stop and buy one on the way to Ipswich. So he'd have it to read on the beach. Don't worry, everything's under control. So Bonnie's fixed up the house, huh?"

"It's perfectly beautiful," said Ellen, letting go of a small urge to correct; she wasn't worried and she didn't doubt that Dan had things under control.

"And how does she seem?" he asked. "I mean apart from being pregnant. How's the whole scene?"

"Honestly, I'm not sure," Ellen said. "It's still too early to tell. Pastor doesn't seem especially hellfire-and-damnation. So far he's not handling snakes or speaking in tongues."

"That's always good," said Dan.

"I've just been inexplicably tired since we arrived," she said. "Everything's so emotionally loaded, it's exhausting. Everything *evokes*."

"Sounds like home," he said. "Sounds like poetry."

"I guess that's right," she said, strangely touched, even saddened, by his observation. "Are you doing okay, my darling?"

"I'm great," he said. "We're having quality time, even if Willie hears only about half of what I say to him. What about you? Are you okay?"

"A little anxious," she said, "mostly about Morris. But yes, I'm okay."

"Well, good."

"I wish you were here," she added. "You and Willie both. Summer's going to be over soon, and it feels like I won't have spent enough time with either of you."

It occurred to her that here he could have mentioned the three weeks in July she'd chosen to spend alone on the Cape, but she knew that even if it had crossed his mind, he would keep it to himself out of kindness. "We'll plan a couple of things when you get back," he said. "The three of us, before school starts."

After they'd hung up, she stretched out on the bed, vaguely aware of not caring about wrinkling the slacks and blouse she was wearing; she arranged the pillow behind her head and pulled a corner of the bedspread up over her legs. In the print on the wall near the foot of the bed, Audubon's trumpeter swan seemed to gaze back at her. She closed her eyes, thinking how the sound of Dan's voice, and of Willie's, had relaxed her. Soon, in a dream, the silent blue-green sheers billowed into the room and slid across her face. Then Morris stood outside the now open window, shirtless and speaking through the screen. "Look," he said, pointing backward with his thumb like a hitchhiker. "Night comes first under the oak." She climbed out of bed and moved toward the window, which was suddenly at the upper landing of a steep flight of stairs. Morris must be standing on a ladder, she thought, noting that the stairs beneath her were trick stairs, new steps added at the top as you mounted the ones below. She kept tripping over the hem of the nightgown she wore, which Willie had given her for Mother's Day. With tremendous effort, she drew closer to the landing, where she could see that Morris was not standing on anything but clung, white-knuckled, to the window-sill, struggling to pull himself up and keep from falling. She tried to call to him, but she was too winded to make a sound. "Something less comical," she heard him say, as his face dropped below the rim of the sill.

Pastor had spread out the blueprints for the Christ Center on the dining room table, weighting down the curled edges and corners with two brass candlesticks and a crystal vase. Morris, who'd recently risen from an afternoon nap, wiped his eyes and tried to focus on the drawings, which he judged to be of poor quality, grayish and smudged. Mostly he'd been saying *Hmm* a lot, and though it didn't seem to hinder

Pastor's enthusiasm, Morris was beginning to feel like a moron. "Sure looks big," he ventured at last, a marginal improvement over *Hmm.*

"Oh, it's big, all right," Pastor said, turning to look him dead in the eye and smiling proudly. "Just shy of sixty-three thousand square feet."

"Goodness," Morris said, though he had no frame of reference for sixty-three thousand square feet.

"These are all classrooms over here," Pastor said, running his index finger along two rows of small rectangles on either side of a much larger one. "And various activity rooms where we'll be housing all our youth and college ministries. This big area off to the south is a full commercial kitchen, everything state-of-the-art."

He pointed to a box at one end of the large central rectangle and said, "This is going to be our stage. Everything you need for a full-scale theatrical production."

"Well, the Oberammergau people will be glad to hear about that," Morris said.

"The who?" Pastor asked.

"Not important," said Morris. "What's the big empty space right in the middle here?"

Pastor smiled again and said, "Can't you tell? Look at it closer."

Morris bent forward. He could see lines and circles that made him think of a basketball court, but it seemed too silly a thing to say.

Pastor arched his eyebrows and said, "Well?"

"Basketball court?" said Morris.

"Two of them," said Pastor. "Two full-sized courts, side by side, see?"

Now Morris had a frame of reference and said, "That really is big." Then he said, "I didn't know Jesus played basketball — although I guess, in a way, the whole disciple thing was sort of like a pickup game. It's easy to imagine them wandering the desert, pitching camp somewhere, rigging hoops onto — I don't know — date palms or something."

Pastor laughed and said, "That's good, a pickup game. I'm going to use that."

He fiddled with the candlesticks and the vase and rolled back the top page of the plans. "Here's the second story," he said. He traced the tip of his finger around an oval shape imposed over the periphery of the basketball courts. "Look at that, Morris," he said. "What do you think that is?"

Morris shrugged.

"That's an elevated track," said Pastor, cocking his head and turning down the corners of his mouth, waiting for Morris's reaction.

"I think I'm beginning to see the racket here," Morris said. "The architects create these designs for Bally Total Fitness and Gold's Gym and then resell them to churches."

"That's probably true," Pastor said, laughing again.

"This takes multitasking to a whole new level," Morris went on. "You can attend church and do your cardio workout at the same time. Who would've thought to combine religious worship and physical fitness? Well, I suppose that's what the whirling dervishes were all about, inadvertently. It's ingenious. It's —"

He stopped himself for he'd noticed that Pastor, whose laughter had faded to a vestigial smile, was now nodding uncertainly. "Well, I mean, it's great, Pastor," Morris said. "It's wonderful. You must be very excited."

"I am, I am," Pastor said. "I try not to get too carried away — I know the real church is not the building; I'm not as foolish as all that — but I do get pretty excited about it."

"And well you should," said Morris, afraid now that he might sound patronizing.

"You see," added Pastor, "half of it's about

whatever brings 'em in. And the other half's about create community any way you can."

"I think I understand," Morris said.

Macy now appeared at the dining room door, wearing a bib apron with an underwater scene of sea fans and angelfish. "Now, y'all have got to clear out of here," she said. "And Pastor, I need you to take whatever that is with you. I'm gonna need to get in here and set the table in a minute."

"Where do you mean for us to go?" Morris said. "You've already banned us from the kitchen and —"

"You got about eight or nine other rooms to use," said Macy. "Not counting the screen porch. Now, where's the girls?"

"Sleeping," said Morris. "Or pretending to."

"Why would they be pretending to?" asked Macy.

"That's a good question," said Morris. "Each in her own way, Ellen and Bonnie have always tended to shrink from reality."

"I have no earthly idea what you're talking about, Morris," said Macy, "but if you see them, please tell them supper's at seven o'clock sharp."

As Pastor rolled up the blueprints, he said, "Something sure does smell good, Macy."

"Something *is* good, Pastor," she said, all

business and no time for compliments.

"Let's sit out on the porch," Pastor said to Morris, and as they moved into the hallway, the grandfather clock in the living room struck five. On the screen porch, Morris shooed the cat from one of the chairs and sat down, leaving the couch for Pastor. As soon as they were settled, they heard a small crashing sound from the kitchen, and Pastor told Morris about the day a few weeks ago when Macy had dropped a frying pan and scared China so bad the cat had come flying through the porch window.

"Macy's always had a penchant for dropping things," said Morris. "When she first came to work for us a hundred years ago, our mother used to forbid her to put away the good crystal."

"Well," said Pastor, after a moment. "How did you and your sisters pass the time today?"

"Oh, it was a typical day in the lives of the rich but not at all famous," Morris answered. "We rose and chatted for a while before breakfast. We ate breakfast and chatted some more. The girls took a long bubble bath and chatted in the tub. We strolled up to the hotel and chatted over lunch. Then we came home and napped, lest we be too tired for supper."

Pastor smiled and asked if they'd had something decent to eat at the hotel.

"I'm afraid we weren't very adventurous," said Morris. "I think we were too intimidated by the credentials of the hotel chefs."

"What credentials?" asked Pastor.

"We learned that they'd prepared meals for the likes of Elton John, Madonna, Marlon Brando, John Travolta, Joan Rivers, and . . . I forget who all else. . . . Oh, I know: P. Diddy, LL Cool J, and the Fourteenth Dalai Lama, Tenzin Gyatso."

Pastor laughed and said he didn't even know who some of those people were.

"There's no reason you should," said Morris. He pointed to the rolled-up blueprints, which Pastor had leaned against an arm of the couch, and said, "So what do you think it's going to cost, the new Christ Center?"

Pastor hesitated.

"I mean, ballpark," Morris added, as if the question would seem less prying if he were asking only for an approximation.

"Well, you see, there's five different phases to the development," Pastor said. "We're just in Phase One, the design phase, which'll cost us close to fifty thousand. We're blessed to have some professionals in the congregation, folks with experience in fund-raising work, and they've helped us to map out a long-range plan. We just kicked off the campaign last month, which'll stretch out over the next four years."

Since Pastor had so clearly skirted the actual question, Morris decided to let it drop. He asked Pastor about the church's history and learned that it had been started eighteen years ago by a group of about two dozen people who'd splintered off from a United Methodist congregation in Fairhope. Pastor was vague about the nature of the instigating dispute, saying only that the group found themselves constantly bumping up against national conference policies and that they were interested in starting an independent organization. They'd called themselves the Free Church of the Gospel and met on Sunday mornings for the first two years in a movie theater. One of the founding members had served as minister, and the membership had grown slowly but steadily. They abandoned the movie theater when they bought an old schoolhouse and the land that came with it, about seventeen acres five miles due east of Point Clear. Six years later they built a new sanctuary, the one still in use today, and converted the old schoolhouse into a fellowship hall. They changed their name to the Church of the

Blessed Hunger, which was based on the line in the Sermon on the Mount where Jesus says, "Blessed are they that hunger and thirst after righteousness." Five years after that, and one year after Pastor began attending the church, they built the new education and administrative facility. Pastor officially joined the church at the age of nineteen and soon signed up to teach Sunday school. He also led the youth group on Sunday evenings and, because he wasn't much older than the members, they seemed to relate to him easily. He didn't think he'd ever had so much fun. He was still living at home with his parents then, selling appliances at the store in Fairhope where his dad had always worked. A girl had broken his heart just before high school graduation; she was destined for Tuscaloosa and the University of Alabama and she figured she might as well hook up with somebody who had a similar destiny, rather than a refrigerator salesman who wasn't even sure he wanted to go to college. A broken heart, he said, was an open window to the Lord, and when he joined the Blessed Hunger he'd already given up dating, as well as drinking and smoking and anything else that defiled his body. After about two years with the church, he'd begun to think privately that

God was calling him to preach, but he didn't breathe a word of it to a single soul. And then the Blessed Hunger's forty-four-year-old minister dropped dead of a heart attack in the bread-products aisle of Food World, over in Foley, Alabama, and the church elders approached Pastor and asked him if he would consider taking over the pulpit. He was twenty-one years old. He had no formal religious training and had only completed half a year of community college. After one day and one night of prayerful discernment, he accepted the call. In the four years since, the membership at the Blessed Hunger had taken off like a rocket. They were bursting at the seams. Pastor took no credit for the church's dramatic growth. He said it was God's will and that was all.

"I preach about it from time to time," he said. "I remind everybody that what's happened at the Blessed Hunger is grace, pure and simple. If folks start thinking it's on account of me or my preaching, then the whole thing's just a house of cards. I could pull out of the driveway tomorrow morning in my little red wedding present and get run over by an eighteen-wheeler. And then where would the Blessed Hunger be? You see what I'm getting at?"

"I do see," said Morris, "in principle. But I think you're being a touch modest. Have you looked in the mirror lately?"

"What do you mean?" said Pastor.

"I mean there's fire in your eyes, Pastor. If the church chose a twenty-one-year-old with no formal training, I would guess it's because you have charisma."

"Well, I don't know about that," said Pastor. "But whatever I have, it's coming through me and not of me." He looked at Morris and added, "That much I know."

Morris noticed that the fire to which he'd just attributed so much effect had suddenly been clouded over with tears. Pastor gazed out at the bay and the sky, and Morris struggled with himself not to be quite so enthralled by the little-boy sadness that overtook the young man's face. Thinking it best not to indulge such tendencies in himself, he said, "What's wrong, my friend?"

"Nothing's wrong," Pastor said and smiled enthrallingly, still misty-eyed. "I'm wondering if I ought to go wake up Bonnie girl."

"Oh, don't do that," said Morris. "You should let her sleep as long as possible, in her delicate condition."

"So she told you!" said Pastor.

"Apparently Ellen guessed it," Morris

said. "I don't know when Bonnie was planning to tell us. Nor do I understand her motive in holding it back."

"Sometimes she runs these little TV shows in her head," said Pastor. "Y'all were supposed to get down here today, not yesterday, and Macy was going to make your special welcome-home supper, and Bonnie was going to make her special announcement at the supper table."

"Our father was like that," said Morris. "Constantly staging things. Before we went anywhere or did anything, he would tell us item by item what was going to be happening. What was expected of us. What we mustn't do. He occasionally read us a story — *The Boxcar Children* or *Call of the Wild* — and you would've thought you'd stumbled into auditions for the Joe Jefferson Players. Anytime there were people over, he'd tell everybody where they had to sit, and he had that awful habit of directing conversation. 'Morris, tell Mr. So-and-so about your history class.' 'I think Ellen has something to tell us about a certain blue ribbon.' Depending on how much he'd had to drink, he would start to repeat himself and you'd have to say, 'But Daddy, I already told them about that.' And then the long brooding silences would set in, equally dramatic but quieter."

"They sure are a powerful force over us, dads are," said Pastor. "I'm a little nervous about the whole thing, if you want to know the truth: becoming one myself. But I guess it's like having to learn to swim by getting thrown into the river. I once heard somebody say that the purpose of marriage wasn't that it produces children but that children produce adults."

"I would say that's only sometimes true," said Morris.

"Well," said Pastor, "I tell myself you can't go too far wrong if you just love them enough."

"Rex told us yesterday that you were the light of their lives," Morris said. "He said they'd never known anything like the love they felt for you."

"Did he really say that?" asked Pastor.

Morris nodded. "I believe he said it was like a bolt of lightning."

"A bolt of lightning, huh?" said Pastor, crossing one leg over the other and brushing a smudge from the heel of his boot. He appeared pleased but with considerable reservation. Something about him made Morris think of a medical waiting room: The receptionist had just told the young preacher that the doctor would see him in a few minutes, and he'd smiled politely and returned his attention to the magazine he'd been reading.

At last Pastor looked up from his boot and grinned at Morris impishly. "You really think I have charisma?" he asked.

"I think you *probably* do," said Morris. "But you mustn't let it go to your head. In fact, you mustn't even think about it. The thing about charisma is that it's always strongest in those who don't know they have it."

Pastor made a halting gesture with his hands. "I won't give it another thought," he said, and returned his gaze to the bay.

The sun on the water was still so bright it caused Pastor to squint, creating delicate lines at the corner of his eyes. He folded his hands in his lap, intertwining his fingers, and Morris observed the lovely ridge of a vein in the top of Pastor's golden right forearm. He believed, in the stillness that seemed to be settling around them, that he could see the vein gently pulsing. A gull cried, raucous and penetrating, somewhere nearby, and Pastor looked at Morris so suddenly, Morris was afraid he'd been caught staring.

"I need to tell you something," Pastor said.

"I'm all ears," Morris said, noting a slight

burning sensation precisely there, in his ears.

"I've invited Bobby Delk over for supper this evening," said Pastor. "Our Newcomers minister."

"I know," said Morris. "Bonnie told us."

"Well, it might've been a mistake," Pastor said. "It seemed like a good idea at the time, but now I'm afraid it —"

"What, is he going to try to recruit Ellen and me?" asked Morris.

"No, no," said Pastor, "nothing like that."

"What then?"

"Bobby's a good man. A good Christian. And like most of us, he's got himself a past. The long and the short of it is, he used to be like you, Morris."

Morris recalled Richard's voice over the telephone, saying, "You best come right home." It was so vivid, he almost thought Richard had stepped onto the porch and spoken.

"What do you mean, like me?" said Morris.

"You know," said Pastor. "He used to be living in the gay lifestyle."

"I don't know what that means," Morris said.

"You don't?" said Pastor, apparently perplexed.

"No," said Morris. "I have no idea."

"Well, he used to be . . . you know . . . homosexual."

"I see," said Morris. "And what happened to him? As if I don't already know."

"What do you think happened to him?" Pastor asked.

"Listen, Pastor," said Morris. "If we're going to have this conversation, which is regrettable, I'm certainly not going to help you. You have to say what you have to say. I mean, you have to say every single word of it yourself."

"Now, you see there, this is just what I was afraid of," said Pastor. "You're upset already. It's the reason I said I might've made a mistake."

"I'm not upset," said Morris.

"Well, you're mad at me," said Pastor.

"Not at all," said Morris.

"I just wanted y'all to meet," said Pastor. "Bobby's story is . . . well, it just shows the strong possibility of something. He's a kind of walking talking living proof of something. I just wanted y'all to meet."

"So we'll meet," Morris said.

"I got Bobby on the phone this afternoon and told him that's all I wanted. I said I didn't want him to take up any causes at the supper table."

"I get it," said Morris. "He's to teach by example rather than persuasion."

"Did I do wrong?" asked Pastor.

"I think so," said Morris. "But probably not for the reasons you imagine."

"Tell me," said Pastor. "Let me learn."

Morris laughed.

"You're laughing at me," Pastor said.

"Yes, I'm laughing at you," said Morris. "But not too unkindly, I hope. I'm laughing at your plight, really."

"My plight?" said Pastor. "What's my plight?"

"Well, how would *you* describe it?" asked Morris.

Pastor knitted his brow, making a kind of drawbridge with his beautiful black eyebrows. He said, "You're my kin now, you and Ellen. I already feel close to you. It pains me to see somebody I love living in error, and I'd like to do what I can to help. I see it as my Christian duty."

"No," said Morris, "that's not your plight, Pastor, that's something else. That's your dilemma . . . or your problem, maybe. Your plight is your strong desire — your very deep need — to be loved. It's an endearing plight, but it's a plight nonetheless."

"I don't understand," said Pastor.

"I know," said Morris. "That's endearing too."

"I'm not as smart as you, Morris," said Pastor. "Not so educated. But don't look down on me."

"You've got yourself a deal," said Morris. "Don't look down on me either."

"I don't," said Pastor. "It's not like that. I'm not one of those folks standing out on the street corner with a burn-in-hell sign."

"That's true," said Morris. "It could be a lot worse, couldn't it? I could've returned to my childhood home and been required to cross a picket line to get inside the house."

Pastor looked away, shaking his head. "I just wish you could be a little bit more open-minded."

Morris laughed again. "Surely, even you can see the irony of that," he said.

"Okay, okay," Pastor said. "Let's just let it go for now."

"Happily," said Morris.

"I can't very well un-invite Bobby at this late date," Pastor added. "I'm pretty sure you'll like him. At least I think it was the right thing for me to talk to you like this, ahead of time."

"Yes," said Morris. "A kind of warning, which I appreciate. Yesterday, your father gave me a kind of warning too."

"About what?" asked Pastor.

"About you," said Morris. "He told me you were likely to try and save me. The way you saved Bonnie."

Pastor nodded quickly, as if this required no elaboration, as if it might even have been expected. "All right," he said, planting both feet on the floor and cupping his hands over his knees. "If I've hurt you, Morris, I ask your forgiveness."

"Whatever," said Morris, and made a priestly gesture of absolution with one hand. "I've never met an actual ex-gay before. It might be interesting."

"Good," said Pastor, and smiled sadly. "We can talk about this some more later. I think I better get Bonnie out of the bed."

"Right," said Morris, standing and moving to the screen door. "But Pastor — if we do talk about it more, later, I think you're going to have to say the words."

"What words?"

"What you truly believe," said Morris. "You need to look me in the eye and say what you believe."

Without affording Pastor a chance to respond, Morris left the porch and headed for the gate at the front of the yard.

Pastor called out to him, "Where are you going?"

Morris answered that he wanted to take a walk on the beach before supper. He went through the gate, across the promenade, and onto the sand, where he paused to remove his sandals.

The sand was pleasantly warm beneath his feet. A short way along the waterline, toward the hotel, he saw an old black man raking the pristine beach that belonged to the pier with the fancy pavilion. The man — who wore a long-sleeved blue chambray shirt, baggy pants, and a straw sun hat — was the sole occupant of the entire beach, which now struck Morris as a wasteland, inhospitable to flora and fauna alike. He decided to make a beeline for the old man and find out his name. He was feeling weighed down, weak in the knees, and he thought maybe the venerable act of asking a stranger's name might steady him and lighten his heart. Halfway there he imagined that if he were to look back at the house, he would see Pastor; when he did look back, sure enough, Pastor was standing at the screen door, obscured by the shade of the rain porch and watching him go.

"Hello," said Morris, once he'd reached the old man's side.

Right away he saw that the person he'd taken for an old man was actually a youngster, a teenager, impaired somehow, perhaps with Down's. At the sound of *hello,* he'd stopped raking and now turned slowly toward Morris; he seemed quite interested in Morris's bare feet, which he allowed himself to dwell on for some time before lifting his eyes to see the face of the man they belonged to. At last he touched one hand to the brim of his straw hat and nodded. "I'm not shy," he said, shaking his head quickly.

Morris smiled and said, "My name's Morris. What's your name?"

"Folks call me Robert," said the young man, leaning for a moment against the rake handle. "I'm not shy."

He returned to his raking, studiously combing the sand in one spot, over and over, before moving on. "Folks call me Robert," he repeated, not looking up from his work. "I'm not shy . . . I'm not shy," he said, inflected in a way that suggested he was defending himself against having been accused of shyness.

"Well, bye, Robert," Morris said, starting to walk away. He'd decided to visit the Birdcage Lounge, one of the bars at the hotel, and he took a roundabout path back to the promenade, careful not to leave footprints in any of the already-raked sand. He became pointedly aware of the sandals he carried in one hand, the thin leather straps looped over two fingers, and he felt overwhelmed by a kind of self-consciousness that was at once strange and familiar — a brand of a common enough feeling, but particular to the place and nearly forgotten. In order to put his sandals back on, he sat down on the ground, where he contended with the straps and buckles, thinking, *I'm not lonely, I'm not lonely, I'm not lonely.*

CHAPTER 9

Macy believed the only purpose of appetizers was to spoil the appetite, and she didn't see why she should spend all day preparing a delicious meal if people were going to show up at the supper table too full of pigs in a blanket to enjoy it. When Bonnie wandered into the kitchen around six-thirty and asked her what she intended to serve for hors d'oeuvres, Macy didn't answer at first. Bonnie had spoken to her back, as Macy was at the stove, busy with a potato masher; when she turned, ready to espouse her dim view of hors d'oeuvres, she halted at the sight of Bonnie. "Well, would you look at Miss America!" she exclaimed.

Bonnie, who was wearing an ankle-length black silk shift with green glass beads for straps, smiled and said, "Do you like it?"

"You look like a movie star," said Macy. "I just hope —"

"Macy," Bonnie interrupted, pointing to

the counter to Macy's left. "What is that?"

"Just what it looks like," answered Macy. "A bottle of wine."

"But what's it doing there?" asked Bonnie.

"Well, according to Morris," said Macy, "it's *breathing*."

Bonnie moved to the counter, took the bottle in her hands, and read the label. "My God," she said, "that's a good wine."

Macy, who'd returned to mashing the potatoes, said, "I wouldn't know anything about it. As far as I'm concerned, wine is for Communion."

Morris entered the kitchen, wearing khakis, a light blue sport shirt, and a black leather bolo tie with a carved silver clasp. "You look beautiful," he said to Bonnie. "Where did you get that dress?"

"I bought it at Barneys a couple of years ago," said Bonnie. "Where did you get that ridiculous tie?"

"Pastor let me borrow it," said Morris. "This little silver guy here is a Navaho fertility deity. Don't you think it has a certain . . . I don't know . . . confusing but oddly comforting quality?"

"If you say so," said Bonnie. "And where did you get this bottle of wine?"

"Ah, that," said Morris. "That's a fine

Merlot, sold to me by the surprisingly knowledgeable bartender at the Birdcage Lounge. You don't mind, do you?"

"Of course not," said Bonnie. "I think it's nice."

He moved alongside her and whispered, "I mean: You don't mind, do you?"

She kissed him on the cheek and whispered, "Wine was never my drug of choice, Morris. And besides, I'm pregnant, remember?"

"I don't know what you two are whispering about over there," said Macy, "but I'd thank you to take it out of the kitchen. Your guests are gonna be here in fifteen minutes and I need to concentrate. And would you please get Cricket out from under that table and put him in the yard?"

In the hallway, they met a worried-looking Ellen. She'd done her hair and makeup, but she still wore a cotton bathrobe. "Have you seen the sky?" she asked them. "It looks like the end of the world."

"I thought it had gotten unusually dark in here," said Bonnie. "Why aren't you dressed?"

"I'm having trouble," said Ellen. "I was just coming to get you to help. Suddenly I don't seem to know who I am."

Bonnie took her by the arm and began

escorting her down the hall. At the door to Ellen's room, Ellen turned to Morris and said, "What is that tie supposed to be?"

"You disappoint me," he said. "I thought surely you would recognize a fertility god when you saw one."

Just before the two women disappeared into the bedroom, Morris heard Bonnie say, "He doesn't know who he is either."

To the dog, Morris said, "Come on, Cricket, let's go have a look at that sky."

On the screen porch, Morris noticed that the temperature had dropped considerably and saw that the bay had turned a kind of eerie luminous slate-gray. He held open the screen door for Cricket, who lumbered reluctantly out and sat down sphinxlike near a post of the rain porch. Morris moved into the yard, where he stood for a minute under the oak, whose stout limbs rocked stiffly in the wind off the water and whose coarse leaves clattered and whistled. He flattened one hand above his eyes and looked out at the bay; he could see now that the eerie luminous quality was a product of the water's being choppy — it appeared that the odd and changing light of the sky was reflected by trillions of tiny quavering mirrors. At the horizon, the slate gray abutted an orange-tinted band of air, over which hung dark drooping storm clouds, bloated-looking, green around the edges, and nearly stationary; above these, scrims of vapor roiled alternately in silver, gold, and brown toward the shore from the west, out of Mississippi.

A gust of wind loosed from the oak a braid of Spanish moss, which blew past Morris and onto the ground near his feet. As he bent to retrieve it, China the cat came trotting out from the hydrangeas to see what had landed in the grass. Morris dangled the moss above her head and allowed her to bat the end of it around a few times with her paw. When next he looked up, he saw Pastor coming toward him from around a corner of the house.

"We got a string of bad storms headed our way," Pastor called. Once he'd got to where Morris stood, he reached for Morris's tie and hitched up the clasp a half inch. "One of them's already spun off a tornado north of Gulfport," he said.

"Careful with those hands," said Morris. "They're dirty."

Pastor brushed his palms against each other and then wiped them on his jeans. "Sorry," he said. "I was just putting the top on the Jeep. The tie suits you. You look good."

Morris thanked him, flinging the strand of moss into the air and letting the wind sail it toward the house, where it settled in a bed of ferns and palmettos. "I've never known why it's called Spanish moss," he said. "Did it come from Spain?"

"Not only did it not come from Spain," said Pastor, "but it's not even a real moss. It's related to the pineapple, of all things. The Indians used to call it *tree hair.* Back in the days when the French and the Spanish were rivals over here, the French started calling it *Spanish beard,* to make fun of the Spaniards' looks. I guess it got changed somewhere along the way to *Spanish moss* and that's what stuck."

"Interesting," said Morris. "How did you come to know all that?"

"My daddy was always filling me up with stuff like that," said Pastor. "He was fond of saying that everyone and everything's got a story. Have you by any chance seen Bonnie?"

"She's in Ellen's room," said Morris. "Helping Ellen decide what to wear."

"How do you think she seems?" asked Pastor. "Bonnie, I mean."

"Haven't you seen her?" said Morris. "Don't you share a room?"

"She let me talk to her for about ten

minutes," said Pastor. "Then she dis-appeared while I was in the shower. She's still mad at me about inviting the Delks over."

"She seemed in good enough spirits to me," said Morris.

"She's acting strange," Pastor said. "I can't tell if she's going to behave herself tonight."

"Is she in the habit of misbehaving?" asked Morris.

"No," said Pastor. "But like I said, she's acting strange."

"Strange how?"

Pastor shrugged his shoulders and turned away without an answer. "Come on," he said. "We better get these animals back in-side."

When Pastor opened the inside door from the porch, they could see up the hall that Ruth Delk was already standing in the entryway, where Macy had switched on the overhead light and opened the door for her and Bobby. Ruth had not yet abandoned her outdoor voice and was declaring how lucky they were to have got there before the bottom fell out of the sky. Pastor cast Mor-ris a quick apprehensive look and started up the hallway to greet them.

Morris followed him as far as Ellen's

room, where he stopped and knocked but received no reply. He opened the door a crack and found the room empty, so he continued up the hall, arriving at the kitchen the same moment as Macy, coming from the opposite direction.

Ellen and Bonnie were at the kitchen table, putting ivory-colored tapers into two silver candelabras. "I can finish that," said Macy. "I don't know why you think you need candles anyway, but y'all ought to get on in there and not leave Pastor by himself."

Ellen had changed into a dress similar to the one Bonnie wore, but in navy blue, with fabric straps, and not nearly as low-cut. "Well, here we go," she said, as she stood and moved toward the hall.

"You look nice," Morris said to Ellen. He'd remained near the door and now held it open for her and Bonnie. "Is that a new dress?"

"It's Bonnie's," said Ellen. "She didn't approve of anything I'd brought."

"It's very becoming," said Morris. "And now do you know who you are?"

"Well," said Ellen, "for the evening at least, I'm Bonnie's sister. And yours, of course."

"And who shall I be?" asked Morris.

"You need to be my brother," said Bonnie, hooking her arm inside Morris's.

"Okay," he said and suddenly caught Macy's eye as she stood at the table, taper in hand, staring at them. Ellen and Bonnie turned and looked at her too.

"I don't know what's got into y'all," said Macy, "but if I didn't know different I'd think the three of you just got out of the booby hatch. Now kindly get on in there and try acting like grown-ups."

Ruth Delk, who knew nothing of the accidental nature of her being invited to supper, rather seemed to think that if she were not the evening's primary guest, at least she'd been enlisted to deliver Bobby, and since she'd visited the house before, she meant to act as a guide for her son, who hadn't. Her intention was evident in all her passing remarks, which she addressed to him in a stage whisper. "See the sconces," she said, as they moved down the hallway, "and did you ever see a runner as long as this?" Pausing at the dining room door, she informed him that there were seven more leaves for that table, stored in the attic. "Oh, look, Bobby," she said, at the threshold to the living room, "there's the old grandfather clock I told you about." She didn't see, as everyone else did, that each of these remarks, and the several others like them, caused Bobby to blush. He blushed easily and obviously, but since he'd done it all his life — and since she'd learned when he was a little boy that for his own sake she mustn't allow it to alter her behavior — she no longer took it into account.

Bobby had arrived at the Owen house wearing a pair of tan linen slacks, cordovan loafers, and a starched white dress shirt over a white T; on his breast pocket was pinned a caution-yellow button with black lettering that read WHAT'S MISSING IN CH RCH? He had a big smile, extremely white teeth, and thin blond hair cropped very close to the scalp, all of which emphasized his frequent redness. Still, he made a point of looking you in the eye with a great deal of noticeable warmth and composure. When, in the hallway, he was greeted by Bonnie and introduced to her brother and sister from Massachusetts, a shadow of uncertainty crossed his face; the way the two women were dressed had given him pause, but it was a very brief pause. Right away, as if to account (if not apologize) for Bonnie's bare shoulders and visible cleavage, Pastor said, "These two girls have been playing dress-up this afternoon." Ruth said that the two of them together looked pretty as a picture and how nice it must be to be young and beautiful and able to buy and wear such glamorous-looking clothes.

Not fifteen minutes after the Delks arrived — after everyone had reached the porch, started to peer out the screens, and remark about the impending bad weather and how dark the day had grown — Macy announced that supper was served. They moved back into the hall, Pastor closed the front door against the wind, and the grandfather clock began to strike seven. As if to smooth out the social roughness of Macy's precipitate announcement, Ruth entered the dining room saying, "Oh, I'm so happy to eat!" She further declared that Bonnie's china and flatware were gorgeous, the silver candelabras exquisite, and that "nobody but nobody sets an elegant table like this any-more."

At Bonnie's request, Macy had turned off the air-conditioning and opened the tall window in the dining room. She'd switched on the sconces in the hall as well as the chandelier over the enormous table. She'd arranged the six place settings at one end, three on each side, so that people might easily pass the several dishes — a boneless rib-eye roast, mashed potatoes with pan gravy, string beans, fried corn, and sliced tomatoes

— which she served family-style. Bonnie told everyone to sit wherever they liked, but once Bobby had placed himself on the far side of the table between Ellen and Morris, Bonnie appeared to make a point of putting Mrs. Delk between herself and Pastor on the side nearer the door.

When they were all seated, Ellen immediately reached for the bowl of beans, but Pastor cleared his throat loudly and bowed his head. Morris reached across in front of Bobby and slapped the back of Ellen's hand as she withdrew it from the dish, and then Pastor asked Bobby if he would please lead everyone in prayer.

"Lord Jesus," Bobby began, "who fed the multitudes with five loaves and two fish, and who died on the Cross for our salvation: Everything we have comes from You and the Father. Make us grateful for this food and bless it to the nourishment of our bodies that we may more fully love and serve You, repenting of our sins. Help us to honor and glorify You in all that we think and say and do as we fellowship together here tonight. Amen."

While the dishes were passed about, Ruth said, "Doesn't everything look delicious! Y'all are so lucky to have a good cook. Bobby's wife, Brenda, puts me to shame in the kitchen. She is a super cook and a super woman. Brenda's what my mother use to call an original cook, one that can take a recipe as a jumping-off place and turn it into something all her own. Myself, I can cook all right, but I never learned to season well. That's the secret, knowing how to season. Anybody can heat food up, which is basically what cooking is if you think about it. But you've got to be able to taste it and know what it needs. You've also got to have the instinct for what foods to put with what other foods. That's what an original cook can do that the rest of us can't. I'm afraid Brenda's never going to forgive me and Bobby for coming over here to supper when she was out of town."

Morris narrowed his eyes at Ruth, as if he were contemplating the substance of her long introductory monologue, but then he turned toward Bobby and said, "I have a question: Can you really use 'fellowship' that way, as a verb?"

Bobby blushed, and Morris leaned forward so he could look past him to Ellen. "What do you think, Ellen?" he said.

"What I think, Morris," said Ellen, "is that you are very rude."

"Oh, no, he's not, it's okay," said Bobby, and smiled broadly. "I learned to say it that way from Pastor. If it's not grammatically correct, Pastor's the one to blame, not me."

"I don't even get the question," said Pastor, loading a heap of sliced meat onto his plate. "You have fellowship with one another. You fellowship together. What's the problem?"

"Well, you see," said Morris, "that's like saying that because we're having food together, we're fooding together."

Pastor shrugged his shoulders and received the platter of tomatoes from Ruth. Bonnie said, "Morris, I thought you meant to offer people a glass of wine with supper?"

"Wine?" said Ellen. "We don't have any wine."

"Oh, but we do," said Morris, gazing about the room. "How does one call the help in this house? Didn't we used to have a velvet bellpull in here, hanging down from the ceiling or something?"

Bonnie laughed and said, "I'll get the wine."

As she rose from her chair, a burst of air hissed through the screen of the large window at the opposite end of the table, causing the white sheers to balloon into the room. The ten flames on the ten tapers in the candelabras bent in unison toward the east wall. Pastor stood and moved quickly to the window, where he lowered the sash. He paused for a moment to look out at the bay and said, "We're in for some weather, all right."

Before Pastor took his seat at the table, Bonnie arrived with the bottle of Merlot and said, "Pastor, would you get some wineglasses for us from the china cabinet?"

An odd calculating look passed between her and Pastor, as if she'd thrown down a kind of challenge. Then Pastor said, "Well, who all's drinking?"

"Not I," said Bobby. "It just makes me sleepy."

"You know *I'm* not allowed," said Bonnie, placing the bottle on the table before Morris and sitting down.

Ruth said that she was happy as a clam with the ice tea she already had, but she said it with a sigh of disappointment, so Bobby said, "Go ahead and have some, Mama. How often do you get the chance?"

"Well, all right," said Ruth. "I guess it's okay if Bobby says it's okay and if Pastor doesn't have any objection. But only a sip. I wouldn't know a good wine from a bad one. It would be a shame to waste it on me."

At the china cabinet, Pastor opened the glass doors and reached inside, saying, "So that's one, two, three then."

"Oh, not those, Pastor," said Bonnie. "Those are for champagne. And not those either. You want the goblets. Ellen, would you show him?"

"He doesn't need to be *shown*," said Ellen, glaring at Bonnie. "What possible difference does it make?"

Ruth said, "You know, I believe these are the best mashed potatoes I've ever tasted. I wonder what it is she puts in them. Do you think she would mind me asking her for the recipe?"

"It's cinnamon," said Morris. "She puts in a dash of cinnamon."

"Cinnamon?" said Ruth. "Now you see, that's exactly what I was talking about a minute ago. It wouldn't ever occur to me to do such a thing, put cinnamon in mashed potatoes. Did y'all hear about that teenage girl who got almost sixty thousand dollars in a lawsuit against a supermarket chain because her hand was sucked under the conveyor belt at the checkout counter? I can't for the life of me understand how anybody could have a hand thin enough to get sucked under the conveyor belt. I mean, if it sucked her hand under it, it seems like it would've sucked all kinds of food items too. And what was she doing with her hands on the conveyor belt in the first place?"

Morris said he recalled a book from childhood in which a little girl went through a wringer washer and got mashed so flat she could slide under closed doors. Ruth looked at him as if she couldn't quite figure out how his remark related to the story of the girl at the supermarket. Then she said, "Bonnie, I was happy to see you at choir practice last night. Isn't Jeannie Hart just so much fun? You know, about half the people in the choir can't even read music, but Jeannie really knows how to make everybody understand it. I hope you enjoyed yourself because everybody was thrilled to see you there. Pastor, don't you think Jeannie Hart's just so much fun?"

Pastor, who'd placed the goblets on the table next to the wine bottle and returned to his chair, said, "Well, I know we're fortunate to have her, Ruth, that's for sure."

"I did enjoy it," said Bonnie to Ruth, "but I'm not sure the timing is right for me to join anything new right now. I'm not sure it's a good time for me to take on any new commitments."

"Well, I bet this house alone is plenty to keep you busy," said Ruth. "Even if you do have help."

Morris passed a goblet across the table to Ruth, who said, "Oh, honey, that's too much, but thank you. Now, what church do you and Ellen attend up north?"

"Ellen and I are lapsed Episcopalians," said Morris, "but I'm a good deal more lapsed than she. I'm so lapsed I'm null and void."

Ruth's smile faltered and the thin lines of her plucked eyebrows rose ever so slightly; she appeared to be scanning Morris's reply for the single thing in it she could make any sense of, and then, having found it, she said, with an odd conclusiveness, "Episcopalian," and turned to her right to address Bonnie. "Well, sweetheart," she said, "for what it's worth — and I am not trying to influence you in any way — I was standing close enough to you last night to hear your voice . . . and you have a lovely singing voice. Of course I expected you to, coming from the theater and all."

"What was that song you used to sing?" said Morris to Bonnie. "The one about the clock. How did it go?"

Bonnie rolled her eyes and said, "Morris, I hated it — as you well know — when Daddy made me sing for company, and I'm certainly not —"

"Yes, yes, but how did it go?" said Morris. "Just tell me how it went."

"My grandfather's clock was too large for

the shelf," said Ellen.

"That's it," said Morris. *"So it stood ninety years on the floor."*

The two of them began to sing, stumbling over words now and again, and at last Bonnie joined in too:

"It was taller by half than the old man himself,
Though it weighed not a pennyweight more.
It was bought on the morn of the day that he was born,
And was always his treasure and pride.
But it stopped, short, never to go again,
When the old man died."

"That's delightful!" cried Ruth. "I never heard it before."

"There are quite a few verses," said Morris. "*And* a chorus."

"Bonnie, what's the verse about the faithful servant?" said Ellen. "That was my favorite."

Bonnie rolled her eyes again, but sat up straight in her chair and began to sing:

"My grandfather said that of those he could hire,
Not a servant so faithful he found.

326

*For it wasted no time and had but one
    desire,
At the close of each week to be wound.
And it kept in its place, not a frown upon
    its face,
And its hands never hung by its side."*

During Bonnie's solo, Ellen had leaned forward and beamed at Morris, and they both joined in to sing the last lines:

*"But it stopped, short, never to go again,
When the old man died."*

"How absolutely precious!" cried Ruth, clapping her hands. "And do you see what I mean? Doesn't she have a beautiful voice?"

They all clapped for Bonnie and then Ruth said, "You know the other person who hides his light under a bushel is this young man sitting on my left. Have y'all ever heard *him* sing? He got his musicality from his mother. I went to school with Sheila Pastor, and we sang together in the glee club about a hundred years ago. She was the —"

"Wait a minute," said Morris. "You mean Pastor was Sheila's maiden name?"

"That's right," said Ruth. "Didn't you know that? The Pastors lived about a half mile down the road from us when I was a girl."

"You thought my folks named me Pastor in the hopes I'd grow up to be a preacher, didn't you?" said Pastor. "That's what a lot of people think. Mama's fond of saying that if she'd known I was going to grow into my name like that, she'd have named me *Doctor* Vandorpe."

"Sheila's grandparents were named Pastorini," said Ruth, "which sounds Italian to me, but they came from Argentina. I guess her grandfather changed it to Pastor so it would sound more American. And my goodness, what a beauty Sheila was! Well, still is, I guess, but you should've seen her when she was young. I'm ashamed to admit it, but I was secretly jealous of her. It just didn't seem fair that somebody could be that beautiful and sing so beautifully too. Anyway, y'all can hear Pastor sing on the AM radio every Saturday morning at eight o'clock."

"Really," said Morris.

"Uh-huh," said Ruth. "He gives a five-minute devotional and sings a hymn every Saturday. Bobby and Brenda and me never miss it. Y'all ought to tune in if you're still here on Saturday. Well, Bonnie, everybody's gonna be disappointed if you don't come back to the choir, but I'm sure they'll understand. Besides, there's a lot of different opportunities at the Blessed Hunger to get involved. What was it you were telling me yesterday, Bobby? How many different opportunities was it you counted up?"

"Fifty-seven," answered Bobby. "Fifty-seven volunteer positions to fill every week."

"Fifty-seven?" said Ellen. "That seems impossible."

"It's a lot," said Bobby, "no doubt about it. But just take my ministry alone, for example, the Newcomer Ministry. Every week we have to line up people to answer the phones on Sunday morning, to give out information about the church and what time the services begin; people to drive the carts from the new parking lot, and —"

"Carts?" said Morris. "What kind of carts?"

"Oh, just regular golf carts," said Bobby. "The new parking lot's a long ways from the sanctuary, so we shuttle people over after they've parked their cars. Then you've got to get greeters for the various Sunday school classes and for both of the worship services. And guides to help folks, especially first-timers, find where they're supposed to be or show them where the nursery is. These are the little things that can make the difference between whether a person comes back a second time or not. If you want to attract new members, which we always do, you have to anticipate people's needs before they arise."

Morris, who'd gulped his first glass of wine, poured another; he looked at Ruth, who was gazing at Bobby starry-eyed from across the table. "Why, Ruth," said Morris, "you look as if you could just about pop your buttons."

"Guilty as charged," said Ruth, laughing and raising her hand in the air like a person on a witness stand in a courtroom. "I admit it. I can't hide it and why should I? If I can't be proud of him, who can? I'm just so grateful. . . . Well, anyway, Pastor's the one that found Bobby and gave him this important work to do. Saved his life too."

"It was God that did that, Ruth," said Pastor. "I just ran the necessary errand."

"Mmm, that *is* good wine," said Ruth, and set down her glass, never to touch it again throughout the evening. She smiled across the table, first at Morris and then at Ellen, and said, "Now, you-all know that when Pastor says things like that . . . he just ran the necessary errand . . . it's just his humility shining through."

"What confuses me, though," said Bonnie, "is how do you know you're running the right errand? I mean, it's not like you receive a written memo from God, telling you exactly what you're supposed to do."

Bonnie had addressed no one in particular, but rather appeared to speak directly into her dinner plate. A moment of silence followed, in which everyone looked at her save Pastor, who was entirely absorbed in eating and only tilted his head to one side, as if he were eavesdropping on the conversation.

At last Ruth said, "Well, I really should let Pastor answer that question, honey, but I think that's where prayer comes in. And of course the scriptures."

"Yes, but I'm sure there are lots of people who pray regularly and read the Bible regularly and still do plenty of bad things," said Bonnie. "Things that hurt other people."

"It may seem too trivial to mention," said Morris, "but the Inquisition comes to mind. Ellen, could you please pass me the gravy boat?"

"And what do you mean," said Bonnie to Ruth, "that Pastor *found* Bobby?" She looked at Bobby and said, "Where were you?"

Bobby glanced at Pastor, and Pastor looked from Bobby to Morris and held Morris's eye for a moment. Bonnie observed all this business with the eyes and said, "What did I say? What's going on?"

"Actually," said Pastor, "Bobby found me. He was attending services at the church already, and one day he came to see me and we talked."

"I don't understand," said Bonnie. "What did you talk about? Were you looking for a job, Bobby?"

Bobby, who appeared to be having some trouble swallowing, reached for his glass and took a drink of tea. Before he could answer, Pastor said, "I think you might be making Bobby uncomfortable, Bonnie. After all, what passes between a person and his pastor is generally considered private."

"I'm sorry," said Bonnie. "Bobby, I didn't mean to make you uncomfortable. I only —"

"No, no," said Bobby, "you didn't. It's okay, really."

Bonnie leaned forward and said, "I didn't make him uncomfortable, Pastor."

Macy entered with a fresh pitcher of tea and said, "Did I hear y'all singing that old clock song in here? I reckon that one takes me back."

Pastor said, "Everything's delicious, Macy, as usual," and everyone chimed in with similar accolades. Macy moved around the table, refilling glasses as required, and when she'd finished and was about to leave, Ruth said that those mashed potatoes were the best she'd ever tasted and she was going to do whatever it took to get Macy to give her the recipe.

Macy stopped in the wide doorway and said she was glad Mrs. Delk enjoyed the potatoes but there wasn't any recipe. "I just make them as I go," she said. "Like some people play music by ear."

"Isn't that always the way," Ruth said, as Macy left. "True artists never reveal their secrets."

"Morris," said Bobby, "speaking of true artists . . . you being an English professor and all . . . I wondered what you thought of Eudora Welty."

Morris, surprised by what seemed an abrupt transition, only turned and looked at Bobby.

"I was just wondering," said Bobby, blushing. "Do you like her . . . Eudora Welty?"

Morris blinked his eyes slowly and said, "I assume you mean, do I like her work. And by her work, I assume you mean her writing and not her photography. And by her writing, I assume you mean her stories and not her novels and criticism."

"Oh, God, Morris," said Ellen, "give it a

rest. This is why you shouldn't drink wine. Or anything." She saw that Bonnie was quietly laughing in the chair next to Ruth. "And please don't encourage him, Bonnie," she added.

"Sorry," said Morris. "Yes, Bobby, I do like her. I especially like —"

"Bobby, isn't that the old woman you bumped into all those years ago over in Jackson?" said Ruth.

"I met her for just a few minutes when I was fifteen," Bobby answered. "It was the Christmas vacation and I was visiting my Aunt Rhea, who lives in Jackson. We went to a local bookstore one afternoon to buy somebody a present, and there she was, Eudora Welty, standing right there in the mystery aisle."

"You mean you recognized her?" said Ellen. "When you were only fifteen?"

"She was already my favorite writer," said Bobby. "I recognized her from her pictures. She was just this stoop-shouldered old lady in a beige trench coat. I would never have intruded on her, but I told Aunt Rhea who it was and she took me by the elbow and dragged me over and said, 'Miz Welty, this is my nephew Bobby and he's your biggest fan.' It just about embarrassed the life out of me."

"Well, that's Rhea up one side and down the other," said Ruth. "Outgoing to a fault. Always was."

"What was she like?" asked Ellen. "Welty, I mean."

"Cordial as could be," said Bobby. "And funny. We chatted for a good few minutes. She told me about how people sometimes turned up on her doorstep to give her their ideas for stories and how she was always trying to find a polite way of explaining to them that she preferred to write stories using her *own* ideas. And she told me about a time once when she'd been the guest of honor at a ladies' club luncheon and how the club president introduced her and said, 'Now, Miz Welty, why don't you just *tell* us one of your stories . . . in your own words?' "

Everybody laughed except for Pastor, who took a long drink of tea, wiped his mouth with his napkin, and seemed in every way to be distracted by his own thoughts.

"What's your favorite story of hers?" said Bobby to Morris.

"I'm not inclined to have favorites except in things like shoes," said Morris. "But I do especially like a little story that no one ever talks about much, called 'A Memory.' "

" 'A Memory'?" said Bobby. "I don't believe I know that one."

"As I said," said Morris, "no one talks about it much."

"What's it about?" Bobby asked.

"A young girl is lying by a lake one summer day," said Morris. "She's in love for the first time, with a boy at school who hardly knows she exists. Since it's summer now, she carries around a small memory of him — a time when she'd touched his wrist on the stairs at school. It's very short . . . almost like a poem, the way every word, every moment in it has purpose. The girl carefully observes the world around her at the lake, and what she sees —"

"Oh, I think I know this story," said Ellen. "Is it the one where she has a habit of making a little frame with her fingers and viewing everything through it?"

Morris made just such a frame with his fingers, leaned forward, and looked at Ellen through it. "That's the one," he said. "Almost nothing happens. Some low-class people show up and she watches them roughhouse with one another in the sand."

"It's been years," said Ellen, reaching for the bottle of wine, pouring more into her glass, "but I think the young girl wants everything to conform to what she believes to be true. She wants everything to conform to what she *wants* to be true . . . but of course it doesn't . . . it won't. I believe it's a kind of loss-of-innocence story."

"I think so," said Morris. "She's growing up — waking up to reality, if that doesn't sound too trite — and losing the ability to take refuge in any kind of childish fantasy that life is simple. For example, she sees that to love something means to fear losing it. She's starting to experience the uneasiness of knowing there's so little we can ever be sure of. Everything she —"

"My goodness," interrupted Ruth. "It almost sounds like a religious story."

"Why do you say that?" asked Morris.

"Well," said Ruth, turning toward Pastor, as if for support, "I just mean . . . the way you tell it . . . that girl might find faith on the next page. Is that what happens? Does she find faith?"

"No," said Morris, "not the way you mean, anyway. But she bursts into tears near the end, if that's an indication of anything."

"It's more like she loses faith," said Ellen. "She loses faith in —"

"What a sad story!" said Ruth.

"Well, I guess it is kind of sad," said Ellen. "I don't remember for sure. Is it sad, Morris?"

"I would describe it as sad but true," said Morris. "But more true than sad. The total effect of it is —"

"Oh, honey . . . Bonnie, my heavens . . . what's the matter?" said Ruth suddenly, for she'd noticed that Bonnie was crying. She put her arm around Bonnie's shoulders and then turned back to Pastor for a second, to see if perhaps he had the answer.

Bonnie laughed and wiped her eyes delicately with a corner of her napkin. "It's nothing," she said, "it's nothing. I'm pregnant, and it's probably just my hormones going lunatic."

Ruth opened her mouth wide and again turned to Pastor. "You mean y'all are going to have a baby?" she said. "How much fun!"

"Yeah," said Bonnie, examining the smudges of mascara on her napkin. "A regular barrel of monkeys so far."

Ruth said, "Well, isn't this the most exciting news, Pastor? Are me and Bobby the first from the church to know?"

"We're just starting to tell people," said Pastor. He leaned forward and said, "Bonnie, do you want to go and lie down for a while, sweetheart? I'm sure everybody would —"

"I'm fine, Pastor," said Bonnie, "I don't need to go lie down. Would you *like* for me to go lie down? Or maybe you would prefer for me to stay, so you can go on treating me like a child."

"Oh, Bonnie," said Ellen, and reached her hand across the table.

There was a violent staccato sound at the window, as if someone had slapped pebbles against the glass, and then, all at once, a noise like the thrumming of a combustion engine engulfed the room, a rough static coming from the roof of the house. "Sounds like a cloudburst," said Pastor, and stood up quickly. "I better run around and make sure all the windows are shut."

Both Bobby and Morris said that they would help and also left the table and the room. As soon as they were gone there was a three-pronged flash of lightning, and Ruth said, "Oh, my, did y'all see that? The whole bay just lit up."

A long rumble of thunder, which seemed to commence somewhere out over the water and move in to shore, invaded the house end to end. Ruth turned to Bonnie and put her hand on Bonnie's arm, a gesture of sympathy and confidentiality. Her voice low, she said, "I need to explain something, honey. When I said Pastor had found Bobby and saved his life, I was referring to Bobby's struggle, which apparently you don't know about. You see, he used to be like your brother Morris is. He struggled the better part of his twenties with it, but through the love of Jesus, he's come out the other side. I shouldn't have said what I did — not because Bobby keeps it a secret, he doesn't — but Pastor told him we shouldn't talk about it here tonight. I'm just as sorry as I can be, me and my big mouth . . . I do wish I could learn to think more before I speak. My mother used to say it was better to keep your mouth shut and let people think you're a fool than to open it and remove all doubt. But I guess that was one of her lessons that just didn't sink in."

Ellen and Bonnie stared at each other across the table, as if they were decoding Ruth's remarks and trying to determine who should speak next. At last Bonnie said, "Do you mean that Bobby's gay, or was gay, and now he's straight?"

Ruth nodded and said, "Through Christ's love. Pastor wanted him and Morris to meet, for obvious reasons, I guess. But, honey, please don't tell him I talked to you. I think I'm doing the right thing, but like I said, he asked us not to —"

"I don't believe this," Bonnie said to Ellen.

"Oh, have I gone and made things worse now?" said Ruth. "I was trying to just —"

"How dare he?" said Bonnie.

Ellen said, "Okay, let's not —"

"Now everything's starting to make a little more sense," said Bonnie.

"Bonnie," said Ellen sternly, "we're going to have dessert, we're going to get through the evening, and then you and Pastor can hash out whatever you need to hash out privately. Okay?"

Bonnie looked at her, then averted her eyes. The clock across the hall began to strike the hour, and Bonnie stood without a word and started gathering dishes. Ruth shook her head at Ellen, apologetically, hopelessly, and then she and Ellen began to help with clearing the table.

The tall dining room window groaned in a gust of wind. The chandelier overhead flickered and went out, as did the lights in the hallway. "There goes the power," said Ellen.

Under her breath, Bonnie said, "Great . . . just great."

Ruth moved around to the opposite side of the table and began to collect the silverware. "But isn't it so beautiful in here now," she said, "with the candles and the —"

All at once there was another flash of lightning, and Ruth cried out, dropping a large serving spoon to the floor and pressing her hand to her heart. China the cat had leaped onto the table and now crouched there, near the middle, her orange hair standing on end and glistening in the candlelight. The cat opened her mouth and hissed at the window as thunder rattled the rain-streaked panes. Ruth backed against the wall, muttering, "Oh, please don't let it jump on me, don't let it jump on me, please don't let it jump on me."

A stir of activity immediately followed the power outage and China's harrowing performance. Everyone searched for and lit candles and helped Macy get the two pies, the cake, and the coffee to the dining room — and then, once they'd all resettled at the table, it seemed to Ellen that the evening had taken a spill and was doomed to limp to the finish. Otherwise she found her thoughts diffused across the bleak prospect of rescuing everyone. She fretted about Morris and how Pastor's manipulations, well-intentioned or not, might hurt him; about their Point Clear visit overall and how it might affect Bonnie's marriage; and even about the Delks, who, though she hardly knew them, induced in her the kind of sheltering instinct one feels for small animals. The cat fright appeared to have put Ruth on tenterhooks despite reassurances about China's being locked up in the mudroom — or, equally possible, the poor woman was cowed by the smoldering hush that emanated from Bonnie in the chair next to her. Ellen took Bonnie's silence as a resentful obedience to her earlier directive about waiting to hash things out with Pastor in private. This indoor storm, so pointedly postponed, hung in the air, made all the more vibrant by the actual weather outdoors; rain continued to pelt the roof, wind shook the windows, and the recurrent lightning and thunder jangled everyone's nerves. Most of all, Ellen didn't like the wine flush of Morris's face and the way his peculiar questions regarding Bobby Delk's wife and marriage seemed to have a hidden purpose, as if he knew about Bobby's recent religious conversion to heterosexuality. More likely, she thought, Morris had picked up on Bobby's *former* orientation, and his probing was mischievous. In a pitiful attempt to intervene, she spoke over Morris and said, "I'm still mortified by the bad manners of our cat. I've never seen China do anything like that before."

Bobby laughed and said, "It's just Mama's bad luck. Wherever she goes, it seems to be some cat's stalking her. That's the way it is with folks who are afraid of them."

"It's true," said Ruth. "They find me wherever I go. No matter how hard I try, I can't avoid them. They gravitate to me because they seem to know I hate them. Bobby says it's because I was a cat in a previous life, but I don't believe in previous lives. I just pray to the Lord that when I die and go to Heaven there won't be any cats. Pastor, do you think there's gonna be cats in Heaven?"

A few minutes earlier, Morris had observed that Pastor seemed generally uneasy and disappointed, conditions he thought Pastor deserved, though his choice of whole milk in lieu of coffee, along with his very earnest overeating, made Morris feel some sympathy for him. Pastor had already devoured a piece of each of Macy's pies and was reaching for a slice of pineapple upside-down cake when Ruth spoke to him. He took a long drink of milk, pumping his beautiful Adam's apple three times, blinked his impossible eyelashes, and grinned — as if the question not only delighted him but also tapped in him a deep well of warmth and affection. Morris's poor opinion of Bonnie's petulance at the supper table shifted a bit toward admiration: Surely it was difficult to oppose someone who could so thoroughly disarm you with a smile.

"Now, Ruth," said Pastor, "you know I haven't been to seminary, so I can't say for sure. But I expect there'll be plenty of cats in Heaven. You'll just no longer be afraid of them."

Ruth, clearly moved, turned first without thinking to Bonnie but quickly deflected her eye across the table, as if her gaze had ricocheted off stone. "Isn't that the most beautiful answer you ever heard," she said, settling her focus at last on Ellen. "Here I am asking him the silliest question in the world and he comes back at me with something that could make a person cry."

"Well, I would've said the same thing, Mama," said Bobby, poking Morris in the ribs with his elbow. "But you didn't think to ask me."

"Very interesting," said Morris, nodding and staring meaningfully at Pastor.

Pastor halted a cake-laden fork halfway to his mouth and said, "What?"

"Oh, nothing important," said Morris, shrugging. "It just occurred to me that you could say the same thing about gay people, and I never before thought of gay people as having anything especially in common with cats." Since no one immediately responded — and since even the rain on the roof seemed to hit a temporary dry patch —

Morris laughed and said, "I'll give you all a moment to mull that one over."

At last Ellen said quietly, "There'll be plenty of gay people in Heaven —"

"Polishing the gold-paved streets," interjected Morris, "giving harp lessons to the young —"

"But you'll no longer be afraid of them," finished Ellen.

Bonnie, suddenly animated, said, "Now, you see, Ruth asked the silliest question in the world, and Morris comes back at us with an answer that could make a person cry."

Though Bonnie had not mimicked Ruth's voice or drawl, her echoing the woman's words was enough like mocking to give everyone pause, especially Ruth herself, who removed her napkin from her lap and began to fold it into quarters. She turned toward Bonnie and smiled doubtfully, then looked across the table at Bobby. Pastor heaved a great sigh and pressed his lips together, as if he meant to prohibit himself from speaking.

"Well," said Ruth, with forced cheerfulness. "I think maybe it's time for us to say our good-byes to these folks, Bobby."

"Oh, please don't go," said Bonnie. "It's still terrible out. You don't want to drive in this weather. Please stay a while longer. I'm sorry if —"

"Sweetheart," said Ruth, touching Bonnie's wrist, "you don't know this because you've never had a baby before, but it makes you tired, tired, tired. It takes a lot of energy to create a new life. You need to get lots and lots of rest, and Bobby and me are not going to be the ones to deprive you of it."

This response, for all its would-be solicitude, appeared to irritate Bonnie, the way it artfully exploited her unborn child. She looked across the table at Ellen and said, "But if you and Bobby go now, Ruth, it'll defeat the whole purpose of the evening . . . from Pastor's viewpoint, anyway."

"Bonnie, don't," Ellen said.

"But Bonnie's right, Ellen," said Morris. "Pastor, you'll have to forgive us, but your plan to have Bobby and me meet . . . and pretend we don't know why . . . has put an unnecessary strain on the evening. Inadvertently, it's created a big fat taboo subject, and —"

"Wait a minute," said Ellen. "You mean you knew about that from the start?"

"Yes," said Morris, "Pastor told me this afternoon. But I had the impression that you and Bonnie didn't know."

"We didn't," said Ellen.

"Not until Ruth told us," said Bonnie. She

turned to Ruth and added, "Sorry, Ruth."

Another silence fell over the table. Bobby and Ruth were looking alternately at each other and at Pastor, but Pastor only resumed eating his cake, twice glancing solemnly across the table at Morris. At last Morris said, "Well, now, doesn't that feel better? Doesn't it feel as if we've cleared the air?"

Bonnie said that she for one felt *much* better, which prompted Pastor to take another long drink of milk and then wipe his mouth with his napkin, resolute gestures that seemed to suggest that he'd absorbed the new conditions Morris had established and was prepared now to get down to business.

"First of all," he said, "I want to apologize to everybody. Morris is dead right. I didn't mean to, but I have put an unnecessary strain on our time together. I think my heart was in the right place, but my head must've been a little off to one side."

"Now don't you worry, Pastor," said Ruth, unfolding her napkin but leaving it ambiguously on the tabletop. "Nobody blames you for a thing. If Bobby and me hadn't come to supper tonight we wouldn't have learned about your and Bonnie's wonderful news. As far as I'm concerned, that alone was worth the price of admission. We're happy as can be for both of you, and we have loved meeting Bonnie's family. There's no need to apologize for anything. And the *food!* That's without doubt the best blackberry pie I've ever had, and I've had quite a few in my day. Start to finish everything was absolutely —"

"Mama," said Bobby softly, "let Pastor say what he was gonna say."

"Oh, I'm sorry, Pastor," said Ruth. "There I go again . . ."

Pastor placed his hand over Ruth's on the table, as if he meant to console and restrain her at once. "I did want Bobby and Morris to meet," he said. "I love Bobby like a brother. I love the way he's faced the tough challenges laid in his path. I love his courage and his faith, and most of all I love his example, his witness. In the last twenty-four hours or so, I've come to love Ellen and Morris too, with all my heart. I'm proud to call them family and I pray they'll come to feel the same way about me if they don't already. The last thing in the world I would ever want is for us to find ourselves standing on opposite sides of the river. It's not necessary for us to agree about every little thing in life. We can stand beside one another even in conflict and confusion, knowing we're united in God's all-encompassing love, which is all that matters in the end. What do *you* think, Bobby?"

Ellen noted that Bonnie was staring slump-shouldered into her coffee cup now, as if her moment of animation had been found disorderly and beaten back into its cage: In a pinch, Pastor could always resort to preaching. Impulsively, Ellen said, "Oh, I wish the lights would come back on!" which caused Morris to laugh out loud and then to lean forward and smile at her.

"What I honestly think, Pastor," said Bobby, with a very pointed seriousness, "is that our knowledge of Heaven is pretty limited. But scripture tells us we'll be given a new body and I assume a new mind will be part of it. I expect that homosexual people in Heaven won't be homosexual anymore."

Morris had allowed his eyes to drift upward for a moment to study the candlelit crystals of the chandelier. "I like the idea of a new body," he said. "It would be a bit grim otherwise. But I do have to say that I'm a little embarrassed to find myself in an actual conversation about the possibilities of gay life in Heaven . . . which, frankly, conjures for me comical, slightly campy images."

Bonnie, straightening one of the beaded straps on her dress, said, "I've always thought angels were *very* gay."

Morris looked at her and smiled. He noticed that Ruth had turned to look at her too, with a kind of charitable eye she might usually have reserved for children in wheel-chairs; most oddly, the pink tip of the woman's tongue was showing between her lips. "My remark comparing gay people and cats," said Morris, "was meant in a pictur-esque way — or rhetorically, to make a point. I didn't mean to introduce a topic for debate. What really interests me is Pastor's suggestion that we can stand on the same side of the river, even though we may not agree about 'every little thing in life.' "

"I'm interested in that too," said Bonnie tentatively. "What did you mean by that, Pastor?"

"I was just reminding us of God's love," said Pastor. "Its power of reconciliation. The tie that binds our hearts. That's all."

"But you see," said Morris, "in this case, what you refer to as a little thing is actually quite a big one. It only seems little because of our tacit agreement not to speak about it outright."

"I don't follow you," said Pastor.

"Well, we're all pleasant people here," said Morris. "We like each other, and that makes us happy. Naturally we don't want to jeopardize that happiness. But it comes at a price."

"I'm still not sure I follow you," said Pastor.

"He means that standing on the same side of the river, as you put it, requires different things of different people," said Ellen. "There are different prices to pay."

"Exactly," said Morris.

"I guess I'm being thick," said Pastor, "but I still don't understand."

"No, Pastor, I don't understand either," said Bobby. "But I want to."

Ruth leaned her head toward Bonnie and whispered, "Bobby got his brains from his father, not from me. Matters this deep I leave to folks better equipped to handle them."

"It's what I mentioned to you on the porch this afternoon," said Morris to Pastor. "If you were required to say out loud what you really believe about me, it would be a lot harder for you to paint this cozy little picture of us arm in arm down at the river. You're comfortable enough *referring* to what you believe and *alluding* to what you believe — even making decisions and taking actions based on it — but the harsh reality remains unspoken."

"What harsh reality?" said Pastor, upturning his palms, his voice rising.

"Oh, really, Pastor," said Bonnie, "don't you get it? Half the people at this table believe Morris is going to burn in Hell."

"Well, there it is in one of its simpler forms," said Morris. "And you see, part of the price I pay for standing next to you at the river is to pretend that's perfectly all right . . . not a problem."

"Yeah," said Bonnie, leaning past Ruth to look at Pastor. "And what you get to feel is what a good man you are for loving a real live gay person. Maybe, with God's help, you can even *save* him."

"Okay, okay, I just want to say one thing," said Bobby, as if he meant to come to Pastor's defense. "Y'all are talking like there's no options available, but I'm sitting here in this chair as living proof that there is: If I can walk away from bondage, Morris, if I can come out of the lifestyle, anybody can. I guarantee you that, because I don't mind telling you . . . I was a serious captive."

Bobby had gone quite red and tears had filled his eyes.

Morris patted Bobby on the shoulder and said, "Good for you, Bobby. Good for you."

Bobby turned to see if Morris had spoken with irony, which he clearly had not. His face close to Morris's, he spoke softly, uncertainly. "Now my mind's filled with nothing but Kingdom thoughts," he said.

"That's good," said Morris.

Bobby reached for his water glass and took a drink.

"Listen, everyone," said Ellen. "The rain's stopped."

Not only had the rain stopped, but the wind had all but died as well. In the few ensuing seconds of quiet, the deep woody thump of the grandfather clock across the hall was heard. An unexpected peace descended on the house, outside and in, which everyone was eager to savor except for Pastor, who rose from his chair with a good deal of noise, went to the window, and raised the sash. "It's gotten warm in here," he said.

The flames on all the candles in the room quivered in the change of air, creating a fluttering mosaic of firelight on the walls and ceiling. Pastor stood at the window, looking out at the darkness, his hands clasped at the small of his back. "I just wonder, Morris," he said, "what you'd say to someone who happened to bring up Leviticus Eighteen, Romans One, or First Corinthians Six."

Bonnie let out an audible groan, pushed her dessert things to one side with a clatter, and lowered her head to the table. Pastor turned and looked at her, briefly, with barefaced misery. Ruth glanced at Pastor, as if seeking his permission for something, then laid her hand on Bonnie's back.

"What I would say," said Morris, "is that someone hasn't been watching his after-school specials."

Bonnie raised her head from the table and laughed, the smoky exaggerated bray of a seasoned actress.

Pastor moved right up to the end of the table and crossed his arms against his chest. "Oh, I guess that answer makes perfect sense to you, Bonnie," he said. "Just sharp enough to tickle your funny bone and clever enough to go over my head. I guess that's the kind of thing you learn in college maybe, so you're in a position to laugh at people and feel superior. But there's more than one kind of education and more than one kind of ignorance too. You don't even know what those verses say, do you, Bonnie? Bobby can tell you. Ruth can tell you. Ruth and Bobby have deigned to go to Bible Study. What you don't seem to appreciate is that I'm a man of the Bible, which obligates me in certain ways. I can't just shut my eyes and act like I don't know what I know. If the Bible tells me that a man who —"

"What you don't appreciate, Pastor," cried Bonnie, "is that I don't *care* what the Bible says!" She stood, pushing her chair back roughly behind her. "Now if everyone will excuse me," she added, with less volume, "I have to go powder my nose."

She tossed her napkin onto the table and left the room.

Ruth looked pleadingly across the table and said, "Bobby, honey? Sweetheart?"

"All right, Mama," said Bobby, and began to stand up. "All right."

Bonnie powdered her nose for an exceedingly long time, too long for the Delks to wait before taking their leave. But her sudden and extended absence enabled the rest of them to make her welfare the focus of their farewells, a comfortable place to put their anxieties about how the evening had gone. Ruth firmly charged the family with taking good care of Bonnie, and even Pastor, temporarily at least, bought into the idea that Bonnie's delicate condition was what mostly accounted for the occasion's going so astray. The minute the Delks had left, Morris said something about needing to find his cell phone and disappeared. Ellen, with Pastor's approval, withdrew to the master bedroom to see after her sister.

A little while later, when the two women reemerged and found Pastor sitting on the screen porch, they'd changed their elegant attire for jeans, T-shirts, and rubber sandals. Ellen had brought a candlestick to the porch, but when she saw the loveliness of the near-dark, she blew out the flame. The night had a subdued feel to it, the cool air steeped with the rain-pummeled windswept spirits of everything in nature; flowers, trees, grasses, soil, and sea seemed to emit sharp perfumes stunned out of them by violence. On the screen porch, regret and contrition dominated the human air, though they all three were reluctant to speak; words, after all, were what had got them here. Bonnie sat next to Pastor on the rattan couch while Ellen took the nearby chair. After a moment Bonnie reached for Pastor's hand, which he allowed her to hold in her lap. A minute later, he sighed, leaned close to her, and kissed her cheek. Soon Ellen asked Pastor where Morris had gone, and Pastor said he believed that might be Morris out on the pier. Ellen stood and went to the screen, where she saw — sitting cross-legged, about a quarter of the pier's length into the water — a slightly darker silhouette in the darkness. She said she thought she would go check on him, and Bonnie suggested they all go.

"It's such a beautiful night," said Bonnie, standing up, and then she seemed doubtful and self-conscious, as if she'd too rashly thrown down a certain card in a game of hearts. She shoved her fingers into the pockets of her jeans and looked at Pastor.

"Y'all go on and go," he said. "I think I'll stay put."

"Are you sure?" said Bonnie, and Pastor smiled and nodded.

After they'd left, Cricket, having heard the squeak of the screen door, wandered onto the porch, sat on his haunches, and stared at Pastor. Pastor rose from the couch, stepped around the dog, and watched through the screen as the two women made their way across the strip of sand toward the pier. Ellen must have said something funny, for Bonnie laughed and staggered around in the sand as if she'd lost her balance. He watched as they climbed the wooden steps and trod along the diminishing gray ramp over the water. He continued to watch, as they reached Morris and lingered for a moment and then as Morris stood and the three of them set out side by side for the boat shed at the end of the pier. As they moved into the distance and the

dark, he could hear the occasional discon-
nected note of their chatter, and it made
him want to join them. He whistled for
Cricket, and the dog stood, sauntered to
Pastor's side, and shook himself, a ripple
from nose to tail that seemed to leave him
dazed. Pastor pushed open the screen door
and moved out from under the rain porch.
Overhead, a blanket of innocuous clouds
glowed a tarnished silver, backlit by the
moon. When Pastor had got only as far as
the stone wall at the edge of the lawn, he
had a deflating vision of himself hurrying to
catch up to the others, and he stopped and
rested his hands on the curved top rail of
the gate. The old bird dog, beside him,
poked his head through the vertical bars.
They remained there as the figures on the
pier grew fainter and faded altogether. If
Bonnie or either of the two others turned to
glance back at the house, Pastor wasn't able
to see it.

CHAPTER 10

After the storms, three days of dazzling summer weather moved in. Ellen very much wanted to visit Dauphin Island, the barrier island off the other side of the bay, so they planned a trip to the beach for Saturday. Morris rose early in the morning in order to catch Pastor's devotional on the radio; tiptoed into the bathroom, washed his face, and brushed his teeth; then went in his pajamas to the kitchen, where Macy poured him a cup of coffee and offered the breakfast she'd prepared earlier for Pastor (ham steak and biscuits), which Morris spurned by covering his face with the back of his hands as if Macy intended to hurl the food at him. He asked Macy if there was a radio in the house, and she gave him an old transistor she found in her apartment. Morris returned with the coffee and the radio to his room, where he'd already opened the French windows that gave onto a small brick stoop (sheltered by banana trees) and the expansive lawn that stretched between the house and the road. He sat down at the maple desk a few steps in from the windows and plugged the radio into a nearby wall socket. He didn't know the call numbers he wanted, but he remembered Ruth Delk's saying it was an AM station, and he figured he would find it easily enough.

Since supper with the Delks on Wednesday, Pastor had been busy and absent, even at night, as there were functions at the church he said he couldn't duck; on Friday he asked Morris to join him for a Men-in-Christ golf outing and barbecue, but Morris thought the invitation was extended in the spirit of knowing it would be declined. Morris and his sisters felt, as Bonnie had put it, "really badly" about supper with the Delks, especially the lasting effect of its having united the three of them as a sort of gang while setting Pastor apart. That night, on the pier immediately afterward, Morris had phoned Ipswich and interrupted Richard and Dan and Willie watching a baseball game on NESN. They'd not been able to bring themselves to turn down the volume on the TV, or even to leave the room in order to talk, and they'd passed the telephone among themselves like a hot potato.

Once the call was over, Morris chastised himself for having yielded to such a vague and childish impulse without first thinking it through, and because he'd sat down on the rain-drenched planks of the pier to use the phone, he'd got the seat of his pants soaking wet. A few minutes later, inside the boat shed with Bonnie and Ellen, he asserted that he and Ellen should just go home. There was some sound reason to the idea, but since he'd said it in the foul temper of a child who'd recently sat down in something wet, neither Bonnie nor Ellen gave it the consideration it deserved. They each took a turn at self-blame for the unfortunate evening — Bonnie lamented her rudeness, Morris his stubbornness, Ellen her powerlessness to change the course of things — and each resolved in unspecified ways to make it up to Pastor. As they were returning to shore and about midway along the pier, the power came back on in Point Clear, igniting the windows in all the houses on the promenade and throwing down quivering splinters of yellow light across the water, an unaccountable thrill that seemed an intimation of new beginnings. By noon the following day, however, it was plain to Morris that the notion of new beginnings lived on largely as it had been conceived, symbolically, for no one really knew (aside from generic remorse) what exactly it should comprise. Meanwhile, the remorse vested itself in an undeclared conspiracy to stick to trivial themes when Pastor was around. Though it helped that Pastor was so taken up by pastoral duties, Morris did have a mounting sense that more and more verboten tones populated the air, humming like the sympathetic strings of a sitar. Most memorable was the shrill note that had ended the evening with the Delks (coda of good-byes notwithstanding): Bonnie's declamation that she didn't *care* what the Bible said. Morris readily saw this as something to be sorted out between husband and wife, but the trouble, in his view, was that Bonnie's attitude would be overly determined by his and Ellen's proximity.

As Morris turned the knob on the radio bit by bit, scanning for anything that sounded like Pastor's voice, he was distracted by the arrhythmic chirp of hedge clippers somewhere outside. The gardeners, two brothers from El Paso, whom Morris had met at the funeral last year, had arrived and set about tidying up the two islands of azaleas in the field; the older of the brothers (Miguel, maybe as old as thirty) had already removed his shirt, revealing beautiful brown arms and torso and a wide band of red boxer shorts above baggy low-slung khaki work pants. When Morris eventually found Pastor on the radio, his message, which had to do with the inerrancy *and* infallibility of Holy Scripture, was a peculiar sound track to the lovely view through the open windows. Morris recalled, from past sporadic visits to the Anglican mass, an idea that the liturgy, spoken or sung, could sometimes be experienced discrete from its content, enjoyed merely as sound, washing over the worshiper. Pastor's voice on the radio, a younger version altered by the airwaves, entered this realm for Morris; he'd missed Pastor the last couple of days, and part of the pleasure now, hearing him, was the pleasure of his company, a happiness to which his actual words were secondary if not irrelevant. "Thus saith the Lord" became a leitmotif for the pruning ballet of the gardeners in the field as the younger Rey bent to trim a low branch and Miguel leaned across him, raising the shears over his own head to reach the topmost leaves. Morris soon found himself wondering at how many little pictures we paint in our minds, up close, as it were, without the benefit of stepping back to see what we've painted. He'd imagined, for example — not knowing he'd imagined it until this moment — that the advent of middle age would bring with it certain freedoms, among them liberation from the whole sexual question, answered for years by the fact of Richard. He'd thought that dwelling so long and habitually in the answer would eradicate the question, and it disquieted him now, cropping up in this old form, as it sometimes used to with busboys in hotel bistros or with the Pakistani brute who came to read the water meter at the townhouse in Brookline. At least in this instance, he thought, blame it on the thousand-and-a-half miles that separated him from Richard: This wasn't the horny compulsion of earlier years but a hunger for the particular physical touch that confirmed rightness with one's world; stranded here and deprived of it, the body reached for a poor but alluring semblance.

The shirtless Miguel suddenly dropped his shears and headed toward the house on a path that would land him on the stoop outside Morris's room; as he neared the shadow of the roofline, he reached up to change the tilt of his baseball cap and sweat glistened in the sunlight on his arms. On the radio, Pastor (who, as it turned out, did have the voice of an angel) launched a cappella into the first verse of "Abide with Me," which Morris thought an eccentric choice for the early morning, though it lent an appealing spirit to the gardener's steady approach. Once Miguel had entered the shadow of the house and was no longer blinded by the sun, he saw Morris and stopped, startled, then quickly waved and made a right turn, disappearing from view — a view replaced in Morris's mind by a dreary one of himself, as a patient in a posh sanatorium, listening in pajamas to a hymn on the radio.

For the Dauphin Island adventure, Morris chose a pair of plaid microfiber swim shorts, a cultural compromise to the Speedo briefs he would have worn to the beach in Ipswich. He packed a mesh shoulder bag (supplied to him by Macy) with the things he wanted to take and stepped into the hallway to look for his fellow travelers. Partway down the hall toward the porch, he heard Pastor's voice coming from the dining room, and some familiar note in it caused him to stop and eavesdrop. He softly lowered the shoulder bag to the floor, where he squatted and — should anyone discover him there — pretended to search for something inside it.

". . . classrooms and activity rooms over

here," he heard Pastor saying, "where we'll be housing our youth and college ministries. And over here is a full commercial kitchen, everything state-of-the-art."

After a beat or two of silence, Morris heard Ellen's voice. "Very nice," she said, with the buttery tone of someone trying to trick a jailor into giving her the keys. "*Very* nice, Pastor."

"And this big area here will be our production stage. Everything you need for a full-scale theatrical production."

"How wonderful," said Ellen. "A real theater."

"Now you can probably guess what this is in the middle if you take a close look at it," said Pastor.

A longer silence now, in which Morris imagined Ellen making an effort but ultimately having to give up and shrug her shoulders.

"It's basketball courts," said Pastor at last. "Two of them, full courts, side by side. See?"

"Of course," said Ellen. "I see now. Wow, Pastor, this is really impressive."

Morris heard the rustle of the blueprints as the top sheet was folded back to reveal the one beneath, and Ellen repeated, "Really impressive."

"Well," said Pastor, "I have to watch I don't get carried away — I know the real church is not the building — but I do get pretty excited about it. You see, about half of this is all about whatever brings 'em in, and the other half is all about create community any way you can."

"I get it," said Ellen, and Morris stood and returned quietly to his room, where he sat down on his boyhood bed.

On the nightstand was the Forster he'd read the first night in Point Clear and an old paperback of *A Separate Peace* that Morris had found earlier on the floor of his closet; inside the Knowles novel was a single loose page from a thesaurus, folded in half and used (by Morris himself, years before?) as a bookmark. As he pulled the yellowed and frayed slip from the book, he saw — in a weirdly mimetic moment — the word *page:* "*n.* 1. leaf, sheet, folio, recto, verso. 2. (*of history*) event, incident, affair, matter, period." He dimly recalled his father's zealousness for synonyms and etymologies (and some browbeating little lectures on the Importance of Words), and this memory blended somehow with what Morris had overheard the minute before in the hallway. He believed there'd been a recurrent visitor to the house — not a single person, but a type of visitor, a composite of several persons — who'd come to show his wealthy father plans for one project or another, hoping for financial backing. He believed he'd sometimes overheard their conversations and that even as a boy he'd disliked the give-and-take of the disparate tones of voice, the one fervent, fawning, the other blasé, bored. From outdoors, now, there came the sudden roar of a combustion engine and then Miguel bumped by the windows bestride a bright green lawn tractor. Morris moved to the windows, shut them, and returned to the bed, where he lay down and read *A Separate Peace* until Ellen knocked on the door twenty minutes later and told him it was time to go.

About a hundred yards down the beach, four skinny teenage boys had planted an enormous rebel flag in the sand next to their disordered jumble of coolers and cheap aluminum chairs. The flag snapped vigorously and sometimes even audibly in the sea breeze, and Morris toyed with the idea of going down there and asking the teenagers what — nearly a hundred and fifty years after Robert E. Lee's crybaby surrender at Appomattox — the flag meant to them exactly. He thought he would either have to sashay over or swagger, and he was having trouble choosing.

It had taken better than an hour and a half to drive to the island, including a stop for Pastor to fill the tank of the red Wrangler. At the gas station, a homemade sign hung above the pumps that read "YOU" ARE OUR BEST CUSTOMER, and Morris, next to Ellen in the backseat, leaned close and whispered, "Observe the ubiquitous misuse of quote marks; it makes me doubt my very existence." Because Pastor had removed the Wrangler's top for the trip, they'd enjoyed what (according to Pastor) the Jeep people called Wind-in-Your-Hair Freedom, a relentless assault of gale-force exhaust fumes, with conversation restricted to what might reasonably be shouted at the top of one's lungs, imparting to the most quotidian remarks a flavor of panic. As they'd crossed the three-mile-long bridge from the mainland to the island, Pastor had screamed an account of its history — the original drawbridge, destroyed by Hurricane Frederic in 1979, was replaced by this altogether better concrete high-rise model — and Morris had the irrational feeling throughout that he was supposed to *do* something in response, perhaps start throwing heavy items from the back of the car to lighten the load. Pastor had secured for the day a beach cottage owned by a Church of the Blessed Hunger deacon, a dismal little five-room board-and-batten box on stilts that nonetheless provided them with the use of a private stretch of beach as well as a toilet and shower. Macy had sent them off with an elaborate picnic — turkey sandwiches, potato salad, sliced cantaloupe and watermelon, oranges, lemon meringue pie, and a huge jug of sweet tea — which was fabulous except that it made for an ice chest weighing about two hundred pounds that had to be lugged (together with tote bags, towels, chaise longues, and umbrellas) nearly a quarter mile to the beach from the borrowed cottage.

This portion of the beach was sparsely populated, but in the far westerly distance, beyond the boys with the rebel flag and at the end of a gentle curve, you could see the trembling colorful bloom of the overcrowded public sector. The sky was a uniform cloudless sky-blue, the sand sugar-white, and the water changed hues three times as it moved away from the shore, from pale green to blue-green to blue. Once they'd established the umbrellas in the sand, Morris took a quick dip, a kind of purging of the punishing journey in the Jeep, and then, soon after the others came in, he went ashore and settled himself on a chaise in the sun; he'd fancied the watchful meditative role of lifeguard, though of course he contemplated the lives of the loved ones in the water more than guarded them. Because getting there from Point Clear required driving around the entire bay, he and Ellen hadn't often visited the island as kids — they'd gone to the closer beaches of Gulf Shores — and he didn't remember the place very well. He'd wondered why she was keen to see it again, but after they'd crossed the sound and arrived at the main intersection at Bienville Boulevard, the island's essential character came back to him: It was a long narrow sandbar, really, three miles into the Gulf of Mexico, just the sort of removed and birdy scene Ellen would find enticing. Too bad, thought Morris, about the array of oil rigs visible only a few miles farther out, a kind of ghostly pale-blue Futureworld on the once-clear horizon.

He dug into the bag he'd brought and found his sunglasses, for he realized he'd been squinting in the glare; the three others had swum far enough from shore that their heads resembled the vertices of a watery triangle, bobbing hypnotically in the waves. He heard laughter from the direction of the rebel flag — the group of teenagers seemed to be in a constant state of hilarity as they lounged about and chain-smoked cigarettes — and he again considered paying them a visit to discuss the various symbolisms of the red-white-and-blue "Southern Cross."

Soon he saw that Bonnie had drifted apart from Ellen and Pastor, and after a minute Ellen turned from Pastor and began to swim toward shore. She swam with the speed and form of a person who regarded swimming, even short distances, as very serious business. Once she'd gained her footing on the sea floor, she paused to slick back her hair from her forehead, and as she walked out of the water in her conservative black one-piece from Lands' End, Morris noticed that Pastor watched her rather too carefully from behind. He reflected that Ellen was still fetching, though he seldom thought of her that way, and that she had — he now noted and recalled — million-dollar legs and an especially beautiful walk, the kind of graceful swing of the arms from side to side that counterpointed the sway of the hips, quietly and unignorably sexy. He thought for some illusive reason of Bobby Delk, of his red-faced sweetness and sincerity, of how Morris from time to time had glimpsed in the young man's radiant smile the undead sparkle of sadness, and of how it seemed there was no sadness quite like sexual sadness. How strange, the absurdity of sex, he thought, the animal starkness of it, and how strange that humans brought to it so much brouhaha, angst, and legislation.

He handed Ellen a towel. As she used it to dry her face and hair, she maintained the residual simpleton's smile often consequent to a swim in the sea. She dragged a chaise into the shade of an umbrella and aligned it close enough to Morris that they might talk, but once settled she seemed entirely content with the surf-suffused silence and the pleasure of her own breathing; Morris observed that she closed her eyes with each inspiration, the better to relish it, and at last he asked her whether she was doing some sort of Hindu respiratory exercise. She pointedly did not move her head to look at him, as if the energy it would require was a good deal more than he merited, and Morris welcomed what he hoped was the return of her edge — since Wednesday night with the Delks, she'd been maddeningly maternal toward him, as if he'd taken ill. Now she kept her eyes shut, impervious to anything that might disrupt her extreme serenity. Soon Morris asked her if she would like something to drink, and without opening her eyes, she cried *yes* in the passionate tone of someone who'd forgotten there was such a thing in the world as liquid refreshment. Morris moved to the cooler and poured them each a clear plastic cup of Macy's sweet tea with lemon. He had to bump Ellen's wrist with the cup in order to shake her from her trance, but once she'd taken a good long drink, she found her own sunglasses and trained her gaze on Bonnie and Pastor, who now rode the waves face-to-face, Bonnie hanging on to him with her hands clasped behind his neck in a way that suggested she had him in an underwater leg lock. Pastor boosted her higher in the water and tilted his head back to receive her down-angled kiss, and Morris wondered if one mightn't be tempted to cross Pastor on a regular basis for the sake of delicious rounds of peacemaking; he thought it just the sort of twisted behavior the young preacher was capable of inciting in a person.

Ellen, suddenly down to earth, surprised Morris by saying, "You know, we still have to talk about money."

And so began one of those beach dialogues conducted aboard adjacent reclining chairs — words directed upward and outward at sky and sea — which for some reason always made Morris think of space travel. "Yes," he said, "I suppose we do."

"This isn't the part we have to talk about," said Ellen, "and it's really none of our business, but did you know she's given something to the church?"

"It crossed my mind that she probably would have," said Morris. "But no, I didn't know."

"I can't quite figure why," said Ellen, "but it feels disappointing."

"I imagine you feel that way because it's so hopelessly unoriginal," said Morris. "Did she tell you about it?"

"No, Pastor did, just this morning. I think it was meant to encourage me to follow suit."

"Really. He hit you up?"

"Not overtly," said Ellen. "Well, pretty overtly, I guess."

"I'm hurt," said Morris. "He didn't hit on me. I guess I don't rate."

"He showed me the plans for the new Christ Center," she said.

"Yes, he showed them to me too. . . . As far as I can tell, it's a kind of religious resort and spa."

"He talked about the various phases of the fund-raising campaign, and somehow we ended up at Bonnie's having made a very generous gift."

"But he didn't say how much."

"No," said Ellen. "But he did say she'd made it anonymously."

"Oh, dear," said Morris. "That's not a good sign."

"Well, as I said, it's really none of our business. But I wouldn't mind sorting out the house. I don't really care about the money involved, it just feels odd to me — if they're planning to live there permanently — for you and me to part-own it."

"Then you don't mind giving up your share of your childhood home?"

For an answer, Ellen remained silent, and so, after a moment, Morris said, "You don't quite know if you mind."

"I think it has to do with the way things have happened," said Ellen. "If she'd approached us with a proposition, I could have considered it and —"

"But Ellen," said Morris, "do you really think that if she'd written a letter, or telephoned and offered to buy you out, you would have said okay?"

"I might have," said Ellen. "I've thought off and on about something Dan said in Wellfleet — how the house is the physical thing that binds us to one another, the three of us. It didn't mean much to me when he said it, but since you and I have been down here, I've felt. . . ."

"Felt what?"

"I don't know . . . *good,* in a way. And now I'm —"

"Well, you do already have two other houses," said Morris, "in which to feel good."

After another silence, during which Morris tried to assess the damage his curt remark might have inflicted, Ellen said, "Why do you have to do that, Morris? Why, when I'm trying to talk to you about something the tiniest bit emotional, do you have to resort to a silly barb? It makes you seem so much weaker than you are."

"Sorry," he said, "it just popped out . . . because we were talking about houses. It makes me nervous."

"Talking about houses makes you nervous?"

Now Morris was the one to remain silent, for he didn't know what he meant by what he'd just said. He could feel Ellen's gaze, so he turned to look at her: She'd raised herself onto one elbow, angled toward him, and pushed her sunglasses to the top of her head. He mirrored these maneuvers, facing her and moving his glasses to his head, but since he still couldn't think of what to say, he only smiled and shrugged.

Because Ellen sat beneath the umbrella, and because the umbrella was red, she appeared to be horribly sunburned. She squinted at him and said, "You mean talking about *that* house makes you nervous. Our house, in Point Clear."

"I guess so," he said.

They each lowered their sunglasses again and resumed their former positions on the chaises.

After a moment, she said, "What I was going to say, Morris, is that now I feel confused."

"Now that we've come down here," he said.

"Now that we've come down here, yes, but also following my little chat with Pastor this morning."

"Ah," he said, "I see. The what's-what-in-Point-Clear question. Part of what we came to ascertain was whether or not Bonnie had taken in another stray. It was comforting to find Pastor so well situated, President and CEO of JesusCorp. And now it's not only disappointing to learn she's given him a large sum of money, it's also alarming."

"I think it changes things a little," said Ellen. "I think it affects my feelings. And maybe explains things a little too."

"You refer to the obvious ambivalence

between them," said Morris.

"Yes."

"Notwithstanding the amorous aquatics we're witnessing at the moment."

"Yes."

"Well," said Morris, "you know there's that odd effect a gift of money can have . . . the way it can create resentment on both ends of the bargain. It does seem to increase with the size of the gift."

"I might be reading too much into it," said Ellen. "It's still new — the information, I mean. It's so perplexing . . . how she seems both happier than I've ever seen her and unhappy at the same time."

"Different and also the same."

"That's right."

"Very Gertrude Stein."

Ellen laughed. "God, I haven't heard that name in years."

"Well, there's nothing fresh or surprising about old Gertie anymore," said Morris. "We live in an *age* of solipsism. Today she'd just be one more blogger on the World Wide Web."

"By the way," said Ellen, "did you really listen to Pastor's radio show this morning?"

"How did you know?"

"In the water, just now, he asked me about it. When Bonnie had swum out of earshot, he asked me if I'd listened to it with you."

"Macy must've said something to him about my borrowing her damned radio," said Morris. He looked away from the water for a moment and down the beach. "Well, I'm not bringing it up if he doesn't," he said.

"And he's *assuming* we're coming to church services tomorrow morning," Ellen said. "The jazz combo is playing, whatever that means, and the Sunday school's putting on a puppet show."

"Jazz combo?" said Morris. "Puppet show? Are we actually planning to go?"

"I think we should," said Ellen. "Do you really not want to?"

"I don't know," said Morris. "I fear the sermon."

"I don't imagine it will kill us," said Ellen. "And it obviously means a lot to him. We'll go and sit with Bonnie."

"Ellen," said Morris, "do you think I should walk down there and ask those boys what their intentions are . . . what exactly they're trying to say with that rebel flag?"

"By all means," said Ellen.

"Are you serious?"

"Of course I'm not serious."

"Okay," said Morris, "do you want me to tell you something the tiniest bit emotional . . . to make up for before?"

"Yes," said Ellen, turning toward him.

"I've been thinking about the house," he said. "It's much more pleasant now, of course — that's plain — with what she's done to it. But being here has confirmed something I've been thinking for a while already: that the *world* feels more pleasant now too." He turned his face toward hers and added, "Pleasant may not be the right word, but definitely . . . improved. Is that a terrible thing to say?"

"You mean the world with Daddy no longer in it."

He nodded. "Actually, I've been waiting most of a year to say that to you," he said.

She returned her gaze to the water and then closed her eyes. At last she said, "No, Morris, it's not a terrible thing to say. You should have been able to say it sooner. I'm sorry I made you wait so long."

"That's all right," he said, "But returning to our former subject . . . I have the feeling she was happier before we arrived and she'll start to get happier again as we go out the driveway Monday morning."

"That's probably true," said Ellen. "Sad but true."

"*I* expect to be happier too," said Morris. "Not that it hasn't been great fun. . . . Not that it hasn't been a real blast, being the controversy that threatens to break up my baby sister's marriage."

"Oh, Morris," said Ellen, "you're not the only controversy. There's a world of things they're going to have to work out."

"And they'll work them out better when we're gone."

"I imagine so. Are you sorry you came?"

"Not exactly," he said. "Are you?"

"Not exactly," she said. "I only hope Bonnie's not sorry."

"Yes," he said. Then: "I can't tell if your eyes are open or closed, but you should probably know that she and Pastor are coming out of the water now."

Pastor wore orange-and-green swim trunks (the fashionable knee-length and absurdly copious style that, once wet, clung annoyingly to the thighs), and Morris thought he looked somehow older in them, as they revealed the well-proportioned physique and the pattern of body hair (delicate black blossom on a slender black stem) of a grown man. There was no ambiguity whatsoever about Bonnie's grown-woman status, in her skimpy pink bikini that left virtually nothing to the imagination.

Ellen sat up straighter and smiled. She said, "Did you notice the little bulge below her belly button?"

"You mean my future niece or nephew?" said Morris. "Of course I noticed. But seriously, Ellen, how big do you think it might have been, what she gave him, the gift she made to the church?"

"I have no idea. And I'm certainly not going to ask."

"It occurred to me that it might help to find out."

"Or hurt," said Ellen. "I don't think I want to know."

Morris watched Bonnie's wobbly approach, arm in arm with Pastor, up the low incline of the sand. After a moment, he said, "No, I don't think I want to know either."

"I've been thinking about you," said Pastor, and then took a stupendous bite out of a turkey sandwich.

"What a coincidence," said Morris. "I've been thinking about you too."

The women had put on cover-ups and straw hats and sandals and walked to the cottage for the bathroom. Soon after they'd gone, Pastor quickly and carelessly applied some tanning lotion, remarked at how *hungry* swimming made a person, and tore into the ice chest. First he squatted by the cooler and took a plastic fork to a Tupperware container of potato salad — his upper lip still gleamed with oily bits — and then he uncapped a brown bottle of root beer, sat next to Morris in Ellen's chair, and removed the plastic wrap from a sandwich.

"Have you really?" he said now.

"Well, I've been thinking about you and me," said Morris. "Both of us. Actually, I've been thinking about everybody."

Pastor upturned the bottle to his lips, polished off about half the root beer, and then gave Morris a blank look. "Well, anyway," he said, after a moment, "I was thinking about how you don't have to work — for money, I mean — but how you work anyway. How you teach school even though you don't have to . . . and how great that is."

"Thank you," said Morris, "but I assure you my motives are selfish."

"That doesn't matter," said Pastor. "That's true of most of what we do. But since your selfish reason's not to make money, what is it?"

"It gets me out of the house," said Morris. "I get to be onstage three days a week in an atmosphere where I'm the one who knows the most. And at cocktail parties, when somebody asks the rude inevitable question, 'What do you do?' it supplies me with an acceptable answer."

"But you must enjoy it too," said Pastor.

"I thought enjoyment was what I just described," Morris said. "I don't imagine salary's the main impetus behind your chosen field either."

Pastor laughed and said, "Not hardly."

Morris, bewildered to find himself in a second conversation about money in less than half an hour, said, "What do you think about those boys down there with the rebel flag? What point do you think they're trying to make?"

Pastor leaned forward and gazed down the beach, squinting at the glare. "Oh, it's just kids," he said. "I'd be surprised if they could tell you the first thing about it. To them it's just a we're-proud-to-be-southern thing."

Pastor's tone suggested he couldn't be less interested in the subject, but Morris decided he was most likely just taken up by the grave urgency of eating. "Well, if they're that ignorant," he said, "don't you think somebody should go down there and enlighten them, tell them a thing or two about history?"

Pastor laughed again and said, "You remind me of my daddy, Morris. What is it you want them to know?"

"Nothing too complicated," said Morris. "One or two things about what the flag represents."

"And what does it represent?"

"Are you playing devil's advocate?"

"Not me," said Pastor. "I just think it represents different things to different people, and I'm curious to know what you think it represents."

"Well, obviously, for starters, it was the flag of the Confederacy, and at best it's a kind of sore-loser emblem of —"

"Not really," said Pastor, shaking his head.

"What do you mean?"

"That was just one of several battle flags the rebel soldiers used. Granted, it got to be the most popular, but it was never the flag of the Confederacy . . . or even the Confederate Army."

"Hmm," said Morris. "I didn't know that."

Pastor, who'd already gulped down the turkey sandwich in five or six bites, leaned away from Morris and reached for the lid to the ice chest, lifted it, and then began to feel blindly around inside. At last he fished out an orange, sat up straight, and dug his thumb into the peel. "I wouldn't make too much of that flag if I were you, Morris," he said. "It's just a piece of cloth."

"Of course I'm only speculating," said Morris, "but I bet the ease with which you embrace that concept is determined in part by the color of your skin."

"No doubt," said Pastor. "But think about this, Morris: What flag are you gonna fly that *doesn't* conjure up something to be ashamed of?"

Morris looked at him, surprised. "Come to think of it," he said, "a neighbor of mine in Ipswich flies a bright yellow flag with a smiley face on it . . . and even that embarrasses me a little when friends come over."

Pastor nodded and smiled and wiped his mouth with the back of his hand. "Down there at the other end of the island," he said, "is where Farragut ran the gauntlet between the two forts to capture Mobile Bay. Once he got through the bottleneck, he watched the U.S.S. *Tecumseh* blow up and go down in about three minutes and realized the whole bay was mined. That's where *Damn the torpedoes — full speed ahead* comes from."

"I've always liked the rhythm of that expression," said Morris, "but I've never entirely understood it. *Full speed ahead* is clear enough, but what does *damn the torpedoes* mean?"

"Torpedoes was what they used to call mines back in those days," answered Pastor. "Once the admiral realized he was going to have to navigate a minefield, he had a decision to make: turn back or forge ahead. So he was saying, Never mind about the mines, keep going."

"I see," said Morris. "Further evidence that history often records foolhardiness as bravery."

"Depending on the outcome," said Pastor.

"Yes, depending on the outcome."

"Now, tell me what you thought of my radio broadcast this morning," said Pastor. "And I don't mean the singing part."

"Speaking of minefields," said Morris. "Isn't that a rather loaded question?"

"I don't mean it to be," said Pastor.

"Given the unpleasantness at supper Wednesday night?"

"No," said Pastor. "I honestly want to know your opinion."

Morris couldn't quite see a way to explain about the open French windows, the sexy gardeners pruning the azaleas, and how he'd allowed Pastor's devotional to wash over him like the liturgy in the Anglican mass, so he said, "Which opinion do you want? As it turns out, I have several. I'm sure you could anticipate that we'll disagree about the topic itself, so do you want my opinion of your delivery? Or what I think about your choosing that particular topic on this particular day? Or my psychological assessment of people who believe what you apparently believe? What exactly are you looking for?"

"I did figure you'd disagree," said Pastor, "but I'm curious about *how* you disagree."

"I get it," said Morris. "You just want to kick it around as if it has no bearing on me or you or our friendship; as if it has no personal aspect."

"Is that possible?"

Morris watched as a brown pelican plunged into the gulf, surfaced after a moment with a full pouch dripping water, tipped its head back — and then a gull dive-bombed it and stole its prey before it had a chance to swallow. "No," he said to Pastor, "I don't think so."

Pastor had spread his legs apart so he could drop the pieces of orange peel through the webbing of the chair onto the sand. Now that he'd finished, he tore the peeled orange in two and offered half to Morris. His hair, still wet, hung to his eyebrows, and as he held out the lovely little golden hemisphere in his palm — which seemed also to hold the mixed aromas of orange oil, salty sea air, and coconut from the lotion he'd applied to his chest and arms — the look on his face was so let down and hopeful at once, his eyes, half closed in the glare, so bright, Morris accepted, sighed, and said,

"Oh, I suppose we can try."

"Well, then," said Pastor, and waited.

"What I think is that you take a complex issue and reduce it so it feels nice and cozy. Constantly having to question things is tiring. And one way to make something that's inherently ambiguous into something clear is to place it beyond the realm of questioning. Do you see what I mean?"

"You're saying the reason I believe the Word of God's infallible is so I can understand it better," said Pastor. "But my belief makes it *harder* to understand, Morris . . . because I don't have any loopholes or wiggle room. Just because I don't question the truth of it doesn't mean I don't question the meaning."

"Well, those two questions are inextricably linked," said Morris. "The unnerving thing about truth is that it's historically mutable — and capitalizing the *T* doesn't make it not so. It used to be true that the sun revolves around the earth and that the earth is flat and held up by columns. The church famously put a few folks to death for saying otherwise. *Is it true?* asks you to think about how and when something written thousands of years ago . . . translated from languages people don't even speak anymore . . . still applies today. And that's the stuff of soul-searching and scholarship."

Morris noted that Pastor appeared stung by these last words, and he imagined it was because *scholarship* implied *seminary*. After a moment, Pastor said, "That's exactly what I meant by loopholes and wiggle room. To me the Bible's as timeless as it is true. Every word applies today. I don't get to pick and choose."

"But of course you do anyway," said Morris. "I have to say, Pastor, your hair looks a bit long for a man who calls himself a Christian. And why do you let your wife run around so often with nothing covering her head? And by the way — though it's unseemly of me to bring it up — my sister, according to her gynecologist, is eleven weeks pregnant. By my calculations, that means she was six weeks pregnant on her wedding day."

"That's between me and Bonnie and God," said Pastor, in a deep voice meant, Morris guessed, to ward off any challenge. "And we don't have any problems with it, Morris. It's private and I'm not going to talk about it, but rest assured, we wouldn't have stood up there at the altar if there'd been any kind of a problem."

Morris smiled but immediately felt a bit ashamed, for it was an unkind smile. He said, "It doesn't feel very good when the conversation turns to your private life, does it, Pastor? You don't like it very much, do you?"

"I just thought we could have a conversation about my devotional," Pastor said, "without stirring anything up . . . without breeding contempt . . . without making it personal."

"Ah, your little plight rears its ugly head again," said Morris. "I think I'll take a swim. It's hot."

"No, wait," said Pastor.

Morris, standing already, turned and looked down at Pastor, whose face was disagreeably pleading. "What did you mean before," he said, "when you mentioned me choosing this particular topic on this particular day?"

"Well, if you really want to know," said Morris, tossing his sunglasses onto the chaise, "I was disappointed in you, Pastor. I would've thought it beneath you, exploiting your position the way you did this morning. It's not quite a level playing field, is it, when one of us has both a pulpit *and* a radio station. I don't think it's the sort of thing one should use for the purpose of having the last word . . . especially in a domestic dispute. Lucky for you, Bonnie's a late sleeper. Lucky for her too."

Morris had been franker than he'd meant to, and now, as he walked toward the water with Pastor's eyes boring into his backside, he felt thoroughly foolish, surprised at how cross he'd sounded. About twenty feet from the water's edge, a tingle went up his spine just before he was struck from behind, at the bend in his knees, and suddenly he was face down on the ground with a mouthful of sand. The next minute or so was a rollicking commotion in which the sun seemed to play a stroboscopic role: As he and Pastor tumbled over and over in the sand, Morris couldn't tell if Pastor intended him harm or was only trying to pull him into an embrace, though he instinctively tried to throw him off; within the repeated abrasion of sand and the hot shock of flesh against flesh, he sensed a subtle headward logic to Pastor's maneuvers, as if he meant to straddle Morris's chest and pin his arms to the ground with his knees. Then there was the peculiar intrusion of female cries nearby, followed by Pastor's even more peculiar laughter — false, forced, nearly perverse; the alarmed arrival of Bonnie and Ellen, their silhouettes eclipsing the sun; Bonnie, most peculiarly of all, holding an enormous beach ball; and finally, Pastor's sudden release.

As Morris twisted onto all fours, he heard Pastor saying, "We were just horsing around," and he twisted a second time, into a sitting position cross-legged on the sand, and looked around, woozy. Pastor stood right next to him, hands on his hips, and repeated, "We were just horsing around." Bonnie and Ellen appeared incredulous, and Morris thought irrationally it might have something to do with a patch of sand, in the shape of South America, caked to Pastor's stomach. "Come on, Morris," he said, offering Morris his hand. "How about that swim?" Without looking at his face, looking only at his hand, Morris waved him away, and then Pastor punched the beach ball out of Bonnie's grasp, kicked it hard so that it sailed into the water, and chased after it, leaping into the surf.

Morris stood and began to brush sand away from his eyes and mouth as Bonnie moved silently toward the water. Ellen said, "Are you okay?"

"A little stunned," Morris answered.

"What was that about?" she asked.

"He *tackled* me," said Morris. "From *behind.*"

"We saw," said Ellen.

A worried look came over her face as she gazed past him toward the gulf, and when

Morris turned in that direction he saw that the wind had got hold of the beach ball, which was skimming across the water at a good clip away from shore, and that Pastor, swimming after it, was already quite far out. When they moved to Bonnie's side, she turned to them and said, "He's going too far." Morris, despite the fear in Bonnie's eyes, reflected that "too far" was only an idea, determined by circumstances and intuition. He noticed a pale suggestion of mist hovering on the surface of the water. Pastor was swimming hard and fast, ever farther from shore, but the ball always stayed a few feet ahead, occasionally spinning its primary colors round and round, as if to show that it could outrun him and do tricks at the same time. Bonnie cupped her hands on either side of her mouth and yelled, "Pastor, let it go!" and though it seemed Pastor was surely too far away to hear her, he stopped. He appeared to swivel in the water and turn toward shore. "Thank God," Bonnie said softly, but instead of starting to swim back, Pastor remained in the same spot. One arm went up, then the other — did he mean to wave to them? There was the brief illusion of his drifting toward them, caused by the ongoing progress of the ball out to sea, and then the three of them continued to watch as Pastor's arms vanished and resurfaced several times and he appeared somehow to fall backward in the water, his face aimed at the sky. Though no one spoke a word, it began to dawn on them that he was in trouble, and soon Ellen, by far the strongest swimmer of the three, threw her hat to the sand and tore off her cover-up and sandals. She ran into the surf, dove over a breaker, and started swimming. Bonnie never averted her eyes from the water but with a quiet note of accusation in her voice said, "Morris, what happened? Tell me what's happening?"

CHAPTER 11

The instant before the pain, he'd seen it, but he didn't *know* he'd seen it until he felt the pain: a graceful shape like a large bubble of clear oil in the water, which, with the stroking motion of his right hand, he'd pulled into contact with his chest and stomach. He'd been stung before, maybe a half-dozen times, but this was by far the worst — like a blowtorch to his ribs, and then there was a second or two of disbelief, the panic of trying to get away from something virtually invisible, the stupidity of waving for help, and the crazy temporary paralysis brought on by fear of getting stung again. Ellen had covered almost half the distance from shore by the time the initial shock wore off and he was able to grasp the facts — he'd run up on a jellyfish; he was in terrible pain; he'd swallowed a lot of salt water; but he was okay, he could still swim. Most of all, he wanted to cut Ellen off as quickly as possible and avoid the risk of her getting stung too. As he swam toward her, he never looked back, never saw the damned beach ball again, but he thought of it as a devil, made of air, carried by air, that had lured him into peril and punishment and then gone on about its business elsewhere.

Everything that followed was humiliation and more humiliation, from the physical wound itself (ugly welts on the right side of his rib cage and reaching up into his armpit) to the several spiritual ones that would swell and fester some hours afterward. Everybody had been kind and efficient. He was escorted to the cottage, where Ellen found a bottle of white vinegar, which Bonnie used for bathing the wound; Morris brought him two Advil tablets from the medicine chest and a glass of water; they all three insisted he stay put in the shade of the cottage's screen porch while they got the things from the beach and loaded the car; and it seemed that in a matter of minutes Bonnie was backing the Jeep out of the driveway and they were on their way home. She stopped at a convenience store to buy a tube of cortisone cream, which Pastor cautiously rubbed onto himself as they crossed the bridge. By the time they reached the mainland, the red patch on his side looked more like a rash than a wound and itched more than burned.

But everybody was also noticeably subdued, as if a tragedy had befallen them, and it seemed that any semblance of cheerfulness had gone out of the day. A few miles north on the parkway, the sky grew overcast, and Pastor wished he'd left the top on the Jeep, for the roar of the wind, which had seemed so right on the way out, now felt all wrong, almost an aggravation. During the long stretch of the Interstate he nodded off and didn't wake up until they'd already crossed the bay into Baldwin County. The rest of the way to the house he had a feeling that the three others had been talking about him while he slept — ridiculous, since they would've had to yell anything they wanted to say.

At the house, he and Morris each took an end of the ice chest and carried it inside to the kitchen. Once they'd set it down on the counter next to the sink, where Pastor uncorked it to let the ice water drain out, Morris gave him a kind of arched-eyebrow look, as if to say, What next?

Pastor shrugged his shoulders, and Morris said, "How do you feel, Pastor?"

"I'm okay," he answered, and then they both headed back through the mudroom to help the girls with the rest of the things.

Bonnie and Ellen, who'd already removed the umbrellas and chairs and laid them on the ground next to the car, now stood at the rear end of the Jeep reorganizing the contents of the several beach bags. When Pastor asked Bonnie if she knew where his shirt and his cell phone had got to, she looked at him sadly and said, "How do you feel, Pastor?"

"Yes," said Ellen, beside her, "how *do* you feel, Pastor?"

"It's just about stopped hurting," he said. "I feel good enough to put on my shirt. . . . I guess that's a positive sign."

In one of the bags, Bonnie found his phone and his white short-sleeved sport shirt and gave them to him. He quickly checked the phone for missed calls (none), dropped it into the pocket of his trunks, put on the shirt (but left it unbuttoned), and then set about gathering up the umbrellas and beach chairs, which he carried to the nearby garden shed to put away. As he stacked the chairs against a wall inside the dark shed, he found himself worried about how Macy's lemon meringue pie, still untouched inside the ice chest, had survived the trip. He was in the shed maybe thirty seconds, and when he returned to the yard, the others had apparently gone into the house already. He paused for a moment midway between the garden shed and the house and looked at the stand of pines that lined the north border of the field; not a branch or needle on them moved. He heard no bird, nor saw the flight of any. The red Jeep, cooling down a few feet away, uttered three short metallic pops. The sun broke through the clouds in a flash of brilliance and sharp shadows, disrupting the eerie stillness, and then went directly back into hiding.

He expected to find the others in the kitchen, but all that greeted him there was the hum of the fridge and the repetitive whir of the ceiling fan. He checked the answering machine that hung next to the phone on the kitchen wall, but there were no new messages. He sat for a minute at the table and crossed his arms on the fresh white linen tablecloth. He wondered where Macy could be and then recalled that Saturday afternoon to Sunday afternoon was her regular time off. He reflected that he was the only one who'd eaten any of Macy's picnic lunch. He guessed maybe rich people didn't need to eat as much as regular folks, but he was quickly ashamed of himself for such meanness of mind. He put his left hand inside his shirt and touched with his fingertips the skin under his right arm. Its tenderness mixed with the greasy feel of the cortisone cream made it seem cooked, which caused him to shudder. He stood, moved to the ice chest, and took out Macy's Tupperware pie keeper. Through the translucent plastic he could see white blotches of meringue where the pie had banged against the sides of the container.

After he'd cut a good-sized piece and slid it onto a plate, he found a fork in the silverware drawer, poured a glass of cold milk, and returned to the table. He took the first bite, and the cool delicious lemony flavor made him close his eyes. From the hall came the lazy *click-click* of toenails against wood and then Cricket appeared in the doorway, stopped, and stared at him. "I got stung by a jellyfish," Pastor said to the dog. "That's why we're home so early." As he went to cut a second bite of pie, the fork somehow slipped from his fingers, banged against the plate, and fell off the edge of the table onto the floor. The old bird dog ambled over and began to lick it, scooting it inch by inch across the linoleum, and Pastor watched this for a moment, feeling inexplicably sad. He placed his elbows on the tabletop and held his head in his hands for a few seconds, thinking about the little bin of identical forks inside the silverware drawer, and — even more inexplicably — this made him feel sad too.

Around six o'clock, Bonnie came to the den, where he lay on the couch watching stock-car races on TV. She was barefoot, wore very short shorts and a sexy green tank top. She'd pulled her hair back from her face in a new way and she smelled good, like a mixture of apples and roses, but Pastor could see that she was still in the same distant mood she'd brought home with her from the island. Now she conveyed it by leaning against the frame of the door, as if it would kill her to actually be in the same room with him. She glared at the TV for a second, and he used the remote to mute the sound. "How do you feel?" she asked, for about the hundredth time in the last four hours.

"I'm plenty sore," he said, and for an instant it seemed as if he meant he was angry, so he added, "I mean, it's tender, but I'm okay."

"You still don't want to change?" she said.

This too she'd asked him more than once already, and he'd explained, more than once, that you didn't want to put fresh water on a jellyfish sting right away, so he would wait awhile before taking a shower, and there wasn't any point in changing his clothes until he was ready to take the shower. "In a little while," he said now, which is what he'd said the last time she asked.

"Well," she said, sighing as if he'd disappointed her again, "do you want to come with us to the hotel? We're going to get dressed and walk over in about an hour or so."

Later, he thought about how unwanted this invitation (if you could call it that) caused him to feel. The three of them had made their plans already, and then Bonnie had come to see if he would like to tag along. And when he'd declined, saying simply that he was feeling worn out, she hadn't questioned his decision even a little bit. Before they left the house, the three of them arrived together at the door of the den, dressed to the nines, to say good-bye. The races on TV were over by then and Pastor was watching the tail end of a program about deep-sea fishing out of Carrabelle, Florida. The charter company had a nice-looking boat with an air-conditioned cabin and two fighting chairs on the deck, and Pastor had been thinking he and Bonnie might drive over to Fort Walton Beach and pick up his folks and take them deep-sea fishing one day before the baby came. Morris, who apparently didn't care for fish or fishing, poked his head into the room and made a face at the TV screen, where the boat's captain was helping a man haul a fifty-pound amberjack onto the deck. They made their farewells and nobody bothered to ask if Pastor might like them to bring back something from the hotel for him to eat. After they'd already started to go, Bonnie returned to the door to say that they would likely stay late and hang out at the piano bar. She said he should come and join them if he felt better later.

"You know that's not the sort of thing I enjoy," he said.

"Oh," she said, playacting surprise. "Well, if you change your mind, you know where we'll be."

This she said as if they'd begged him to come and he'd stubbornly and repeatedly refused. She did not enter the room to kiss him, and when he heard the faraway slam of the screen door out on the porch, he felt like crying.

In truth, she hadn't been herself since her brother and sister arrived, which from Pastor's viewpoint had been a kind of rollercoaster ride, minus the fun. A lot of the time she'd seemed generally dissatisfied with him; sometimes downright angry; then, as if she'd temporarily forgotten how vile he truly was, affectionate again (despite the fact that they hadn't made love all week long); and finally distant, in this you-figure-it-out kind of way. He supposed it had primarily to do with Morris. Even though he'd bent over backward to be kind and welcoming to Morris, Pastor guessed that for Bonnie nothing would do short of his signing on to homosexual marriage. Meanwhile, nobody had made even the smallest attempt to appreciate his side of things — which in his opinion amounted to their not making any attempt to appreciate who he was. Since supper on Wednesday night, a little fantasy had replayed in his mind, in which he shouted at the three of them, "What y'all don't understand is that this is my *life* we're talking about! It's who I *am!*"

Pastor sat up on the edge of the couch and turned off the TV. Bonnie would not want to drive down to Florida and take his parents deep-sea fishing, not before the baby came or after.

Once he'd showered and shaved and applied fresh cortisone cream to the sting to alleviate the itching, he found himself wishing he'd gone to the hotel with them, and he considered getting dressed and joining them after all. But when he imagined the sudden halt in their conversation as he approached their table, and their pretending to be glad to see him, he decided against it. Was he sulking? He couldn't be sure. Mostly, he felt strange — a blend of fidgetiness and exhaustion that reminded him of his teen years, when he'd sometimes partied all night on Friday and then popped an upper to get through Saturday morning on the sales floor of Fairhope Appliance. Now, as he stood before his bureau in the master bedroom, a bath towel wrapped around his waist, he admitted to himself that the real reason he hadn't gone with the others to the hotel restaurant was because he needed some time alone. And then it hit him, the full weight of his self-centeredness: He hadn't honestly wanted to be with them, but he'd wanted them to want to be with him. Not since high school, and the early years of high school at that, had he suffered such idiocy in himself. He opened the bureau's middle drawer and stared at the stacks of clean boxer shorts and white T-shirts, washed and perfectly folded by Macy, neatly put away by Bonnie, and the bounty of blessings this represented — in the face of his pettiness — moved him almost to tears. He put on the baggiest T-shirt he could find and lightweight khakis with his beaded Navaho belt. He went to the nightstand on his side of the bed, lifted his Bible and spiral notebook from the tabletop, and carried them to the screen porch, where he sat on the rattan couch and observed in the sky the promise of a spectacular sunset. This is why he needed to be alone. When he got this much out of whack, when he'd drifted this far astray, the only thing for it was scripture, prayer, and meditation. He was grateful not only to know the remedy but to have it so close to hand.

Pride, he decided, had been the chief culprit. Earlier, on the beach, Morris had nailed him and he hadn't liked it. The personal remark about the timing of the wedding had only been a warm-up; it had rankled Pastor, but he felt he stood on firm enough spiritual ground there. What really got under his skin was what Morris had said about the radio show. Pastor *had* used it as a means of having the last word, used his minister's position to argue, to an unseen audience, something he should've argued in the privacy of his home, to his wife. He'd taken to the airwaves what he hadn't been man enough to take directly to Bonnie: the lingering effects of her Wednesday-night declaration that she didn't care what the Bible said. A declaration that could've shaken the very foundations of their marriage, if for one minute he believed it, which he didn't. People often said things they didn't mean, and even if it was what she felt then, in the heat of the moment, he knew she would feel differently later. The real source of her remark had been the desire to hurt him, born out of what she thought to be his rejection of her gay brother, and what could she possibly have done that would hurt him more? Shaming him in front of the Delks, attacking in this dramatic fashion the very Bible he'd given her for a wedding present. Afterward, he'd reminded himself of her clear joy the morning of their wedding day, when she unwrapped the Bible and saw her new name, BONNIE OWEN VANDORPE, engraved in gold on its black leather cover. No, she had only meant to hurt him and he'd deemed it best to sit tight, let it go, and once Ellen and Morris went back home to Massachusetts, Bonnie and he would sort out whatever needed to be sorted out. He'd phoned Bobby Delk from the church on Thursday and apologized, blaming hormones for Bonnie's behavior at supper and expressing his hope that the Delks would keep to themselves what had happened, and Bobby had reassured him he needn't worry on that account.

Pastor was convinced that once her sister and brother left, Bonnie would return to reading her Bible and she would be the same again as before. *Things* would be the same as before. Still, though he had neglected these last three days to broach with her the subject of her outburst, and though she seemed perfectly happy with this arrangement, it had continued to eat at him. And then he'd gone and chosen for the radio devotional what Morris called "that particular subject on this particular day." Even if Bonnie never heard the Saturday-morning show, he was having his way, having the last word, making his view official, to as broad an audience as possible. And what Morris *didn't* know was even worse: Pastor had chosen the same topic for tomorrow's sermon, which he would now, obviously, have to scrap.

"Pride goeth before the fall" would be his new subject. In his heart of hearts he knew he'd gone after Morris on the beach — and brought down a much older man, a man in his forties, whom he might easily have hurt — out of nothing but sheer pique. He'd disguised it as horseplay, called it horseplay, even almost convinced himself it was horseplay, but he knew better in his heart of hearts. Likewise, he couldn't fool himself entirely about chasing after that beach ball. He'd swum a good minute or more, thinking *I'm going out too far, they'll be worried about me* and relishing the prospect. He guessed God had sent that stinging jellyfish to turn him around, and not just physically. Back home, he'd tried zoning out with the TV, but even stock-car races and deep-sea fishing couldn't hold off the truth forever.

Fortunately, the sermon's title, already printed in tomorrow morning's bulletin, was "Thus Saith the Lord," a title you could do just about anything with. The gospel reading, also already printed, was the opening verses of John: "In the beginning was the Word, and the Word was with God" and so on, a passage he'd intended to use as a springboard for a discussion about how God's Word, like Christ himself, was the embodiment of God. He figured the passage was poetical enough to lend itself to any number of uses; he could cite it in the new sermon in a different way, then add to it the Old Testament verse about pride and anything he could find that Jesus might have said on the subject. He consulted the concordance at the back of his Bible and learned first that the verse from the Book of Proverbs actually said, "Pride goeth before destruction, and an haughty spirit before a fall." And when he searched the concordance for a gospel reading on the topic, all he found was the passage from Mark in which Jesus talks about how everything that defiles a man comes from within his own heart. It was a fairly comprehensive list, which, besides the sin of pride, included evil thoughts, adulteries, fornications, murders, thefts, covetousness, wickedness, deceit, lasciviousness, an evil eye, blasphemy, and foolishness. The point Jesus was making had to do with the old Jewish traditions concerning food and eating; he meant to teach the disciples not to worry about what they put into their stomachs but to worry about what came out of their hearts. Pastor found this interesting enough, but it didn't really relate to what he wanted to talk about in his new sermon.

For the next hour and a half or so, during which the promise of a nice sunset turned into an ordinary cloudy dusk, he made some rambling notes in his spiral notebook, read random passages from the gospels (hoping for inspiration), and generally got nowhere. He supposed he could always fall back on the two parables in Luke that exemplified "For whosoever exalteth himself shall be abased; and he that humbleth himself shall be exalted" — the one about the Pharisees and the publican, and the other about choosing the "lowest room" at a wedding feast. But these familiar stories captured a familiar kind of pride, in which a person puts himself on a pedestal. The kind of pride Pastor wanted to explore was when a person secretly feels inferior and seeks to have *others* put him on a pedestal.

At last he closed the notebook and the Bible, shut his eyes, and silently asked Jesus to show him the way. On the back of his eyelids he first saw the afterimage of the stone wall out front of the house and the ancient oak tree. Soon he tasted salt water on his tongue and felt the sweet pressure of Bonnie's breasts against his chest, her nipples hard beneath the wet fabric of her bikini top; he saw Morris's face, very close to his own, the shiny black orbs of his sunglasses — "Your little plight," he heard him say; and then for some unimaginable reason he saw Morris naked on a bed with Bobby Delk, the two of them kissing each other on the mouth and their hairy legs braided together on top of a tangled white sheet. . . .

He opened his eyes and closed them again quickly, as if he were turning a TV set that had gone haywire off and back on. Now the face of Jesus loomed up, a gray shadowy likeness of the Savior, bearded, long-haired (but somehow looking very pale white and feminine), embossed on a silver coin. Pastor concentrated on the coin and it slowly began to turn on a vertical axis. He found to his pleasure that he could make it stop turning and start again with his will. When he'd turned it 180 degrees, he saw that it was blank on the other side, which felt to him both surprising and not-surprising; there followed a gap — nothing, nowhere, no time — and then he was sitting in the twilight, on the rattan couch, on the screen porch, with the full and sure knowledge that his main problem was not spiritual but physical and resided not in his mind but in his stomach; he was famished.

As he started up the hallway, China crossed in front of him, trotting from the dining room into the living room. He paused at the door and saw in the near-dark that the cat was resting on its haunches in the middle of the Oriental rug, staring up at the old grandfather clock, as if she were waiting for it to chime. She turned her head and looked at Pastor over her yellow shoulder. "What are you up to, you crazy old alley cat?" he said, but for an answer she only shifted her position an inch or two on the rug and put her back to him more fully. He continued up the dark hall, the floor creaking beneath his bare feet, and once he reached the kitchen, he pushed open the swinging door and began to pass his hand in a circle on the inside wall, searching for the light switch. His face touched the doorjamb, which felt suddenly like the cold blade of a knife flat against his cheek, and a certain unexpected misery invaded his heart: *It was not his house, and he didn't belong in it.* Cricket growled at him from underneath the table, and then Pastor switched on the light, a circular fluorescent tube that sputtered to life over the sink. Somebody had turned the now-empty ice chest upside down, at an angle, with one end resting in the sink and the other on the countertop, and for a moment, it seemed to Pastor that the whole room was off-kilter. "Man, I need to eat," he said aloud, and moved to the refrigerator, where he opened the door and stood, head lowered, gazing in. Through the raised windows behind the sink, he heard music coming from somewhere beyond the lush wall of oleanders and dogwoods and vine-covered trellises on the kitchen side of the property — an old dance-orchestra tune with a clarinet, the kind of smooth tinny-sounding music from the 1940s his folks used to like to listen to when his daddy was grilling hamburgers and they were having their Tom Collinses on the patio.

A little before ten o'clock, he turned off the TV in the den and gathered up his dirty supper dishes to carry them back to the kitchen. He'd found in the fridge what was left of Macy's picnic and eaten so much he felt ashamed of himself afterward. He'd watched about an hour of an army movie about men going through basic training at the hands of a brutal drill sergeant, but the language was so persistently vulgar he finally gave up on it. His hands full, he pushed open the kitchen door with his shoulders and backed his way into the room.

Macy was sitting at the table with a cup of hot tea. She immediately stood to take the dishes from him, but he told her to sit back down, he could manage, and went straight for the sink.

"Well, I wondered who that was in there watching TV on a Saturday night," she said, as he rinsed the dishes. "You're not here by yourself, are you, Pastor?"

"Yes, ma'am, I am," he said, placing his supper things in the dishwasher.

"How come?" said Macy.

He closed the dishwasher and looked directly at her. She appeared to be fresh out of the bath and ready for bed — her white hair was still wet, her face was shiny with some kind of bedtime lotion, and she wore a purple housecoat.

"I got stung by a jellyfish today at the island," said Pastor, "and I didn't feel like going out with the others."

"I thought you looked a little poorly," said Macy. "Lord, I hate those things. I got stung so bad once when I was a girl they had to take me to the doctor, and I never really enjoyed swimming in the gulf again. You tell me, Pastor . . . you're a man of God . . . why in the world did God make such horrible things and put them out in the ocean like that? What possible purpose do they serve?"

Pastor smiled. "It's too big a design for us to fully see or understand, Macy."

"Or too small," she said. "Do you want some tea? It's chamomile, my bedtime drink, very soothing."

"No, thank you," said Pastor, but sat opposite her at the table. "What do you mean, *too small?*"

"Oh, nothing," she said, waving her hand. "I just sometimes wonder if we don't think there's more of a design than there really is."

"Well," said Pastor, "you can read on the very first page of your Bible that He made every living creature that moveth and saw that it was good."

"Yeah," said Macy, "but it doesn't say good for what, does it."

Pastor laughed and said that was true, that was true. He noticed how Macy was holding her tea mug with both hands, her elbows propped on the tabletop, and moving it around in little circles near her chin, as if to savor the tea's aroma. She was a curiosity to him, this devoutly Catholic woman who seemed so gratified by small pleasures, who'd never married or had children of her own, who'd been content to live in two rooms off the back of somebody else's house. She was not much older than his own mother but different in every possible way. He thought his mother took a dim view of women like Macy but that she would be hard pressed to say why. When his mother had suggested that she could come and live with him and Bonnie and take Macy's place, he'd felt, besides the implication that Macy was an unnecessary indulgence, an implication that she was unnecessary altogether. He thought his mother was a perfectly decent person and had been a decent enough mother to him, but he also thought she seemed shallow compared to a woman like Macy, and he believed his mother had long ago ceased to have anything useful to teach him. He'd recently persuaded Bonnie to give Macy a raise in salary because he was afraid she would leave them now that she'd got some money from Bonnie's father's will and Bonnie had got herself squared away. Certainly he would have missed Macy's cooking and everything else she did for them, but no doubt, with time and diligence, a substitute could be found. Her other qualities were the real reason he didn't want her to leave: Besides the fact that Macy was the nearest thing to a mother Bonnie had ever had, Pastor believed he could learn something from the woman. He recognized that there were some potential lessons for him in the simple way she went about serving others, with modest compensation and with little or no thought to what others were doing for her in return. Now he felt especially warmly disposed toward her in this vein, and he was about to put a question to her, but before he could speak, she said, "Where'd they go, Bonnie and them?"

"Over to the hotel to eat," he answered. "She said they'd probably hang out at the piano bar for a while . . . but I did think they'd be home by now."

"Not at ten o'clock," Macy said. "I expect that piano-bar scene's just about getting started."

"I don't think anybody's going to be in any shape for church in the morning," he said, and felt a small flutter of anxiety inside his chest. At this late hour, he still had only the vaguest notion of a sermon.

"Oh, I imagine they'll rally to the cause," said Macy.

"I'm curious about something, Macy," said Pastor. "I was wondering what you think — I mean, as a religious woman — about Morris and his situation."

He could see that the question surprised her. She lowered her mug to the table and drew her mouth into a straight line, and it struck Pastor suddenly just what an unfair position he'd put her in. He flattened his hands on the tabletop and said, "Never mind, Macy. I shouldn't have asked you that."

Now she smiled, as if he'd caused her to

remember something happy. "Oh, I don't mind," she said. "You just have to understand that I've known those kids since . . . well, since they were kids; Bonnie since the day she was born. When you ask me a question like that about Morris, you're asking about a grown man you've met recently. But when I start to answer it, I'm thinking of him mostly as a little boy. You made me think of what we were just talking about a minute ago — about God's plan. It never did make any sense to me that God would've given a little boy like Morris a father like Roy Owen. I know next to nothing about what life was like for Morris after he went up north to boarding school. But my guess is that getting out of this house and away from Roy was the best thing that could've happened to him. There wasn't a day went by that Roy didn't let that child know — oh, sometimes just by a look in his eye — that he was a disappointment to his father. So what do I think as a religious woman?"

Pastor nodded. "If it's not too personal," he said. "I promise anything you say won't leave this room."

She smiled again, but this time Pastor had a sense she was smiling at him with a kind of tolerance, the way adults sometimes smiled at children.

"As a religious woman," she said, "I think God doesn't make mistakes. But if God *did* make mistakes, Morris being the way he is would be a small one compared to him being born into this house and then losing his mother at the age of ten. It might come as a surprise to you, Pastor, but I'm not a very good Catholic. I'm a *practicing* Catholic, and I intend to go on practicing, but I don't expect to ever get very good at it. I do my best. There's some of the teaching that comes into conflict with my heart and there always has been. I guess there's either something wrong with the teaching or something wrong with my heart. What I know for sure is that I love Jesus, I love the mass and the sacraments, and I love Morris. I believe God gave me all these things to love because for some reason He wanted me to have a lot to love. I'm not gonna take one part of what He gave me and turn it against another, I just can't. Don't you want a piece of lemon meringue pie or something, Pastor? It ain't like you to sit in the kitchen and not eat something. It causes me to worry."

"If you saw how much I already had, you wouldn't be asking," he said.

"Did you wash that jellyfish sting with

white vinegar? It's the best thing for it."

"We did," he said. "And cortisone cream for the itching."

"Where did it get you, on the leg?"

"No," he said, "up here on my side and stomach."

Macy winced. "Oh, that's gotta hurt," she said. "You sure there ain't something I can get for you?"

"Macy," he said, "if I'm not mistaken, this is your time off."

"That's right," she said, pretending to have forgotten. "Well, in that case, I believe I'll go on to bed. I'll just let the animals back inside first."

She rose from the table, moved into the mudroom, opened the outside door, and whistled for Cricket. But the cat came in first. It ran urgently into the kitchen and then stopped and looked around wide-eyed, as if it didn't know where it had arrived or why it had been so anxious to get there. The old bird dog eventually came too, and then Macy closed the door and turned back to the kitchen. She looked at Pastor, who remained at the table.

"It used to be that I spent a good bit of time in this big old dark house by myself," she said. "All those years, living here with Roy, who depended on me for everything under the sun but love and money. He would've been utterly lost without me, and yet for the most part he didn't even notice me. Some days I would be out in the living room, dusting the same old things I'd been dusting for thirty years or more. This place can get quiet as a tomb, and I'd catch myself thinking, What in the world is it all about, Macy? What in the world is your life about? But I would go on about my business, doing my work, and pretty soon I'd just forget the question. It must've happened to me a hundred times like that over the years. I guess I thought I would just go on and on and one day Roy would die and I'd have to find a different situation. I'd go to mass and continue to see my church friends, and maybe the Owen kids would come and visit me from time to time. But then Roy had his last stroke and Bonnie came down to help take care of him. After a while he died, and she fixed up the house and stopped all those drugs she was taking. Then you came along with your Bible and your hearty appetite, and now there's a baby on the way. It feels like I have a whole new life. It just goes to show, you never know what's in store. I'm afraid I'm not much deeper than that, Pastor, but my goodness. . . . I ain't talked to anybody like this since I don't know when. You must bring it out in a person."

"Thank you," he said, though he wasn't entirely sure of what he was thanking her for. Everything she'd said had somehow made him feel frustrated and uneasy. What he'd thought he admired in her and even envied a little, her apparent peace of mind, now smacked to him of complacency. Faced with a difficult question or a spiritual dilemma, you just went on about your business, happy enough not to know the answer, happy enough to wait for what life might have in store — a strategy a good bit easier to apply if your business was cooking and cleaning house. It didn't work so well if your business, like his, happened to *be* the business of difficult questions and spiritual dilemmas. He guessed Macy's brand of contentment was a luxury denied him by virtue of his calling. He wanted to ask her another question about Morris, or return to the original one, but he couldn't see the way. When he looked at her, he saw that she was looking back at him with concern, almost as if she knew how utterly alone he felt, and when next she spoke, she even seemed to indicate as much. "Now, if I was you," she said, "I would go on to bed. All Bonnie and them's got to do is sit up straight in a pew tomorrow morning, but you've got to preach."

In the dream, he stood barefoot in the cold sand at the base of the steps to the pier, trying to figure out how he could climb to the top without getting stung. It was nighttime, but he could see in the moonlight that the steps were made of marble, patterned with many cracks, in and out of which thousands of yellow jackets crawled, obscenely rubbing together their black furry hindmost legs. As they twitched their clear-veined wings, they glistened in the moonlight and made terrible *click-click* noises like electrical sparks. The water in the bay appeared to be oily, so that there was something sickening about how it licked heavily against the pier's creosote pilings. At the extreme end, beneath the tin roof of the boat shed, he could see the small dim outline of his wife and her brother and sister, standing with their arms around one another, facing the western shore. He called out each of their names but couldn't make himself heard. As he started to shout again, a yellow jacket spiraled up to his face, flew into his mouth, and startled him awake.

He was still on the couch in the den, where he'd apparently fallen asleep. Somebody had switched off the TV and put a cotton bedspread over his legs. He immediately sensed that his T-shirt had stuck to the jellyfish wound and he reached down and slowly peeled the cloth away from the skin, which, to his surprise, produced an almost pleasant feeling. He reached up and turned on the small lamp on a table beside the couch and then shielded his eyes with his hand. After a moment, he lifted his head and saw that in the armchair near his feet the bird dog lay curled up sleeping, its nose tucked beneath its hip. On the chair's matching ottoman the cat lay on its back, the fur of her stomach fanned apart, accordion-like, her head hanging off the edge as if she'd been shot. A sheet of paper stood tented on the coffee table at Pastor's left elbow, next to it a glass of water and a saucer, on the saucer a brownie. He reached for the brownie first and took a bite, then pulled the paper close to his face and read *Didn't have the heart to wake you. ♡ Bonnie.* He took a sip of the water, switched off the lamp, and closed his eyes. He told himself he should get up off the couch and go to bed. He heard Macy saying, "This place can get quiet as a tomb," and then the sermon he still hadn't written — or the thought of the sermon he still hadn't written — glided through his mind like a silent jet airplane, leaving behind it a vapor trail that was only mildly disturbing. Maybe he would turn the den into a study for himself, he thought. After all, he should have a place to work at home . . . he could create a little nest for himself, a place where he could take phone calls, work on his sermons, pray, and meditate in private. He adjusted the throw pillow beneath his head and took a deep satisfying breath. Again he told himself he should go to bed, and he decided that was just what he would do; in a minute, he would get up and go to bed.

When next he woke he recalled no dream but he felt he'd been sleeping, alone, on top of a mountain somewhere, and so deeply he'd nearly slipped into a coma. As he lifted his head a couple of inches off the pillow, he noticed that both animals had left the room, a detail that inexplicably caused his heart to race. Through the den's open door, he could see, out in the foyer, an odd greenish light — or the suggestion of a light — and at first he thought, *dawn,* but then he saw that the single window in the den, covered only with white sheers, was still black. He threw the bedspread from his legs and sat up, and the moment his feet touched the floor, an unnatural stillness swept over him, very like the moment he'd experienced that afternoon, outdoors, as he'd paused on his way from the garden shed to the house. Now he was struck by the strange but convincing idea that the stillness had invaded the woodwork in the house, petrified it, and yet, deep within the stillness, everything moved, more agitated than usual. As if this contradiction in the physical world, once noted, was bound to produce a sound, Pastor heard a faint humming noise coming from somewhere beyond the foyer, from somewhere down the long hallway. He thought, *I'm still asleep, dreaming,* but as he stood and started toward the door he knew with absolute certainty that he was not asleep and he was not dreaming. Once he'd gained a view of the hallway and saw at its end that the odd light came from the living room, he knew with equal certainty that a stranger was in the house.

As he moved slowly down the hall the deep hum grew gradually more distinct, a vibration that seemed to enter his body and calm him, just as the light, growing brighter, seemed to bathe and comfort him. He looked at his bare arms and saw that his skin was tinted pale green, as if by sunlight filtered through leaves. Drawing nearer to the living room, the peculiar quality of these particulars vanished, and the only thing he found unusual was the fact that he was crying, not unhappily but in a neutral way; the tears trickling down his cheeks were the body's natural response to the light and the vibration, as sweat was to heat and humidity.

Once he reached the wide threshold to the room, he saw a small dark-skinned man standing near the grandfather clock, any threat his unexpected presence might have posed erased by his sheer smallness. He was not much over five feet tall, not much over a hundred pounds; not much older than Pastor himself, with dark curly hair and a short scraggly beard; thin, wiry, and wearing what looked like brown pajama pants. The glass door over the face of the old clock stood open, and the little man was going up on tiptoe to touch the brass dial and Roman numerals. The animals, who'd been sitting in adoration poses on the rug, now turned their eyes toward Pastor, then rose and came to him as if they meant to console him. The dog stood next to him, leaning against his right leg, and the cat rubbed her head against his ankles and settled near his feet. The little man at the grandfather clock strained an inch higher on tiptoe to close the clock's glass door, revealing, as he did so, a ladder of ribs in his back. He ran his hand along the length of the clock's trunk, bending to touch the little ledge at its base, then straightened up and turned toward the room. He gazed down at the rug for a moment, thoughtfully, upturned a palm, and spoke a word in a language Pastor did not understand, though he sensed that he'd said something about the clock. He lifted his eyes and looked briefly at Pastor and the animals in the hall before lowering his eyes again to the rug, and Pastor fell to his knees, causing the dog and the cat to scrabble away from him a foot or two. "Oh, ohhh," he said, and as he struggled to form additional words, all he managed to get out was "Precious . . . precious . . ."

A warmth spread through his body, from the top of his head down into his arms and hands. His heart beat hard for a moment but immediately abated. He struggled to catch his breath and then breathed easily. His penis rose and fell. "Precious . . . precious," he said again, and his breath, green-tinted molecules of vapor, dispersed through the room and fogged the windows onto the screen porch. The dank crawl space beneath the house rose up to press against Pastor's knees, and the earth under it; the hot air of the attic over the ceiling came down to rest on his shoulders, and the sky above the roof. He began to weep: a wailing baby in a crib, a pockmarked teenage boy alone at the side of a dirt road, a middle-aged man in the backseat of a bus, an old woman in a shadowy hospital room. He wept and wept, resting on his heels, covering his face with his hands, and bending forward so that his knuckles nearly met his knees, and when next he lifted his head Macy was coming down the hall in her nightgown. When he looked at her, she gasped and crossed herself. "Oh, my Lord," she said, reaching out her hand, but Pastor cried, "No, no, Macy, don't touch me yet . . . don't touch me. . . ."

CHAPTER 12

Shortly before dawn, when Bonnie, in tears, awakened Ellen and asked her to come to the master bedroom — when it became evident that Pastor had suffered some kind of breakdown — Ellen immediately thought that, whatever had happened, it was somehow connected to their abandoning him the night before.

After Pastor's encounter with the jellyfish, they'd all felt a swell of sympathy for him, which, it seemed to Ellen, they'd then discarded in favor of a night of fun, a final fling before the mandatory sobriety of church on Sunday and the sweet sorrow of parting on Monday. Ellen had sensed, the minute the three of them had set off down the stone walkway toward the Grand Hotel, a guilty freedom — Bonnie's young husband was a problem from which, temporarily, they'd loosed themselves. At the hotel restaurant, they ordered rather recklessly from the dinner menu, and Ellen purchased an absurdly expensive bottle of Puligny-Montrachet. They further postponed any conversation about money by spending a great deal of it, and if a distressing memory lingered of Pastor's dropping Morris to the sand at Dauphin Island, they managed to get through the entire evening without the slightest allusion to it. In the piano bar after dinner, Morris ordered a virgin daiquiri for Bonnie, and two snifters of Armagnac for himself and Ellen. They stayed quite late and joined in the sing-along, song after song after song, and around 1 a.m. Morris persuaded Bonnie to take the little stage, where she leaned into the curve of the baby grand and delivered a steamy rendition of "Whatever Lola Wants." During the applause and whistles that followed, Morris had cried into Ellen's ear, "What do you think the folks at the Blessed Hunger would think about *that?*"

Some hours later, Ellen, her head pounding, followed Bonnie to the master bedroom and watched helplessly as Bonnie sat with Pastor on the edge of the bed and tried to comfort him, one arm around his shoulders, Pastor rocking back and forth, weeping and repeating again and again, "I don't know what it means. . . . I don't know what it

435

means. . . ." Ellen — bewildered, distressed, and groggy — imagined that whatever terrible thing had happened wouldn't have happened if only they'd been less selfish. And some hours later still, close to noon on Sunday, when she found herself sitting on the screen porch single-handedly entertaining Pastor's parents, it felt a kind of punishment.

The Vandorpes, at Bonnie's behest, had driven up that morning from Fort Walton Beach. The day, which had started out sunny, had now grown overcast; a cool breeze blew in from the bay and occasionally whistled softly in the porch screens. Sheila Vandorpe, obviously delighted, even under odd circumstances, to reassume her former position on the rattan couch, seemed on a deeper level gratified to have been summoned to Point Clear — still to be needed, despite her boy's recent marriage and general elevation in the world.

"It happened to him twice when he was ten years old," she said to Ellen, seated next to her on the couch. "He woke up one morning and found a big white bird perched at the foot of his bed. He said it looked at him with a big silver eye and spread its wings clear up to the ceiling and spoke his name. Well, he was convinced it was the

Holy Spirit, which worried me and Rex but we weren't sure what to do about it. You know you have to be careful who you talk to about such things."

Sheila, who'd arrived in her church clothes — white slacks, red blouse, white bag and heels — paused for a moment to examine the overlapping traces of red lipstick she'd left on her coffee cup.

"Then about a month later," she continued, "he woke us up crying in the middle of the night and said a circle had opened up in his bedroom wall. He said rings of all different colors had come floating out of the wall and landed on top of him and pinned him to the bed. It was the breath of God, he told us, and it didn't let him up off the bed for three full hours. Well, we thought we needed to get some help after that and we decided to go see the minister of our church, even though Rex didn't much like him. And I guess we would've, but nothing like it ever happened again. The problem . . . if you could call it that . . . just went away all by itself."

"Or he just stopped talking about it," said Rex, sitting in the chair catercorner to Sheila and Ellen. He took a sip of coffee while gazing meaningfully at Sheila over the rim of the cup. In his blue-and-white seersucker suit, he made Ellen think of the country doctor in a William Carlos Williams story she couldn't quite recall; she wished he would simply take charge of things and tell everybody what they should do.

"I think we would've known it if that had been the case, Rex," said Sheila. "Upset as he used to get."

"Maybe," said Rex, "and maybe not."

Sheila pointedly turned toward Ellen and away from Rex, as if to cut off any further challenges from that direction. "How long have Bonnie and him been sleeping?" she asked.

Ellen explained that Pastor had finally got to sleep around seven o'clock, and that Bonnie had gone back to bed after putting in calls to the Vandorpes and to the church.

"Oh, what did she tell the people at the church?" asked Sheila.

"I think she just told them Pastor had come down with something during the night and wouldn't be able to preach," answered Ellen.

"Well, that's true enough, I guess," said Sheila. "For the life of me I can't see where he gets it from. I mean, we made sure he went to Sunday school when he was a boy, that sort of thing, but Rex and me weren't anything like . . . well, we were just normal, if you know what I mean . . . normal church-goers. I'm not at all sure Bonnie needs this kind of excitement right now, what with her —"

She stopped, put her hand over her mouth, and looked apologetically at Rex. Rex stared back at her and shook his head, but Ellen smiled and told them that she and Morris knew about the baby.

"Oh," cried Sheila, putting her hand now over her heart, "I am so glad! Pastor and Bonnie had sworn us to secrecy, so we couldn't say anything about it to y'all when we met you . . . and that was *hard*."

She leaned forward and reached for the coffeepot, but Ellen quickly intervened and replenished Sheila's cup herself.

"I'll just go freshen this up," said Ellen, even though the pot was only about half empty.

On her way to the kitchen, she stopped and knocked at Morris's door. He opened it a crack, standing behind it and tilting his head to one side, affording her a partial view of his face. "What in the world are you *do-ing?*" she whispered.

"What do you *think* I'm doing?" he said, mimicking Ellen's vehement stage whisper. "I'm getting dressed."

She pushed on the door and he stepped

back to allow her inside, where she saw that he was in fact fully dressed except for shoes. He wore another in his series of below-the-knee shorts and short-sleeved checked sport shirts. "They've been here for nearly half an hour," she said. "Macy hasn't come back from mass yet, Bonnie's still sleeping, and I'm wondering if you plan to emerge any time soon and help me."

"Do calm yourself," said Morris. "And give me that pot of coffee before you hurl it somewhere and scald somebody."

She pulled the pot away from his outstretched hand. "I've got to go and make more," she said. "They drink it like . . . like I don't know what. I wonder if you'd be kind enough to put on some shoes and go out to the porch and *talk* to them."

"All right," said Morris, "but in all frankness I can't quite figure out what they're doing here."

He moved to the bed, where he sat down and began to pull on his sandals.

"They're here because Bonnie asked them to come," said Ellen.

"I know that," he said, "but I don't know why. He's not a child, you know."

"At around six a.m.," said Ellen, "and with him crying like a baby, it seemed like a good idea."

440

"I suppose," said Morris. "Isn't that your traveling outfit you're wearing? Has there been a change of plans? Are we leaving a day early?"

"No," said Ellen. "I mean, yes, these are my traveling clothes . . . and no, there hasn't been a change of plans. I just reached for what was easiest, Morris. What possible difference can it make?"

"Well, it's just that you were wearing that last Tuesday, the last time you saw the Vandorpes," he said. "You don't mind their thinking you own only one thing?"

"I'm worried to death," she said. "I'll probably lose sleep over it . . . if I ever have an opportunity."

"God, I know," he said, falling backward onto the bed like a rag doll and staring at the ceiling. "Are you as exhausted as I am? I'm utterly fried."

"Morris," she said, "I imagine I'm more exhausted than you are, since I've had even less sleep. And I refuse to do this all by myself, so will you please get up and go out to the porch."

She opened the door.

He sat up and looked at her, squinting. "But tell me what you really think, Ellen," he said. "What are we actually dealing with?"

She moved into the open doorway, where she shook her head and shrugged. "I honestly don't know," she said. "But I'm not sure we can very well leave and go back home tomorrow."

"Oh, of course we can leave tomorrow," said Morris.

"How can you be so certain?"

"Just ask Bonnie," said Morris, standing and starting to move toward the door. "Just see what Bonnie says."

In the kitchen, as she sat at the table and waited for the new pot of coffee to brew, Ellen returned to the image of Pastor and Bonnie in the master bedroom, Pastor weeping and rocking on the edge of the bed, and she could feel herself resigning from the job of managing, worrying about, or in any manner interfering in Bonnie's life. She felt her heart and soul shrinking from it, and she was suddenly overtaken by a longing to be home, in her own house, in the company of her own husband and child. She knew she was suffering from a lack of sleep, and also a bit hung over from last night's wine and cognac, but she felt herself retreating heart and soul from Point Clear and all the unfinished business it represented, past, present, and future. By way of a roundabout path — one she didn't especially care to review — she seemed to have decided (though it didn't feel exactly like a decision) simply to leave things be. She recalled Dan's saying on the telephone that when she returned home they would plan a couple of things with Willie before school started. Impossible to think that Willie would be entering the eighth grade, growing minute by minute toward independence . . . and what, she asked herself, was she doing *here?*

Of course Morris had been right; Bonnie would want them to leave tomorrow morning as planned. The question of staying longer had arisen in Ellen's mind earlier, as she witnessed the daybreak drama in the master bedroom and again as she fetched food and drink and consulted with Bonnie about what to do, what phone calls to make, and so forth. But once Bonnie finally got Pastor to sleep, Ellen thought she'd seen in her young sister's face the answer: Bonnie had straightened the covers over Pastor and stood for a moment gazing down at him, as if to drink in his extraordinary beauty, the passionate angel in repose; she tiptoed away from the bed and closed the shutters at the nearby window, where gray light was falling through the slats; she moved to Ellen, who waited bleary-eyed on the vanity bench, took her hands and pulled her up, smiled warmly, hugged her, and whispered, "I never have shown you what I wore at my wedding." At the time, it hadn't even surprised Ellen, for it seemed only the next tiny creak of a slow-grinding wheel of abnormality. Bonnie led her to the walk-in closet and switched on the light inside. She found a certain navy blue hanging bag, unzipped it, and produced a beautiful knee-length dress of white silk, with a band of pearl-strewn lace at the neckline and individual pearls sewn into the bodice like little white stars. She allowed Ellen to hold the dress as she reached into the bottom of the bag and removed a veil, a burst of fine white net fanning from a central flower of lace. "Isn't it lovely?" Bonnie whispered, touching the lace petals with her fingertips. Whatever had happened to Pastor, something had also happened to Bonnie. She'd been called to the cause of him with absolute abandon, the way a mother sets aside all other concerns for a gravely sick child. She was without ambivalence, and even the nature of his experience gave her no pause; its element of the supernatural only drew her all the more thoroughly. Pastor was unusual, different from everyone else, his gift the source and object of her devotion.

For Ellen and Morris to linger around the edges of this scene would only cloud an otherwise entirely clear — entirely clarified — picture.

"Well," said Morris to the Vandorpes, on the porch, "if *I* had wandered into the living room at four a.m. and found Jesus of Nazareth standing by the old grandfather clock, I would've had a few questions for him. Unfortunately, I slept through the whole thing."

Morris noticed that while Rex appeared adequately amused (he'd gone crinkly around the eyes), Sheila looked as if she'd taken a bite of something unexpectedly fishy. Was Morris ridiculing Pastor's alleged episode? Did he mean to lampoon Pastor's status as a bona fide religious ecstatic? Apparently, she couldn't quite tell, and in the face of such a various audience, Morris's only idea was to push ahead. "You know, the clock is frozen at four-ten," he said. "It appears to be fully wound, but it simply won't go. It's as if the works have somehow locked."

"How very peculiar!" said Sheila, turning quickly to Rex and back to Morris. "That gives me chills."

Rex, who now sat next to Sheila on the

rattan couch, reached behind her and delivered one of his one-armed squeezes. "Well, I reckon if the Lord broke it," he said, winking at Morris, "He'll just have to come back again tonight and fix it."

"I hope so," said Morris. "It would seem the responsible thing to do."

Sheila turned again toward Rex and pushed him away with both her hands. "You better be careful, Rex Vandorpe," she said. "There's some things you oughtn't to make jokes about."

"All I said —" began Rex.

"And besides," said Sheila, "if He did break that clock, I'm sure it was for a reason." To Morris she said, "What did Pastor say about it . . . I mean, what did he say specifically about the clock?"

"I'm afraid Pastor wasn't able to say very much," answered Morris. "He was too . . . overcome."

Sheila pressed her lips together, narrowed her eyes, and nodded, a mask of pained compassion suggesting that she was not entirely unacquainted with certain forms of rapture.

"I hope he'll have more to tell us when he wakes up," Morris went on. "I imagine the injury to the clock was a kind of collateral damage, though intentional mischief isn't totally out of the question. You know, there are accounts of such things."

"Of what such things?" asked Sheila, and Morris observed that she now looked at him with the unthreatened curiosity of a person viewing an exotic plant.

"Well, not in the Bible, of course," Morris said. "But elsewhere, among the myriad texts that didn't make it into the Bible, there are accounts of Jesus using his supernatural powers . . . especially when he was young . . . to wreak all kinds of havoc. You know the famous gap in the biography, between infancy and thirty-something — well, except for the scene in the temple at the age of twelve, where he sets the Pharisees straight about a thing or two — apparently the rest of his childhood was purposefully expurgated. Apparently he was the Original Holy Terror. Seems, for example, he was keen on killing other children. He killed one child for no other reason than that the child was running and bumped him in the shoulder. Rather extreme, I'd say, even if he did sometimes raise them back from the dead afterward. More distressing to me personally, he also killed a couple of his school-teachers, for giving lessons he judged to be false."

As Morris had spoken the last sentence or

two, Ellen stepped onto the porch with a fresh pot of coffee and refilled the Vandorpes' empty cups. "Who are you-all talking about?" she now said, cheerfully, and placed the pot in the middle of the little barn-wood table.

"We're talking about Whom," said Morris, smiling. "With a capital *W.*"

Rex looked at his wristwatch, reached for his cup, and said, "Ellen, thank you, sweetheart. Now tell us, what's your best guess about when those two are gonna get out of bed?"

"I don't know," said Ellen, taking the chair opposite Morris. "But don't you think we could wake them pretty soon?"

"I think we could," said Shelia. "I'm just about beside myself with waiting. I'm dying to *talk* to him."

Morris, feeling more slighted than petty, thought Rex's tack had been to dismiss him out of hand, and he wondered if Ellen mightn't have been right about what she'd suggested in the library a few days ago — perhaps Morris did want all roads to lead to himself. He and Pastor had been varyingly but ongoingly at odds during their stay in Point Clear, and despite any amount of complaining on Morris's part, perhaps (he thought now) he'd not truly minded being at the heart of a domestic squabble. He'd already imagined removing himself from it physically — a few hours hence, on an airplane to Boston — but leaving behind a kind of echo of himself, to be reckoned with in his absence. Now Pastor had pulled a stunt sufficiently melodramatic not only to derail the falling action of Morris's daydream but also to enlist the overwrought attentions of the entire household. When Ellen had awakened Morris earlier, astonishingly at around five-thirty in the morning, and told him about Pastor's mystical ordeal, he'd desired only to go back to sleep. Morris's subsequent visit to the master bedroom had been brief, for the scene had made him exceedingly uneasy. He thought it possessed the unsavory aspect of a circus sideshow, with Pastor, inconsolable and gibbering at the center; Bonnie, finally settled into the plummy role that had eluded her for a decade of auditions in New York; and everyone else, including Macy and even the four-legged animals, looking on from the peripheral gloom. And for Morris it had raised the immanent sideshow question: What was more depraved, the exhibitionism or the voyeurism? While these judgments, in review, still seemed to hold water, Morris wondered if beneath them crouched an infantile frustration (rekindled by the disregard of the father figure, Rex) at being cast out of the spotlight. He comforted himself with the idea that for all his narcissism he, unlike Pastor, wouldn't have stooped to invoke a Manifestation of the Christ to call attention to himself.

Macy now arrived at the interior porch door, dressed as always in one of her floral smocks but sans apron. She hung deferentially in the doorway as she greeted the Vandorpes and seemed to Morris unusually anxious. Sheila, somehow agitated by the arrival of the other woman, said, "Oh, Macy, I understand you're the one who discovered Pastor last night . . . I mean, you found him right after —"

"Yes, ma'am," said Macy. "Something woke me up. Is there anything I can get for y'all? Have you had anything to eat yet?"

Morris knew (because Macy had told him, in whispers, in the early morning shadows of the master bedroom) that Macy in fact had been awakened by Pastor's own voice calling out to her for help in a dream, a dream in which he'd fallen into a deep well and was drowning. So vivid it was, and so vivid Pastor's cry for help, Macy had left her bed and her apartment to walk through the house. She'd found Pastor kneeling and sobbing on the floor of the hallway, near the entrance to the living room, and she could tell right away that something strange had happened, something — she'd said to Morris — *special*. Morris, in his pajamas, had absorbed as best he could Macy's account of events and then turned to leave the master bedroom. Macy, still in her nightgown and robe, followed him to the door. "Here's the oddest thing about it," she whispered, touching Morris's arm. "When I remember it, I see the whole thing happening in bright sunlight. But it was before dawn and not a single light was on in the house. Isn't that the oddest thing?"

Now Macy's deliberate deflection of Sheila's question indicated to Morris a reluctance to be interviewed, and since to him it felt like opposition to the Vandorpes, he decided to support her. He quickly said, No, they'd not yet had anything to eat, that he for one was famished, and he would come to the kitchen with Macy and help throw something together. With that, he stood, glanced back at Ellen, and started for the door.

"Macy," called Ellen, before Morris had quite reached the hall. "We're thinking about waking Bonnie and Pastor. I imagine they'll want some kind of breakfast, even though —"

"Oh, they're awake already," said Macy. "Bonnie met me in the mudroom just now when I was coming into the house. She put in Pastor's order for scrambled eggs and sausage. I don't guess anybody else wants eggs at this time of the day, do they?"

Five minutes later, Morris returned to the porch and found Ellen there alone, standing near the screen door and staring out at the bay. When he moved next to her and put his arm around her waist, she leaned her head against his shoulder and sighed, deeply and audibly. They remained like that for a few seconds, silent, and it seemed to Morris they stood on the prow of an enormous ship inching into port; he closed his eyes and felt the hesitant sway of the boards under his feet. At last Ellen said, "I thought you were helping Macy."

"I intended to," he said, "but she told me she'd do better without my getting in her way. Have Sheila and Rex gone in . . . *there?*"

"Yes," said Ellen, and sighed again.

"Did you see Bonnie?"

"Only for a second," she said. "She came out here to get them; then took them into the bedroom."

"Rather like an ostiary," said Morris.

"What's that?"

"A doorkeeper," said Morris. "The lowliest of ranks. Opens and closes the doors of the church."

"It's very confusing," said Ellen. Then, after a moment, she lifted her head from his shoulder and said, "Since I'm not going to be needed for a while, I think I'll go take a nap."

"You don't want to eat first?"

Ellen shuddered and said, "I may never eat again. I'm not the least bit hungry."

"I know," said Morris. "Neither am I. The very idea of food repels me."

"I thought a minute ago you said you were famished."

"I lied."

"But why?"

"I don't know," said Morris. "Something about the situation, I suppose. Do you ever walk into a room and everything's just so perfect, you feel an urge to put something out of place? It was like that. I felt an urge to tell a lie. Not a big one. A little one, and I hate little lies."

"I also thought you liked perfect rooms," said Ellen. "I think of you as someone who loves extreme order."

"Well, yes," said Morris, "I do. But my

own. . . . I love my own order."

He followed her into the house, and once she'd gone to her room he retired to his. He closed the door and leaned against it, gazing about the room as if he meant to assess it in some way. He then went to the closet, found his suitcase, and set about the business of packing.

The rented green Volvo had sat in the yard for five days untouched, which seemed a waste; Morris was completely ready for tomorrow's journey, so he decided to slip out through the French doors and escape for a few minutes the property and its inhabitants. Out of the oyster-shell drive, he pulled onto the highway behind a dusty black pickup truck with a bumper sticker that read REAL MEN PRAY, and only two minutes later, after he'd turned onto Dixie Road, he passed a large billboard that read GOT FAITH? Something about the uniform grayness of the day made these details seem more implicating than their authors even intended them to be. He had no particular destination in mind, and as he increased his speed, up to over sixty, he felt a dim (and dimly familiar) satisfaction at knowing he was headed east, inland and away from the house.

He passed three small (and also dimly familiar) red-brick houses he judged to have been erected in the fifties, sad little boxes with picture windows, carports, and camellia bushes, and then a thing came into view that made him put on the brakes. He pulled the car onto the grassy shoulder of the road, came to a stop, and found the button that lowered the passenger-side window. Set back about a hundred feet from the pavement rose a huge contemporary monstrosity built of pink-colored bricks, with a roof that swooped in two curved lines, back to front, upward to a peak, front and center, where two tall narrow panels of smoked glass formed the backdrop for a brilliant white cross. On the neatly trimmed lawn, a marquee:

THE CHURCH OF THE BLESSED
HUNGER
PASTOR VANDORPE, SENIOR MINISTER
MIKE JORDAN, PASTORAL MINISTER
SUNDAY WORSHIP 9:30 & 11 A.M.
"THUS SAITH THE LORD"
SUNDAY SCHOOL 10 A.M.
ALL WELCOME

The building was flanked on either side by two enormous parking lots, and it appeared that an asphalt driveway led to yet another lot quite a distance beyond, in back. Only four or five cars remained, parked to the right of the sanctuary, near the side entry, and no sign of people, but Morris thought the place still hummed with the energy of singing and praise, jazz combos and puppet shows. "Well, well," he said to himself, and then began to move the car slowly back onto the road.

As he reached the mouth of the asphalt driveway, he quickly turned into it, for a second building had come into view, farther from the road and resting behind a stand of tall pines. When he'd arrived at the cracked concrete sidewalk that led to the building's front entrance, he stopped again, got out, and stood next to the open car door. He gazed at the old one-story structure of ocher bricks and double-hung windows with yellow shades; a hand-painted sign next to the entrance read:

CHURCH OF THE BLESSED HUNGER
CHRISTIAN FELLOWSHIP HALL

"Impossible," Morris whispered, suddenly invaded by the two-headed memory of the dread with which he'd entered this very same building each morning, nine months out of twelve as a boy, and the relief with which he'd left it each afternoon. It was where he and Ellen had attended elementary school, and where, to his awe and hidden sense of betrayal, Ellen had managed somehow to fit in. "Will wonders never cease," he said now, as he got back into the car and shut the door.

When he'd turned the car around and started out the church driveway, he recalled another August day some twenty-nine years ago, when he and Ellen were to leave for Connecticut to attend boarding school; his getting ready too early and waiting in the backseat of his father's Cadillac and, most acutely, the great windfall, the miraculous prospect of salvation.

When Morris entered the kitchen, Macy was putting down bowls of food for the cat and dog, whose morning meals had apparently been forgotten in all the hubbub. "Macy, my Macy," he said, "Earth Mother, feeding the nation. Give me your tired, your hungry —"

"Where did you go?" she said, rather crossly. "He's been asking for you."

"Oh, dear," said Morris, and left the kitchen through the swinging door.

Halfway up the hall, Ellen called to him from inside the library. She was sitting in one of the two gold wing chairs that faced the fireplace. "Where did you go?" she said to him as he entered the room. "He's been asking for you."

"So I hear," said Morris, taking the other chair and observing that Ellen appeared a bit less haggard than she had earlier. "What are you doing in here?"

"That's a good question," she said. "Waiting for you, I guess . . . vaguely."

"Where are the Vandorpes?" he asked.

"They just left, five minutes ago," she answered.

"Left?"

"I'm not sure what happened," she said. "I dozed for a little while, and when I got up, they were leaving already. It felt . . . awkward."

"Did they seem angry?"

"More sad than angry," she said. "They asked me to tell you good-bye. Where did you go?"

"Oh, I just took the poor rent car for a spin," said Morris. "It was looking so neglected."

"Where to?"

"Nowhere special."

"Nowhere special, or you won't say?"

"I won't say."

"Why not?"

"Because it's delightful, ironic, and amazing, but finally trivial, and I want to hold on to it for a while before sharing."

Ellen smiled, almost, Morris thought, a smile of approval. "Okay," she said.

"Now, what does this *he's been asking for you* mean?" said Morris.

"I don't know," she said. "Bonnie only said that he wanted to see you, and I should tell you, when I saw you, to please come to the bedroom."

"How does he seem? He's not still bawling his eyes out, is he?"

"No," said Ellen. "He seems calm but — I don't know — worried."

"Worried?"

"Well, wouldn't you be?"

"You mean, if I'd been having religious visions."

"Yes."

"I suppose so," said Morris, "but I don't think I believe in religious visions . . . or at least I don't think I believe in the ones that come to religious people. What about you?"

"So far," she said, "the only thing that's completely clear to me is that he's not pretending, and I'm grateful. I mean, I'm grateful that *something's* completely clear. Now, what are we going to do about *that?*"

She indicated with her eyes the marble

urn on the mantel.

"I rather like it where it is," said Morris.

"Do you really think we could just do nothing?"

"I don't see why not," he said. "There'd be something interestingly reciprocal about doing nothing."

After a moment, Ellen uttered a neutral *Mmm,* then said, "And do you really think we can get on that plane tomorrow morning? I feel I should be concerned about Bonnie, even if I can't quite stir it up."

"Bonnie's going to be fine," said Morris. "She's going to have babies with astonishing midnight-blue eyes and long black eyelashes. She's going to become a star in community theater and sing the lead in — I don't know — *Once Upon a Mattress* or something."

"I can't tell if that's real optimism speaking or just a kind of expediency."

Morris thought for a moment. "I surprise even myself," he said, "but I believe it's real optimism."

Just then Bonnie appeared at the library door, still in her nightclothes and looking, Morris thought, frazzled, yet almost frazzled by design and very beautiful. As she'd done a few days before, she wandered into the room and made for his lap, but now, rather than flinging herself down and draping herself over him, she settled herself gingerly and leaned into his chest; she took each of his hands, one at a time, pulled his arms forward, and wrapped them around her waist. He noticed, too, as she placed her hands over his, that her choice of sleepwear seemed to come from the Sunday Best department, a long sleeveless affair with ruffles and tiny pink embroidered flowers sewn randomly here and there. If Pastor had taken to his bed, she'd taken to it with him, and apparently she meant to bring some style to the enterprise.

"Where have you been?" she said, and tilted her head backward to kiss the underside of his chin. "I haven't seen you all day, Morris, and you're leaving tomorrow."

Morris cast Ellen a knowing glance across the top of Bonnie's head. "I took a drive," he said. "What did Pastor say to Rex and Sheila to make them leave so abruptly?"

Bonnie didn't move an inch but Morris thought he felt her stop breathing. She said nothing for quite a few seconds; then she sighed and said softly, "It was a mistake to call them."

"He didn't want to see them," said Morris.

"Not even a little bit," she said.

"Well, Ellen said it seemed like a good idea at the time."

Bonnie now sat up, turned, and looked at Ellen. "Did you say that?"

"Of course it seemed like a good idea," Ellen said. "He was inconsolable."

"Thank you," said Bonnie, and then slumped again against Morris. "He wasn't rude to them," she said, after another pause. "He just told them he wished I hadn't gotten them involved. He made it sound like he was sorry to have inconvenienced them . . . sorry they had to drive all the way up here . . . but I'm afraid it still hurt their feelings. Especially Sheila's. In retrospect, though, I see how — under the circumstances — he wouldn't want a lot of people filing in and out of the master bedroom."

"They're not people, Bonnie," said Ellen. "They're his parents."

"I know," she said. "But do you see what I mean? I mean, from Pastor's point of view. On the other hand, Morris, he really wants to talk to you."

"I'm honored," said Morris.

"I suppose you're being sarcastic," said Bonnie.

"I suppose I am," he said.

"If you were more humble you wouldn't need to resort to sarcasm," she said.

"I'm sure I don't know what that means," said Morris.

"Well, what *I* mean," said Bonnie, "is that I know all this must seem weird to you, but I wish you would go in and be sweet to him. He wants to talk to you, and you're only here for another eighteen hours, and I wish you could just be sweet to him . . . for me."

"Oh, all right," said Morris. "I just hope he doesn't start to cry again."

"But Morris," said Ellen, "you've never been one to shy away from tears. You've never minded it when —"

"I hate it when *men* cry," said Morris. "I find it very unnecessary and . . . upsetting."

Morris had of course expected to find Pastor in the bed — sitting up with many pillows piled behind his back — but he hadn't expected him to be shirtless. His skin glowed pink from yesterday's beach outing, and in the dark aquamarine room, drenched now with the soft light of an overcast day and smelling faintly of roses, Pastor appeared to have been recently hand-bathed, perhaps even sprinkled ritualistically with rose water. He seemed to Morris both younger and older, changed in more than one direction. He smiled at Morris, the dewy-eyed smile of someone greeting a long-lost friend. He extended a perfect bare arm, inviting a hug, and as Morris leaned toward him, Pastor put a hand at the back of Morris's head and drew him into a bit more skin contact than Morris wanted. Morris retreated from the embrace with a mixture of apprehensions, including something left over from the alarming scuffle in the sand at Dauphin Island.

As if Pastor somehow intuited this, he said, "I'm sorry about that nonsense on the beach yesterday. I hope you can forgive me. It was thoughtless and foolish. I haven't been myself the last couple of days. Why don't you pull that rocking chair over here by the bed so we can talk."

Once Morris was settled he said, "Don't worry, Pastor, I forgive you. How are you?"

"I'm all shook up," said Pastor, holding out his hands palms upward, as if to say, *Look at me.*

But Morris saw in his mind's eye the marquee on the lawn of the Church of the Blessed Hunger and pictured little white letters pressed into the black felt:

SUNDAY WORSHIP 9:30 & 11 A.M.
"ALL SHOOK UP"

"*You* shook me up," added Pastor.

464

"Well, I'm not sure what you're referring to," said Morris, "but whatever I might have done to . . . shake you up . . . I didn't mean to."

Pastor tilted his head to one side and peered at Morris from beneath his eyebrows, a look, inadvertently, more enchanting than incredulous.

"Well, I certainly didn't want to," said Morris.

Pastor repeated the look.

"Well, I didn't come here with any such intention."

"That I believe," said Pastor.

"And besides," said Morris, "I assumed it was your . . . vision, or whatever you call it, that —"

"No doubt," said Pastor. "But you were my John the Baptist, Morris. Crying in the wilderness."

"I'm afraid you lift me to a place way above my talents or capacities," said Morris. "Which I don't especially mind as long as I don't have to *dress* like John the Baptist."

Pastor smiled and blinked and folded his hands in his lap, a mingling of gestures that Morris found insanely moving.

"And as long as I'm not beheaded at the

whim of some slutty palace dancer," Morris added.

Pastor looked away, toward the window, his face growing serious. He said, "Morris, He was here. He was definitely here, but I don't know what to make of it. I want you to help me figure out what it means."

"Oh, Pastor, how would I know what it means?" said Morris. "I was sound asleep."

Pastor, silent, conveyed with his eyes his disappointment. Morris could see what he already knew, that he would be unable to entertain Pastor's ordeal with as much gravity as Pastor wanted. Pastor reached for the glass of water on the nearby nightstand and took a drink. He looked at Morris and said, "You don't believe me, do you. I can tell that you don't believe me."

"Don't be tiresome, Pastor," said Morris. "Of course I believe you. If I didn't believe you, I would have to think you were lying, wouldn't I."

"But you don't believe He was really here."

"I'm sure everything happened exactly the way you experienced it," said Morris.

"Which isn't the same as saying I experienced everything exactly the way it happened."

"That's far too tricky for me," said Morris. "I don't think this is the sort of thing we need to split hairs over."

"If I'm sitting in my car," said Pastor, "not moving . . . and a car next to me starts to move . . . I might have the *experience* of my own car moving. But that doesn't mean my car really moved. And what I'm saying to you is, *He was really here.* He stood out yonder in the living room next to that old clock just as real as you sitting there in that rocking chair. I just don't know how to interpret it, Morris. I'm struggling with what it means."

"Well, what does it usually mean?" said Morris. "It's not as if you're the first person it's ever happened to. You can hardly pick up a tabloid newspaper without reading an item about somebody who's seen the face of Jesus somewhere."

"I didn't see Bigfoot and I didn't see Elvis on my refrigerator, Morris," said Pastor. "I saw *Him.*"

"Okay," said Morris. "You saw *Him,* but —"

"And He didn't look like any picture of Him I ever saw. He was a little wiry thing, about five feet tall and dark-skinned. I saw *Him.*"

Pastor's description gave Morris pause. "Really," he said.

"Tough as leather too," said Pastor, nodding. "Short curly hair and a little scraggly beard."

"That's very interesting and surprising," said Morris. "But I —"

"And He spoke to me," said Pastor.

"Oh," said Morris. "What did He say?"

"I don't know," answered Pastor, shaking his head, almost in disgust, as if this was his main frustration. "It was just a word, in a foreign language. I had a feeling He was saying something about the old grandfather clock."

"Hmm," said Morris. "I wonder how one says *I broke it,* in Aramaic."

Pastor looked at him blankly, so Morris went on.

"Still, Pastor, I return to the former question: What does it usually mean, this kind of . . . sighting or . . . visitation?"

Morris thought he noted in Pastor's face a glimmer of the hurt look he'd seen there yesterday. After a moment, Pastor said, "Well, generally it's a conversion experience."

"So there you have it," said Morris. "You had a conversion experience."

"But, Morris, I'm already a Christian."

"Are you sure?"

"Of course I'm sure. Through and

through."

"But are you *really* sure?"

"Why would you ask me such a thing?" said Pastor. "Of course I'm really sure."

"Well, then, I guess you had a *pointless* conversion experience," said Morris. "There's nothing in you that needs converting, Pastor, nothing that needs to change. It didn't mean anything. You can go in peace now."

He hadn't intended to sound quite so impatient, though impatient was what he felt, impatient and a touch exasperated. It was exactly the sort of dialogue he'd hoped to avoid, and to make matters much worse, Pastor now appeared wounded. His eyes welled with tears. Soon tears actually sprang from his eyes and landed on the white sheet that covered his lap. Morris had never seen tears actually spring from anybody's eyes; if one of his students had written it in a story, he would have called it overstatement. He was startled, and he noticed too that a tear had landed disconcertingly at the edge of Pastor's navel, hung there glistening among the downy hairs on his stomach.

"*Now* look who's crying in the wilderness," said Morris, without conviction. He averted his own eyes, then closed them and lowered his head. "Please don't cry," he said at last. "I don't like it. I don't. . . ."

When next he looked at Pastor, Pastor was hanging his head and letting out a series of sobs that sounded more like coughing than crying. Morris leaned forward in the rocker and said, "I'll go get Bonnie."

"No, don't," said Pastor, not lifting his head but extending one hand in Morris's direction. "Don't leave me."

Morris stared at Pastor's outstretched hand and felt himself grow cold. He recognized it as the moment in which he might move to the bed and comfort Pastor, and he hoped above all that the moment would pass quickly. It occurred to him that if Pastor had wanted someone to hold his hand, he shouldn't have chased away his mama and daddy — a reflection so harsh and bleak it stunned even Morris himself. And again, as if Pastor had intuited Morris's thoughts, he sat up straight, took another long drink from the water glass, and composed himself. He cleared his throat; Morris half expected him to pull the sheet up around his shoulders, compromised and humiliated by rejection. His beautiful face was a mess, blotchy and shut-down, and Morris could see that his nose badly needed blowing. Suddenly a shocking grid of light and shadow fell onto the carpet next to the

470

rocking chair — sunlight shot through the slats of the shuttered window — then faded away. This brought to Morris's mind the passing of time, and he knew that in the near and distant future, he would review this scene and feel heartbroken at not having been somehow more effective in it, and at not being able, from that future vantage, to revise it. He leaned forward again, reached into the hip pocket of his shorts, and pulled out a clean white handkerchief. He meant only to offer it as a means of tending to the sorry state of Pastor's nose, but he found himself unfurling it and waving it in the air like a flag of truce. He moved to the bed and sat down, facing Pastor, whose hands were now balled into fists at his sides. Morris took hold of one, unclasped it finger by finger, and placed the handkerchief in it.

"You need to blow your nose," he said, and soon he went on to tell Pastor about the drive he'd taken earlier down Dixie Road, about coming upon the church, and about the amazing coincidence involving the old schoolhouse from his miserable boyhood. Pastor wept a bit more throughout, but it seemed he truly couldn't help it, and Morris, to his surprise, found he didn't especially mind.

CHAPTER 13

Around one o'clock on the Friday before Labor Day, Ellen, barefoot and wearing a long white T over her swimsuit, sat at the kitchen table in the Wellfleet house; spiral notebook and pencil in hand, she was doing what she called "doodling," tinkering with some lines of a new poem. She and Willie had driven down from Cambridge earlier that morning, and Dan, who'd left Cambridge later in his own car, had only just arrived about half an hour ago. He'd given Richard a ride down from Brookline, and the two of them had stopped to buy a stockpile of groceries, which Dan was now putting away, occasionally pausing to read the fine-print Nutrition Facts on a label. To his back, Ellen said, "Are you sure you don't want me to help you?"

"I'm sure," he said, without turning around. "This way I know where everything is. Now read to me."

"Read to you?" she said. "Read what?"

"Whatever you've got written down there," he said.

"It's nothing," she said. "Just fragments . . . not ready for —"

"Let me hear it," he said, noisily folding a paper sack and shoving it into a drawer.

"It doesn't even make sense yet," said Ellen. *"The earth scent of geranium . . . the year's turned . . . watch for the sudden thaw . . . ice that splinters under a skater . . . a rise in the draw."*

After a silence, in which Dan placed four cans of chicken broth on a shelf, he turned toward her and said, "That's it?"

Ellen shrugged and said, "I told you."

"Read it again," he said.

She reread the lines.

"I like it," said Dan. "It's sort of what's happening now, isn't it. I mean, I know you're writing about spring there, but . . . I love the way it makes me see red, green, and white."

Ellen laughed as he passed her on his way to the refrigerator. After a moment, she felt his arms encircling her from behind and then his lips on the top of her head. "I'm really glad you're back," he said.

She took one of his hands and kissed it. "I'm really glad to be back," she said, smiling up at him.

He released her and returned to the groceries at the counter opposite the table. Facing away from her again, he said, "I don't mean just from Point Clear. I mean I'm glad you're . . . you know . . . *back.*"

She waited for a few seconds, until he turned toward her, and then said, "I *know* what you mean. And thank you . . . for everything."

"You're welcome," he said, and looked past her through the garden windows. "Is that Morris out there in the garden?"

She stood and moved to the windows, where she stopped briefly, then went to Dan and kissed him on the mouth. "Yes," she said, "that would be Morris. And do you know what *I* mean . . . by everything?"

She took the dirt path from the kitchen stoop into the garden and sat next to Morris on the wooden bench, from which they could see, past the tall asters bundled with kite string, down the slope of golden waist-high grasses, the glare of the salt marsh, nearly full and shimmering in the afternoon sun. The morning fog (through which Ellen and Willie had driven earlier, from Cambridge) had burned off, and now the day was very hot. Morris, who'd arrived in

474

Wellfleet four days ahead of everyone else, had, in Dan's words, "gone native," which meant he'd developed the habit of parading around in nothing but a tiny navy-blue Speedo and flip-flops. This habit went unaltered by anyone else's arrival — not that of Ellen and Willie; not that, more recently, of Dan and Richard; and not even, only fifteen minutes earlier, that of Gaston, the chimney sweep, who'd come to repair the damper in the upstairs fireplace. Since Tuesday, Morris had spent most of his solitary time lying in the sun, reading in preparation for his fall classes, and he was very brown. The last several minutes, he'd been rapt in thought, which had somehow made him feel physically heavy, and the slats of the bench had left red bars across his back and on the undersides of his thighs. Ellen passed him a glass of lemonade with seltzer water, which he accepted with gratitude and asked where everybody had disappeared to.

"You're the one who disappeared," she said. "Everyone else is still in the house. Richard's napping on the porch, Dan's putting away groceries, and Willie's upstairs with Gaston, helping him fix the broken damper."

"We're hardly going to need any fires,"

said Morris.

"Yes, well, brace yourself, darling," said Ellen, "summer's almost over. How's it been for you, down here alone?"

"Wonderful," he said. "Lonely at night —"

"Yes."

"But even that had a kind of wonderfulness to it. It was so quiet and . . . I don't know . . . sharp."

"You've had the *space* you felt you needed?"

"Yes, thank you," he said.

"And Richard didn't mind being left alone again, so soon?"

"Not at all," said Morris. "He was relieved I didn't ask him to go back to Brookline so I could have Ipswich to myself. This was truly ideal. Everyone should have a sister with an antique Greek Revival on Cape Cod. And what about Cambridge, for you?"

"Very good," said Ellen. "The three of us did a kind of in-town vacation. Went to the science museum, went to Fenway for a game. Did takeout all week. Lay around at night watching horrible action movies on DVD."

"Why horrible?"

"Chosen by Willie," she said. "Well, not all horrible, but very . . . loud."

Just then, behind them, Dan pushed open

the kitchen's screen door and stepped onto the stoop. "I forgot to give you this," he called, waving a white envelope in his hand. "Came in the mail after you left this morning." He laid the envelope on the top step and went back inside.

Ellen walked to the stoop, retrieved the piece of mail, and returned to the garden bench. She passed the envelope into Morris's hands, a letter addressed to herself, with *and Morris* in parentheses after her name.

"Hmm," said Morris. "I don't suppose I mind *too* terribly being parenthetical. Though it does make me feel a little like your child . . . or perhaps your pet. Shall I open it?"

Ellen suggested he read it aloud, which he did:

Point Clear
    Sunday evening

Dear Ellen,
I'm afraid I have something sad to tell you. I should probably have called on the phone, but this is my coward's way of doing unpleasant things, I guess. Cricket died suddenly yesterday afternoon.

Here Morris paused, for about five seconds, to allow the two of them to absorb the news; he did not look up from the letter but began reading again:

Around 3 o'clock he came wandering into the bedroom where Pastor and I were in bed reading. He seemed to want to get up onto the bed with us, which he's never been allowed to do and which he's never even asked to do. Pastor said to go ahead and let him, so we did, and he just curled up at our feet and went to sleep. About 20 minutes later, I felt him shudder, the bed shook a little, and that was it. He didn't make a sound or anything, just that little shuddering thing and it was over. I insisted we take him to the animal hospital, even though Pastor said it was no use. The vet said he'd most likely had a heart attack and then talked about what a nice long life he'd had and how he hadn't suffered, etc. It's crazy how sad it makes me, but it feels like the end of something bigger, if you know what I mean. I feel sadder than when Daddy died, which I guess is terrible of me. Honestly, I think Macy's the one who's going to have the hardest time with it. And China has just moped around all day today, though she does a fair amount of moping anyway and I might be projecting. I stayed home from church this morning but Pastor was back in the pulpit, said there was no way he was going to miss two Sundays in a row. Even though he went to his office Wednesday and preached this morning, it has definitely not been business as usual. He's changed, and I think it's going to be awhile before I can say much more about exactly how. It's like his world has been turned upside down and he's figuring out how to proceed. He's even mentioned "going back to school," whatever that means, seminary I guess, though I'm not sure how he can do that and continue at the church. Symptomwise, he still cries easily. He cried at the vet's and then he went with me to the doctor on Friday and I had the sonogram and when we saw the little image of the baby on the screen he started crying, but I guess neither of those things is all that unusual. I felt like crying too, in both instances, but something about Pastor crying made me hold back. (BTW, the baby's fine and gender undetermined as yet.) Oh: I had to search and search before I found somebody who could fix the grandfather clock. Finally called a man in Mobile, scheduled an appointment for him to come to the house on Thurs., and Wed. night the old clock just started running again, spontaneously. I was on my way to the screen porch after supper and heard it chime, I went on out onto the porch and sat down, and about 30 seconds later I went, Oh, my God, the clock just chimed! All I had to do was adjust the hands to the right place, and then I called the clock man and told him not to come after all. I LOVED LOVED LOVED it that you and Morris came down. I know it wasn't perfect and a little weird at times but it meant everything to me that you came. More and more I realize what lucky people we are in life, not just to have everything we have materially but also to have each other, and I'm determined not to ever take any of this for granted. When you come back down in Feb., after the baby's born, I want us to talk some more about this. In the meantime, please share this letter with Morris and kiss him for me (and Richard) and yourself and sweet

Willie and Dan.

> All my love,
> Bonnie

P.S. Something you and M will find interesting: The other day I received a large box of papers in the mail from Mr. Barrie (you remember, Daddy's accountant). Said he was cleaning out his files. Mostly old tax returns, and guess what? Daddy's date of birth was July 12, not July 4. Wasn't that a silly thing to lie about, I mean his whole life? I guess his real birthday didn't feel important enough to him.

P.P.S. Ellen, I just want to mention this so you can consider it and then we'll talk about it on the phone. I'm thinking that your old room would be the best candidate for a nursery (because of its size and location), but I will definitely make other plans if you have even the smallest objection. Think about it and we'll talk.

Morris folded the letter, sighed, and said, "Well." He spied a photograph inside the envelope and took it out — a snapshot of Bonnie and Pastor on their wedding day. He passed it to Ellen and said, "They certainly make a lovely couple, you have to give them that."

"Yes," said Ellen. "You have to give them that."

Now he passed the folded letter to Ellen, and she put both it and the photo back into the envelope, which she then held in her lap. They sat in silence for quite a long time, and at last Morris sighed and repeated, "Well."

"Poor old Cricket," said Ellen.

"Mmm," said Morris. "Sort of like old married folks, when one dies and the other goes a few months after."

"We should phone her," Ellen said.

"Later," said Morris. "How do you feel about the room?"

"I love the idea," said Ellen. "I can't think of a better use for it."

"I think my room would be better actually," said Morris.

After a moment, Ellen said, "I've got to get out of the sun," but made no move to do so.

"Technically," said Morris, "*horticulturally,* it's only partial sun."

A neon-blue damselfly came and lit on Ellen's knee, perched there for a couple of seconds, and flew away. A fleeting breeze rattled the leaves in the nearby birch and bent the heads of the many coneflowers. At last, Ellen took out the photograph again, looked at it briefly, and returned it to the envelope. After another long silence, she said, "I wish you would put on some clothes, Morris. I'm worried that it might make Willie uncomfortable."

"I don't mind," said Morris, "but in my opinion it would be better if conformity flowed in the other direction . . . if the rest of you took some of your clothes *off.* You really are growing more and more conservative by the minute, Ellen."

"I'm sure you're right," she said. "I'm nervous . . . worried about the advent of Willie's teens."

"He already has everything he needs to survive," said Morris.

She looked at him and said, "What a sweet thing to say. Thank you."

"I didn't say it to be sweet," said Morris. "I meant it as a cold clinical observation of truth."

"What have you said to Richard about Point Clear?" she said.

"Funny you should ask," said Morris. "Amazingly very little. He keeps asking how it went in one form or another, and I seem to keep answering in one-word sentences.

It's very peculiar. What have you said to Dan?"

"I might've done better to confine myself to one-word sentences," she said. "I have the impression my answers have mostly perplexed him. Last night I felt very proud of myself when I finally managed to say that the visit, overall, had a very unfinished quality."

"And what did he say?"

"He said, *Hmm . . . an unfinished quality, huh?*"

"Well," said Morris, "I suppose we can comfort ourselves with the idea that some of our greatest works of art have an unfinished quality."

"Is that true?" said Ellen.

"I believe so," said Morris. "Think about it."

Ellen gazed out at the marsh, thinking, and at last said, "Yes, I guess that's true. But Point Clear . . . some of it's dreamlike too."

"Yes," said Morris. "And that's less true of great art, I think."

"What did you say to Richard, specifically about Pastor?"

"You mean specifically about the Mysterious Incident of the Clock?"

"Yes."

Morris bent forward and pulled a single blade from a tuft of chives near his feet. He tasted it thoughtfully, pinching it between his front teeth, then tossed it away. "Nothing," he said. "I haven't mentioned it."

"Me either," she said. "Why do you think that is? Are we protecting him?"

"I suppose," said Morris. "It would feel like a thing taken out of context, wouldn't it . . . and misrepresent him somehow."

"Exactly," said Ellen. Then, after a moment, "Well, maybe not exactly, but close. Do you want to go swimming?"

"I do want to go swimming," he said. "But it's odd of you to tell me to put on clothes one minute and then ask me to go swimming the next."

"I *feel* odd," she said. "Increasingly. Just ignore what I said before. Wear what you like . . . as little as you like."

"Do me a favor," said Gaston to Willie, at the hearth upstairs. "Bend down and look where I'm pointing the flashlight. You see that little pie-shaped piece there? Tell me, does it look bigger to you than this one I just took out of the box?"

Willie — dressed in baby-blue basketball shorts, basketball jersey, and basketball shoes, as if he were fresh off the court —

knelt on the hearthstones, lowered his head, and gazed up the chimney to the spot where Gaston shone the light. "Definitely," he said. "Definitely bigger."

Gaston switched off the flashlight and placed it on the hearth. He rested back on his heels and shook his head. "They sent me the wrong damn part," he said. He wiped sweat from his nose, leaving a smudge of soot in its place. "Actually, that's not true," he added. "I *ordered* the wrong damn part."

"What's wrong with the old one?" said Willie.

"Cracked," answered Gaston. "Probably happens once every two hundred years or so. It won't hold the damper rod, just lets it slip out."

He pushed on the rod, slid it into the notch where it was meant to catch, and then allowed the damper to slam shut with a clang. Willie watched as a blizzard of black snow fell into the grate. "See?" said Gaston.

"Well, it's not like we're needing any extra heat," said Willie.

"That's true enough," said Gaston.

"You can order another one . . . the right one."

"That's just what I'll do," said Gaston, putting the part back into its cardboard box.

"You must be getting ready for school. When do you start, on Tuesday?"

"Wednesday," said Willie, "but I've been ready for a while."

"Oh, you like school," said Gaston.

Willie shrugged his shoulders and nodded.

"I liked it too, when I was a boy," said Gaston. "I've got a grandson about your age, doesn't care for it at all."

"Where does he go?" asked Willie.

"Somewhere way the hell out in Fresno, California," said Gaston. "To tell you the truth, he was about six years old the last time I saw him. Could be he likes school just fine now. I haven't seen him since then."

"How come?" said Willie.

Gaston, whose blue work shirt had come undone all the way down to his chest, rebuttoned it and said, "I used to be a drinker, you see. Didn't do a very good job with my own boy. And when he grew up he didn't want to have anything to do with me. Got as far away from here as he could, and I don't blame him."

"You mean you were an alcoholic?" asked Willie.

Gaston nodded. "Still am," he said. "Always will be, but I haven't touched a drop in over eleven years."

"I have a couple of friends who are alco-holics," said Willie.

Gaston looked at him. "How old are you?" he said.

"Thirteen."

"How old are your alcoholic friends?"

"Thirteen."

"That's awful young."

Willie said, "I know."

"And what about you?"

"I don't drink," said Willie, shaking his head.

"Well, good," said Gaston. "Don't start is my advice."

"I figure I'll start when I go to college," Willie said.

"Put it off for as long as you can," said Gaston.

He stood and gave Willie a hand up from the hearth. "Now, I've got to go downstairs and tell your dad I ordered the wrong part."

"He won't mind," said Willie. "He doesn't mind stuff like that. If you haven't touched a drop in over eleven years, it seems like he'd forgive you and come for a visit . . . or invite you out to California."

"Oh, maybe he will, someday," said Gaston, bending down to gather his things. "You never know what might happen."

Willie descended the creaky stairs ahead

of Gaston and led him into the kitchen, where Dan sat at the table reading something in a cookbook. Willie said, "Dad, the fireplace people sent Gaston the wrong damn part. He'll have to order another one and come back later."

Dan looked up from the cookbook, over the top of his reading glasses, and appeared to replay in his mind what he'd just heard. "That's okay," he said, after a moment. He stood and moved to the refrigerator. "I bet you boys could use something cold to drink."

Willie turned toward Gaston, who stood near the doorway to the hall. "I told you," he said.

"Told him what?" asked Dan.

Ellen and Morris entered the kitchen from the outside door, each carrying an empty glass, Ellen crying, "God, it's hot out there!" Seeing Gaston, she said, "Oh, Gaston, have you met my brother, Morris?"

Gaston shook Morris's hand, giving him the once-over, then looked at Ellen and said, "Have you been swimming?"

"No," said Ellen. "But we were just thinking of it. Was Willie a help or a hindrance?"

"A help," said Gaston. "A big help."

"Gaston," she said. "You have soot on

your nose again. It must be a kind of trademark with you."

Willie, who'd taken a seat at the table, turned toward Morris and smiled. "I like your swimsuit, Morris," he said, in a mock awestruck voice. "*Very* cool."

Dan placed a glass of lemonade on the table for Willie and gave another to Gaston.

"Oh, Gaston," said Ellen. "Do you think you might have time to take a look at the stovepipe in the cabin? I can't remember the last time we had it cleaned."

Gaston emptied his glass before answering. "I'll do it right now," he said, handing Ellen the glass.

As Gaston left the kitchen, Morris moved behind Willie and wrapped one arm around the top of the boy's head. He leaned down and whispered into his ear, "You do realize, don't you, that I could twist that little head right off your neck if I wanted to."

Willie stood quickly, shoving his chair into Morris and ducking out from under his wrestling hold. Willie appeared to be headed for the hallway, but he paused when Ellen said, "Look, Willie, here's a picture of your new uncle."

She passed him the photo of Bonnie and Pastor. "Wow," he said, "he's young," and passed the photo on to Dan. He moved into the hallway and out the front door, letting the screen door slam.

"And good-looking," said Dan. "And Bonnie looks as beautiful as she does happy."

He slid the photo under a magnet on the refrigerator, amid a messy collage of other snapshots, advertising flyers, and take-out menus. When he turned back to the room, he saw that both Ellen and Morris had moved into the hallway and stood at the front door, looking through the screen. He joined them there and they all three watched as Willie jogged down the slope, caught up to Gaston about halfway to the cabin, and fell into step alongside the old man. After a moment, Gaston put a hand on the boy's shoulder.

"Looks like Willie's made a new friend," Ellen said at last.

"He's got skills," Morris said.

When they turned away from the door, they saw Richard standing shirtless and dazed in the middle of the living room. "It's kind of noisy around here," he said. "What were you all looking at?"

They spent the whole afternoon at their favorite pond in the woods, which, for the most part, they had to themselves. The pond, which was almost perfectly round and had roughly the circumference of a baseball stadium, was close to the ocean beach, separated from it by dunes and a strip of piney woods and connected to it by a path that started out as dirt and straw and ended as sand. Not long after they arrived, a British family who'd rented one of the three houses on the far side of the pond came rowing over in two canoes, on their way to the ocean beach. There were five of them altogether: a mother and father, a girl in her early twenties, a boy about Willie's age, and a grandmother with snow-white hair done up in a French twist. The girl, who sat in one of the canoes between the father and the grandmother and who'd apparently been attending college somewhere in the States, was going on about the food at her school. "The most peculiar thing," she said, in a loud outdoor voice, "is that they never seemed to have any ba*nah*nas," pronouncing the middle syllable with the strongest possible emphasis and the broadest possible *a*. "I mean, I love ba*nah*nas, and they never had any. They had all sorts of other fruits, but never any ba*nah*nas. Mummy, you know ba*nah*nas are my favorite." They approached the shore (where Willie and his family were picnicking), landed, disembarked, gathered their beach things from the canoes, and set off through the woods, the single notice of Willie's family paid by the boy, a lingering look, at Willie, as they passed. Their voices faded away in the woods, and the old grandmother could be heard saying that when she was a girl in Cornwall she had a nice ba*nah*na every morning with her cereal.

The rest of the afternoon, Willie made repeated references to ba*nah*nas and complained several times that his mummy never bought him any. She bought him other fruits, he said, but never any ba*nah*nas. Between swims, he lay on the shore and read his Steinbeck novel for school, which he took to calling *The Banahnas of Wrahth,* and the adults read their own books, except for Dan, who'd brought along some work, a thick folder of quarterly financial reports, which he pored over with a pencil in one hand but on which he never made any marks. As the sun began to fall behind the trees on the western side of the pond, they heard New Age music coming from another of the houses across the water — a repetitious composition with no identifiable instruments — and a large woman in a long white robe appeared on the deck. She struck a pose, arms lifted in the air like a circus performer acknowledging the applause of the audience, but just then the music stopped abruptly. She stalked back inside, and after a moment, they heard the sounds of a squabble from within the house, a man and a woman at odds over the choice of music. Ellen took a solitary swim around the perimeter, and Dan set his work aside and watched her progress for the duration. Richard, who'd brought along the backgammon, engaged Willie in a series of games and twice accused the boy of cheating, of somehow having loaded the dice. Morris waded in the mucky reeds at the edge of the water, stalking turtles and frogs, and occasionally Richard looked up from the backgammon board to cast a worried look in his direction.

When it was time to leave, they persuaded Dan to forgo the elaborate mixed grill he'd planned for dinner — it was too hot to cook, they said — and drove back through the woods along the bumpy dirt road, to the highway and into town, where they bought burgers and lobster rolls at a joint near the harbor. They sat at a wooden picnic table right at the edge of the water, and while they ate, Ellen said she remembered when Willie was a little boy and they'd come to this same place for cheeseburgers, and Willie, talking a mile a minute about something, had dropped his cheeseburger in the sand, picked it up, brushed it off, took a bite, and went on talking. A few minutes later, Ellen said she remembered when Willie was a little boy and wouldn't wear anything to the beach except a tiny blue Speedo like Morris's. She said she remembered when Willie was born and how the doctor who'd delivered him had exclaimed at the size of his feet and the length of his toes. She said that when he was a toddler people used to laugh at what a goofy smile he had — and Willie finally reached across the picnic table, placed his hand over hers, and said, "Mom, knock it off," which caused the other adults to laugh. They all sat quietly then and watched the sun set over the bay.

The house had grown very hot over the course of the afternoon, and at bedtime the night was still humid. Shortly after dark, clouds blanketed the sky, and the few stars that had already pierced the dusk disappeared. The upstairs rooms were particularly unpleasant, and Dan set up electric fans in the master bedroom and in Willie's room. Richard and Morris opted for the sleeping porch, since there, as Morris put it, one had at least a *sense* of air.

Around eleven-thirty, Ellen and Dan lay

side by side in bed, atop the covers and naked, though neither of them had yet initiated anything. The oscillating fan, steadfast and vigilant, oscillated in the corner nearest the door to the hallway (closed now for privacy, despite the heat) and pleasantly rippled the hems of the bedsheets with each pass. At last Ellen said softly, "What are you thinking about, my darling?"

He stared straight up at the ceiling. "I was trying to think of a way to make love," he said, "without actually having to touch each other."

"Well," she said, "I suppose we could try to do it touching each other as little as possible."

"Mmm, that's kinky," he said. "Okay."

He slid off the bed to the floor, onto his knees.

"Oh," she whispered, "I forgot to tell you that Cricket died."

"Who's Cricket?"

"Daddy's old bird dog," she said. "And oh, my God, I forgot to call Bonnie."

"Call her tomorrow," he said, and began to crawl on all fours around to her side of the bed.

"Okay," she said, "but what's that sound I'm hearing?"

He stopped, near her bare hipbone, and

reared his head like a gopher out of its hole, listened for a moment, and said, "Sounds to me like the outdoor shower. Somebody's having another shower."

Outdoors, Richard was standing naked inside the cedar stall of the shower at the back corner of the house; he was fiddling with the faucets, adjusting the water temperature as Morris, also naked, waited by the opening in the stall. Spearmint, which grew between the boards on the ground, sent up its sharp scent, and Morris whispered, "Well, if anybody's going to save me I would prefer it to be you. I just wish I could put him out of my mind . . . it's driving me crazy."

"Come on in," whispered Richard. "It's just right now . . . not too hot, not too cold. And shut up about it. He just managed to get under your skin somehow. You probably won't see him again for a long time. It'll fade."

Morris stepped into the spray of lukewarm water and said, "You always have such a simple solution, don't you: Just shut up about it."

"Yeah," said Richard, which was the last word spoken for quite a while on the subject of Pastor Vandorpe or any other matter. They fooled around in the shower like schoolboys then, soaping each other up and backing each other into the corners of the stall, and when they returned at last to the porch, and to bed, they were able to fall asleep.

Upstairs, about five hours later, Willie awakened to the sound of rain in his window. He thought he'd been dreaming about rain, or a waterfall, or something having to do with water, and somehow it had left him ravenously hungry. He went down the hall to use the bathroom, careful to avoid the particularly squeaky floorboards, and then downstairs in the dark, in his boxer shorts, groping his way along the wall and the handrail. In the living room, he saw a light burning out on the sleeping porch and crept quietly over to the door.

"What are you doing?" he whispered from the doorframe to Morris, who was sitting, in pajama bottoms, on one of the beds. Morris had switched on a pin-up lamp on the wall behind the bed and held a large book in his lap.

"Studying the atlas," whispered Morris. "The rain woke me up and I couldn't get back to sleep."

"Why the atlas?" Willie whispered. "What are you looking for?"

"Nothing special," said Morris. "It's what

I could reach without getting out of bed."

"Where's Richard?"

Morris tilted his head to one side, indicating Richard, asleep on the adjacent bed. "He moved over there a while ago," Morris said. "These old beds are really bouncy."

Willie stepped out of the doorway and onto the porch, where he could look past Morris at Richard, who was lying on his back with his lips slightly parted, a white sheet pulled up to his waist. "He looks dead," Willie whispered.

"I know," Morris said. "He always looks dead when he's sleeping."

"I guess everybody does," Willie said.

"Well, there are degrees," said Morris. "Richard looks especially dead. What are *you* doing?"

"I was hungry," said Willie, moving to the bed and sitting next to Morris. Morris put his arm behind the boy so he could comfortably see the atlas, which was opened to a two-page spread of the United States. Willie pointed to the scorpion's-tail shape that was Cape Cod and said, "Here we are."

"Yes," said Morris. "Here we are. And right down here is your Aunt Bonnie and her new husband, Pastor Vandorpe."

"And here's Kool-Aid, my friend from camp," said Willie.

"Right," said Morris. "Home of the Tar-heels."

"And where's Fresno, California?" asked Willie.

Morris touched California with his finger. "It's not big enough to show up here," he said, "but I think it's right around this area. Who's in Fresno?"

"Gaston's son," said Willie.

"Oh," said Morris. "The chimney sweep?"

"Mmm," said Willie. "And his grandson."

Morris drew circles with his finger throughout the Midwest. "And here's a whole bunch of people we never met," he said.

"But might meet someday," said Willie.

"But might meet someday," repeated Morris. "You never know. Now, tell me what you think about this lovely rain on the roof over our heads."

The boy shrugged and whispered, "I like it." He looked out at the dark screen, where the rain was falling off the eaves in perfectly straight lines, lit gold by the light of their lamp.

AUTHOR'S NOTE

For their kind help and advice, I thank Janet Baker, Jennifer Barth, Tessa Blake, Peter Bryant, Michael Downing, Rick Gradone, Nancy Hausman, Gail Hochman, Richard Hoffman, Larry Keane, Fran Kiernan, Mike Lew, Jeff and Monique McFarland, Katharine McFarland, Sam McFarland, Maggie Richards, Lindsay Ross, John Sterling, Ian Williams, and Ira Ziering. A special thanks to my wife, Michelle Blake, for her many contributions and for allowing me to derive some lines from her poem "Delicate Matters."

ABOUT THE AUTHOR

Dennis McFarland is the bestselling author of *Prince Edward, Singing Boy, A Face at the Window, School for the Blind,* and *The Music Room.* His fiction has appeared in *Best American Short Stories, The American Scholar, The New Yorker,* and elsewhere. He lives with his family in Massachusetts.